PRAISE FOR ELENA FERRANTE'S NEAPOLITAN NOVELS

FROM THE UNITED STATES

"Ferrante can do a woman's interior dialogue like no one else, with a ferocity that is shockingly honest, unnervingly blunt."
— Minna Proctor, *Booklist*

"Elena Ferrante's gutsy and compulsively readable new novel, the first of a quartet, is a terrific entry point for Americans unfamiliar with the famously reclusive writer, whose go-for-broke tales of women's shadow selves—those ambivalent mothers and seething divorcées too complex or unseemly for polite society (and most literary fiction, for that matter)—shimmer with Balzacian human detail and subtle psychological suspense . . . The Neapolitan novels offer one of the more nuanced portraits of feminine friendship in recent memory—from the make-up and break-up quarrels of young girls to the way in which we carefully define ourselves against each other as teens—Ferrante wisely balances her memoir-like emotional authenticity with a wry sociological understanding of a society on the verge of dramatic change." —Megan O'Grady, *Vogue*

"Elena Ferrante will blow you away." —Alice Sebold, writer

"The Neapolitan novel cycle is an unconditional masterpiece . . . I read all the books in a state of immersion; I was totally enthralled. There was nothing else I wanted to do except follow the lives of Lila and Lenù to the end."
— Jhumpa Lahiri, Pulitzer-prize winning author of *The Lowland*

"*My Brilliant Friend* is a sweeping family-centered epic that encompasses issues of loyalty, love, and a transforming Europe. This gorgeous novel should bring a host of new readers to one of Italy's most acclaimed authors." —The *Barnes and Noble Review*

"[Ferrante's Neapolitan Novels] don't merely offer a teeming vision of working-class Naples, with its cobblers and professors, communists and mobbed-up businessmen, womanizing poets and downtrodden wives; they present one of modern fiction's richest portraits of a friendship."   —John Powers, Fresh Air, *NPR*

"The feverish speculation about the identity of Elena Ferrante betrays an understandable failure of imagination: it seems impossible that right now somewhere someone sits in a room and draws up these books. Palatial and heartbreaking beyond measure, the Neapolitan novels seem less written than they do revealed. One simply surrenders. When the final volume appears—may that day never come!—they're bound to be acknowledged as one of the most powerful works of art, in any medium, of our age."
                      —Gideon Lewis-Kraus, author of *A Sense of Direction*

"Ferrante tackles girlhood and friendship with amazing force."
                      —Gwyneth Paltrow, actor

"Ferrante draws an indelible picture of the city's mean streets and the poverty, violence and sameness of lives lived in the same place forever . . . She is a fierce writer."   —*Shelf Awareness*

"Ferrante transforms the love, separation and reunion of two poor urban girls into the general tragedy of their city."
                      —*The New York Times*

"Elena Ferrante: the best angry woman writer ever!"
                      —John Waters, director

"Beautifully translated by Ann Goldstein . . . Ferrante writes with a ferocious, intimate urgency that is a celebration of anger. Ferrante is terribly good with anger, a very specific sort of wrath harbored by women, who are so often not allowed to give voice to it. We are angry, a lot of the time, at the position we're in—whether it's as wife, daughter, mother, friend—and I can think of no other woman writing who is so swift and gorgeous in this rage, so bracingly fearless in mining fury."   —Susanna Sonnenberg, The *San Francisco Chronicle*

"Elena Ferrante's *The Story of a New Name*. Book two in her Naples trilogy. Two words: Read it."   —Ann Hood, writer (from Twitter)

"The through-line in all of Ferrante's investigations, for me, is nothing less than one long, mind-and-heart-shredding howl for the history of women (not only Neapolitan women), and its implicit *j'accuse* . . . Ferrante's effect, critics agree, is inarguable. 'Intensely, violently personal' and 'brutal directness, familial torment' is how James Wood ventures to categorize her—descriptions that seem mild after you've encountered the work."
                    —Joan Frank, The *San Francisco Chronicle*

"Lila, mercurial, unsparing, and, at the end of this first episode in a planned trilogy from Ferrante, seemingly capable of starting a full-scale neighborhood war, is a memorable character."
                                        —*Publishers Weekly*

"Ferrante's own writing has no limits, is willing to take every thought forward to its most radical conclusion and backwards to its most radical birthing."   —*The New Yorker*

FROM THE UNITED KINGDOM

"*The Story of a New Name*, like its predecessor, is fiction of the very highest order."   —*Independent on Sunday*

"*My Brilliant Friend*, translated by Ann Goldstein, is stunning: an intense, forensic exploration of the friendship between Lila and the story's narrator, Elena. Ferrante's evocation of the working-class district of Naples where Elena and Lila first meet as two wiry eight-year-olds is cinematic in the density of its detail."
                                —*The Times Literary Supplement*

"This is a story about friendship as a mass of roiling currents—love, envy, pity, spite, dependency and Schadenfreude coiling around one another, tricky to untangle."   —*Intelligent Life*

"Elena Ferrante may be the best contemporary novelist you have

never heard of. The Italian author has written six lavishly praised novels. But she writes under a pseudonym and will not offer herself for public consumption. Her characters likewise defy convention . . . Her prose is crystal, and her storytelling both visceral and compelling."
—*The Economist*

From Italy

"*Those Who Leave and Those Who Stay* evokes the vital flux of a heartbeat, of blood flowing through our veins." —*La Repubblica*

"We don't know who she is, but it doesn't matter. Ferrante's books are enthralling self-contained monoliths that do not seek friendship but demand silent, fervid admiration from her passionate readers . . . The thing most real in these novels is the intense, almost osmotic relationship that unites Elena and Lila, the two girls from a neighborhood in Naples who are the peerless protagonists of the Neapolitan novels." —*Famiglia Cristiana*

"Today it is near impossible to find writers capable of bringing smells, tastes, feelings, and contradictory passions to their pages. Elena Ferrante, alone, seems able to do it. There is no writer better suited to composing the great Italian novel of her generation, her country, and her time." —*Il Manifesto*

"Regardless of who is behind the name Elena Ferrante, the mysterious pseudonym used by the author of the Neapolitan novels, two things are certain: she is a woman and she knows how to describe Naples like nobody else. She does so with a style that recalls an enchanted spider web with its expressive power and the wizardry with which it creates an entire world." —*Huffington Post* (Italy)

"A marvel that is without limits and beyond genre." —*Il Salvagente*

"Elena Ferrante is proving that literature can cure our present ills; it can cure the spirit by operating as an antidote to the nervous attempts we make to see ourselves reflected in the present-day of a country that is increasingly repellent." —*Il Mattino*

"*My Brilliant Friend* flows from the soul like an eruption from Mount Vesuvio."   *—La Repubblica*

From Australia

"No one has a voice quite like Ferrante's. Her gritty, ruthlessly frank novels roar off the page with a barbed fury, like an attack that is also a defense . . . Ferrante's fictions are fierce, unsentimental glimpses at the way a woman is constantly under threat, her identity submerged in marriage, eclipsed by motherhood, mythologised by desire. Imagine if Jane Austen got angry and you'll have some idea of how explosive these works are."   —John Freeman, *The Australian*

"One of the most astounding—and mysterious—contemporary Italian novelists available in translation, Elena Ferrante unfolds the tumultuous inner lives of women in her thrillingly menacing stories of lost love, negligent mothers and unfulfilled desires." *—The Age*

"Ferrante bewitches with her tiny, intricately drawn world . . . *My Brilliant Friend* journeys fearlessly into some of that murkier psychological territory where questions of individual identity are inextricable from circumstance and the ever-changing identities of others."
—The Melbourne Review

"The Neapolitan novels move far from contrivance, logic or respectability to ask uncomfortable questions about how we live, how we love, how we singe an existence in a deeply flawed world that expects pretty acquiescence from its women. In all their beauty, their ugliness, their devotion and deceit, these girls enchant and repulse, like life, like our very selves."   —The *Sydney Morning Herald*

ALSO BY

ELENA FERRANTE

The Days of Abandonment
Troubling Love
The Lost Daughter
My Brilliant Friend
The Story of a New Name
The Story of the Lost Child

THOSE WHO LEAVE
AND THOSE WHO STAY

Elena Ferrante

THOSE WHO LEAVE
AND THOSE WHO STAY

Book Three, The Neapolitan Novels
Middle Time

*Translated from the Italian
by Ann Goldstein*

Europa
editions

Europa Editions
214 West 29th Street
New York, N.Y. 10001
www.europaeditions.com
info@europaeditions.com

Copyright © 2013 by Edizioni E/O
First Publication 2014 by Europa Editions
Seventh printing, 2015

Translation by Ann Goldstein
Original title: *Storia di chi fugge e di chi resta*
Translation copyright © 2014 by Europa Editions

Library of Congress Cataloging in Publication Data is available
ISBN 978-1-60945-233-9

Ferrante, Elena
Those Who Leave and Those Who Stay

Book design by Emanuele Ragnisco
www.mekkanografici.com

Cover photo © J Wheeler and V Laws/Corbis

Prepress by Grafica Punto Print – Rome

Printed in Italy

THOSE WHO LEAVE
AND THOSE WHO STAY

INDEX OF CHARACTERS AND NOTES ON THE EVENTS
OF THE EARLIER VOLUMES

The Cerullo family (the shoemaker's family):

Fernando Cerullo, shoemaker, Lila's father. He wouldn't send
  his daughter beyond elementary school.

Nunzia Cerullo, Lila's mother. Close to her daughter, but without sufficient authority to support her against her father.

Raffaella Cerullo, called Lina, or Lila. She was born in
  August, 1944, and is sixty-six when she disappears from
  Naples without a trace. A brilliant student, at the age of
  ten she writes a story titled *The Blue Fairy*. She leaves
  school after getting her elementary-school diploma and
  learns to be a shoemaker. She marries Stefano Carracci at
  a young age and successfully manages first the grocery
  store in the new neighborhood and then the shoe store in
  Piazza dei Martiri. During a vacation on Ischia she falls in
  love with Nino Sarratore, for whom she leaves her husband. After the shipwreck of her relationship with Nino
  and the birth of her son Gennaro (also called Rino), Lila
  leaves Stefano definitively when she discovers that he is
  expecting a child with Ada Cappuccio. She moves with
  Enzo Scanno to San Giovanni a Teduccio and begins
  working in the sausage factory belonging to Bruno
  Soccavo.

Rino Cerullo, Lila's older brother, also a shoemaker. With his
  father, Fernando, and thanks to Lila and to Stefano
  Carracci's money, he sets up the Cerullo shoe factory. He
  marries Stefano's sister, Pinuccia Carracci, with whom he

has a son, Ferdinando, called Dino. Lila's son bears his name, Rino.
Other children.

The Greco family (the porter's family):

Elena Greco, called Lenuccia or Lenù. Born in August, 1944, she is the author of the long story we are reading. Elena begins to write it when she learns that her childhood friend Lina Cerullo, whom she calls Lila, has disappeared. After elementary school, Elena continues to study, with increasing success; in high school her abilities and Professor Galiani's protection allow her to survive unscathed a clash with the religion teacher about the role of the Holy Spirit. At the invitation of Nino Sarratore, with whom she has been secretly in love since childhood, and with valuable help from Lila, she writes an article about this clash, which, in the end, is not published in the magazine Nino contributes to. Elena's brilliant schoolwork is crowned by a degree from the Scuola Normale, in Pisa, where she meets and becomes engaged to Pietro Airota, and by the publication of a novel in which she reimagines the life of the neighborhood and her adolescent experiences on Ischia.

Peppe, *Gianni*, and *Elisa*, Elena's younger siblings.

The *father* is a porter at the city hall.

The *mother* is a housewife. Her limping gait haunts Elena.

The Carracci family (Don Achille's family):

Don Achille Carracci, the ogre of fairy tales, dealer in the black market, loan shark. He was murdered.

Maria Carracci, wife of Don Achille, mother of Stefano, Pinuccia, and Alfonso. She works in the family grocery store.

Stefano Carracci, son of Don Achille, husband of Lila. He manages the assets accumulated by his father and over time becomes a successful shopkeeper, thanks to two profitable grocery stores and the shoe store in Piazza dei Martiri, which he opens with the Solara brothers. Dissatisfied by his stormy marriage to Lila, he initiates a relationship with Ada Cappuccio. He and Ada start living together when she becomes pregnant and Lila moves to San Giovanni a Teduccio.

Pinuccia, daughter of Don Achille. She works in the family grocery store, and then in the shoe store. She is married to Lila's brother, Rino, and has a son with him, Ferdinando, called Dino.

Alfonso, son of Don Achille. He is Elena's schoolmate. He is the boyfriend of Marisa Sarratore and becomes the manager of the shoe store in Piazza dei Martiri.

The Peluso family (the carpenter's family):

Alfredo Peluso, carpenter. Communist. Accused of killing Don Achille, he was convicted and sent to prison, where he dies.

Giuseppina Peluso, wife of Alfredo. A worker in the tobacco factory, she is devoted to her children and her imprisoned husband. After his death, she commits suicide.

Pasquale Peluso, older son of Alfredo and Giuseppina, construction worker, militant Communist. He was the first to become aware of Lila's beauty and to declare his love for her. He detests the Solaras. He was the boyfriend of Ada Cappuccio.

Carmela Peluso, also called *Carmen,* sister of Pasquale. She is a salesclerk in a notions store but is soon hired by Lila to work in Stefano's new grocery store. She was the girlfriend of Enzo Scanno for a long time, but he leaves her without explanation at the end of his military service. She subsequently becomes engaged to the owner of the gas pump on the *stradone*.

Other children.

The Cappuccio family (the mad widow's family):

Melina, a relative of Nunzia Cerullo, a widow. She washes the stairs of the apartment buildings in the old neighborhood. She was the lover of Donato Sarratore, Nino's father. The Sarratores left the neighborhood because of that relationship, and Melina has nearly lost her mind.

Melina's *husband*, who unloaded crates in the fruit and vegetable market, and died in mysterious circumstances.

Ada Cappuccio, Melina's daughter. As a girl she helped her mother wash the stairs. Thanks to Lila, she is hired as a salesclerk in the Carraccis' grocery. She is the girlfriend of Pasquale Peluso, and becomes the lover of Stefano Carracci: when she gets pregnant she goes to live with him. From their relationship a girl, Maria, is born.

Antonio Cappuccio, her brother, a mechanic. He is Elena's boyfriend and is very jealous of Nino Sarratore. The prospect of leaving for military service worries him deeply, but when Elena turns to the Solara brothers to help him avoid it, he is humiliated, so much so that he breaks off their relationship. During his military service he has a nervous breakdown and is discharged early; back in the neighborhood, driven by poverty, he goes to work for Michele Solara, who at a certain point sends him to Germany on a long and mysterious job.

Other children.

The Sarratore family (the railway-worker poet's family):

Donato Sarratore, train conductor, poet, journalist. A great womanizer, he was the lover of Melina Cappuccio. When Elena goes on vacation to Ischia, and is a guest in the same house where the Sarratores are staying, she is compelled to leave in a hurry to escape Donato's sexual molestations. The following summer, however, Elena gives herself to him on the beach, driven by the suffering that the relationship between Nino and Lila has caused her. To exorcise this degrading experience, Elena writes about it in the book that is then published.

Lidia Sarratore, wife of Donato.

Nino Sarratore, the oldest of the five children of Donato and Lidia. He hates his father. He is an extremely brilliant student and has a long secret affair with Lila. They live together briefly when Lila becomes pregnant.

Marisa Sarratore, sister of Nino. The girlfriend of Alfonso Carracci.

Pino, *Clelia*, and *Ciro Sarratore,* younger children of Donato and Lidia.

The Scanno family (the fruit-and-vegetable seller's family):

Nicola Scanno, fruit-and-vegetable seller, died of pneumonia.

Assunta Scanno, wife of Nicola, died of cancer.

Enzo Scanno, son of Nicola and Assunta, also a fruit-and-vegetable seller. Lila has felt a liking for him since childhood. Enzo was for a long time the boyfriend of Carmen Peluso, whom he leaves without explanation upon his return from military service. During his military service he started to study again, and he earns an engineering diploma. When Lila finally decides to leave Stefano, he takes responsibility for her and her son, Gennaro, and the three of them go to live in San Giovanni a Teduccio.

Other children.

The Solara family (the family of the owner of the Solara bar-pastry shop):

Silvio Solara, owner of the bar-pastry shop, Monarchist-fascist and Camorrist tied to the illegal trafficking in the neighborhood. He opposed the Cerullo shoe factory.

Manuela Solara, wife of Silvio, moneylender: her red book is much feared in the neighborhood.

Marcello and Michele Solara, sons of Silvio and Manuela. Braggarts, arrogant, they are nevertheless loved by the neighborhood girls, except Lila and Elena. Marcello is in love with Lila but she rejects him. Michele, a little younger than Marcello, is colder, more intelligent, more violent. He is engaged to Gigliola, the daughter of the pastry maker, but over the years develops a morbid obsession with Lila.

The Spagnuolo family (the baker's family):
Signor Spagnuolo, pastry maker at the Solaras' bar-pastry shop.
Rosa Spagnuolo, wife of the pastry maker.
Gigliola Spagnuolo, daughter of the pastry maker, engaged to Michele Solara.
Other children.

The Airota family:
Guido Airota, professor of Greek literature.
Adele Airota, his wife. She works for the Milanese publishing house that publishes Elena's novel.
Mariarosa Airota, the older daughter, professor of art history in Milan.
Pietro Airota, university colleague of Elena's and her fiancé, destined for a brilliant academic career.

The teachers:
Maestro Ferraro, teacher and librarian. He gave both Lila and Elena prizes when they were young, because they were diligent readers.
Maestra Oliviero, teacher. She is the first to notice the potential of Lila and Elena. At the age of ten, Lila writes a story titled *The Blue Fairy*. Elena, who likes the story a lot, gives it to Maestra Oliviero to read. But the teacher, angry because Lila's parents wouldn't send their daughter beyond elementary school, never says anything about it. In fact, she stops

concerning herself with Lila and concentrates only on the success of Elena. She dies after a long illness soon after Elena graduates from the university.

Professor Gerace, high-school teacher.

Professor Galiani, high-school teacher. She is a very cultured woman and a Communist. She is immediately charmed by Elena's intelligence. She lends her books, protects her in the clash with the religion teacher, invites her to a party at her house given by her children. Their relations cool when Nino, overwhelmed by his passion for Lila, leaves her daughter Nadia.

Other characters:

Gino, son of the pharmacist. Elena's first boyfriend.

Nella Incardo, the cousin of Maestra Oliviero. She lives in Barano, on Ischia, and rents rooms during the summer to the Sarratore family. Elena stays with her for a vacation at the beach.

Armando, medical student, son of Professor Galiani.

Nadia, student, daughter of Professor Galiani, and girlfriend of Nino, who leaves her, sending her a letter from Ischia when he falls in love with Lila.

Bruno Soccavo, friend of Nino Sarratore and son of a rich industrialist in San Giovanni a Teduccio, near Naples. He gives Lila a job in his family's sausage factory.

Franco Mari, student and Elena's boyfriend during her first years at the university.

MIDDLE TIME

1.

I saw Lila for the last time five years ago, in the winter of 2005. We were walking along the *stradone,* early in the morning and, as had been true for years now, were unable to feel at ease. I was the only one talking, I remember: she was humming, she greeted people who didn't respond, the rare times she interrupted me she uttered only exclamations, without any evident relation to what I was saying. Too many bad things, and some terrible, had happened over the years, and to regain our old intimacy we would have had to speak our secret thoughts, but I didn't have the strength to find the words and she, who perhaps had the strength, didn't have the desire, didn't see the use.

Yet I loved her, and when I came to Naples I always tried to see her, even though, I have to say, I was a little afraid of her. She had changed a great deal. Age had had the better of us both by then, but while I fought a tendency to gain weight she was permanently skin and bones. She had short hair that she cut herself; it was completely white, not by choice but from neglect. Her face was deeply lined, and increasingly recalled her father's. She laughed nervously, almost a shriek, and spoke too loudly. She was constantly gesturing, giving to each gesture such fierce determination that she seemed to want to slice in half the houses, the street, the passersby, me.

We had gone as far as the elementary school when a young man I didn't know overtook us, out of breath, and shouted to her that the body of a woman had been found in a flowerbed next to the church. We hurried to the gardens, and Lila dragged me into the knot of curious bystanders, rudely opening a path. The woman was lying on one side; she was extraordinarily fat, and was wearing an unfashionable dark-green raincoat. Lila recognized her immediately, but I did not: it was our childhood friend Gigliola Spagnuolo, the ex-wife of Michele Solara.

I hadn't seen her for several decades. Her beautiful face was ruined, and her ankles had become enormous. Her hair, once brown, was now fiery red, and long, the way she'd had it as a girl, but thin, and spread out on the loose dirt. One foot was shod in a worn, low-heeled shoe; the other was encased in a gray wool stocking, with a hole at the big toe, and the shoe was a few feet beyond, as if she had lost it kicking against some pain or fear. I burst into tears; Lila looked at me in annoyance.

Sitting on a bench nearby, we waited in silence until Gigliola was taken away. What had happened to her, how she had died, for the moment no one knew. We went to Lila's house, her parents' old, small apartment, where she now lived with her son Rino. We talked about our friend; Lila criticized her, the life she had led, her pretensions, her betrayals. But now it was I who couldn't listen. I thought of that face in profile on the dirt, of how thin the long hair was, of the whitish patches of skull. How many who had been girls with us were no longer alive, had disappeared from the face of the earth because of illness, because their nervous systems had been unable to endure the sandpaper of torments, because their blood had been spilled. For a while we sat in the kitchen listlessly, neither of us decisive enough to clear the table. Then we went out again.

The sun of the fine winter day gave things a serene aspect. The old neighborhood, unlike us, had remained the same. The low gray houses endured, the courtyard of our games, the dark mouths of the tunnel, and the violence. But the landscape around it had changed. The greenish stretch of the ponds was no longer there, the old canning factory had vanished. In their place was the gleam of glass skyscrapers, once signs of a radiant future that no one had ever believed in. I had registered the changes, all of them, over the years, at times with curiosity, more often carelessly. As a child I had imagined that, beyond the neighborhood, Naples was full of marvels. The skyscraper at the central station, for example, had made a great impression, decades earlier, as it rose, story by story, the skeleton of a building that seemed to us extremely tall, beside the ambitious railroad station. How surprised I was when I passed through Piazza Garibaldi: look how high it is, I said to Lila, to Carmen, to Pasquale, to Ada, to Antonio, to all the companions of those days, as we made our way to the sea, to the edges of the wealthy neighborhoods. At the top, I thought, live the angels, and surely they delight in the whole city. To climb up there, to ascend—how I would have liked that. It was *our* skyscraper, even if it was outside the neighborhood, a thing that we saw growing day by day. But the work had stopped. When I came back from Pisa, the station skyscraper no longer seemed the symbol of a community that was reviving but, rather, another nest of inefficiency.

During that period I was convinced that there was no great difference between the neighborhood and Naples, the malaise slid from one to the other without interruption. Whenever I returned I found a city that was spineless, that couldn't stand up to changes of season, heat, cold, and, especially, storms. Look how the station on Piazza Garibaldi was flooded, look how the Galleria opposite the museum had collapsed; there was a landslide, and the electricity didn't come back on. Lodged in my memory were dark streets full of dangers, unregulated traffic, broken pavements, giant puddles. The clogged sewers splattered, dribbled over. Lavas of water and sewage and garbage and bacteria spilled into the sea from the hills that were burdened with new, fragile structures, or eroded the world from below. People died of carelessness, of corruption, of abuse, and yet, in every round of voting, gave their enthusiastic approval to the politicians who made their life unbearable. As soon as I got off the train, I moved cautiously in the places where I had grown up, always careful to speak in dialect, as if to indicate *I am one of yours, don't hurt me.*

When I graduated from college, when, in a single burst, I wrote a story that in the space of a few months became, surprisingly, a book, the things of the world I came from seemed to me to deteriorate even further. In Pisa, in Milan, I felt good, at times even happy; upon every return to my own city I feared that some unexpected event would keep me from escaping, that the things I had gained would be taken away from me. I would be unable to reach Pietro, whom I was soon to marry; the tidy space of the publishing house would be barred to me; I would no longer enjoy the refinements of Adele, my future mother-in-law, a mother as mine had never been. Already in the past the city had seemed to me crowded, a crush from Piazza Garibaldi to Forcella, to Duchesca, to Lavinaio, to the Rettifilo. In the late sixties the crush seemed to intensify, while impatience, aggressiveness spread without restraint. One morning I ventured out to Via Mezzocannone, where some years earlier I had worked as a clerk in a bookstore. I went because I was curious to see the place where I had toiled, and also to see the university, where I had never been. I wanted to compare it with the university in Pisa, the Normale, I was even hoping I might run into the children of Professor Galiani—Armando, Nadia—and boast of what I had accomplished. But the street, the university buildings had distressed me. They were teeming with students from Naples and the province and the whole South, well-dressed, noisy, self-confident youths, and others, rough yet inferior. They thronged the entrances, the classrooms, stood in long, often quarrelsome lines in front of the secretaries. Without warning, three or four started hitting each other a few steps from me, as if the mere sight of one another were sufficient for an explosion of insults and blows, a fury of boys shouting their craving for blood in a dialect that I myself had difficulty understanding. I left in a hurry, as if something threatening had touched me in a place that I had imagined safe, inhabited only by good reasons.

Every year, in other words, it seemed to me worse. In that season of rains, the city had cracked yet again, an entire building had buckled onto one side, like a person who, sitting in an old chair, leans on the worm-eaten arm and it gives way. Dead, wounded. And shouts, blows, cherry bombs. The city seemed to harbor in its guts a fury that couldn't get out and therefore eroded it from the inside, or erupted in pustules on the surface, swollen with venom against everyone, children, adults, old people, visitors from other cities, Americans from NATO, tourists of every nationality, the Neapolitans themselves. How could one endure in that place of disorder and danger, on the outskirts, in the center, on the hills, at the foot of Vesuvius? What a brutal impression San Giovanni a Teduccio had left on me, and the journey to get there. How brutal the factory where Lila was working, and Lila herself—Lila with her small child, Lila who lived in a run-down building with Enzo, although they didn't sleep together. She had said that he wanted to study computers, and that she was trying to help him. I still remember her voice, as it tried to erase San Giovanni, the salami, the odor of the factory, her situation, by citing with false expertise abbreviations like: Cybernetics Center of the State University of Milan, Soviet Center for the Application of Computer Science to the Social Sciences. She wanted to make me believe that a center of that type would soon be established even in Naples. I had thought: in Milan maybe, certainly in the Soviet Union, but here no, here it is the folly of your uncontrollable mind, into which you are dragging even poor, devoted Enzo. Leave, instead. Get away for good, far from the life we've lived since birth. Settle in well-organized lands where everything really is possible. I had fled, in fact. Only to discover, in the decades to come, that I had been wrong, that it was a chain with larger and larger links: the neighborhood was connected to the city, the city to Italy, Italy to Europe, Europe to the whole planet. And this is how I see it today: it's not the neighborhood that's sick, it's not Naples, it's the entire earth, it's the universe, or universes. And shrewdness means hiding and hiding from oneself the true state of things.

I talked about it with Lila that afternoon, in the winter of 2005, emphatically and as if to make amends. I wanted to acknowledge openly that she had understood everything since she was a girl, without ever leaving Naples. But I was almost immediately ashamed, I heard in my words the irritable pessimism of someone who is getting old, a tone I knew she detested.

In fact, in a nervous grimace of a smile that showed her old teeth, she said: "Are you playing the know-it-all, the moralizer? What do you intend to do? You want to write about us? You want to write about me?"

"No."

"Tell the truth."

"It would be too complicated."

"You've thought about it, though, you're thinking about it."

"A little, yes."

"Let me be, Lenù. Let us all be. We ought to disappear, we deserve nothing, neither Gigliola nor me, no one."

"That's not true."

She had an ugly expression of discontent, and she scrutinized me, her pupils hardly visible, her lips half parted.

"All right," she said, "write, if you want, write about Gigliola, about whoever you want. But about me no, don't you dare, promise."

"I won't write about anyone, not even you."

"Careful, I've got my eye on you."

"Yes?"

"I'll come look in your computer, I'll read your files, I'll erase them."

"Come on."

"You think I'm not capable of it?"

"I know you're capable. But I can protect myself."

She laughed in her old mean way.

"Not from me."

2.

I have never forgotten those three words; it was the last thing she said to me: *Not from me.* For weeks now I've been writing at a good pace, without wasting time rereading. If Lila is still alive—I imagine as I sip my coffee and look out at the Po, bumping against the piers of the Principessa Isabella bridge—she won't be able to resist, she'll come and poke around in my computer, she'll read, and, cantankerous old woman that she is, she'll get angry at my disobedience, she'll want to interfere, correct, add, she'll forget her craving to disappear. Then I wash the cup, go back to the desk to write, starting from that cold spring evening in Milan, more than forty years ago, in the bookstore, when the man with the thick eyeglasses spoke derisively about me and my book in front of everyone, and I replied in confusion, shaking. Until suddenly Nino Sarratore stood up and, almost unrecognizable with his unruly black beard, harshly attacked the man who had attacked me. Right then my whole self began to silently shout his name—how long had it been since I'd seen him: four, five years—and although I was ice-cold with tension I felt myself blushing.

As soon as Nino stopped talking, the man, with a slight gesture, asked to respond. It was clear that he was offended, but I was too agitated by violent emotions to immediately understand why. I was aware, naturally, that Nino's words had shifted the conversation from literature to politics, and in an aggressive, almost disrespectful way. Yet at the moment I gave that little importance; I couldn't forgive myself for my failure to stand up to the challenge, for having been ineffectual in front of a sophisticated audience. And yet I was clever. In high school I had reacted to my disadvantages by trying to become like Professor Galiani, I had adopted her tones and her language. In Pisa that model of a woman hadn't been enough; I had had to deal with highly experienced people. Franco, Pietro, all the best students, and of course the renowned teachers at the Normale expressed themselves in a complex manner: they wrote with deliberate artifice, they had an ability to classify, a logical lucidity, that Professor Galiani didn't possess. But I had trained myself to be like them. And often I succeeded: it seemed to me that I had mastered words to the point of sweeping away forever the contradictions of being in the world, the surge of emotions, and breathless speech. In short, I now knew a method of speaking and writing that—by means of a refined vocabulary, stately and thoughtful pacing, a determined arrangement of arguments, and a formal orderliness that wasn't supposed to fail—sought to annihilate the interlocutor to the point where he lost the will to object. But that evening things didn't go as they should have. First, Adele and her friends, whom I imagined as very sophisticated readers, and then the man with the thick eyeglasses intimidated me. I had become again the eager little girl from the poor neighborhood of Naples, the daughter of the porter with the dialect cadence of the South, amazed at having ended up in that place, playing the part of the cultured young writer. So I had lost confidence and expressed myself in an unconvincing, disjointed manner. Not to mention Nino. His appearance had taken away any self-control, and the very quality of his speech on my behalf had confirmed to me that I had abruptly lost my abilities. We came from backgrounds that were not very different, we had both worked hard to acquire that language. And yet not only had he used it naturally, turning it easily against the speaker, but, at times, when it seemed to him necessary, he had even dared to insert disorder into that polished Italian with a bold nonchalance that rapidly managed to make the professorial tones of the other man sound out of date and perhaps a little ridiculous. As a result, when I saw that the man wished to speak again, I thought: he's really angry, and if he said bad things about my book before, now he'll say something even worse to humiliate Nino, who defended it.

But the man seemed to be gripped by something else: he did not return to my book; he didn't bring me into it at all. He focused instead on certain formulas that Nino had used incidentally but had repeated several times: things like *baronial arrogance, anti-authoritarian literature*. I understood only then that what had made him angry was the political turn of the discussion. He hadn't liked that vocabulary, and he emphasized this by inserting a sudden sarcastic falsetto into his deep voice (*And so pride in knowledge is today characterized as pretension, and so literature, too, has become anti-authoritarian?*). Then he began to play subtly with the word *authority*, thank God, he said, a barrier against the uncultured youths who make random pronouncements on everything by resorting to the nonsense of who knows what student-run course at the state university. And he spoke at length on that subject, addressing the audience, never Nino or me directly. In his conclusion, however, he focused first on the old critic who was sitting next to me and then directly on Adele, who was perhaps his true polemical objective from the beginning. I have no argument with the young people, he said, briefly, but with those educated adults who, out of self-interest, are always ready to ride the latest fashion in stupidity. Here at last he was silent, and he prepared to leave with quiet but energetic "Excuse me"s, "May I"s, "thank you"s.

The audience rose to let him pass, hostile and yet deferential. It was utterly clear to me by now that he was an important man, so important that even Adele answered his dark nod of greeting with a cordial *Thank you, goodbye.* Maybe for that reason Nino surprised everyone a little when, in an imperative and at the same time joking tone, evidence that he was aware who he was dealing with, he called him by the title of professor—*Professor, where are you going, don't run off*—and then, thanks to the agility of his long legs, cut off his path, confronted him, spoke to him in that new language of his that I couldn't really hear from where I was, couldn't really understand, but that must be like steel cables in a hot sun. The man listened without moving, showing no signs of impatience, and then he made a gesture with his hand that meant move aside, and headed toward the door.

3.

I left the table in a daze, struggling to take in the fact that Nino was really there, in Milan, in that room. And yet he was, already he was coming toward me, smiling, but at a restrained, unhurried pace. We shook hands, his was hot, mine cold, and we said how glad we were to see each other after so long. To know that finally the worst of the evening was over and that now he was before me, real, assuaged my bad mood but not my agitation. I introduced him to the critic who had generously praised my book, saying that he was a friend from Naples, that we had gone to high school together. The professor, although he, too, had received some jabs from Nino, was polite, praised the way he had treated that man, and spoke of Naples with fondness, addressing him as if he were a gifted student who was to be encouraged. Nino explained that he had lived in Milan for some years, his field was economic geography, he belonged—and he smiled—to the most wretched category in the academic pyramid, that is to say lecturer. He said it sweetly, without the almost sullen tones he had had as a boy, and it seemed to me that he wore a lighter armor than that which had fascinated me in high school, as if he had shed any excess weight in order to be able to joust more rapidly and with elegance. I noted with relief that he wasn't wearing a wedding ring.

Meanwhile some of Adele's friends had come over to have their books signed, which made me nervous: it was the first time I had done this. I hesitated: I didn't want to lose sight of Nino even for an instant, but I also wanted to mitigate the impression I must have made of a clumsy girl. So I left him with the old professor—his name was Tarratano—and greeted my readers politely. I intended to do this quickly, but the books were new, with an odor of ink, so different from the dog-eared, ill-smelling books that Lila and I took out from the library in the neighborhood, and I didn't feel like marring them carelessly with the pen. I displayed my best handwriting, from the time of Maestra Oliviero, I invented elaborate dedications that caused some impatience in the women who were waiting. My heart was pounding as I wrote, with an eye on Nino. I trembled at the idea that he would leave.

He didn't. Now Adele had gone up to him and Tarratano, and Nino spoke to her confidently and yet with deference. I remembered when he used to talk to Professor Galiani in the corridors of the high school, and it took me a while to consolidate in my mind the brilliant high school student of then with the young man of now. I vehemently discarded, on the other hand, as a pointless deviation that had made all of us suffer, the university student of Ischia, the lover of my married friend, the helpless youth who hid in the bathroom of the shop on Piazza dei Martiri and who was the father of Gennaro, a child he had never seen. Certainly Lila's irruption had thrown him off, but—it now seemed obvious—it was just a digression. However intense that experience must have been, however deep the marks it had left, it was over now. Nino had found himself again, and I was pleased. I thought: I have to tell Lila that I saw him, that he's well. Then I changed my mind: no, I won't tell her.

When I finished the dedications, the room was empty. Adele took me gently by the hand, she praised the way I had spoken of my book and the way I had responded to the terrible intrusion—so she called it—of the man with the thick eyeglasses. Since I denied having done well (I knew perfectly well that it wasn't true), she asked Nino and Tarratano to give their opinion, and both were profuse with compliments. Nino went so far as to say, looking at me seriously: *You don't know what that girl was like in high school, extremely intelligent, cultivated, very courageous, very beautiful.* And while I felt my face burning, he began to tell with exaggerated courtesy the story of my clash with the religion teacher years earlier. Adele laughed frequently as she listened. In our family, she said, we understood Elena's virtues right away, and then she said she had made a reservation for dinner at a place nearby. I was alarmed, I said in embarrassment that I was tired and not hungry, I would happily take a short walk with Nino before going to bed. I knew it was rude, the dinner was meant to celebrate me and thank Tarratano for his work on behalf of my book, but I couldn't stop myself. Adele looked at me for a moment with a sardonic expression, she replied that naturally my friend was invited, and added mysteriously, as if to compensate for

the sacrifice I was making: I have a nice surprise in store for
you. I looked at Nino anxiously: would he accept the invitation? He said he didn't want to be a bother, he looked at his
watch, he accepted.

4.

We left the bookstore. Adele, tactfully, went ahead with
Tarratano, Nino and I followed. But I immediately found that I
didn't know what to say to him, I was afraid that every word
would be wrong. He made sure there were no silences. He
praised my book again, he went on to speak with great respect
of the Airotas (he called them "the most civilized of the families
who count for something in Italy"), he said he knew Mariarosa
("She's always on the front lines: two weeks ago we had a big
argument"), he congratulated me because he had learned from
Adele that I was engaged to Pietro, whose book on Bacchic
rites he seemed to know, amazing me; but he spoke with respect
especially of the father, Professor Guido Airota, "a truly exceptional man." I was a little annoyed that he already knew of my
engagement, and it made me uneasy that the praise of my book
had served as an introduction to the far more insistent praise of
Pietro's entire family, Pietro's book. I interrupted him, I asked
him about himself, but he was vague, with only a few allusions
to a small volume coming out that he called boring but obliga-
tory. I pressed him, I asked if he had had a hard time during his
early days in Milan. He answered with a few generic remarks
about the problems of coming from the South without a cent in
your pocket. Then out of the blue he asked me:

"Are you living in Naples again?"

"For now, yes."

"In the neighborhood?"

"Yes."

"I've broken conclusively with my father, and I don't see anyone in my family."

"Too bad."

"It's better that way. I'm just sorry not to have any news of Lina."

For a moment I thought I'd been wrong, that Lila had never gone out of his life, that he had come to the bookstore not for me but only to find out about her. Then I said to myself: if he had really wanted to find out about Lila, in so many years he would have found a way, and I reacted violently, in the sharp tone of someone who wants to end the subject quickly:

"She left her husband and lives with someone else."

"Did she have a boy or a girl?"

"A boy."

He made a grimace of displeasure and said: "Lina is brave, even too brave. But she doesn't know how to submit to reality, she's incapable of accepting others and herself. Loving her was a difficult experience."

"In what sense?"

"She doesn't know what dedication is."

"Maybe you're exaggerating."

"No, she's really made badly: in her mind and in everything, even when it comes to sex."

Those last words—*even when it comes to sex*—struck me more than the others. So Nino's judgment on his relationship with Lila was negative? So he had just said to me, disturbingly, that that opinion included even the sexual arena? I stared for some seconds at the dark outlines of Adele and her friend walking ahead of us. The disturbance became anxiety, I sensed that *even when it comes to sex* was a preamble, that he wished to become still more explicit. Years earlier, Stefano, after his marriage, had confided in me, had told me about his problems with Lila, but he had done so without ever mentioning sex—

no one in the neighborhood would have in speaking of the woman he loved. It was unthinkable, for example, that Pasquale would talk to me about Ada's sexuality, or, worse, that Antonio would speak to Carmen or Gigliola about my sexuality. Boys might talk among themselves—and in a vulgar way, when they didn't like us girls or no longer liked us—but among boys and girls no. I guessed instead that Nino, the new Nino, considered it completely normal to discuss with me his sexual relations with my friend. I was embarrassed, I pulled back. Of this, too, I thought, I must never speak to Lila, and meanwhile I said with feigned indifference: water under the bridge, let's not be sad, let's go back to you, what are you working on, what are your prospects at the university, where do you live, by yourself? But I certainly overdid it; he must have felt that I had made a quick escape. He smiled ironically, and was about to answer. But we had arrived at the restaurant, and we went in.

5.

Adele assigned us places: I was next to Nino and opposite Tarratano, she next to Tarratano and opposite Nino. We ordered, and meanwhile the conversation had shifted to the man with the thick glasses, a professor of Italian literature—I learned—a Christian Democrat, and a regular contributor to the *Corriere della Sera*. Adele and her friend now lost all restraint. Outside of the bookstore ritual, they couldn't say enough bad things about the man, and they congratulated Nino for the way he had confronted and routed him. They especially enjoyed recalling what Nino had said as the man was leaving the room, remarks they had heard and I hadn't. They asked him what his exact words were, and Nino retreated, saying that he didn't remember. But then the words emerged, maybe reinvented for the occasion, something like: *In order to safeguard authority in all of its manifestations, you suspend democracy.* And from there the three of them took off, talking, with increasing ardor, about the secret services, about Greece, about torture in the Greek prisons, about Vietnam, about the unexpected uprising of the student movement not only in Italy but in Europe and the world, about an article in *Il Ponte* by Professor Airota—which Nino said that he agreed with, word for word—about the conditions of research and teaching in the universities.

"I'll tell my daughter that you liked it," Adele said. "Mariarosa thought it was terrible."

"Mariarosa gets passionate only about what the world can't give."

"Very good, that really is what she's like."

I knew nothing of that article by my future father-in-law. The subject made me uneasy, and I listened in silence. First my exams, then my thesis, then the book and its rapid publication had absorbed much of my time. I was informed about world events only superficially, and I had picked up almost nothing about students, demonstrations, clashes, the wounded, arrests, blood. Since I was now outside the university, all I really knew about that chaos was Pietro's grumblings, his complaints about what he called literally "the Pisan nonsense." As a result I felt around me a scene with confusing features: features that, however, my companions seemed able to decipher with great precision, Nino even more than the others. I sat beside him, I listened, I touched his arm with mine, a contact merely of fabrics which nevertheless agitated me. He had kept his fondness for figures: he was giving a list of numbers, of students enrolled in the university, a crowd by now, and of the capacity of the buildings; of the hours the tenured professors actually worked, and how many of them, rather than doing research and teaching, sat in parliament or on administrative committees or devoted themselves to lucrative consulting jobs and private practice. Adele agreed, and so did her friend; occasionally they interrupted, mentioning people I had never heard of. I felt excluded. The celebration for my book was no longer at the top of their thoughts, my mother-in-law seemed to have forgotten even the surprise she had announced for me. I said that I had to get up for a moment; Adele nodded absently, Nino continued to speak passionately. Tarratano must have thought that I was getting bored and said kindly, almost in a whisper:

"Hurry back, I'd like to hear your opinion."

"I don't have opinions," I said with a half smile.

He smiled in turn: "A writer always invents one."

"Maybe I'm not a writer."

"Yes, you are."

I went to the bathroom. Nino had always had the capacity, as soon as he opened his mouth, to demonstrate to me my backwardness. I have to start studying, I thought, how could I let myself go like this? Of course, if I want I can fake some expertise and some enthusiasm. But I can't go on like that, I've learned too many things that don't count and very few that do. At the end of my affair with Franco, I had lost the little curiosity about the world that he had instilled in me. And my engagement to Pietro hadn't helped, what didn't interest him lost interest for me. How different Pietro is from his father, his sister, his mother. And how different he is from Nino. If it had been up to him, I wouldn't ever have written my novel. He was almost irritated by it, as an infraction of the academic rules. Or maybe I'm exaggerating, it's just my problem. I'm so limited, I can only concentrate on one thing at a time, excluding everything else. But now I'll change. Right after this boring dinner I'll drag Nino with me, I'll make him walk all night, I'll ask him what books I should read, what films I should see, what music I should listen to. And I'll take him by the arm, I'll say: I'm cold. Confused intentions, incomplete proposals. I hid from myself the anxiety I felt, I said to myself only: It might be the only chance we have, tomorrow I'm leaving, I won't see him again.

Meanwhile I gazed angrily into the mirror. My face looked tired, small pimples on my chin and dark circles under my eyes announced my period. I'm ugly, short, my bust is too big. I should have understood long ago that he never liked me, it was no coincidence that he preferred Lila. But with what result? *She's made badly even when it comes to sex*, he said. I was wrong to avoid the subject. I should have acted curious, let him continue. If he talks about it again I'll be more open-minded, I'll say: what does it mean that a girl is made badly when it comes to sex? I'm asking you, I'll explain laughing, so that I can correct myself, if it seems necessary. Assuming that one can correct it, who knows. I remembered with disgust what had happened with his father on the beach at the Maronti. I thought of making love with Franco on the little bed in his room in Pisa—had I done something wrong that he had noticed but had tactfully not mentioned to me? And if that very evening, let's say, I had gone to bed with Nino, would I make more mistakes, so that he would think: she's made badly, like Lila, and would he speak of it behind my back to his girl-friends at the university, maybe even to Mariarosa?

I realized the offensiveness of those words; I should have rebuked him. From that mistaken sex, I should have said to him, from an experience of which you now express a negative opinion, came a child, little Gennaro, who is very intelligent: it's not nice for you to talk like that, you can't reduce the question to who is made badly and who is made well. Lila ruined herself for you. And I made up my mind: when I get rid of Adele and her friend, when he walks me to the hotel, I'll return to the subject and tell him.

I came out of the bathroom. I went back to the dining room and discovered that during my absence the situation had changed. As soon as my mother-in-law saw me, she waved and

said happily, her cheeks alight: the surprise finally got here.
The surprise was Pietro, he was sitting next to her.

6.

My fiancé jumped up, he embraced me. I had never told
him anything about Nino. I had said a few words about
Antonio, and had told him something about my relationship
with Franco, which, besides, was well known in the student
world of Pisa. Nino, however, I had never mentioned. It was a
story that hurt me, it had painful moments that I was ashamed
of. To tell it meant to confess that I had loved forever a person
as I would never love him. And to give it an order, a sense,
involved talking about Lila, about Ischia, maybe even going so
far as to admit that the episode of sex with an older man, as it
appeared in my book, was inspired by a true experience at the
Maronti, by a decision that I had made as a desperate girl and
which now, after so much time had passed, seemed to me
repugnant. My own business, therefore. I had held on to my
secrets. If Pietro had known, he would have easily understood
why I was greeting him without pleasure.

He sat down again at the head of the table, between his
mother and Nino. He ate a steak, drank some wine, but he
looked at me in alarm, aware of my unhappiness. Certainly he
felt at fault because he hadn't arrived in time and had missed
an important event in my life, because his neglect could be
interpreted as a sign that he didn't love me, because he had left
me among strangers without the comfort of his affection. It
would have been difficult to tell him that my dark face, my
muteness, could be explained *precisely* by the fact that he hadn't
remained completely absent, that he had intruded between me
and Nino.

Nino, meanwhile, was making me even more unhappy. He

was sitting next to me but didn't address a word to me. He seemed happy about Pietro's arrival. He poured wine for him, offered him cigarettes, lighted one, and now they were both smoking, lips compressed, and talking about the difficult journey by car from Pisa to Milan, and the pleasure of driving. It struck me how different they were: Nino thin, lanky, his voice high and cordial; Pietro thick-set, with the comical tangle of hair over his large forehead, his broad cheeks scraped by the razor, his voice always low. They seemed pleased to have met, which was unusual for Pietro, who was generally reserved. Nino pressed him, showing a real interest in his studies (*I read an article somewhere in which you compare milk and honey to wine and every form of drunkenness*), and urging him to talk about them, so that my fiancé, who tended not to talk about his subject, gave in, he corrected good-humoredly, he opened up. But just when Pietro was starting to gain confidence, Adele interrupted.

"Enough talk," she said to her son. "What about the surprise for Elena?"

I looked at her uncertainly. There were other surprises? Wasn't it enough that Pietro had driven for hours without stopping, to arrive only in time for the dinner in my honor? I thought of my fiancé with curiosity, he had a sulky expression that I knew and that he assumed when circumstances forced him to speak about himself in public. He announced to me, but almost in a whisper, that he had become a tenured professor, a very young tenured professor, with a position at Florence. Like that, by magic, in his typical fashion. He never boasted of his brilliance, he was scarcely aware of his value as a scholar, he kept silent about the struggles he had endured. And now, look, he mentioned that news casually, as if he had been forced to by his mother, as if for him it meant nothing. In fact, it meant remarkable prestige at a young age, it meant economic security, it meant leaving Pisa, it meant escaping a political and cultural climate that for months, I don't know why, had exasperated him. It meant finally that in the fall, or at the beginning of the next year, we would get married and I would leave Naples. No one mentioned this last thing, instead they all congratulated Pietro and me. Even Nino, who right afterward looked at his watch, made some acerbic remarks on university careers, and exclaimed that he was sorry but he had to go.

We all got up. I didn't know what to do, I uselessly sought his gaze, as a great sorrow filled my heart. End of the evening, missed opportunity, aborted desires. Out on the street I hoped that he would give me a phone number, an address. He merely shook my hand and wished me all the best. From that moment it seemed to me that each of his gestures was deliberately cutting me off. As a kind of farewell I gave him a half smile, waving my hand as if I were holding a pen. It was a plea, it meant: you know where I live, write to me, please. But he had already turned his back.

7.

I thanked Adele and her friend for all the trouble they had taken for me and for my book. They both praised Nino at length, sincerely, speaking to me as if it were I who had contributed to making him so likable, so intelligent. Pietro said nothing, he merely nodded a bit nervously when his mother told him to return soon, they were both guests of Mariarosa. I said immediately: you don't have to come with me, go with your mother. It didn't occur to anyone that I was serious, that I was unhappy and would rather be alone.

All the way back I was impossible. I exclaimed that I didn't like Florence, and it wasn't true. I exclaimed that I didn't want to write anymore, I wanted to teach, and it wasn't true. I exclaimed that I was tired, I was very sleepy, and it wasn't true.

Not only that. When, suddenly, Pietro declared that he wanted to meet my parents, I yelled at him: you're crazy, forget my parents, you're not suitable for them and they aren't suitable for you. Then he was frightened, and asked:

"Do you not want to marry me anymore?"

I was about to say: *No, I don't want to,* but I restrained myself in time, I knew that that wasn't true, either. I said weakly, I'm sorry, I'm depressed, of course I want to marry you, and I took his hand, I interlaced my fingers in his. He was an intelligent man, extraordinarily cultured, and good. I loved him, I didn't mean to make him suffer. And yet, even as I was holding his hand, even as I was affirming that I wanted to marry him, I knew clearly that if he hadn't appeared that night at the restaurant I would have tried to sleep with Nino.

I had a hard time admitting it to myself. Certainly it would have been an offense that Pietro didn't deserve, and yet I would have committed it willingly and perhaps without remorse. I would have found a way to draw Nino to me, with all the years that had passed, from elementary school to high school, up to the time of Ischia and Piazza dei Martiri. I would have made love with him, even though I hadn't liked that remark about Lila, and was distressed by it. I would have slept with him and to Pietro I would have said nothing. Maybe I could have told Lila, but who knows when, maybe as an old woman, when I imagined that nothing would matter anymore to her or to me. Time, as in all things, was decisive. Nino would last a single night, he would leave me in the morning. Even though I had known him forever, he was made of dreams, and holding on to him forever would have been impossible: he came from childhood, he was constructed out of childish desires, he had no concreteness, he didn't face the future. Pietro, on the other hand, was of the present, massive, a boundary stone. He marked a land new to me, a land of good reasons, governed by rules that originated in his family and endowed everything with meaning. Grand ideals flourished, the cult of the reputation, matters of principle. Nothing in the sphere of the Airotas was perfunctory. Marriage, for example, was a contribution to a secular battle. Pietro's parents had had only a civil wedding, and Pietro, although as far as I knew he had a vast religious knowledge, would never get married in a church; rather, he would give me up. The same went for baptism. Pietro hadn't been baptized, nor had Mariarosa, so any children that might come wouldn't be baptized, either. Everything about him had that tendency, seemed always to be guided by a superior order that, although its origin was not divine but came from his family, gave him, just the same, the certainty of being on the side of truth and justice. As for sex, I don't know, he was wary. He knew enough of my affair with Franco Mari to deduce that I wasn't a virgin, and yet he had never mentioned the subject, not even an accusatory phrase, a vulgar comment, a laugh. I didn't think he'd had other girlfriends; it was hard to imagine him with a prostitute, I was sure he hadn't spent even a minute of his life talking about women with other men. He hated salacious remarks. He hated gossip, raised voices, parties, every form of waste. Although his circumstances were comfortable, he tended—in this unlike his parents and his sister—to a sort of asceticism amid the abundance. And he had a conspicuous sense of duty, he would never fail in his commitments to me, he would never betray me.

No, I did not want to lose him. Never mind if my nature, coarse in spite of the education I had had, was far from his rigor, if I honestly didn't know how I would stand up to all that geometry. He gave me the certainty that I was escaping the opportunistic malleability of my father and the crudeness of my mother. So I forced myself to repress the thought of Nino, I took Pietro by the arm, I murmured, yes, let's get married as soon as possible, I want to leave home, I want to get a driver's license, I want to travel, I want to have a telephone, a televi-

sion, I've never had anything. And he at that point became
cheerful, he laughed, he said yes to everything I randomly
asked for. A few steps from the hotel he stopped, he whispered
hoarsely: Can I sleep with you? That was the last surprise of
the evening. I looked at him bewildered: I had been ready so
many times to make love, he had always avoided it; but having
him in the bed there, in Milan, in the hotel, after the traumatic
discussion in the bookstore, after Nino, I didn't feel like it. I
answered: We've waited so long, we can wait a little longer. I
kissed him in a dark corner, I watched him from the hotel
entrance as he walked away along Corso Garibaldi, and every
so often turned and waved timidly. His clumsy gait, his flat
feet, the tangle of his hair moved me.

8.

From that moment life began to pound me without respite,
the months were rapidly grafted onto one another, there was
no day when something good or bad didn't happen. I returned
to Naples, thinking about Nino, and that encounter without
consequences, and at times the wish to see Lila was strong, to
go and wait for her to come home from work, tell her what
could be told without hurting her. Then I convinced myself
that merely mentioning Nino would wound her, and I gave it
up. Lila had gone her way, he his. I had urgent things to deal
with. For example, the evening of my return from Milan I told
my parents that Pietro was coming to meet them, that probably we would be married within the year, that I was going to
live in Florence.

They showed no joy, or even satisfaction. I thought that
they had finally grown used to my coming and going as I
liked, increasingly estranged from the family, indifferent to
their problems of survival. And it seemed to me normal that

only my father became somewhat agitated, always nervous at the prospect of situations he didn't feel prepared for.

"Does the university professor have to come to our house?" he asked, in irritation.

"Where else?" my mother said angrily. "How can he ask you for Lenuccia's hand if he doesn't come here?"

Usually she seemed more prepared than he, concrete, resolute to the point of indifference. But once she had silenced him, once her husband had gone to bed and Elisa and Peppe and Gianni had set up their beds in the dining room, I had to change my mind. She attacked me in very low but shrill tones, hissing with reddened eyes: We are nothing to you, you tell us nothing until the last minute, the young lady thinks she's somebody because she has an education, because she writes books, because she's marrying a professor, but my dear, you came out of this belly and you are made of this substance, so don't act superior and don't ever forget that if you are intelligent, I who carried you in here am just as intelligent, if not more, and if I had had the chance I would have done the same as you, understand? Then, on the crest of her rage, she first reproached me saying that because I had left, and thought only of myself, my siblings hadn't done well in school, and then asked me for money, or, rather, demanded it: she needed it to buy a decent dress for Elisa and to fix up the house a bit, since I was forcing her to receive my fiancé.

I passed over my siblings' lack of success in school. The money, on the other hand, I gave her right away, even if it wasn't true that she needed it for the house—she continually asked for money, any excuse would do. Although she had never said so explicitly, she still couldn't accept the fact that I kept my money in a post-office savings account, that I hadn't handed it over to her as I always had, ever since I first took the stationer's daughters to the beach, or worked in the bookstore on Via Mezzocannone. Maybe, I thought, by acting as if my money belonged to her she wants to convince me that I myself belong to her, and that, even if I get married, I will belong to her forever.

I remained calm, I told her as a sort of compensation that I would have a telephone put in, that I would buy a television on the installment plan. She looked at me uncertainly, with a sudden admiration that clashed with what she had just been saying.

"A television and telephone in this house here?"

"Yes."

"You'll pay for it?"

"Yes."

"Always, even after you're married?"

"Yes."

"The professor knows that there's not a cent for a dowry, and not even for a reception?"

"He knows, and we're not having a reception."

Again her mood changed, her eyes became inflamed.

"What do you mean, no reception? Make him pay."

"No, we're doing without."

My mother became furious again, she provoked me in every way she could think of, she wanted me to respond so that she could get angrier.

"You remember Lila's wedding, you remember the reception she had?"

"Yes."

"And you, who are much better than she is, don't want to do anything?"

"No."

We went on like that until I decided that, rather than taking her rage in doses, it would be better to have it all at once, one grand fury:

"Ma," I said, "not only are we not having a party but I'm

not even getting married in church, I'm getting married at city hall."

At that point it was as if doors and windows had been blown open by a strong wind. Although she wasn't religious, my mother lost control and, leaning toward me, red in the face, began yelling insults at me. She shouted that the marriage was worthless if the priest didn't say that it was valid. She shouted that if I didn't get married before God I would never be a wife but only a whore, and, despite her lame leg, she almost flew as she went to wake my father, my siblings, to let them know what she had always feared, that too much education had ruined my brain, that I had had all the luck and yet I was treated like a whore, that she would never be able to go out of the house because of the shame of having a godless daughter.

My father, stunned, in his underwear, and my siblings sought to understand what other trouble they had to deal with because of me, and tried to calm her, but in vain. She shouted that she wanted to throw me out of the house immediately, before I exposed her, too, *her, too,* to the shame of having a concubine daughter like Lila and Ada. Meanwhile, although she wasn't actually hitting me, she struck the air as if I were a shadow and she had grabbed a real me, whom she was beating ferociously. It was some time before she quieted down, which she did thanks to Elisa. My sister asked cautiously:

"But is it you who want to get married at city hall or is it your fiancé?"

I explained to her, but as if I were explaining the matter to all of them, that for me the Church hadn't counted for a long time, but that whether I got married at city hall or at the altar was the same to me; while for my fiancé it was very important to have only a civil ceremony, he knew all about religious matters and believed that religion, however valuable, was ruined precisely when it interfered in the affairs of the state. In other words, I concluded, if we don't get married at city hall, he won't marry me.

At that point my father, who had immediately sided with my mother, suddenly stopped echoing her insults and laments.

"He won't marry you?"

"No."

"And what will he do, leave you?"

"We'll go and live together in Florence without getting married."

That information my mother considered the most intolerable of all. She completely lost control, vowing that in that case she would take a knife and cut my throat. My father instead nervously ruffled his hair, and said to her:

"Be quiet, don't get me mad, let's be reasonable. We know very well that someone can get married by the priest, have a fancy celebration, and still come to a bad end."

He, too, was obviously alluding to Lila, the ever-vivid scandal of the neighborhood, and my mother finally understood. The priest wasn't a guarantee, nothing was a guarantee in the brutal world we lived in. So she stopped shouting and left to my father the task of examining the situation and, if necessary, letting me have my way. But she didn't stop pacing, with her limp, shaking her head, insulting my future husband. What was he, the professor? Was he a Communist? Communist and professor? Professor of that shit, she shouted. What kind of professor is he, one who thinks like that? A shit thinks like that. No, replied my father, what do you mean shit, he's a man who's educated and knows better than anyone what disgusting things the priests do, that's why he wants to go and say "I do" only at city hall. Yes, you're right, a lot of Communists do that. Yes, you're right, like this our daughter doesn't seem married. But I would trust this university professor: he loves her. I can't believe that he would put Lenuccia in a situation where she seems like a whore. And anyway if we don't want to trust him—but I do trust him, even if I don't know him yet: he's an important person, the girls here dream of a match like that— at least we can trust the city hall. I work there, at the city hall, and a marriage there, I can assure you, is as valid as the one in church and maybe even more.

He went on for hours. My siblings at a certain point collapsed and went back to sleep. I stayed to soothe my parents and persuade them to accept something that for me, at that moment, was an important sign of my entrance into Pietro's world. Besides, it made me feel bolder than Lila. And most of all, if I met Nino again, I would have liked to be able to say to him, in an allusive way: See where that argument with the religion teacher led, every choice has its history, so many moments of our existence are shoved into a corner, waiting for an outlet, and in the end the outlet arrives. But I would have been exaggerating, in reality it was much simpler. For at least ten years the God of childhood, already fairly weak, had been pushed aside like an old sick person, and I felt no need for the sanctity of marriage. The essential thing was to get out of Naples.

9.

My family's horror at the idea of a civil union alone certainly was not exhausted that night, but it diminished. The next day my mother treated me as if anything she touched—the coffee pot, the cup with the milk, the sugar bowl, the fresh loaf of bread—were there only to lead her into the temptation to throw it in my face. Yet she didn't start yelling again. As for me I ignored her; I left early in the morning, and went to start the paperwork for the installation of the telephone. Having taken care of that business I went to Port'Alba and wandered through the bookstores. I was determined, within a short time, to enable myself to speak with confidence when situations like the one in

Milan arose. I chose journals and books more or less at random, and spent a lot of money. After many hesitations, influenced by that remark of Nino's that kept coming to mind, I ended up getting *Three Essays on the Theory of Sexuality*—I knew almost nothing of Freud and the little I knew irritated me—along with a couple of small books devoted to sex. I intended to do what I had done in the past with schoolwork, with exams, with my thesis, what I had done with the newspapers that Professor Galiani passed on to me or the Marxist texts that Franco had given me. I wanted to *study* the contemporary world. Hard to say what I had already taken in at that time. There had been the discussions with Pasquale, and also with Nino. There had been some attention paid to Cuba and Latin America. There was the incurable poverty of the neighborhood, the lost battle of Lila. There was school, which defeated my siblings because they were less stubborn than I was, less dedicated to sacrifice. There were the long conversations with Franco and occasional ones with Mariarosa, now jumbled together in a wisp of smoke. (*The world is profoundly unjust and must be changed, but both the peaceful coexistence between American imperialism and the Stalinist bureaucracies, on the one hand, and the reformist politics of the European, and especially the Italian, workers' parties, on the other, are directed at keeping the proletariat in a subordinate wait-and-see situation that throws water on the fire of revolution, with the result that if the global stalemate wins, if social democracy wins, it will be capital that triumphs through the centuries and the working class will fall victim to enforced consumerism.*) These stimuli had functioned, certainly they had been working in me for a long time, occasionally they excited me. But driving that decision to bring myself up to date by forced marches was, at least at first, I think, the old urgency to succeed. I had long ago convinced myself that one can train oneself to anything, even to political passion.

As I was paying, I glimpsed my novel on a shelf, and immediately looked in another direction. Whenever I saw the book in a window, among other novels that had just come out, I felt inside a mixture of pride and fear, a dart of pleasure that ended in anguish. Certainly, the story had come into being by chance, in twenty days, without struggle, as a sedative against depression. Moreover, I knew what great literature was, I had done a lot of work in the classics, and it never occurred to me, while I was writing, that I was making something of value. But the effort of finding a form had absorbed me. And the absorption had become *that* book, an object that contained me. Now *I* was there, *exposed*, and seeing myself caused a violent pounding in my chest. I felt that not only in my book but in novels in general there was something that truly agitated me, a bare and throbbing heart, the same that had burst out of my chest in that distant moment when Lila had proposed that we write a story together. It had fallen to me to do it seriously. But was that what I wanted? To write, to write with purpose, to write better than I had already? And to study the stories of the past and the present to understand how they worked, and to learn, learn everything about the world with the sole purpose of constructing living hearts, which no one would ever do better than me, not even Lila if she had had the opportunity?

I came out of the bookshop, I stopped in Piazza Cavour. The day was fine, Via Foria seemed unnaturally clean and solid in spite of the scaffolding that shored up the Galleria. I imposed on myself the usual discipline. I took out a notebook that I had bought recently, I wished to start acting like a real writer, putting down thoughts, observations, useful information. I read *l'Unità* from beginning to end, I took notes on the things I didn't know. I found the article by Pietro's father in *Il Ponte* and skimmed it with curiosity, but it didn't seem as important as Nino had claimed. Rather, it put me off for two reasons: first, Guido Airota used the same professorial language as the man with the thick eyeglasses but even more rigorously; second, in a passage in which he spoke about women students ("It's a new crowd," he wrote, "and by all the evidence they are not from well-off families, young ladies in modest dresses and of modest upbringing who justly expect from the immense labor of their studies a future not of domestic rituals alone"), it seemed to me that I saw an allusion to myself, whether deliberate or completely unconscious. I made a note of that in my notebook as well (*What am I to the Airotas, a jewel in the crown of their broad-mindedness?*) and, not exactly in a good mood, in fact with some irritation, I began to leaf through the *Corriere della Sera*.

I remember that the air was warm, and I've preserved an olfactory memory—invented or real—a mixture of printed paper and fried pizza. Page after page I looked at the headlines, until one took my breath away. There was a photograph of me, set amid four dense columns of type. In the background was a view of the neighborhood, with the tunnel. The headline said: *Salacious Memoirs of an Ambitious Girl: Elena Greco's Début Novel.* The byline was that of the man with the thick eyeglasses.

10.

I was covered in a cold sweat while I read; I had the impression that I was close to fainting. My book was treated as an occasion to assert that in the past decade, in all areas of productive, social, and cultural life, from factories to offices, to the university, publishing, and cinema, an entire world had collapsed under the pressure of a spoiled youth, without values. Occasionally he cited some phrase of mine, in quotation marks, to demonstrate that I was a fitting exponent of my badly brought-up generation. In conclusion he called me "a girl concerned with hiding her lack of talent behind titillating pages of mediocre triviality."

I burst into tears. It was the harshest thing I had read since the book came out, and not in a daily with a small circulation but in the most widely read newspaper in Italy. Most of all, the image of my smiling face seemed to me intolerable in the middle of a text so offensive. I walked home, not before getting rid of the *Corriere*. I was afraid my mother might read the review and use it against me. I imagined that she would have liked to put it, too, in her album, to throw in my face whenever I upset her.

I found the table set only for me. My father was at work, my mother had gone to ask a neighbor for something or other, and my siblings had already eaten. As I ate pasta and potatoes I reread at random some passages of my book. I thought desperately: Maybe it really is worthless, maybe it was published only as a favor to Adele. How could I have come up with such pallid sentences, such banal observations? And how sloppy, how many useless commas; I won't write anymore. Between disgust with the food and disgust with the book I was depressed, when Elisa arrived with a piece of paper. It came from Signora Spagnuolo, who had kindly agreed to let her telephone number be used by anyone who urgently needed to communicate with me. The piece of paper said that there had been three phone calls, one from Gina Medotti, who ran the press office at the publisher's, one from Adele, and one from Pietro.

The three names, written in Signora Spagnuolo's labored handwriting, had the effect of giving concreteness to a thought that until a moment before had remained in the background: the terrible words of the man with the thick eyeglasses were spreading rapidly, and in the course of the day they would be everywhere. They had already been read by Pietro, by his family, by the directors of the publishing house. Maybe they had reached Nino. Maybe they were before the eyes of my professors in Pisa. Certainly they had come to the attention of

Professor Galiani and her children. And who knows, even Lila might have read them. I burst into tears again, frightening Elisa.

"What's wrong, Lenù?"

"I don't feel well."

"Shall I make you some chamomile tea?"

"Yes."

But there wasn't time. Someone was knocking at the door, it was Rosa Spagnuolo. Cheerful, slightly out of breath from hurrying up the stairs, she said that my fiancé was again looking for me, he was on the telephone, what a lovely voice, what a lovely northern accent. I ran to answer, apologizing repeatedly for bothering her. Pietro tried to console me, he said that his mother urged me not to be upset, the main thing was that it talked about the book. But, surprising Signora Spagnuolo, who knew me as a meek girl, I practically screamed, What do I care if it talks about it if it says such terrible things? He urged me again to be calm and added: Tomorrow an article is coming out in *l'Unità*. I ended the call coldly, I said: It would be better if no one worried about me anymore.

I couldn't close my eyes that night. In the morning I couldn't contain myself and went out to get *l'Unità*. I leafed through it in a rush, still at the newsstand, a few steps from the elementary school. I was again confronted by a photograph of myself, the same that had been in the *Corriere*, not in the middle of the article this time but above it, next to the headline: *Young Rebels and Old Reactionaries: Concerning the Book by Elena Greco*. I had never heard of the author of the article, but it was certainly someone who wrote well, and his words acted as a balm. He praised my novel wholeheartedly and insulted the prestigious professor. I went home reassured, maybe even in a good mood. I paged through my book and this time it seemed to me well put together, written with mastery. My mother said sourly: Did you win the lottery? I left the paper on the kitchen table without saying anything.

In the late afternoon Signora Spagnuolo reappeared, I was wanted again on the telephone. In response to my embarrassment, my apologies, she said she was very happy to be able to be useful to a girl like me, she was full of compliments. Gigliola had been unlucky, she sighed on the stairs, her father had taken her to work in the Solaras' pastry shop when she was thirteen, and good thing she was engaged to Michele, otherwise she'd be slaving away her whole life. She opened the door and led me along the hall to the telephone that was attached to the wall. I saw that she had put a chair there so that I would be comfortable: what deference was shown to someone who is educated. Studying was considered a ploy used by the smartest kids to avoid hard work. How can I explain to this woman—I thought—that from the age of six I've been a slave to letters and numbers, that my mood depends on the success of their combinations, that the joy of having done well is rare, unstable, that it lasts an hour, an afternoon, a night?

"Did you read it?" Adele asked.

"Yes."

"Are you pleased?"

"Yes."

"Then I'll give you another piece of good news: the book is starting to sell, if it keeps on like this we'll reprint it."

"What does that mean?"

"It means that our friend in the *Corriere* thought he was destroying us and instead he worked for us. Bye, Elena, enjoy your success."

11.

The book was selling really well, I realized in the following days. The most conspicuous sign was the increasing number of phone calls from Gina, who reported a notice in such-and-such a newspaper, or announced some invitation from a bookstore or cultural group, without ever forgetting to greet me with the kind words: The book is taking off, Dottoressa Greco, congratulations. Thank you, I said, but I wasn't happy. The articles in the newspapers seemed superficial, they confined themselves to applying either the enthusiastic matrix of *l'Unità* or the ruinous one of the *Corriere*. And although Gina repeated on every occasion that even negative reviews were good for sales, those reviews nevertheless wounded me and I would wait anxiously for a handful of favorable comments to offset the unfavorable ones and feel better. In any case, I stopped hiding the malicious reviews from my mother; I handed them all over, good and bad. She tried to read them, spelling them out with a stern expression, but she never managed to get beyond four or five lines before she either found a point to quarrel with or, out of boredom, took refuge in her mania for collecting. Her aim was to fill the entire album and, afraid of being left with empty pages, she complained when I had nothing to give her.

The review that at the time wounded me most deeply appeared in *Roma*. Paragraph by paragraph, it retraced the one in the *Corriere*, but in a florid style that at the end fanatically hammered at a single concept: women are losing all restraint, one has only to read Elena Greco's indecent novel to understand it, a novel that is a cheap version of the already vulgar *Bonjour Tristesse*. What hurt me, though, was not the content but the byline. The article was by Nino's father, Donato Sarratore. I thought of how impressed I had been as a girl by the fact that that man was the author of a book of poems; I thought of the glorious halo I had enveloped him in when I discovered that he wrote for the newspapers. Why that review? Did he wish to get revenge because he recognized himself in the obscene family man who seduces the protagonist? I was tempted to call him and insult him atrociously in dialect. I gave it up only because I thought of Nino, and made what seemed an important discovery: his experience and mine were similar. We had both refused to model ourselves on our families: I had been struggling forever to get away from my mother, he had burned his bridges with his father. This similarity consoled me, and my rage slowly diminished.

But I hadn't taken into account that, in the neighborhood, *Roma* was read more than any other newspaper. I found out that evening. Gino, the pharmacist's son, who lifted weights and had become a muscular young man, looked out from the doorway of his father's shop just as I was passing, in a white pharmacist's smock even though he hadn't yet taken his degree. He called to me, holding out the paper, and said, in a fairly serious tone, because he had recently moved up a little in the local section of the neo-fascist Italian Social Movement party: Did you see what they're writing about you? In order not to give him the satisfaction, I answered, they write all sorts of things, and went on with a wave. He was flustered, and stammered something, then he said, with explicit malice: I'll have to read that book of yours, I understand it's *very* interesting.

That was only the start. The next day Michele Solara came up to me on the street and insisted on buying me a coffee. We went into his bar and while Gigliola served us, without saying a word, in fact obviously annoyed by my presence and perhaps also by her boyfriend's, he began: Lenù, Gino gave me an article to read where it says you wrote a book that's banned for those under eighteen. Imagine that, who would have expected it. Is *that* what you studied in Pisa? Is *that* what they taught you at the university? I can't believe it. In my opinion you and Lina made a secret agreement: she does nasty things and you write them. Is that right? Tell me the truth. I turned red, I didn't wait for the coffee, I waved to Gigliola and left. He called after me, laughing: What's the matter, you're offended, come here, I was joking.

Soon afterward I had an encounter with Carmen Peluso.

My mother had obliged me to go to the Carraccis' new grocery, because oil was cheaper there. It was afternoon, there were no customers, Carmen was full of compliments. How well you look, she said, it's an honor to be your friend, the only good luck I've had in my whole life. Then she said that she had read Sarratore's article, but only because a supplier had left *Roma* behind in the shop. She described it as spiteful, and her indignation seemed genuine. On the other hand, her brother, Pasquale, had given her the article in *l'Unità*—really, really good, such a nice picture. You're beautiful, she said, in everything you do. She had heard from my mother that I was going to marry a university professor and that I was going to live in Florence in a luxurious house. She, too, was getting married, to the owner of the gas pump on the *stradone*, but who could say when, they had no money. Then, without a break, she began complaining about Ada. Ever since Ada had taken Lila's place with Stefano, things had gone from bad to worse. She acted like the boss in the grocery stores, too, and had it in for her, accused her of stealing, ordered her around, watched her closely. She couldn't take it anymore, she wanted to quit and go to work at her future husband's gas pump.

I listened closely, I remembered when Antonio and I wanted to get married and, similarly, have a gas pump. I told her about it, to amuse her, but she muttered, darkening: Yes, why not, just imagine it, you at a gas pump, lucky you who got yourself out of this wretchedness. Then she made some obscure comments: there's too much injustice, Lenù, too much, it has to end, we can't go on like this. And as she was talking she pulled out of a drawer my book, with the cover all creased and dirty. It was the first copy I'd seen in the hands of anyone in the neighborhood, and I was struck by how bulging and grimy the early pages were, how flat and white the others. I read a little at night, she said, or when there aren't any customers. But I'm still on page 32, I don't have time, I have to do everything, the Carraccis keep me shut up here from six in the morning to nine in the evening. Then suddenly she asked, slyly, how long does it take to get to the dirty pages? How much do I still have to read?

The dirty pages.

A little while later I ran into Ada carrying Maria, her daughter with Stefano. I struggled to be friendly, after what Carmen had told me. I praised the child, I said her dress was pretty and her earrings adorable. But Ada was aloof. She spoke of Antonio, she said they wrote to each other, it wasn't true that he was married and had children, she said I had ruined his brain and his capacity to love. Then she started on my book. She hadn't read it, she explained, but she had heard that it wasn't a book to have in the house. And she was almost angry: Say the child grows up and finds it, what can I do? I'm sorry, I won't buy it. But, she added, I'm glad you're making money, good luck.

12.

These episodes, one after the other, led me to suspect that the book was selling because both the hostile newspapers and the favorable ones had indicated that there were some risqué passages. I went so far as to think that Nino had alluded to Lila's sexuality only because he thought that there was no problem in discussing such things with someone who had written what I had written. And via that path the desire to see my friend returned. Who knows, I said to myself, if Lila had the book, as Carmen did. I imagined her at night, after the factory—Enzo in solitude in one room, she with the baby beside her in the other—exhausted and yet intent on reading me, her mouth half open, wrinkling her forehead the way she did when she was concentrating. How would she judge it? Would she, too, reduce the novel to the *dirty pages?* But maybe she wasn't reading it at all, I doubted that she had the money to buy a copy, I ought to take her one as a present. For a while it seemed to me a good idea, then I forgot about it. I still cared more about Lila than about any other person, but I couldn't make up my mind to see her. I didn't have time, there were too many things to study, to learn in a hurry. And then the end of our last visit—in the courtyard of the factory, she with that apron under her coat, standing in front of the bonfire where the pages of *The Blue Fairy* were burning—had been a decisive farewell to the remains of childhood, the confirmation that our paths by now diverged, and maybe she would say: I don't have time to read you, you see the life I have? I went my own way.

Whatever the reason, the book really was doing better and better. Once Adele telephoned and, with her usual mixture of irony and affection, said: If it keeps going like this you'll get rich and you won't know what to do with poor Pietro anymore. Then she passed me on to her husband, no less. Guido, she said, wants to talk to you. I was agitated, I had had very few conversations with Professor Airota and they made me feel awkward. But Pietro's father was very friendly, he congratulated me on my success, he spoke sarcastically about the sense of decency of my detractors, he talked about the extremely long duration of the dark ages in Italy, he praised the contribution I was making to the modernization of the country, and so on with other formulas of that sort. He didn't say anything specific about the novel; surely he hadn't read it, he was a very busy man. But it was nice that he wanted to give me a sign of approval and respect.

Mariarosa was no less affectionate, and she, too, was full of praise. At first she seemed on the point of talking in detail about the book, then she changed the subject excitedly, she said she wanted to invite me to the university: it seemed to her important that I should take part in what she called *the unstop-*

pable flow of events. Leave tomorrow, she urged, have you seen what's happening in France? I knew all about it, I clung to an old blue grease-encrusted radio that my mother kept in the kitchen, and said yes, it's magnificent, Nanterre, the barricades in the Latin Quarter. But she seemed much better informed, much more involved. She was planning to drive to Paris with some of her friends, and invited me to go with her. I was tempted. I said all right, I'll think about it. To go to Milan, and on to France, to arrive in Paris in revolt, face the brutality of the police, plunge with my whole personal history into the most incandescent magma of these months, add a sequel to the journey I'd made years earlier with Franco. How wonderful it would be to go with Mariarosa, the only girl I knew who was so open-minded, so modern, completely in touch with the realities of the world, almost as much a master of political speech as the men. I admired her, there were no women who stood out in that chaos. The young heroes who faced the violence of the reactions at their own peril were called Rudi Dutschke, Daniel Cohn-Bendit, and, as in war films where there were only men, it was hard to feel part of it; you could only love them, adapt their thoughts to your brain, feel pity for their fate. It occurred to me that among Mariarosa's friends there might also be Nino. They knew each other, it was possible. Ah, to see him, to be swept into that adventure, expose myself to dangers along with him. The day passed like that. The kitchen was silent now, my parents were sleeping, my brothers were still out wandering in the streets, Elisa was in the bathroom, washing. To leave, tomorrow morning.

13.

I left, but not for Paris. After the elections of that turbulent year, Gina sent me out to promote the book. I began with

Florence. I had been invited to teach by a woman professor friend of a friend of the Airotas, and I ended up in one of those student-run courses, widespread in that time of unrest in the universities, speaking to around thirty students, boys and girls. I was immediately struck by the fact that many of the girls were even worse than those described by my father-in-law in *Il Ponte:* badly dressed, badly made up, muddled, excitable, angry at the exams, at the professors. Urged by the professor who had invited me, I spoke out about the student demonstrations with manifest enthusiasm, especially the ones in France. I showed off what I was learning; I was pleased with myself. I felt that I was expressing myself with conviction and clarity, that the girls in particular admired the way I spoke, the things I knew, the way I skillfully touched on the complicated problems of the world, arranging them into a coherent picture. But I soon realized that I tended to avoid any mention of the book. Talking about it made me uneasy, I was afraid of reactions like those of the neighborhood, I preferred to summarize in my own words ideas from *Quaderni piacentini* or the *Monthly Review.* On the other hand I had been invited because of the book, and someone was already asking to speak. The first questions were all about the struggles of the female character to escape the environment where she was born. Then, near the end, a girl I remember as being tall and thin asked me to explain, breaking off her phrases with nervous laughs, why I had considered it necessary to write, in such a polished story, a *risqué part.*

I was embarrassed, I think I blushed, I jumbled together a lot of sociological reasons. Finally, I spoke of the necessity of recounting frankly every human experience, including—I said emphatically—what seems unsayable and what we do not speak of even to ourselves. They liked those last words, I regained respect. The professor who had invited me praised them, she said she would reflect on them, she would write to me.

Her approval established in my mind those few concepts, which soon became a refrain. I used them often in public, sometimes in an amusing way, sometimes in a dramatic tone, sometimes succinctly, sometimes developing them with elaborate verbal flourishes. I found myself especially relaxed one evening in a bookstore in Turin, in front of a fairly large audience, which I now faced with growing confidence. It began to seem natural that someone would ask me, sympathetically or provocatively, about the episode of sex on the beach, and my ready response, which had become increasingly polished, enjoyed a certain success.

On the orders of the publisher, Tarratano, Adele's old friend, had accompanied me to Turin. He said that he was proud of having been the first to understand the potential of my novel and introduced me to the audience with the same enthusiastic words he had used before in Milan. At the end of the evening he congratulated me on the great progress I had made in a short time. Then he asked me, in his usual good-humored way: why are you so willing to let your erotic pages be called "risqué," why do you yourself describe them that way in public? And he explained to me that I shouldn't: my novel wasn't simply the episode on the beach, there were more interesting and finer passages; and then, if here and there something sounded daring, that was mainly because it had been written by a girl; obscenity, he said, is not alien to good literature, and the true art of the story, even if it goes beyond the bounds of decency, is never risqué.

I was confused. That very cultured man was tactfully explaining to me that the sins of my book were venial, and that I was wrong to speak of them every time as if they were mortal. I was overdoing it, then. I was submitting to the public's myopia, its superficiality. I said to myself: Enough, I have to be less subservient, I have to learn to disagree with my readers, I shouldn't descend to their level. And I decided that at the first opportunity I would be more severe with anyone who wanted to talk about those pages.

At dinner, in the hotel restaurant where the press office had reserved a table for us, I listened, half embarrassed, half amused, as Tarratano quoted, as proof that I was essentially a chaste writer, Henry Miller, and explained, calling me dear child, that not a few very gifted writers of the twenties and thirties could and did write about sex in a way that I at the moment couldn't even imagine. I wrote down their names in my notebook, but meanwhile I began to think: This man, in spite of his compliments, doesn't consider that I have much talent; in his eyes I'm a girl who's had an undeserved success; even the pages that most attract readers he doesn't consider outstanding, they may scandalize those who don't know much but not people like him.

I said that I was a little tired and helped my companion, who had drunk too much, to get up. He was a small man but had the prominent belly of a gourmand. Tufts of white hair bristled over large ears, he had a red face interrupted by a narrow mouth, a big nose, and very bright eyes; he smoked a lot, and his fingers were yellowed. In the elevator he tried to kiss me. Although I wriggled out of his embrace I had a hard time keeping him away; he wouldn't give up. The touch of his stomach and his winey breath stayed with me. At the time, it would never have occurred to me that an old man, so respectable, so cultured, that man who was such a good friend of my future mother-in-law, could behave in an unseemly way. Once we were in the corridor he hastened to apologize, he blamed the wine, and went straight to his room.

14.

The next day, at breakfast and during the entire drive to Milan, he talked passionately about what he considered the most exciting period of his life, the years between 1945 and 1948. I heard in his voice a genuine melancholy, which vanished, however, when he went on to describe with an equally genuine enthusiasm the new climate of revolution, the energy—he said—that was infusing young and old. I kept nodding yes, struck by how important it was for him to convince me that my present was in fact the return of his thrilling past. I felt a little sorry for him. A random biographical hint led me, at a certain point, to make a quick calculation: the person with me was fifty-eight years old.

Once in Milan I had the driver drop me near the publishing house, and I said goodbye to my companion. I had slept badly and was in something of a daze. On the street I tried to eradicate my disgust at that physical contact with Tarratano, but I still felt the stain of it and a confusing continuity with a kind of vulgarity I recognized from the neighborhood. At the publisher's I was greeted warmly. It wasn't the courtesy of a few months earlier but a sort of generalized satisfaction that meant: how clever we were to guess that you were clever. Even the switchboard operator, the only one there who had treated me condescendingly, came out of her booth and embraced me. And for the first time the editor who had done that punctilious editing invited me to lunch.

As soon as we sat down in a half-empty restaurant near the office, he returned to his emphasis on the fact that my writing guarded a fascinating secret, and between courses he suggested that I would do well to plan a new novel, taking my time but not resting too long on my laurels. Then he reminded me that I had an appointment at the state university at three. Mariarosa had nothing to do with it; the publishing house itself, through its own channels, had organized something with a group of students. Whom should I look for when I get there? I asked. My authoritative lunch companion said proudly: My son will be waiting for you at the entrance.

I retrieved my bag from the office, and went to the hotel. I stayed a few minutes and left for the university. The heat was unbearable. I found myself against a background of posters dense with writing, red flags, and struggling people, placards announcing activities, noisy voices, laughter, and a widespread sense of apprehension. I wandered around, looking for signs that had to do with me. I recall a dark-haired young man who, running, rudely bumped into me, lost his balance, picked himself up, and ran out into the street as if he were being pursued, even though no one was behind him. I recall the pure, solitary sound of a trumpet that pierced the suffocating air. I recall a tiny blond girl, who was dragging a clanking chain with a large lock at the end, and zealously shouting, I don't know to whom: I'm coming! I remember it because in order to seem purposeful, as I waited for someone to recognize me and come over, I took out my notebook and wrote down this and that. But half an hour passed, and no one arrived. Then I examined the placards and posters more carefully, hoping to find my name, or the title of the book. It was useless. I felt a little nervous, and decided not to stop one of the students: I was ashamed to cite my book as a subject of discussion in an environment where the posters pasted to the walls proclaimed far more significant themes. I found to my annoyance that I was poised between opposing feelings: on the one hand, a strong sympathy for all those young men and women who in that place were flaunting, gestures and voices, with an absolute lack of discipline, and, on the other, the fear that the disorder I had been fleeing since I was a child might, now, right here, seize me and fling me into the middle of the commotion, where an incontrovertible power—a Janitor, a Professor, the Rector, the Police—would quickly find me at fault, me, me who had always been good, and punish me.

I thought of sneaking away, what did I care about a handful of kids scarcely younger than me, to whom I would say the usual foolish things? I wanted to go back to the hotel, enjoy my situation as a successful author who was traveling all over, eating in restaurants and sleeping in hotels. But five or six busy-looking girls passed by, carrying bags, and almost against my will I followed them, the voices, the shouts, even the sound of the trumpet. Like that, walking and walking, I ended up outside a crowded classroom from which, just then, an angry clamor arose. And since the girls I was following went in, I, too, cautiously entered.

A sharp conflict involving various factions was under way, both in the packed classroom and in a small crowd that besieged the lectern. I stayed near the door, ready to leave, already repelled by a burning cloud of smoke and breath, by a strong odor of excitement.

I tried to orient myself. I think they were discussing procedural matters, in an atmosphere, however, in which no one—some were shouting, some were silent, some poking fun, some laughing, some moving rapidly like runners on a battlefield, some paying no attention, some studying—seemed to think that agreement was possible. I hoped that Mariarosa was there somewhere. Meanwhile I was getting used to the uproar, the smells. So many people: mostly males, handsome, ugly, well-dressed, scruffy, violent, frightened, amused. I observed the women with interest; I had the impression that I was the only one who was there alone. Some—for example the ones I had followed—stayed close together, even as they distributed leaflets in the crowded classroom: they shouted together, laughed together, and if they were separated by a few meters they kept an eye on each other so as not to get lost. Longtime friends or perhaps chance acquaintances, they seemed to draw from the group the authority to stay in that place of chaos, seduced by the lawless atmosphere, yes, but open to the experience only on the condition that they not separate, as if they had decided beforehand, in more secure places, that if one left they would all leave. Other women, however, by themselves or at most in pairs, had infiltrated the male groups, displaying a provocative intimacy, the lighthearted dissolution of safe distances, and they seemed to me the happiest, the most aggressive, the proudest.

I felt different, there illegally, without the necessary credentials to shout myself, to remain inside those fumes and those odors that brought to mind, now, the odors and fumes that came from Antonio's body, from his breath, when we embraced at the ponds. I had been too wretched, too crushed by the obligation to excel in school. I had hardly ever gone to the movies. I had never bought records, yet how I would have liked to. I wasn't a fan of any singers, hadn't rushed to concerts, collected autographs; I had never been drunk, and my limited sexual experiences had taken place uncomfortably, amid subterfuges, fearfully. Those girls, on the other hand, to varying degrees, must have grown up in easier circumstances, and were more prepared to change their skin; maybe they felt their presence in that place, in that atmosphere, not as a derailment but as a just and urgent choice. Now that I have some money, I thought, now that I'll earn who knows how much, I can have some of the things I missed. Or maybe not, I was now too cultured, too ignorant, too controlled, too accustomed to freezing life by storing up ideas and facts, too close to marriage and settling down, in short too obtusely fixed within an order that here appeared to be in decline. That last thought frightened me. Get out of this place right away, I said to myself, every gesture or word is an insult to the work I've done. Instead I slipped farther inside the crowded classroom.

I was struck immediately by a very beautiful girl, with delicate features and long black hair that hung over her shoulders, who was certainly younger than me. I couldn't take my eyes off her. She was standing in the midst of some combative young men, and behind her a dark man about thirty, smoking a cigar, stood glued to her like a bodyguard. What distinguished her in that environment, besides her beauty, was that she was holding in her arms a baby a few months old, she was nursing him and, at the same time, closely following the conflict, and occasionally even shouting something. When the baby, a patch of blue, with his little reddish-colored legs and feet uncovered, detached his mouth from the nipple, she didn't put her breast back in the bra but stayed like that, exposed, her white shirt unbuttoned, her breast swollen, her mouth half open, frowning, until she realized the child was no longer suckling and mechanically tried to reattach him.

That girl disturbed me. In the noisy smoke-filled classroom, she was an incongruous icon of maternity. She was younger than me, she had a refined appearance, responsibility for an infant. Yet she seemed determined to reject the persona of the young woman placidly absorbed in caring for her child. She yelled, she gesticulated, she asked to speak, she laughed angrily, she pointed to someone with contempt. And yet the child was part of her, he sought her breast, he lost it. Together they made up a fragile image, at risk, close to breaking, as if it had been painted on glass: the child would fall out of her arms or something would bump his head, an elbow, an uncontrolled movement. I was happy when, suddenly, Mariarosa appeared beside her. Finally: there she was. How lively, how bright, how cordial she was: she seemed to be friendly with the young mother. I waved my hand, she didn't see me. She whispered briefly in the girl's ear, disappeared, reappeared in the crowd that was gathered around the lectern. Meanwhile, through a side door, a small group burst in whose mere arrival calmed people down. Mariarosa signaled, waited for a signal in response, grabbed the megaphone, and spoke a few words that silenced the packed classroom. For a few seconds I had the impression that Milan, the tensions of that period, my own excitement had the power to let the shadows I had in my head emerge. How many times had I thought in those days of my early political education? Mariarosa yielded the megaphone to a young man beside her, whom I recognized immediately. It was Franco Mari, my boyfriend from the early years in Pisa.

15.

He had stayed the same: the same warm and persuasive tone of voice, the same ability to organize a speech, moving from general statements that led, step by step, in a logical sequence to ordinary, everyday experiences, revealing their meaning. As I write, I realize that I recall very little of his physical aspect, only his pale clean-shaven face, his short hair. And yet his was the only body that, so far, I had been close to as if we were married.

I went over to Franco after his speech, and his eyes lighted up with amazement, he embraced me. But it was hard to talk, someone pulled him by the arm, someone else had started to criticize, pointing at him insistently, as if he had to answer for terrible crimes. I stayed near the lectern, uneasy; in the crush I had lost Mariarosa. But this time it was she who saw me, and she tugged on my arm.

"What are you doing here?" she asked, pleased.

I avoided explaining that I had missed an appointment, that I had arrived by chance. I said, indicating Franco: "I know him."

"Mari?"

"Yes."

She spoke about Franco enthusiastically, then she whispered: They'll make me pay for it, I invited him, look what a hornets' nest. And since he was going to stay at her house and leave for Turin the following day, she immediately insisted that

I should come and stay with her, too. I accepted, too bad about the hotel.

The meeting dragged on, there were moments of extreme tension, and a permanent sensation of alarm. It was getting dark when we left the university. Besides Franco, Mariarosa was joined by the young mother, whose name was Silvia, and the man around thirty whom I had noticed in the classroom, the one who was smoking the cigar, a Venezuelan painter named Juan. We all went to dinner in a trattoria that my sister-in-law knew. I talked to Franco enough to find out that I was wrong, he hadn't stayed the same. Covering his face—and maybe he had placed it there himself—a mask, which, although it perfectly matched the features of before, had eliminated the generosity. Now he was pinched, restrained, he weighed his words. In the course of a short, apparently confidential exchange, he never alluded to our old relationship, and when I brought it up, complaining that he had never written to me, he cut me off, saying: It had to be like that. About the university, too, he was vague, and I understood that he hadn't graduated.

"There are other things to do," he said.

"What?"

He turned to Marirosa, as if irritated by the too private note of our exchange:

"Elena is asking what there is to do."

Mariarosa answered cheerfully: "The revolution."

So I assumed a mocking tone, I said: "And in your free time?"

Juan, who was sitting next to Silvia, broke in seriously, gently shaking the baby's closed fist. "In our free time we're getting ready for it."

After dinner we piled into Mariarosa's car; she lived in a large old apartment in Sant'Ambrogio. I discovered that the Venezuelan had a kind of studio there, a very untidy room

where he brought Franco and me to show us his work: big can-
vases depicting crowded urban scenes, painted with an almost
photographic skill, but he had spoiled them by nailing to the
surface tubes of paint or brushes or palettes or bowls for tur-
pentine and rags. Mariarosa praised him warmly, but addressing Franco in particular, whose opinion she seemed to value.

I observed, without comprehending. Certainly Juan lived
there, certainly Silvia also lived there, since she moved through
the house confidently with Mirko, the baby. But at first I
thought that the painter and the young mother were a couple
and lived as tenants in one of those rooms, but soon I changed
my idea. The Venezuelan, in fact, all evening showed Silvia an
abstracted courtesy, while he often put an arm around
Mariarosa's shoulders and once he kissed her on the neck.

At first there was a lot of talk about Juan's work. Franco
had always had an enviable expertise in the visual arts and a
strong critical sensibility. We all listened eagerly, except Silvia,
whose baby, until then very good, suddenly began to cry incon-
solably. For a while I hoped that Franco would also talk about
my book, I was sure he would say something intelligent, such
as, with some severity, he was saying about Juan's paintings.
Instead no one alluded to my novel, and, after a burst of impatience from the Venezuelan, who hadn't appreciated a remark
of Franco's on art and society, we went on to discuss Italy's cultural backwardness, the political picture that emerged from
the elections, the chain-reaction concessions of social democracy, the students and police repression, what was termed *the
lesson of France*. The exchange between the two men immediately became contentious. Silvia couldn't understand what
Mirko needed. She left the room and returned, scolding him
harshly as if he were a grown child, and then, from the long
hall where she was carrying him up and down or from the
room where she had gone to change him, shouted out clichéd
phrases of dissent. Mariarosa, after describing the nurseries

organized at the Sorbonne for the children of the striking students, evoked a Paris of early June, rainy and cold, still paralyzed by the general strike—not at first hand (she regretted it, she hadn't managed to get there) but as a friend had described it to her in a letter. Franco and Juan both listened distractedly, and yet never lost the thread of their argument; rather, they confronted each other with increasing animosity.

The result was that we found ourselves, we three women, in the situation of drowsy heifers waiting for the two bulls to complete the testing of their powers. This irritated me. I waited for Mariarosa to intervene in the conversation again; I intended to do so myself. But Franco and Juan left us no space; the baby meanwhile was screaming and Silvia treated him even more aggressively. Lila—I thought—was even younger when she had Gennaro. And I realized that something had driven me, even during the meeting, to establish a connection between Silvia and Lila. Maybe it was the solitude as a mother that Lila had felt after the disappearance of Nino and the break with Stefano. Or her beauty: if she had been at that meeting with Gennaro she would have been an even more captivating, more determined mother than Silvia. But Lila was now cut off. The wave that I had felt in the classroom would reach as far as San Giovanni a Teduccio; but she, in that place where she had ended up, demeaning herself, would never be aware of it. A pity, I felt guilty. I should have carried her off, kidnapped her, made her travel with me. Or at least reinforced her presence in my body, mixed her voice with mine. As in that moment. I heard her saying: If you are silent, if you let only the two of them speak, if you behave like an apartment plant, at least give that girl a hand, think what it means to have a small child. It was a confusion of space and time, of distant moods. I jumped up, I took the child from Silvia gently and carefully, and she was glad to let me.

16.

What a handsome child: it was a memorable moment. Mirko charmed me immediately; he had folds of rosy flesh around his wrists, around his legs. How cute he was, what a nice shape his eyes had, how much hair, what long, delicate feet, what a good smell. I whispered all those compliments, softly, as I carried him around the house. The voices of the men faded, as did the ideas they defended and their hostility, and something happened that was new to me. I felt pleasure. I felt, like an uncontrollable flame, the child's warmth, his motility, and it seemed to me that all my senses became more vigilant, as if the perception of that perfect fragment of life that I had in my arms had become achingly acute, and I felt his sweetness and my responsibility for him, and was prepared to protect him from all the evil shadows lying in wait in the dark corners of the house. Mirko must have understood and he was quiet. This, too, gave me pleasure, I was proud of having been able to give him peace.

When I returned to the room, Silvia, who had settled herself on Mariarosa's lap and was listening to the discussion between the two men, joining in with nervous exclamations, turned to look at me and must have seen in my face the pleasure with which I was hugging the child to me. She jumped up, took him from me with a harsh thank you, and went to put him to bed. I had an unpleasant sensation of loss. I felt Mirko's warmth leaving me, I sat down again, in a bad mood, with my thoughts in confusion. I wanted the baby back, I hoped that he would start crying again, that Silvia would ask for my help. What's got into me? Do I want children? Do I want to be a mamma, nursing and singing lullabies? Marriage plus pregnancy? And if my mother should emerge from my stomach just now when I think I'm safe?

17.

It took me a while to focus on the lesson that was coming to us from France, on the tense confrontation between the two men. But I didn't want to be silent. I wanted to say something about what I had read and thought about the events in Paris, the speech was twisting around in sentences that remained incomplete in my mind. And it amazed me that Mariarosa, so clever, so free, said nothing, that she confined herself to agreeing always and only with what Franco said, with pretty smiles, which made Juan nervous and occasionally insecure. If she doesn't speak, I said to myself, I will, otherwise why did I agree to come here, why didn't I go to the hotel? Questions to which I had an answer. I wanted to show those who had known me in the past what I had become. I wanted Franco to realize that he couldn't treat me like the girl of long ago, I wanted him to realize that I had become a completely different person, I wanted him to say in front of Mariarosa that *this other person* had his respect. Therefore, since the baby was quiet, since Silvia had disappeared with him, since neither one had further need of me, I waited a little and finally found a way of disagreeing with my old boyfriend. It was an improvised disagreement: I wasn't moved by solid convictions, the goal was to express myself *against Franco* and I did it, I had certain formulas in my mind, I combined them with false confidence. I said more or less that I was puzzled by the development of the class struggle in France, that I found the student-worker alliance for the moment very abstract. I spoke with decision, I was afraid that one of the two men would interrupt me to say something that would rekindle the argument between them. Instead, they listened to me attentively, all of them, including Silvia, who had returned almost on tiptoe, without the baby. And neither Franco nor Juan gave signs of impatience while I spoke, in fact the Venezuelan agreed when, two or three times,

I uttered the word "people." This annoyed Mari. You're saying that the situation *isn't objectively* revolutionary, he said emphatically, sarcastically, and I recognized that tone, it meant that he would defend himself by making fun of me. So the sentences piled up, mine on top of his and vice versa: I don't know what *objectively* means; it means that to act is inevitable; so if it's not inevitable, you sit on your hands; no, the task of the revolutionary is always to do what's possible; in France the students have done the impossible, the mechanism of instruction is broken and will never be fixed; admit that things have changed and they will change; yes, but no one asked you or anyone else for certification on official paper or for a guarantee that the situation is *objectively* revolutionary, the students have acted and that's all; it's not true; it is true. And so on. Until at the same moment we were silent.

It was an odd exchange, not in its content but in its heated tones, the rules of etiquette abandoned. In Mariarosa's eyes I glimpsed a flash of amusement: she understood that if Franco and I talked to each other like that there had been something more than a friendship between university colleagues. Come, give me a hand, she said to Silvia and Juan. She had to get a ladder, to find sheets for me, for Franco. The two followed her, Juan whispered something in her ear.

Franco stared at the floor for a moment, he pressed his lips together as if to restrain a smile, and said affectionately: "You've remained the petit bourgeois you always were."

That was the way, years earlier, he had often made fun of me when I was afraid of being caught in his room. In the absence of the others, I said impetuously: "You're the petit bourgeois, by origin, by education, by behavior."

"I didn't mean to offend you."

"I'm not offended."

"You've changed, you've become aggressive."

"I'm the same as ever."

"Everything all right at home?"

"Yes."

"And that friend of yours who was so important to you?"

The question came with a logical leap that disoriented me. Had I talked to him about Lila in the past? In what terms? And why did she come to mind now? Where was the connection that he had seen somewhere and I hadn't?

"She's fine," I said.

"What is she doing?"

"She works in a sausage factory on the outskirts of Naples."

"Didn't she marry a shopkeeper?"

"The marriage didn't work."

"When I come to Naples you must introduce me."

"Of course."

"Leave me a number, an address."

"All right."

He looked at me to assess what words would be least hurtful, and asked: "Has she read your book?"

"I don't know, did you read it?"

"Of course."

"How did it seem to you?"

"Good."

"In what way?"

"There are wonderful passages."

"Which ones?

"Those where you give the protagonist the capacity to put together the fragments of things in her own way."

"And that's all?"

"Isn't that enough?"

"No: it's clear that you didn't like it."

"I told you it's good."

I knew him, he was trying not to humiliate me. That exasperated me, I said:

"It's a book that's inspired discussion, it's selling well."

"So good, no?"

"Yes, but not for you. What is it that doesn't work?"

He compressed his lips again, and made up his mind: "There's not much depth, Elena. Behind the petty love affairs and the desire for social ascent you hide precisely what it would be valuable to tell."

"What?"

"Forget it, it's late, we should go to sleep." And he tried to assume an expression of benevolent irony, but in reality he had that new tone of someone who has an important task to complete and gives only sparingly to all the rest: "You did everything possible, right? But this, objectively, is not the moment for writing novels."

18.

Mariarosa returned just then along with Juan and Silvia, carrying clean towels and nightclothes. She certainly heard that last phrase, and surely she understood that we were talking about my book, but she didn't say a word. She could have said that she had liked the book, that novels can be written at any moment, but she didn't. From that I deduced that, beyond the declarations of liking and affection, in those circles that were so caught up and sucked in by political passions my book was considered an insignificant little thing, and the pages that were helping its circulation either were judged cheap versions of much more sensational texts that I had never read, or deserved that dismissive label of Franco's: *a story of petty love affairs*.

My sister-in-law showed me the bathroom and my room with a fleeting courtesy. I said goodbye to Franco, who was leaving early. I merely shook his hand, and he made no move to embrace me. I saw him disappear into a room with Mariarosa, and from Juan's dark expression and Silvia's unhappy look I understood that the guest and the mistress of the house would sleep together.

I withdrew into the room assigned to me. There was a strong smell of stale smoke, an unmade single bed, no night table, no lamp except the weak ceiling light, newspapers piled up on the floor, some issues of journals like *Menabò*, *Nuovo impegno*, *Marcatré*, expensive art books, some well-thumbed, others evidently never opened. Under the bed I found an ashtray overflowing with cigarette butts; I opened the window, and put it on the sill. I got undressed. The nightgown that Mariarosa had given me was too long, too tight. I went to the bathroom barefoot, along the shadowy corridor. The absence of a toothbrush didn't bother me: I hadn't grown up brushing my teeth, it was a recent habit, acquired in Pisa.

In bed I tried to erase the Franco I had met that night by superimposing the Franco of years earlier, the rich, generous youth who had loved me, who had helped me, who had bought everything for me, who had educated me, who had taken me to Paris for his political meetings and on vacation to Versilia, to his parents' house. But I was unsuccessful. The present, with its unrest, the shouting in the packed classroom, the political jargon that was buzzing in my head and spilling out onto my book, vilifying it, prevailed. Was I deluded about my literary future? Was Franco right, there were other things to do besides write novels? What impression had I made on him? What memory did he have of our love, if he even had one? Was he complaining about me to Mariarosa as Nino had complained to me about Lila? I felt wounded, disheartened. Certainly what I had imagined as a pleasant and perhaps slightly melancholy evening seemed to me sad. I couldn't wait for the night to pass so that I could return to Naples. I had to get up to turn out the light. I went back to bed in the dark.

I had trouble falling asleep. I tossed and turned, the bed and the room had the odors of other bodies, an intimacy similar to that of my house but in this case made up of the traces of possibly repulsive strangers. Then I fell asleep, but I woke suddenly: someone had come into the room. I whispered: Who's there? Juan answered. He said, straight out, in a pleading voice, as if he were asking an important favor, like some form of first aid:

"Can I sleep with you?"

The request seemed to me so absurd that, to wake myself completely, to understand, I asked: "Sleep?"

"Yes, lie next to you, I won't bother you, I just don't want to be alone."

"Absolutely not."

"Why?"

I didn't know what to say. I murmured: "I'm engaged."

"So what? We'll sleep, that's all."

"Go away, please, I don't even know you."

"I'm Juan, I showed you my work, what else do you want?"

I felt him sit down on the bed, I saw his dark profile, I felt his breath that smelled of cigars.

"Please," I said, "I'm sleepy."

"You're a writer, you write about love. Everything that happens to us feeds the imagination and helps us to create. Let me be near you, it's something you'll be able to write about."

He touched my foot with the tips of his fingers. I couldn't bear it, I leaped up and turned on the light. He was still sitting on the bed, in underpants and undershirt.

"Out," I hissed and in such a peremptory tone, so clearly close to shouting, so determined to attack and to fight with all my energy, that he got up, slowly, and said with disgust:

"You're a hypocrite."

He went out. I closed the door behind him, there was no key.

I was appalled, I was furious, I was frightened, a bloodthirsty dialogue was whirling in my head. I waited a while before going back to bed, and I didn't turn out the light. What had I intimated about myself, what sort of person did it seem that I was, what legitimatized Juan's request? Was it the reputation of a free woman that my book was giving me? Was it the political words I had uttered, which evidently were not only a dialectical jousting, a game to prove that I was as skillful as a man, but defined the entire person, sexual availability included? Was it a sort of membership in the same ranks that had led that man to show up in my room without scruples, and Mariarosa, also without scruples, to lead Franco into hers? Or had I been contaminated myself by the diffuse erotic excitement that I had felt in the university classroom, and that, unaware, I gave off? In Milan I always felt ready to make love with Nino, betraying Pietro. But that was an old passion, it justified sexual desire and betrayal, while sex in itself, that unmediated demand for orgasm, no, I couldn't be drawn into that. I was unprepared; it disgusted me. Why let myself be touched by Adele's friend in Turin, why in this house by Juan, what did I display, what did *they* want to display? Suddenly I thought of what had happened with Donato Sarratore. Not so much the evening on the beach in Ischia, which I had transformed into the episode in the novel, but the time he appeared in Nella's kitchen, when I had just gone to bed, and he had kissed me, touched me, causing a flow of pleasure against my very will. Between the girl of then, astonished, frightened, and the woman attacked in the elevator, the woman who had been subjected to that incursion now, was there a connection? The extremely cultured friend of Adele's Tarratano, the Venezuelan artist Juan, were they of the same clay as Nino's father, train conductor, bad poet, hack journalist?

19.

I couldn't get to sleep. Added to my strained nerves, to the contradictory thoughts, was Mirko, who had started crying again. I recalled the powerful emotion I had felt when I held the child in my arms and, since he didn't calm down, I couldn't restrain myself. I got up, and, following the trail of his wailing, reached a door through which light filtered. I knocked, Silvia answered rudely. The room was more welcoming than mine, it had an old armoire, a night table, a double bed on which the girl was sitting, in baby-doll pink, legs crossed, a spiteful expression on her face. Her arms flung wide, the backs of both hands on the sheet, she was holding Mirko on her bare thighs, like a votive offering: he, too, was naked, violet, the black hole of his mouth opened wide, his little eyes narrowed, his limbs agitated. At first she greeted me with hostility, then she softened. She said she felt she was an incompetent mother, she didn't know what to do, she was desperate. Finally she said: He always acts like this if he doesn't eat, maybe he's sick, he'll die here on the bed, and as she spoke she seemed very unlike Lila—ugly, disfigured by the nervous twisting of her mouth, by her staring eyes. Until she burst into tears.

The weeping of mother and child moved me, I would have liked to embrace them both, hold them tight, rock them. I whispered: Can I take him for a moment? She nodded yes between her sobs. So I took the child off her knees, brought him to my breast, and again felt the flood of odors, sounds, warmth, as if his vital energies were rushing joyfully to return to me, after the separation. I walked back and forth in the room murmuring a sort of ungrammatical litany that I invented on the spot, a long senseless declaration of love. Mirko miraculously calmed down, fell asleep. I laid him gently beside his mother, but with no desire to be separated from him. I was afraid to go back to my room, a part of me was sure of finding Juan there and wanted to stay here.

Silvia thanked me without gratitude, a thank you to which she coldly added a list of my virtues: You're intelligent, you know how to do everything, you know how to be respected, you're a real mother, your children will be lucky. I denied it, I said I'm going. But she had a jolt of anxiety, she took my hand, and begged me to stay: He listens to you, do it for him, he'll sleep peacefully. I accepted immediately. We lay down on the bed with the baby in the middle, and turned off the light. But we didn't sleep, we began to talk about ourselves.

In the dark Silvia became less hostile. She told me of the disgust she had felt when she discovered she was pregnant. She had hidden the pregnancy from the man she loved and also from herself, she was sure it would pass like an illness that has to run its course. Meanwhile, however, her body reacted, changing shape. She had had to tell her parents, wealthy professionals in Monza. There had been a scene, she had left home. But, instead of admitting that she had let months pass, waiting for a miracle, instead of confessing that physical fear had prevented her from considering abortion, she had claimed that she wanted the child, for love of the man who had made her pregnant. He had said to her: If you want him, for love of you I want him, too. Love her, love him: at that moment they were both serious. But after several months, even before the pregnancy reached its end, they had both fallen out of love. Silvia insisted over and over on this point, sorrowfully. Nothing remained, only bitterness. So she had found herself alone and if until now she had managed to get by, it was thanks to Mariarosa, whom she praised abundantly, she spoke of her rapturously, a wonderful teacher and truly on the side of the students, an invaluable companion.

I told her that the whole Airota family was admirable, that I was engaged to Pietro, that we would be married in the fall. She said impetuously: Marriage horrifies me and so does the family, it's all old stuff. Abruptly her tone became melancholy.

"Mirko's father also works at the university."

"Yes?"

"It all began because I took his course. He was so assured,

so competent, very intelligent, handsome. He had all the virtues. And even before the student struggles began he said: Re-educate your professors, don't be treated like beasts."

"Does he take any interest in the baby?"

She laughed in the darkness, she murmured bitterly:

"A male, apart from the mad moments when you love him and he enters you, always remains outside. So afterward, when you no longer love him, it bothers you just to think that you once wanted him. He liked me, I liked him, the end. It happens to me many times a day—I'm attracted to someone. That doesn't happen to you? It lasts a short time, then it passes. Only the child remains, he's part of you; the father, on the other hand, was a stranger and goes back to being a stranger. Even the name no longer has the sound it used to. Nino, I'd say, and I would repeat it, over and over in my head, as soon as I woke up, it was a magic word. Now, though, it's a sound that makes me sad."

I didn't say anything for a while, finally I whispered:

"Mirko's father is named Nino?"

"Yes, everyone knows him, he's very famous at the university."

"Nino what?"

"Nino Sarratore."

20.

I went out early, leaving Silvia sleeping with the child at her breast. Of the painter I found no trace. I managed to say goodbye only to Mariarosa, who had got up very early to take Franco to the station and had just returned. She looked sleepy, and seemed uneasy. She asked:

"Did you sleep well?"

"I talked to Silvia a lot."

"She told you about Sarratore?"

"Yes."

"I know you're friends."

"Did he tell you?"

"Yes. We gossiped a little about you."

"Is it true that Mirko is his son?"

"Yes." She repressed a yawn, she smiled. "Nino is fascinating, the girls fight over him, they drag him this way and that. And these, luckily, are happy times, you take what you want, all the more since he has a power that conveys joy and the desire to act."

She said that the movement needed people like him. She said that it was necessary, however, to look after him, let him grow, direct him. The very capable people, she said, should be guided: in them the bourgeois democrat, the technical manager, the modernizer is always lying in wait. We both regretted that we had spent so little time together and vowed to do better on the next occasion. I picked up my bag at the hotel, and left.

Only on the train, during the long journey to Naples, did I take in that second paternity of Nino's. A squalid desolation extended from Silvia to Lila, from Mirko to Gennaro. It seemed to me that the passion of Ischia, the night of love in Forio, the secret relationship of Piazza dei Martiri, and the pregnancy—all faded, were reduced to a mechanical device that Nino, upon leaving Naples, had activated with Silvia and who knows how many others. The thing offended me, as if Lila were squatting in a corner of my mind and I felt her feelings. I was bitter as she would have been if she had known, I was furious as if I had suffered the same wrong. Nino had betrayed Lila and me. We were, she and I, similarly humiliated, we loved him without ever being truly loved in return. And so, in spite of his virtues, he was a frivolous, superficial man, an animal organism who dripped sweat and fluids and left behind, like the residue of a careless pleasure, living material conceived, nourished, shaped within female bellies. I remembered when he had come to see me in the neighborhood, years earlier, and we had stayed talking in the courtyard, and Melina had seen him from the window and had taken him for his father. Donato's former lover had caught resemblances that had seemed nonexistent to me. But now it was clear, she was right and I was wrong. Nino was not fleeing his father out of fear of becoming like him: Nino *already was* his father and didn't want to admit it.

Yet I couldn't hate him. In the burning-hot train I not only reflected on the time I had seen him in the bookstore but inserted him into events, words, remarks of those days. Sex had pursued me, clawed me, foul and attractive, obsessively present in gestures, in conversations, in books. The dividing walls were crumbling, the shackles of good manners were breaking. And Nino was living that period intensely. He was part of the rowdy gathering at the university, with its intense odor, he was fit for the disorder of Mariarosa's house, surely he had been her lover. With his intelligence, with his desires, with his capacity for seduction, he moved confident, curious within those times. Maybe I was wrong to connect him to the obscene desires of his father; his behavior belonged to another culture, as Silvia and Mariarosa had pointed out; girls wanted him, he took them, there was no abuse of power, there was no guilt, only the rights of desire. Who knows, maybe Nino in telling me that Lila was made badly even when it comes to sex, wished to convey that the time for pretenses was over, that to load pleasure with responsibility was an error. Even if he had his father's nature, surely his passion for women told a different story.

With astonishment, with disappointment, I arrived in Naples at the moment when a part of me, at the thought of how much Nino was loved and how much he loved, had yielded and reached the point of admitting: what's wrong with it, he enjoys life with those who know how to enjoy it. And as I was returning to the neighborhood, I realized that precisely because all women wanted him and he took them all, I who had wanted him forever wanted him even more. So I decided that I would at all costs avoid meeting him again. As for Lila, I didn't know how to behave. Be silent, tell her everything? Whenever I see her, I would decide then.

21.

At home I didn't have, or didn't want to have, time to go back to the subject. Pietro telephoned, he said that he was coming to meet my parents the following week. I accepted it as an inevitable misfortune, I struggled to find a hotel, clean the house, lessen my family's anxiety. That last task was in vain, the situation had grown worse. In the neighborhood the malicious gossip had increased: about my book, about me, about my constant traveling alone. My mother had put up a defense by boasting that I was about to get married, but, to keep my decisions against God from complicating things further, she pretended that I was getting married not in Naples but in Genoa. As a result the gossip increased, which exasperated her.

One night she confronted me harshly, saying that people were reading my book, were outraged, and talking behind her back. My brothers—she cried—had had to beat up the butcher's sons, who had called me a whore, and not only that: they had punched in the face a classmate of Elisa's who had asked her to do nasty things like her older sister.

"What did you write?" she yelled.

"Nothing, Ma."

"Did you write the disgusting things that you go around doing?"

"What disgusting things. Read it."

"I can't waste time with your nonsense."

"Then leave me alone."

"If your father finds out what people are saying about you, he'll throw you out of the house."

"He won't have to, I'll go myself."

It was evening, and I went for a walk so as not to reproach her with things I would later regret. On the street, in the gardens, along the *stradone*, I had the impression that people stared at me insistently, spiteful shadows of a world I no longer inhabited. I ran into Gigliola, who was returning from work. We lived in the same building, we walked together, but I was afraid that sooner or later she would find a way of saying something irritating. Instead, to my surprise, she spoke timidly, she who was always aggressive if not malicious:

"I read your book, it's wonderful, how brave you were to write those things."

I stiffened.

"What things?"

"The things you do on the beach."

"I don't do them, the character does."

"Yes, but you wrote them really well, Lenù, just the way it happens, with the same filthiness. They are secrets that you know only if you're a woman." Then she took me by the arm, made me stop, said softly, "Tell Lina, if you see her, that she was right, I admit it to her. She was right not to give a shit about her husband, her mamma, her father, her brother, Marcello, Michele, all that shit. I should have escaped from here, too, following the example of you two, who are intelligent. But I was born stupid and I can't do anything about it."

We said nothing else important, she stopped on her landing, I went to my house. But those comments stayed with me. It struck me that she had arbitrarily put together Lila's fall and my rise, as if, compared with her situation, they had the same degree of positivity. But what was most clearly impressed in my mind was how she had recognized in the filthiness of my story her own experience of filthiness. It was a new fact, I didn't know how to evaluate it. Especially since Pietro arrived and for a while I forgot about it.

22.

I went to meet him at the station, and took him to Via Firenze, where there was a hotel that my father had recommended and which I had finally decided on. Pietro seemed even more anxious than my family. He got off the train, as unkempt as usual, his tired face red in the heat, dragging a large suitcase. He wanted to buy a bouquet for my mother, and contrary to his habits he was satisfied only when it seemed to him big enough, expensive enough. At the hotel he left me in the lobby with the flowers, swearing that he would return immediately, and reappeared half an hour later in a blue suit, white shirt, blue tie, and polished shoes. I burst out laughing, he asked: I don't look good? I reassured him, he looked very good. But on the street I felt men's gazes, their mocking laughter, maybe even more insistent than if I had been alone, as if to emphasize that my escort did not deserve respect. Pietro, with that big bunch of flowers that he wouldn't let me carry, so respectable in every detail, was not suited to my city. Although he put his free arm around my shoulders, I had the impression that it was I who had to protect him.

Elisa opened the door, then my father arrived, then my brothers, all in their best clothes, all too cordial. My mother appeared last, the sound of her crooked gait could be heard right after that of the toilet flushing. She had set her hair, she had put a little color on her lips and cheeks, and thought, She was once a pretty girl. She accepted the flowers with condescension, and we sat in the dining room, which for the occasion held no trace of the beds we made at night and unmade in the morning. Everything was tidy, the table had been set with care. My mother and Elisa had cooked for days, which made the dinner interminable. Pietro, amazing me, became very expansive. He questioned my father about his work at the city hall and encouraged him to the point where he forgot his labored Italian and began to tell in dialect witty stories about his fellow employees, which my fiancé, although he understood little, appeared to appreciate tremendously. Above all he ate as I had never seen him eat, and not only complimented my mother and sister on every course but asked—he, who was unable even to cook an egg—about the ingredients of every dish as if he intended to get to the stove right away. He showed such a liking for the potato *gattò* that my mother served him a second very generous portion and promised him, even if in her usual reluctant tone, that she would make it again before he left. In a short time the atmosphere became friendly. Even Peppe and Gianni stayed at the table, instead of running out to join their friends.

After dinner we came to the point. Pietro turned serious and asked my father for my hand. He used just that expression, in a voice full of emotion, which brought tears to my sister's eyes and amused my brothers. My father was embarrassed, he mumbled expressions of friendship for a professor so clever and serious who was honoring him with that question. And the evening finally seemed to be reaching its conclusion, when my mother interrupted. She said darkly:

"Here we don't approve of your not getting married in church: a marriage without a priest isn't a marriage."

Silence. My parents must have come to a secret agreement that my mother would take on the job of making this announcement. But my father couldn't resist, and immediately gave Pietro a half smile to indicate that, although he was included in that *we* invoked by his wife, he was ready to see reason. Pietro returned the smile, but this time he didn't consider him a valid interlocutor, he addressed himself only to my mother. I had told him of my family's hostility, and he was prepared. He began with a simple, affectionate, and, according to his usual habit, very clear speech. He said that he understood, but that he wished to be, in turn, understood. He said that he had the greatest respect for all those who sincerely believed in a god, but that he did not feel he could do so. He said that not being a believer didn't mean believing in nothing, he had his convictions and absolute faith in his love for me. He said it was love that would consolidate our marriage, not an altar, a priest, a city official. He said that the rejection of a religious service was for him a matter of principle and that surely I would stop loving him, or certainly I would love him less, if he proved to be a man without principles. He said finally that surely my mother herself would refuse to entrust her daughter to a person ready to knock down even a single one of the pillars on which he had based his existence.

At those words my father made broad nods of assent, my brothers were openmouthed, Elisa was moved again. But my mother remained impassive. For some moments she fiddled with her wedding ring, then she looked Pietro in the eye and instead of going back to the subject to say that she was persuaded, or to continue to argue, she began to sing my praises with cold determination. Ever since I was small I had been an unusual child. I had been capable of doing things that no girl of the neighborhood had been capable of doing. I had been and was her pride, the pride of the whole family. I had never disappointed her. I had won the right to be happy and if someone made me suffer she would make him suffer a thousand times more.

I listened in embarrassment. All the while I tried to understand if she was speaking seriously or if, as usual, she was intending to explain to Pietro that she didn't give a damn about the fact that he was a professor and all his talk, it wasn't he who was doing the Grecos a favor but the Grecos who were doing him one. I couldn't tell. My fiancé instead believed her absolutely and as my mother spoke he simply assented. When at last she was silent, he said that he knew very well how precious I was and that he was grateful to her for having brought me up as I was. Then he stuck a hand in a pocket of his jacket and took out a blue case that he gave me with a timid gesture. What is it, I thought, he's already given me a ring, is he giving me another? Meanwhile I opened the case. There was a very beautiful ring, of red gold, and in the setting an amethyst surrounded by diamonds. Pietro murmured: it was my grandmother's, my mother's mother, and in my family we would all like you to have it.

That gift was the signal that the ritual was over. We began to drink again, my father went back to telling funny stories of his private and work life, Gianni asked Pietro what team he rooted for, Peppe challenged him to arm wrestling. I helped my sister clear the table. In the kitchen I made the mistake of asking my mother:

"How is he?"

"The ring?"

"Pietro."

"He's ugly, he has crooked feet."

"Papa was no better."

"What do you have to say against your father?"

"Nothing."

"Then be quiet, you only know how to be bossy with us."

"It's not true."

"No? Then why do you let him order you? If he has principles, you don't have them? Make yourself respected."

Elisa intervened: "Ma, Pietro is a gentleman and you don't know what a real gentleman is."

"And you do? Be careful, you're small and if you don't stay in your place I'll hit you. Did you see that hair? A gentleman has hair like that?"

"A gentleman doesn't have normal handsomeness, Ma, a gentleman you can tell, he's a type."

My mother pretended she was going to hit her and my sister, laughing, pulled me out of the kitchen, saying cheerfully:

"Lucky you, Lenù. How refined Pietro is, how he loves you. He gave you his grandmother's antique ring, will you show it to me?"

We returned to the dining room. All the males of the house now wanted to arm-wrestle with my fiancé, they were eager to show that they were superior to the professor at least in tests of strength. He didn't back off. He removed his jacket, rolled up his sleeve, sat down at the table. He lost to Peppe, he lost to Gianni, he lost also to my father. But I was impressed by how seriously he competed. He turned red, a vein swelled on his forehead, he argued that his opponents were shamelessly violating the rules of the contest. He held out stubbornly against Peppe and Gianni, who lifted weights, and against my father, who was capable of unscrewing a screw with just his bare hand. All the while, I was afraid that, in order not to give in, he would break his arm.

23.

Pietro stayed for three days. My father and brothers quickly became attached to him. My brothers were pleased that he didn't give himself airs and was interested in them even though school had judged them incompetent. My mother on the other hand continued to treat him in an unfriendly manner and not until the day before he left did she soften. It was a Sunday, and my father said he wanted to show his son-in-law how beautiful

Naples was. His son-in-law agreed, and proposed that we should eat out.

"In a restaurant?" my mother asked, scowling.

"Yes, ma'am, we ought to celebrate."

"Better if I cook, we said we'd make you another *gattò*."

"No, thank you, you've already done too much."

While we were getting ready my mother drew me aside and asked: "Will he pay?"

"Yes."

"Sure?"

"Sure, Ma, he's the one who invited us."

We went into the city center early in the morning, dressed in our best clothes. And something happened that first of all amazed me. My father had taken on the task of tour guide. He showed our guest the Maschio Angioino, the royal palace, the statues of the kings, Castel dell'Ovo, Via Caracciolo, and the sea. Pietro listened attentively. But at a certain point he, who was coming to our city for the first time, began modestly to tell us about it, to make us discover our city. It was wonderful. I had never had a particular interest in the background of my childhood and adolescence, I marveled that Pietro could talk about it with such learned admiration. He showed that he knew the history of Naples, the literature, fables, legends, anecdotes, the visible monuments and those hidden by neglect. I imagined that he knew about the city in part because he was a man who knew everything, and in part because he had studied it thoroughly, with his usual rigor, because it was mine, because my voice, my gestures, my whole body had been subjected to its influence. Naturally my father soon felt deposed, my brothers were annoyed. I realized it, I hinted to Pietro to stop. He blushed, and immediately fell silent. But my mother, with one of her unpredictable twists, hung on his arm and said:

"Go on, I like it, no one ever told me those things."

We went to eat in a restaurant in Santa Lucia that accord-

ing to my father (he had never been there but had heard about
it) was very good.

"Can I order what I want?" Elisa whispered in my ear.

"Yes."

The time flew by pleasantly. My mother drank too much
and made some crude remarks, my father and my brothers
started joking again with each other and with Pietro. I didn't
take my eyes off my future husband; I was sure that I loved
him, he was a person who knew his value and yet, if necessary,
he could forget himself with naturalness. I noticed for the first
time his propensity to listen and his sympathetic tone of voice,
like that of a lay confessor, and they pleased me. Maybe I
should persuade him to stay another day and take him to see
Lila, tell her: I'm marrying this man, I'm about to leave Naples
with him, what do you say, am I doing well? And I was considering that possibility when at a nearby table five or six students began to look at us insistently and laugh. I immediately
realized that they found Pietro funny-looking because of his
thick eyebrows, the bushy hair over his forehead. After a few
minutes my brothers, both at the same time, stood up, went
over to the students' table, and started a quarrel in their usual
violent manner. An uproar arose, shouting, some punches. My
mother shrieked insults in support of her sons, my father and
Pietro rushed to pull them away. Pietro was almost amused; he
seemed not to have understood the reason for the fight. Once
in the street he said ironically: Is this a local custom, you suddenly get up and start hitting the people at the next table? He
and my brothers became livelier and friendlier than before.
But as soon as possible my father drew Peppe and Gianni aside
and rebuked them for the bad impression they had made in
front of the professor. I heard Peppe justifying himself almost
in a whisper: They were making fun of Pietro, Papa, what the
hell were we supposed to do? I liked that he said Pietro and
not the professor: it meant that Pietro was part of the family, at

home, a friend with the best qualities, and that, even if he was rather odd-looking, no one could make fun of him in his presence. But the incident convinced me that it was better not to take Pietro to see Lila: I knew her, she was mean, she would find him ridiculous and would make fun of him like the young men in the restaurant.

In the evening, exhausted by the day outside, we ate at home and then we all went out again, taking my future husband to the hotel. As we parted, my mother, in high spirits, unexpectedly kissed him noisily on each cheek. But when we returned to the neighborhood, saying a lot of nice things about Pietro, she kept to herself, without saying a word. Before she went to her room she said to me bitterly:

"You are too fortunate—you don't deserve that poor boy."

24.

The book sold well all summer, and I continued to talk about it here and there around the country. I was careful now to defend it with a tone of detachment, at times chilling the more inquisitive audiences. Every so often I remembered Gigliola's words and I mixed them with my own, trying to give them a place.

In early September, Pietro moved to Florence, to a hotel near the station, and started looking for an apartment. He found a small place to rent in the neighborhood of Santa Maria del Carmine, and I went right away to see it. It was an apartment with two dingy rooms, in terrible condition. The kitchen was tiny, the bathroom had no window. When in the past I had gone to Lila's brand-new apartment to study, she would often let me stretch out in her spotless tub, enjoying the warm water and the dense bubbles. The bathtub in that apartment in Florence was cracked and yellowish, the type you had to sit upright in. But I smothered my unhappiness, I said it was all right: Pietro's course was starting, he had to work, he couldn't waste time. And, besides, it was a palace compared to my parents' house.

However, just as Pietro was getting ready to sign the lease, Adele arrived. She didn't have my timidity. She judged the apartment a hovel, completely unsuited to two people who were to spend a large part of their time at home working. So she did what her son hadn't done and what she, on the other hand, could do. She picked up the telephone and, paying no attention to Pietro's show of opposition, marshaled some Florentine friends, all influential people. In a short time she had found in San Niccolò, for a laughable rent, because it was a favor, five light-filled rooms, with a large kitchen and an adequate bathroom. She wasn't satisfied with that: she made some improvements at her own expense, she helped me furnish it. She listed possibilities, gave advice, guided me. But I often noted that she didn't trust either my submissiveness or my taste. If I said yes, she wanted to make sure I really agreed, if I said no she pressed me until I changed my mind. In general we always did as she said. On the other hand, I seldom opposed her; I had no trouble going along with her, and in fact made an effort to learn. I was mesmerized by the rhythm of her sentences, by her gestures, by her hair style, by her clothes, her shoes, her pins, her necklaces, her always beautiful earrings. And she liked my attitude of an attentive student. She persuaded me to cut my hair short, she urged me to buy clothes of her taste in an expensive shop that offered her big discounts, she gave me a pair of shoes that she liked and would have bought for herself but didn't consider suitable for her age, and she even took me to a friend who was a dentist.

Meanwhile, because of the apartment that, in Adele's opinion, constantly needed some new attention, because of Pietro, who was overwhelmed by work, the wedding was put off from autumn to spring, something that allowed my mother to prolong her war to get money from me. I tried to avoid serious conflicts by demonstrating that I hadn't forgotten my family. With the arrival of the telephone, I had the hall and kitchen repainted, I had new wine-colored flowered wallpaper put in the dining room, I bought a coat for Elisa, I got a television on the installment plan. And at a certain point I also gave myself something: I enrolled in a driving school, passed the exam easily, got my license. But my mother darkened:

"You like throwing away money? What's the use of a license if you don't have a car?"

"We'll see later."

"You want to buy a car? How much do you really have saved up?"

"None of your business."

Pietro had a car, and once we were married I intended to use it. When he returned to Naples, in the car, in fact, to bring his parents to meet mine, he let me drive a little, around the old neighborhood and the new one. I drove on the *stradone*, passing the elementary school, the library, I drove on the streets where Lila had lived when she was married, I turned back and skirted the gardens. That experience of driving is the only good thing I can remember. Otherwise it was a terrible afternoon, followed by an endless dinner. Pietro and I struggled to make our families less uncomfortable, but they were so many worlds apart that the silences were extremely long. When the Airotas left, loaded with an enormous quantity of leftovers pressed on them by my mother, it suddenly seemed to me that I was wrong about everything. I came from that family, Pietro from that other, each of us carried our ancestors in our body. How would our marriage go? What awaited me? Would the affinities prevail over the differences? Would I be capable of writing another book?

When? About what? And would Pietro support me? And Adele? And Mariarosa?

One evening, with thoughts like that in my head, I heard someone call me from the street. I rushed to the window—I had immediately recognized the voice of Pasquale Peluso. I saw that he wasn't alone, he was with Enzo. I was alarmed. At that hour shouldn't Enzo be in San Giovanni a Teduccio, at home, with Lila and Gennaro?

"Can you come down?" Pasquale shouted.

"What's happening?"

"Lina doesn't feel well and wants to see you."

I'm coming, I said, and ran down the stairs although my mother was shouting after me: Where are you going at this hour, come back here.

25.

I hadn't seen either Pasquale or Enzo for a long time, but they got right to the point—they had come for Lila and began talking about her immediately. Pasquale had grown a Che Guevara-style beard and it seemed to me that it had improved him. His eyes seemed bigger and more intense, and the thick mustache covered his bad teeth even when he laughed. Enzo, on the other hand, hadn't changed, as silent, as compact, as ever. Only when we were in Pasquale's old car did I realize how surprising it was to see them together. I had been sure that no one in the neighborhood wanted to have anything to do with Lila and Enzo. But it wasn't so: Pasquale often went to their house, he had come with Enzo to get me, Lila had sent them together.

It was Enzo who in his dry and orderly way told me what had happened: Pasquale, who was working at a construction site near San Giovanni a Teduccio, was supposed to stop for dinner at their house. But Lila, who usually returned from the factory at four-thirty, still hadn't arrived at seven, when Enzo and Pasquale got there. The apartment was empty, Gennaro was at the neighbor's. The two began cooking, Enzo fed the child. Lila hadn't shown up until nine, very pale, very nervous. She hadn't answered Enzo and Pasquale's questions. The only thing she said, in a terrified tone of voice, was: They're pulling out my nails. Not true, Enzo had taken her hands and checked, the nails were in place. Then she got angry and shut herself in her room with Gennaro. After a while she had yelled at them to find out if I was at home, she wanted to speak to me urgently.

I asked Enzo:

"Did you have a fight?"

"No."

"Did she not feel well, was she hurt at work?"

"I don't think so, I don't know."

Pasquale said to me:

"Now, let's not make ourselves anxious. Let's bet that as soon as Lina sees you she'll calm down. I'm so glad we found you—you're an important person now, you must have a lot to do."

I denied it, but he cited as proof the old article in *l'Unità* and Enzo nodded in agreement; he had also read it.

"Lila saw it, too," he said.

"And what did she say?"

"She was really pleased with the picture."

"But they made it sound like you were still a student," Pasquale grumbled. "You should write a letter to the paper explaining that you're a graduate."

He complained about all the space that even *l'Unità* was giving to the students. Enzo said he was right, and they held forth with arguments not so different from those I had heard in Milan, only the vocabulary was cruder. It was clear that

Pasquale especially wanted to entertain me with arguments worthy of someone who, though she was their friend, appeared in *l'Unità* with a photograph. But maybe they did it to dispel the anxiety, theirs and mine.

I listened. I quickly realized that their relationship had solidified precisely because of their political passion. They often met after work, at party or some sort of committee meetings. I listened to them, I joined in out of politeness, they replied, but meanwhile I couldn't get Lila out of my mind, Lila consumed by an unknown anguish, she who was always so resistant. When we reached San Giovanni they seemed proud of me, Pasquale in particular didn't miss a single word of mine, and kept checking on me in the rear-view mirror. Although he had his usual knowing tone—he was the secretary of the local section of the Communist Party—he ascribed to my agreement on politics the power to sanction his position. So that, when he felt clearly supported, he explained to me, in some distress, that, with Enzo and some others, he was engaged in a serious fight *within* the party, which—he said, frowning, pounding his hands on the wheel—preferred to wait for a whistle from Aldo Moro, like an obedient dog, rather than stop procrastinating and join the battle.

"What do you think?" he asked.

"It's as you say," I said.

"You're clever," he praised me then, solemnly, as we were going up the dirty stairs, "you always were. Right, Enzo?"

Enzo nodded yes, but I understood that his worry about Lila was increasing at every step, as it was in me, and he felt guilty for being distracted by that chatter. He opened the door, said aloud, We're here, and pointed to a door whose top half was of frosted glass, and through which a faint light shone. I knocked softly and went in.

26.

Lila was lying on a cot, fully dressed. Gennaro was sleeping next to her. Come in, she said, I knew you'd come, give me a kiss. I kissed her on the cheeks, I sat on the empty bed that must be her son's. How much time had passed since I'd last seen her? I found her even thinner, even paler, her eyes were red, the sides of her nose were cracked, her long hands were scarred by cuts. She continued almost without a pause, in a low voice so as not to wake the baby: I saw you in the newspapers, how well you look, your hair is lovely, I know everything about you, I know you're getting married, he's a professor, good for you, you're going to live in Florence, I'm sorry I made you come at this hour, my mind's no help to me, it's coming unglued like wallpaper, luckily you're here.

"What's happening?" I asked, and moved to caress her hand.

That question, that gesture were enough. She opened her eyes wide, clenched her hand, abruptly pulled it away.

"I'm not well," she said, "but wait, don't be scared, I'll calm down now."

She became calm. She said softly, enunciating the words:

"I've disturbed you, Lenù, because you have to make me a promise, you're the only person I trust: if something happens to me, if I end up in the hospital, if they take me to the insane asylum, if they can't find me anymore, you have to take Gennaro, you have to keep him with you, bring him up in your house. Enzo is good, he's smart, I trust him, but he can't give the child the things you can."

"Why are you talking like that? What's wrong? If you don't explain I can't understand."

"First promise."

"All right."

She became agitated again, alarming me.

"No, you mustn't say all right; you must say here, now, that you'll take the child. And if you need money, find Nino, tell him he has to help you. But promise: *I will bring up the child.*"

I looked at her uncertainly. But I promised. I promised and I sat and listened to her all night long.

27.

This may be the last time I'll talk about Lila with a wealth of detail. Later on she became more evasive, and the material at my disposal was diminished. It's the fault of our lives diverging, the fault of distance. And yet even when I lived in other cities and we almost never met, and she as usual didn't give me any news and I made an effort not to ask for it, her shadow goaded me, depressed me, filled me with pride, deflated me, giving me no rest.

Today, as I'm writing, that goad is even more essential. I wish she were here, that's why I'm writing. I want her to erase, add, collaborate in our story by spilling into it, according to her whim, the things she knows, what she said or thought: the time she confronted Gino, the fascist; the time she met Nadia, Professor Galiani's daughter; the time she returned to the apartment on Corso Vittorio Emanuele where long ago she had felt out of place; the time she looked frankly at her experience of sex. As for my own embarrassments as I listened, my sufferings, the few things I said during her long story, I'll think about them later.

28.

As soon as *The Blue Fairy* turned to ash in the bonfire of the courtyard, Lila went back to work. I don't know how strong an effect our meeting had on her—certainly she felt unhappy for days but managed not to ask herself why. She had learned that it hurt to look for reasons, and she waited for the unhappiness to become first a general discontent, then a kind of melancholy, and finally the normal labor of every day: taking care of Gennaro, making the beds, keeping the house clean, washing and ironing the baby's clothes, Enzo's, and her own, making lunch for the three of them, leaving little Rino at the neighbor's with a thousand instructions, hurrying to the factory and enduring the work and the abuses, coming home to devote herself to her son, and also to the children Gennaro played with, making dinner, the three of them eating again, putting Gennaro to bed while Enzo cleared up and washed the dishes, returning to the kitchen to help him study, something that was very important to him, and that, despite her weariness, she didn't want to deny him.

What did she see in Enzo? In essence, I think, the same thing she had wanted to see in Stefano and in Nino: a way of finally putting everything back on its feet in the proper way. But while Stefano, once the screen of money vanished, had turned out to be a person without substance and dangerous; while Nino, once the screen of intelligence vanished, had been transformed into a black smoke of pain, Enzo for now seemed incapable of nasty surprises. He was the boy whom, for obscure reasons, she had always respected in elementary school, and now he was a man so deeply compact in every gesture, so resolute toward the world, and so gentle with her that she could be sure he wouldn't abruptly change shape.

Of course, they didn't sleep together. Lila couldn't do it. They shut themselves in their rooms, and she heard him moving on the other side of the wall until every noise stopped and there remained only the sounds of the apartment, the building, the street. She had trouble falling asleep, in spite of her exhaustion. In the dark all the reasons for unhappiness that she

had prudently left nameless got mixed up and were concentrated on Gennaro, little Rino. She thought: What will this
child become? She thought: I mustn't call him Rinuccio, that
would drive him to regress into dialect. She thought: I also
have to help the children he plays with if I don't want him to
be ruined by being with them. She thought: I don't have time,
I myself am not what I once was, I never pick up a pen, I no
longer read books.

Sometimes she felt a weight on her chest. She became
alarmed and turned on the light in the middle of the night,
looked at her sleeping child. She saw almost nothing of Nino;
Gennaro reminded her, rather, of her brother. When he was
younger, the child had followed her around, now instead he
was bored, he yelled, he wanted to run off and play, he said
bad words to her. I love him—Lila reflected—but do I love
him just as he is? An ugly question. The more she observed her
son, the more she felt that, even if the neighbor found him very
intelligent, he wasn't growing up as she would have liked. She
felt that the years she had dedicated to him had been in vain,
now it seemed to her wrong that the quality of a person
depends on the quality of his early childhood. You had to be
constant, and Gennaro had no constancy, nor did she. My
mind is always scattering, she said to herself, I'm made badly
and he's made badly. Then she was ashamed of thinking like
that, she whispered to the sleeping child: you're clever, you
already know how to read, you already know how to write, you
can do addition and subtraction, your mother is stupid, she's
never satisfied. She kissed the little boy on the forehead and
turned out the light.

But still she couldn't sleep, especially when Enzo came
home late and went to bed without asking her to study. On
these occasions, Lila imagined that he had met some prostitute
or had a lover, a colleague in the factory where he worked, an
activist from the Communist cell he had immediately joined.

Males are like that, she thought, at least the ones I've known: they have to have sex constantly, otherwise they're unhappy. I don't think Enzo is any different, why should he be. And besides I've rejected him, I've left him in the bed by himself, I can't make any demands. She was afraid only that he would fall in love and send her away. She wasn't worried about finding no roof over her head, she had a job at the sausage factory and felt strong, surprisingly, much stronger than when she had married Stefano and found herself with a lot of money but was subjugated by him. Rather, she was afraid of losing Enzo's kindness, the attention he gave to all her anxieties, the tranquil strength he emanated and thanks to which he had saved her first from Nino's absence, then from Stefano's presence. All the more because, in her present situation, he was the only one who gave her any gratification, who continued to ascribe to her extraordinary capabilities.

"You know what that means?"

"No."

"Look closely."

"It's German, Enzo, I don't know German."

"But if you concentrate, after a while you'll know it," he said to her, partly joking, partly serious.

Enzo had worked hard to get a diploma and had succeeded, but, even though she had stopped going to school in fifth grade, he believed that she had a much brighter intelligence than he did and attributed to her the miraculous quality of rapidly mastering any material. In fact, when, with very little to go on, he nevertheless became convinced that the languages of computer programming held the future of the human race, and that the élite who first mastered them would have a resounding part in the history of the world, he immediately turned to her.

"Help me."

"I'm tired."

"The life we lead is disgusting, Lina, we have to change."

"For me it's fine like this."

"The child is with strangers all day."

"He's big, he can't live in a bell jar."

"Look what bad shape your hands are in."

"They're my hands and I'll do as I like with them."

"I want to earn more, for you and for Gennaro."

"You take care of your things and I'll take care of mine."

Harsh reactions, as usual. Enzo enrolled in a correspondence course—it was expensive, requiring periodic tests to be sent to an international data processing center with headquarters in Zurich, which returned them corrected—and gradually he had involved Lila and she had tried to keep up. But she behaved in a completely different way than she had with Nino, whom she had assailed with her obsession to prove that she could help him in everything. When she studied with Enzo she was calm, she didn't try to overpower him. The evening hours that they spent on the course were a struggle for him, for her a sedative. Maybe that was why, the rare times he returned late and seemed able to do without her, Lila remained wakeful, anxious, as she listened to the water running in the bathroom, with which she imagined Enzo washing off his body every trace of contact with his lovers.

29.

In the factory—she had immediately understood—over-work drove people to want to have sex not with their wife or husband in their own house, where they returned exhausted and empty of desire, but there, at work, morning or afternoon. The men reached out their hands at every opportunity, they propositioned you if they merely passed by; and women, especially the ones who were not so young, laughed, rubbed against them with their big bosoms, fell in love, and love became a diversion that mitigated the labor and the boredom, giving an impression of real life.

From Lila's first days the men had tried to get close, as if to sniff her. Lila repulsed them, and they laughed or went off humming songs full of obscene allusions. One morning, to make things perfectly clear, she almost pulled off the ear of a man who passing by had made a lewd remark and pressed a kiss on her neck. He was a fairly attractive man in his forties, named Edo, who spoke to everyone in an allusive way and was good at telling dirty jokes. Lila grabbed the ear with one hand and twisted it, pulling with all her strength, her nails digging into the membrane, without letting go her grip even though the man was yelling, as he tried to parry the kicks she was giving him. After which, furious, she went to see Bruno Soccavo to protest.

Lila had seen him only a few times since he hired her—fleetingly, without paying him much attention. In that situation, however, she was able to observe him closely. He was standing behind the desk; he had risen deliberately, the way men do when a woman enters the room. Lila was amazed: Soccavo's face was bloated, his eyes shrouded by dissipation, his chest heavy, and his flushed complexion clashed like magma against his black hair and the white of his wolfish teeth. She wondered: what does this man have to do with the young man, the friend of Nino who was studying law? And she felt there was no continuity between the time on Ischia and the sausage factory: between them stretched a void, and in the leap from one space to the other Bruno—maybe because his father had been ill recently and the weight of the business (the debts, some said) had fallen suddenly on his shoulders—had changed for the worse.

She told him her complaints, he began to laugh.

"Lina," he warned her, "I did you a favor, but don't make

trouble for me. We all work hard here, don't always have your gun aimed: people have to relax every so often, otherwise it causes problems for me."

"The rest of you can relax with each other."

He ran his eyes over her with a look of amusement.

"I thought you liked to joke."

"I like it when I decide."

Lila's hard tone made him change his. He became serious, he said without looking at her: you're the same as ever—so beautiful in Ischia. Then he pointed to the door: go to work, go on.

But from then on, when he met her in the factory, he never failed to speak to her in front of everyone, and he always gave her a good-humored compliment. That familiarity in the end sanctioned Lila's situation in the factory: she was in the good graces of the young Soccavo, and so it was as well to leave her alone. This seemed to be confirmed when one afternoon, right after the lunch break, a large woman named Teresa stopped her and said teasingly: you're wanted in the seasoning room. Lila went into the big room where the salamis were drying, a rectangular space crammed with salamis hanging from the ceiling in the yellow light. There she found Bruno, who appeared to be doing an inspection but in reality wanted to chat.

While he wandered around the room poking and sniffing with the air of an expert, he asked her about Pinuccia, her sister-in-law, and—a thing that irritated Lila—said, without looking at her, in fact as he examined a soppressata: she was never happy with your brother, she fell in love with me that summer, like you and Nino. Then he passed by and, with his back to her, added: it was thanks to her that I discovered that pregnant women love to make love. Then, without giving her the time to comment or make a sarcastic remark or get angry, he stopped in the middle of the room and said that while the place as a whole had nauseated him ever since he was a child, here in the

drying room he had always felt comfortable, there was something satisfying, solid, the product that was nearly finished,
acquiring refinement, spreading its odor, being readied for the
market. Look, touch it, he said to her, it's compact, hard, smell
the fragrance it gives off: it's like the odor of man and woman
when they embrace and touch—you like it?—if you knew how
many girls I've brought here since I was a boy. And just then
he grabbed her by the waist, slid his lips down her long neck,
as he squeezed her bottom—he seemed to have a hundred
hands, he was rubbing her on top of the apron, underneath it,
at a frenetic and breathless speed, in an exploration without
pleasure, a pure intrusive desire.

For Lila everything, except the smell of the salamis,
reminded her of Stefano's violence and for several seconds she
felt annihilated, she was afraid of being murdered. Then fury
seized her, and she hit Bruno in the face and between the legs,
she yelled him, you are a shit of a man, you've got nothing
down there; come here, pull it out so I can cut it off, you shit.

Bruno let go, retreated. He touched his lip, which was
bleeding, he snickered in embarrassment, he mumbled: I'm
sorry, I thought there might be at least a little gratitude. Lila
shouted at him: You mean I have to pay a penalty, or you'll fire
me, is that it? He laughed again, shook his head: No, if you
don't want to you don't want to, that's all, I apologized, what
else should I do? But she was beside herself, only now did she
begin to feel on her body the traces of his hands, and she knew
it would last, it wasn't something she could wash off with soap.
She backed up toward the door, she said to him: You were
lucky right now, but whether you fire me or not, I swear I'll
make you curse the moment you touched me. As she was leaving he muttered: What did I do to you, I didn't do anything,
come here, as if these were real problems, let's make peace.

She went back to her job. At the time she was working in
the steamy vat room, as a kind of attendant who among other

things was supposed to keep the floor dry, a fruitless task. Edo, the one whose ear she had almost torn off, looked at her with curiosity. All of them, men and women, kept their eyes on her as she returned, enraged, from the drying room. Lila didn't exchange a glance with anyone. She grabbed a rag, slammed it down on the bricks, and began to wipe the floor, which was a swamp, uttering aloud, in a threatening tone: Let's see if some other son of a bitch wants to try. Her companions concentrated on their work.

For days she expected to be fired, but she wasn't. If she happened to run into Bruno, he smiled kindly, she responded with a cold nod. No consequences, then, except disgust at those short hands, and flashes of hatred. But since Lila continued to show the same contemptuous indifference toward the supervisors, they suddenly began to torment her again, by constantly changing her job, forcing her to work until she was worn out, making obscene remarks. A sign that they had been given permission.

She didn't tell Enzo anything about almost tearing off the ear, about Bruno's attack, about the everyday harassments and struggles. If he asked her how things were going at the sausage factory, she answered sarcastically: Why don't you tell me how it is where you work? And since he was silent, Lila teased him a little and then together they turned to the exercises for the correspondence course. They took refuge there for many reasons, the most important being to avoid questions about the future: what were they to each other, why was he taking care of her and Gennaro, why did she accept it, why had they been living together for so long while Enzo waited in vain every night for her to join him, tossing and turning in the bed, going to the kitchen with the excuse of getting a drink of water, glancing at the door with the frosted glass to see if she had turned off the light yet and to look at her shadow. Mute tensions—I knock, I let him enter—his doubts, hers. In the end they preferred to dull their senses by competing with block diagrams as if they were equipment for gymnastics.

"Let's do the diagram of the door opening," Lila said.

"Let's do the diagram of knotting the tie," Enzo said.

"Let's do the diagram of tying Gennaro's shoes," Lila said.

"Let's do the diagram of making coffee in the *napoletana*," Enzo said.

From the simplest actions to the most complicated, they racked their brains to diagram daily life, even if the Zurich tests didn't require it. And not because Enzo wanted to but because, as usual, Lila, who had begun diffidently, grew more and more excited each day, and now, in spite of the cold at night, she was frantic to reduce the entire wretched world they lived in to the truth of 0s and 1s. She seemed to aspire to an abstract linearity—the abstraction that bred all abstractions—hoping that it would assure her a restful tidiness.

"Let's diagram the factory," she proposed one evening.

"The whole process?" he asked, bewildered.

"Yes."

He looked at her, he said: "All right, let's start with your job."

An irritated scowl crossed her face; she said good night and went to her room.

30.

That equilibrium, already precarious, changed when Pasquale reappeared. He was working at a construction site in the area and had come to San Giovanni a Teduccio for a meeting of the local section of the Communist Party. He and Enzo met on the street, by chance, and immediately regained their old intimacy. They ended up talking about politics, and manifested the same dissatisfaction. Enzo expressed himself cautiously at first, but Pasquale, surprisingly, although he had an important local post—secretary of the section—proved to be anything but cautious, and he criticized the party, which was revisionist, and the union, which too often closed both eyes. The two spent so long talking that Lila found Pasquale in the house at dinnertime and had to feed him as well.

The evening began badly. She felt herself observed, and had to make an effort not to get angry. What did Pasquale want, to spy on her, report to the neighborhood how she was living? What right did he have to come there to judge her? He didn't speak a single friendly word, he brought no news of her family—of Nunzia, of her brother Rino, of Fernando. Instead he gave her male looks, the kind she got in the factory, appraising, and if she became aware of them he turned his eyes elsewhere. He must have found that she had grown ugly. Surely he was thinking, How could I, as a boy, have fallen in love with this woman, I was a fool. And without a doubt he considered her a terrible mother, since she could have brought up her son in the comfort of the Carracci grocery stores and instead she had dragged him into that poverty. At a certain point Lila said huffily to Enzo, you clean up, I'm going to bed. But Pasquale, to her surprise, assumed a grandiose tone and said to her, with some emotion: Lina, before you go I have to tell you one thing. There is no woman like you, you throw yourself into life with a force that, if we all had it, the world would have changed a long time ago. Then, having broken the ice in this way, he told her that Fernando had gone back to resoling shoes, that Rino had become Stefano's cross to bear, and was constantly begging him for money, that Nunzia he rarely saw, she never left the house. But you did well, he repeated: no one in the neighborhood has kicked the Carraccis and the Solaras in the face as much as you, and I'm on your side.

After that he showed up often, which cut into their studying. He would arrive at dinnertime with four hot pizzas, playing his usual role of someone who knows all about how the capitalist and anti-capitalist world functions, and the old friendship grew stronger. It was clear that he lived without emotional ties; his sister Carmen was engaged and had little time for him. But he reacted to his solitude with an angry activism that Lila liked, that interested her. Although crushed by hard labor at the construction sites, he was involved in union activities: he threw blood-red paint at the American consulate, if there were fascists to be beaten up he was always on the front lines, he was a member of a worker-student committee where he continuously quarreled with the students. Not to mention the Communist Party: because of his critical position he expected at any moment to lose his post as secretary of the section. With Enzo and Lila he spoke freely, mixing personal resentments and political arguments. They tell *me* I'm an enemy of the party, he complained, they tell *me* I make too much of a fuss, I should calm down. But *they* are the ones who are destroying the party, *they* are the ones turning it into a cog in the system, *they* are the ones who've reduced anti-fascism to democratic oversight. But do you know who's been installed as the head of the neighborhood fascists? The pharmacist's son, Gino, an idiot slave of Michele Solara. And must I put up with the fact that the fascists are raising their heads again in my neighborhood? My father—he said, with emotion—gave his entire self to the party, and why: for this watered-down anti-fascism, for this shit we have today? When that poor man ended up in jail, innocent, completely innocent, he got angry—he didn't murder Don Achille—the party abandoned him, even though he had been a loyal comrade, even though he had taken part in the Four Days of Naples, and fought at the Ponte della Sanità, even though after the war, in the neighborhood, he had been more exposed than anyone else. And Giuseppina, his mother? Had anyone helped her? As soon as he mentioned his mother, Pasquale picked up Gennaro and sat him on his lap, saying: See how pretty your mamma is, do you love her?

Lila listened. At times it occurred to her that she should have said yes to that youth, the first who had noticed her, rather than aiming Stefano and his money, rather than getting herself in trouble with Nino: stayed in her place, not committed the sin of pride, pacified her mind. But at other times, because of Pasquale's tirades, she felt gripped again by her childhood, by the ferocity of the neighborhood, by Don Achille, by his murder, which she, as a child, had recounted so often and with so many invented details that now it seemed to her that she had been present. So she remembered the arrest of Pasquale's father, and how much the carpenter had shouted, and his wife, and Carmen, and she didn't like that, true memories mingled with false ones, she saw the violence, the blood. Then she roused herself, uneasily, escaped from the flood of Pasquale's bitterness, and to soothe herself she urged him to recall, I don't know, Christmas and Easter in his family, his mother Giuseppina's cooking. He quickly realized what was going on and maybe he thought that Lila missed the affections of her family, as he missed his. The fact is that one day he showed up without warning and said gaily: Look who I brought you. He had brought her Nunzia.

Mother and daughter embraced, Nunzia cried for a long time, and gave Gennaro a Pinocchio ragdoll. But as soon as she started to criticize her daughter's decisions, Lila, who at first had appeared happy to see her, said: Ma, either we act as if nothing happened or it's better that you go. Nunzia was offended, she played with the child, and kept saying, as if she really were talking to the boy: If your mamma goes to work, what about you, poor thing, where does she leave you? At that point Pasquale realized he had made a mistake, he said it was late and they had to go. Nunzia got up and spoke to her daughter, partly threatening her, partly entreating her. You, she com-

plained. First you had us living the life of rich people and then
you ruined us: your brother felt abandoned and doesn't want
to see you anymore, your father has effaced you; Lina, please,
I'm not telling you to make peace with your husband, that's not
possible, but at least clear things up with the Solaras; they've
taken everything because of you, and Rino, your father, we
Cerullos, now once again we're nothing.

Lila listened and then she practically pushed her out, saying: Ma, it's better if you don't come back. She shouted the
same thing to Pasquale as well.

31.

Too many problems at once: the feelings of guilt toward
Gennaro, toward Enzo; the cruel shifts at work, the overtime,
Bruno's obscenities; her family, who wanted to return to burden her; and that presence of Pasquale, toward whom it was
pointless to be aloof. He never got angry; he burst in cheerfully, sometimes dragging Lila, Gennaro, and Enzo out to a
pizzeria, sometimes driving them in the car to Agerola so the
child could have some fresh air. But mostly he tried to involve
her in his activities. He pushed her to join the union, even
though she didn't want to and did it only to slight Soccavo,
who wouldn't like it. He brought her pamphlets of various
kinds, very clear, concise, on subjects like the pay package,
collective bargaining, wage differentials, knowing that even if
he hadn't opened them Lila would sooner or later read them.
He took her with Enzo and the child to Riviera di Chiaia, to a
demonstration for peace in Vietnam that turned into a general
stampede: rocks flying, fascists stirring things up, police
charging, Pasquale punching, Lila shouting insults, and Enzo
cursing the moment they had decided to take Gennaro into
the middle of that fracas.

But there were two episodes in particular, in that period, that were significant for Lila. Once Pasquale insisted that she come to hear an important comrade, a woman. Lila accepted the invitation; she was curious. But she heard almost none of the speech—a speech more or less about the party and the working class—because the important comrade arrived late and when the meeting finally began Gennaro was fidgety, and she had to amuse him, taking him out to the street to play, bringing him back inside, taking him out again. Yet the little she heard was enough for her to understand how much dignity the woman had, and how distinct she was in every way from the working- and lower-middle-class audience. So when she noticed that Pasquale, Enzo, and some others weren't satisfied with what the speaker was saying, she thought that they were unfair, that they should be grateful to that educated woman who had come to waste her time with them. And when Pasquale made a speech so argumentative that the comrade delegate lost her temper and, her voice cracking, exclaimed, in irritation, That's enough, I'm going to get up and leave, that reaction pleased her, she took her side. But evidently her feelings were, as usual, muddled. When Enzo shouted, in support of Pasquale: Comrade, *without us* you don't even exist, so you stay as long as *we* want you to, and go only when *we* tell you, she changed her mind, with sudden sympathy for the violence of that *we*— it seemed to her that the woman deserved it. She went home angry at the child, who had ruined the evening for her.

Much more lively was a meeting of the committee that Pasquale, with his thirst for engagement, had joined. Lila went not only because it meant a lot to him but because it seemed to her that the restlessness that drove him to try and to understand was good. The committee met in Naples, in an old house on Via dei Tribunali. They arrived one night in Pasquale's car, and climbed up crumbling, monumental stairs. The place was large, and there weren't many people present. Lila noticed how easy it was to distinguish the faces of the students from those of the workers, the fluency of the leaders from the stuttering of the followers. And she quickly became irritated. The students made speeches that seemed to her hypocritical; they had a modest manner that clashed with their pedantic phrases. The refrain, besides, was always the same: We're here to learn from you, meaning from the workers, but in reality they were showing off ideas that were almost too obvious about capital, about exploitation, about the betrayal of social democracy, about the modalities of the class struggle. Furthermore—she discovered—the few girls, who were mostly silent, flirted eagerly with Enzo and Pasquale. Especially Pasquale, who was the more sociable, and was treated with great friendliness. He was a worker who—although he carried a Communist Party card, and was the head of a section—had chosen to bring his experience of the proletariat into a revolutionary meeting. When he and Enzo spoke, the students, who among themselves did nothing but quarrel, always registered approval. Enzo as usual said only a few, loaded words. Pasquale, on the other hand, recounted, with an inexhaustible patter, half in Italian, half in dialect, the progress that the political work was making at the construction sites around Naples, hurling small polemical darts at the students, who hadn't been very active. At the conclusion, without warning, he dragged her, Lila, into it. He introduced her by her name and last name, he called her a worker comrade who had a job in a small food factory, and he heaped praises on her.

Lila furrowed her brow and narrowed her eyes: she didn't like them all looking at her like a rare animal. And when, after Pasquale, a girl spoke—the first of the girls to speak—she became even more annoyed, first of all because the girl expressed herself like a book, second because she kept referring to her, calling her Comrade Cerullo, and, third, because Lila already knew her: it was Nadia, the daughter of Professor

Galiani, Nino's little girlfriend, who had written him love letters on Ischia.

For a moment she was afraid that Nadia had in turn recognized her, but although the girl addressed her as she spoke, she gave no sign of remembering her. Besides, why should she? Who could say how many rich people's parties she had gone to and what crowd of shadows inhabited her memory? For Lila, on the other hand, there had been that one long-ago occasion, and she remained struck by it. She recalled the apartment on Corso Vittorio Emanuele precisely, along with Nino and all those young people from good families, the books, the paintings, and her own agonizing experience of it, the unease it had inspired. She couldn't bear it, she got up while Nadia was still speaking and went out with Gennaro, carrying inside her an evil energy that, finding no precise outlet, writhed in her stomach.

After a while, however, she returned; she had decided to have her say, in order not to feel inferior. A curly-headed youth was speaking with great expertise about Italsider and piecework. Lila waited for him to finish and, ignoring Enzo's look of bewilderment, asked to speak. She spoke for a long time, in Italian, with Gennaro fussing in her arms. She began slowly, then she continued on amid a general silence, perhaps her voice was too loud. She said jokingly that she knew nothing about the working class. She said she knew only the workers, men and women, in the factory where she worked, people from whom there was absolutely nothing to learn except wretchedness. Can you imagine, she asked, what it means to spend eight hours a day standing up to your waist in the mortadella cooking water? Can you imagine what it means to have your fingers covered with cuts from slicing the meat off animal bones? Can you imagine what it means to go in and out of refrigerated rooms at twenty degrees below zero, and get ten lire more an hour—ten lire—for cold compensation? If you imagine this, what do you think you can learn from people who are forced to live like that? The women have to let their asses be groped by supervisors and colleagues without saying a word. If the owner feels the need, someone has to follow him into the seasoning room; his father used to ask for the same thing, maybe also his grandfather; and there, before he jumps all over you, that same owner makes you a tired little speech on how the odor of salami excites him. Men and women both are subjected to body searches, because at the exit there's something called the "partial," and if the red light goes on instead of the green, it means that you're stealing salamis or mortadellas. The "partial" is controlled by the guard, who's a spy for the owner, and turns on the red light not only for possible thieves but especially for shy pretty girls and for troublemakers. That is the situation in the factory where I work. The union has never gone in and the workers are nothing but poor victims of blackmail, dependent on the law of the owner, that is: I pay you and so I possess you and I possess your life, your family, and everything that surrounds you, and if you don't do as I say I'll ruin you.

At first no one breathed. Then other speakers followed, who all quoted Lila devotedly. At the end Nadia came to give her a hug. She was full of compliments, How pretty you are, how clever, you speak so well. She thanked her, and said seriously: You've made us understand how much work we still have to do. But in spite of her lofty, almost solemn tone, to Lila she seemed more childish than she remembered when, that night years earlier, she had seen her with Nino. What did they do, she and the son of Sarratore, did they dance, did they talk, did they stroke each other, did they kiss? She no longer knew. Certainly, the girl had a loveliness that was unforgettable. And now Lila thought, seeing Nadia right before her, she seemed even purer than she had then, pure and fragile and so genuinely open to the suffering of others that she appeared to feel their torments in her own body to an unendurable extent.

"Will you come back?"

"I have the child."

"You have to come back, we need you."

But Lila shook her head uneasily, she repeated to Nadia: I have the child, and pointed to him, and to Gennaro she said, Say hello to the lady, tell her you know how to read and write, let her hear how well you speak. And since Gennaro hid his face against her neck while Nadia smiled vaguely but didn't seem to notice him, she said again to her: I have the child, I work eight hours a day not counting overtime, people in my situation want only to sleep at night. She left in a daze, with the impression of having exposed herself too fully to people who, yes, were good-hearted but who, even if they understood it in the abstract, in the concrete couldn't understand a thing. *I know*—it stayed in her head without becoming sound—*I know what a comfortable life full of good intentions means, you can't even imagine what real misery is.*

Once she was on the street her uneasiness increased. As they went toward the car, she felt that Pasquale and Enzo were sulking, she guessed that her speech had wounded them. Pasquale took her gently by the arm, closing a physical gap that before that moment he had never tried to close, and asked her:

"You really work in those conditions?"

She, irritated by the contact, pulled her arm away, protesting: "And how do you work, the two of you, how do you work?"

They didn't answer. They worked hard, that was obvious. And at least Enzo in front of him, in the factory, women worn out by the work, by humiliations, by domestic obligations no less than Lila was. Yet now they were both angry because of the conditions *she* worked in; they couldn't tolerate it. You had to hide everything from men. They preferred not to know, they preferred to pretend that what happened at the hands of the boss miraculously didn't happen to the women important to

them and that—this was the idea they had grown up with—
they had to protect her even at the risk of being killed. In the
face of that silence Lila got even angrier. "Fuck off," she said,
"you and the working class."

They got in the car, exchanging only trite remarks all the way
to San Giovanni a Teduccio. But when Pasquale left them at
their house he said to her seriously: There's nothing to do, you're
always the best, and then he left again for the neighborhood.
Enzo, instead, with the child asleep in his arms, muttered darkly:

"Why didn't you say anything? People in the factory put
their hands on you?"

They were tired, she decided to soothe him. She said:

"With me they don't dare."

32.

A few days later the trouble began. Lila arrived at work
early in the morning, worn out by her innumerable tasks and
completely unprepared for what was about to happen. It was
very cold, she'd had a cough for days, it felt like flu coming on.
At the entrance she saw a couple of kids, they must have
decided to skip school. One of them greeted her with some
familiarity and gave her not a flyer as sometimes happened but
a pamphlet several pages long. She responded to his greeting
but she was bewildered; she had seen the boy at the committee meeting on Via dei Tribunali. Then she put the pamphlet
in her coat pocket and passed Filippo, the guard, without
deigning to look at him, so he shouted after her: Not even a
good morning, eh.

She worked extremely hard as usual—at that time she was
in the gutting section—and forgot about the boy. At lunchtime
she went into the courtyard with her lunchbox to find a sunny
corner, but as soon as Filippo saw her he left the guard booth

and joined her. He was a man of about fifty, short, heavy, full of the most disgusting obscenities but also inclined to a sticky sentimentality. He had recently had his sixth child, and he easily became emotional, pulling out his wallet to show off a picture of the baby. Lila thought he had decided to show it to her as well, but no. The man pulled the pamphlet out of his jacket pocket and said to her in an extremely aggressive tone:

"Cerù, listen carefully to what I'm telling you: if you said to these shits the things that are written here, you've got yourself in deep trouble, you know?"

She answered coldly:

"I don't know what the fuck you're talking about, let me eat."

Filippo, angrily throwing the pamphlet in her face, snapped:

"You don't know, eh? Read it, then. We were all happy and in harmony here, and only a whore like you could spread these things. I turn on the 'partial' as I please? I put my hands on the girls? I, the father of a family? Look out, or don Bruno will make you pay, and dearly, or by God I'll smash your face myself."

He turned and went back to the guard booth.

Lila calmly finished eating, then she picked up the pamphlet. The title was pretentious: "Investigation Into the Condition of Workers in Naples and the Provinces." She scanned the pages, and found one devoted entirely to the Soccavo sausage factory. She read word for word everything that had come out of her mouth at the meeting on Via dei Tribunali.

She pretended it was nothing. She left the pamphlet on the ground, she went inside without even looking at the guard booth and returned to work. But she was furious with whoever had gotten her into that mess, and without even warning her, especially saintly Nadia. Surely she had written that stuff, it was all tidily in order and full of maudlin emotion. As she worked the knife on the cold meat and the odor made her sick and her rage increased, she felt around her the hostility of the other workers, male and female. They had all known one another a long time, they knew they were complicit victims, and they had no doubt about who the whistleblower was: she, the only one who behaved from the start as if the need to work didn't go hand in hand with the need to be humiliated.

In the afternoon Bruno appeared and soon afterward he sent for her. His face was redder than usual, and he had the pamphlet in his hand.

"Was it you?"

"No."

"Tell me the truth, Lina: there are already too many people out there making trouble, you've joined them?"

"I told you no."

"No, eh? There is no one here, however, who has the ability and the impudence to make up all these lies."

"It must have been one of the office workers."

"The office workers least of all."

"Then what do you want from me, little birds sing, get mad at them."

He snorted, he seemed truly strained. He said:

"I gave you a job. I said nothing when you joined the union, my father would have kicked you out. All right, I did something foolish, there in the drying room, but I apologized, you can't say I persecuted you. And you, what do you do, you take revenge by casting a bad light on my factory and setting it down in black and white that I take my women workers into the drying room? For chrissake, when? Me, the workers, are you mad? You're making me regret the favor I did you."

"The favor? I work hard and you pay me a few cents. It's more the favor I do you than what you do for me."

"You see? You talk like those shits. Have the courage to admit that you wrote this crap."

"I didn't write anything."

Bruno twisted his mouth, he looked at the pages in front of him, and she understood that he was hesitating, he couldn't make up his mind: move to a harsher tone, threaten her, fire her, retreat and try to find out if there were other initiatives like that being prepared? She made up *her* mind, and said in a low voice—reluctantly but with a small charming expression that clashed with the memory of his violence, still vivid in her body—three conciliatory phrases:

"Trust me, I have a small child, I honestly didn't do this thing."

He nodded yes, but he also muttered, unhappily: "You know what you're forcing me to do?"

"No, and I don't want to know."

"I'll tell you just the same. If those are your friends, warn them: as soon as they come back and make a scene out front here, I'll have them beaten to a pulp. As for you, be careful: stretch the cord too far and it will snap."

But the day didn't end there. On the way out, when Lila passed, the red light of the partial went on. It was the usual ritual: every day the guard cheerfully chose three or four victims, the shy girls, eyes lowered, let him feel them up, the savvy older women laughed, saying: Filì, if you have to touch go on, but hurry up, I've got to go make dinner. This time, Filippo stopped only Lila. It was cold, a strong wind was blowing. The guard came out of his booth. Lila shivered, she said: "If you so much as brush me, by God I'll murder you or have you murdered."

Filippo, grim, pointed to a small café table that was always next to the booth.

"Empty your pockets one at a time, put the stuff there."

Lila found a fresh sausage in her coat, with disgust she felt the soft meat inside the casing. She pulled it out and burst into laughter, saying, "What shits you people are, all of you."

33.

Threats to report her for theft. Deductions from her salary, fines. And insults, Filippo's hurled at her, and hers at Filippo. Bruno didn't appear, and yet he was surely still in the factory, his car was in the courtyard. Lila guessed that from then on things would get even worse for her.

She went home wearier than usual; she got angry at Gennaro, who wanted to stay at the neighbor's; she made dinner. She told Enzo that he would have to study on his own and she went to bed early. Since she couldn't get warm under the covers, she got up and put on a wool sweater over her nightgown. She was getting back in bed when suddenly, for no obvious reason, her heart was in her throat and began pounding so hard that it seemed like someone else's.

She already knew those symptoms, they went along with the thing that later—eleven years later, in 1980—she called dissolving boundaries. But the signs had never manifested themselves so violently, and this was the first time it had happened when she was alone, without people around who for one reason or another set off that effect. Then she realized with a jolt of horror that she wasn't alone. From her unstuck head figures and voices of the day were emerging, floating through the room: the two boys from the committee, the guard, her fellow-workers, Bruno in the drying room, Nadia—all moving too rapidly, as in a silent film. Even the flashes of red light from the partial came at very narrow intervals, and Filippo who was tearing the sausage out of her hands and yelling threats. All a trick of the mind: except for Gennaro, in the cot beside her, with his regular breathing, there were no real persons or sounds in the room. But that didn't soothe her, in fact it magnified the fear. Her heartbeats were now so powerful that they seemed capable of exploding the interlocking solidity of objects. The tenacity of the grip that held the walls of the room together had weakened, the violent knocking in her throat was shaking the bed, cracking the plaster, unsoldering the upper part of her skull, maybe it would shatter the child, yes, it would shatter him like a plastic puppet, splitting open his chest and stomach and head to reveal his insides. I have to get him away, she thought; the closer he is to me, the more likely he'll break. But she remembered another baby that she had pushed out, the baby that had never taken shape in her womb, Stefano's child. I pushed him out, or at least that's what Pinuccia and Gigliola said behind my back. And maybe I really did, I expelled him deliberately. Why hasn't anything, so far, really gone well for me? And why should I keep the things that haven't worked? The beating showed no sign of diminishing, the figures of smoke pursued her with the sound of their voices, she got out of the bed again, and sat on the edge. She was soaked with a sticky sweat, it felt like frozen oil. She placed her bare feet against Gennaro's bed, pushed it gently, to move it away but not too far: if she kept him next to her she was afraid of breaking him, if she pushed him too far away she was afraid of losing him. She went into the kitchen, taking small steps and leaning on the furniture, the walls, but repeatedly looking behind her out of fear that the floor would cave in and swallow up Gennaro. She drank from the faucet, washed her face, and suddenly her heart stopped, throwing her forward as if it had braked abruptly.

Over. Objects were sticking together again, her body slowly settled, the sweat dried. Lila was trembling now, and so tired that the walls were spinning around her, she was afraid she would faint. I have to go to Enzo, she thought, and get warm: get in his bed now, press myself against his back while he sleeps, go to sleep myself. But she gave it up. She felt on her face the pretty little expression she had made when she said to Bruno: *Trust me, I have a small child, I didn't do this thing*, a charming affectation, perhaps seductive, the body of a woman acting autonomously in spite of disgust. She was ashamed: how could she behave like that, after what Soccavo had done to her in the drying room? And yet. Ah, to push men and drive them like obedient beasts toward goals that were not theirs. No, no, enough, in the past she had done it for different reasons, almost without realizing it, with Stefano, with Nino, with the Solaras, maybe even with Enzo. Now she didn't want to anymore, she would take care of things herself: with the guard, with her fellow workers, with the students, with Soccavo, with her own mind, which, full of demands, would not resign itself and, worn out by the impact of persons and things, was collapsing.

34.

Upon waking she discovered that she had a fever; she took an aspirin and went to work anyway. In the still dark sky there was a weak bluish light that licked the low buildings, the muddy weeds and refuse. Already as she skirted the puddles on the unpaved stretch of road that led to the factory, she noticed that there were four students, the two from the day before, a third about the same age, and a fat kid, decidedly obese, around twenty years old. They were pasting on the boundary wall placards that called on the workers to join the struggle, and had just begun to hand out a leaflet of the same type. But if, the day before, the workers, out of curiosity, out of courtesy, had taken the pamphlet, the majority now either kept going with their heads down or took the sheet and immediately crumpled it up and threw it away.

As soon as she saw that the youths were there, punctual as if what they called political work had a schedule stricter than hers, Lila was annoyed. The annoyance became hostility when the boy from the day before recognized her and hurried toward her, with a friendly expression, and a large number of leaflets in his hand.

"Everything all right, Comrade?"

Lila paid no attention, her throat was sore, her temples pounding. The boy ran after her, said uncertainly:

"I'm Dario, maybe you don't remember, we met on Via dei Tribunali."

"I know who the fuck you are," she snapped, "but I don't want to have anything to do with you or your friends."

Dario was speechless, he slowed down, he said almost to himself:

"You don't want the leaflet?"

Lila didn't answer, so that she wouldn't yell something hostile at him. But the boy's disoriented face, wearing the expression people have when they feel they are right and don't understand how it is that others don't share their opinion, stayed in her mind. She thought that she ought to explain to him carefully why she had said the things she had said at the meeting, and why she found it intolerable that those things had ended up in the pamphlet, and why she judged it pointless and stupid that the four of them, instead of still being in bed or about to enter a classroom, were standing there in the cold handing out a densely written leaflet to people who had difficulty reading, and who, besides, had no reason to subject themselves to the effort of reading, since they already knew those things, they lived them every day, and could tell even worse: unrepeatable sounds that no one would ever say, write, or read, and that nevertheless held as potential the real causes of their inferiority. But she had a fever, she was tired of everything, it would cost her too much effort. And anyway she had reached the gate, and there the situation was becoming complicated.

The guard was yelling at the oldest boy, the fat one, shouting at him in dialect: You cross that line, cross it, shit, then you're entering private property without permission and I'll shoot. The student, also agitated, replied with a laugh, a broad aggressive laugh, accompanied by insults: he called him a slave, he shouted, in Italian, Shoot, show me how you shoot, this isn't private property, everything in there belongs to the people. Lila passed both of them—how many times had she witnessed bluster like that: Rino, Antonio, Pasquale, even Enzo were masters of it—and said to Filippo, seriously: Satisfy him, don't waste time chattering, someone who could be sleeping or studying and instead is here being a pain in the ass deserves to be shot. The guard saw her, heard her, and, openmouthed, tried to decide if she was really encouraging him to do something crazy or making fun of him. The student had no doubts: he stared at her angrily, shouted: Go on, go in, go kiss the boss's ass, and he retreated a few steps, shaking his head, then he continued to hand out leaflets a few meters from the gate.

Lila headed toward the courtyard. She was already tired at seven in the morning, her eyes were burning, eight hours of work seemed an eternity. Meanwhile behind her there was a noise of screeching brakes and men shouting, and she turned. Two cars had arrived, one gray and one blue. Someone had got out of the first car and begun to tear off the placards that had just been pasted on the wall. It's getting bad, Lila thought, and instinctively went back, although she knew that, like the others, she ought to hurry in and start work.

She took a few steps, enough to identify the youth at the wheel of the gray car: it was Gino. She saw him open the door and, tall, muscular as he had become, get out of the car holding a stick. The others, the ones who were tearing off the posters, the ones who, more slowly, were still getting out of the cars, seven or eight in all, were carrying chains and metal bars. Fascists, mostly from the neighborhood, Lila knew some of them. Fascists, as Stefano's father, Don Achille, had been, as Stefano had turned out to be, as the Solaras were, grandfather, father, grandsons, even if at times they acted like monarchists, at times Christian Democrats, as it suited them. She had hated them ever since, as a girl, she had imagined every detail of their obscenities, since she had discovered that there was no way to be free of them, to clear everything away. The connection between past and present had never really broken down, the neighborhood loved them by a large majority, pampered them, and they showed up with their filth whenever there was a chance to fight.

Dario, the boy from Via dei Tribunali, was the first to move, he rushed to protest the torn-down posters. He was holding the ream of leaflets, and Lila thought: Throw them away, you idiot, but he didn't. She heard him saying in Italian useless things like Stop it, you have no right, and at the same time saw him turn to his friends for help. He doesn't know anything about fighting: never lose sight of your adversary, in the neighborhood there'd be no talk, at most there'd be some yelling, wide-eyed, to inspire fear, and meanwhile you were the first to strike, causing as much injury as possible, without stopping—it was up to others to stop you if they could. One of the youths who were tearing down the posters acted just like that: he punched Dario in the face, with no warning, knocking him to the ground amid the leaflets he had dropped, and then he was on him, hitting him, while the pages flew around as if there were a fierce excitement in the things themselves. At that point the obese student saw that the boy was on the ground and hurried to help him, bare-handed, but he was blocked halfway by someone armed with a chain, who hit him on the arm. The youth grabbed the chain furiously, and started pulling on it, to tear it away from his attacker, and for several seconds they fought for it, screaming insults at one another. Until Gino came up behind the fat student and hit him with the stick, knocking him down.

Lila forgot her fever and her exhaustion, and ran to the gate, but without a precise purpose. She didn't know if she wanted to have a better view, if she wanted to help the students, if she was simply moved by an instinct she had always had, by virtue of which fighting didn't frighten her but, rather, kindled her fury. She wasn't in time to return to the street, she had to jump aside in order not to be run over by a group of workers who were rushing through the gate. A few had tried to stop the attackers, including Edo, certainly, but they hadn't been able to, and now they were escaping. Men and women were running, pursued by two youths holding iron bars. A woman named Isa, an office worker, ran toward Filippo yelling: Help, do something, call the police, and Edo, one of whose hands was bleeding, said aloud to himself: I'm going to get the hatchet and then we'll see. So by the time Lila reached the unpaved road, the blue car had already left and Gino was getting into the gray one, but he recognized her and paused, astonished, saying: Lina, you've ended up here? Then, pulled in by his comrades, he started the engine and drove off, but he shouted out window: You acted the lady, bitch, and look what the fuck you've become.

35.

The workday passed in an anxiety that, as usual, Lila contained behind an attitude that at one moment was contemptuous, the next threatening. They all made it clear that they blamed her for the tensions that had emerged suddenly in a place that had always been peaceful. But soon two parties formed: one, a small group, wanted to meet somewhere during the lunch break and take advantage of the situation to urge Lila to go to the owner with some cautious wage demands; the other, the majority, wouldn't even speak to Lila and was opposed to any undertaking that would complicate a work life that was already complicated. Between the two groups there was no way to reach agreement. In fact Edo, who belonged to the first party and was worried about the injury to his hand, went so far as to say to someone who belonged to the second: If my hand gets infected, if they cut it off, I'm coming to your house, I'll pour a can of gasoline on it, and set you and your family on fire. Lila ignored both factions. She kept to herself and worked, head down, with her usual efficiency, driving away the conversation, the insults, and the cold. But she reflected on what awaited her, a whirl of different thoughts passed through her feverish head: what had happened to the injured students, where had they gone, what trouble had they got her into; Gino would talk about her in the neighborhood, he would tell Michele Solara everything; it was humiliating to ask Bruno for favors, and yet there was no other way, she was afraid of being fired, she was afraid of losing a salary that, even though it was miserable, allowed her to love Enzo without considering him fundamental to her survival and that of Gennaro.

Then she remembered the terrible night. What had happened to her, should she go to a doctor? And if the doctor found some illness, how would she manage with work and the child? Careful, don't get agitated, she needed to put things in order. Therefore, during the lunch break, oppressed by her cares, she resigned herself to going to Bruno. She wanted to tell him about the nasty trick of the sausage, about Gino's fascists, reiterate that it wasn't her fault. First, however, despising herself, she went to the bathroom to comb her hair and put on a little lipstick. But the secretary said with hostility that Bruno wasn't there and almost certainly wouldn't be all week. Anxiety gripped her again. Increasingly nervous, she thought of asking Pasquale to keep the students from returning to the gate, she said to herself that, once the boys from the committee disappeared, the fascists, too, would disappear, the factory would settle back into its old ways. But how to find Peluso? She didn't know where he worked, she didn't want to look for him in the neighborhood—she was afraid of running into her mother, her father, and especially her brother, with whom she didn't want to fight. So, exhausted, she added up all her troubles and decided to turn directly to Nadia. At the end of her shift she hurried home, left a note for Enzo to prepare dinner, bundled Gennaro up carefully in coat and hat, and set off, bus after bus, to Corso Vittorio Emanuele.

The sky was pastel-colored, with not even a puff of a cloud, but the late-afternoon light was fading and a strong wind was blowing in the violet air. She remembered the house in detail, the entrance, all of it, and the humiliation of the past intensified the bitterness of the present. How brittle the past was, continually crumbling, falling on her. From that house where she had gone with me to a party that had made her suffer, Nadia, Nino's old girlfriend, had tumbled out to make her suffer even more. But she wasn't one to stay quiet, she walked up the hill, dragging Gennaro. She wanted to say to that girl: You and the others are making trouble for my son; for you it's only an amusement, nothing terrible will happen to you; for me, for him, no, it's a serious thing, so either do something to fix it or I'll bash your face in. That was what she intended to say, and she coughed and her rage mounted; she couldn't wait to explode.

She found the street door open. She climbed the stairs, she remembered herself and me, and Stefano, who had taken us to the party, the clothes, the shoes, every word that we had said to each other on the way and on the way back. She rang, Professor Galiani herself opened the door, just as she remembered her, polite, orderly, just like her house. In comparison Lila felt dirty, because of the odor of raw meat that clung to her, the cold that clogged her chest, the fever that confused her feelings, the child whose whining in dialect irritated her. She asked abruptly:

"Is Nadia here?"

"No, she's out."

"When will she be back?"

"I'm sorry, I don't know, in ten minutes, in an hour, she does as she likes."

"Could you tell her that Lina came to see her?"

"Is it urgent?"

"Yes."

"Do you want to tell me?"

Tell her what? Lila gave a start, she looked past the professor. She glimpsed the ancient nobility of furniture and lamps, the book-filled library that had captivated her, the precious paintings on the walls. She thought: This is the world that Nino aspired to before he got mixed up with me. She thought: What do I know of this other Naples, nothing; I'll never live there and neither will Gennaro. Let it be destroyed, then, let fire and ashes come, let the lava reach the top of the hills. Then finally she answered: No, thank you, I have to talk to Nadia. And she was about to leave, it had been a fruitless journey. But she liked the hostile attitude with which the professor had spoken of her daughter and she exclaimed in a suddenly frivolous tone:

"Do you know that years ago I was in this house at a party? I don't know what I expected, but I was bored, I couldn't wait to leave."

36.

Professor Galiani, too, must have seen something she liked, maybe a frankness verging on rudeness. When Lila mentioned our friendship, the professor seemed pleased, she exclaimed: Ah yes, Greco, we never see her anymore, success has gone to her head. Then she led mother and son to the living room, where she had left her grandson playing, a blond child whom she almost ordered: Marco, say hello to our new friend. Lila in turn pushed her son forward, she said, go on, Gennaro, play with Marco, and she sat in an old, comfortable green armchair, still talking about the party years ago. The professor was sorry she had no recollection of it, but Lila remembered everything. She said that it had been one of the worst nights of her life. She spoke of how out of place she had felt, she described in sarcastic tones the conversations she had listened to without understanding anything. I was very ignorant, she exclaimed, with an excessive gaiety, and today even more than I was then.

Professor Galiani listened and was impressed by her sincerity, by her unsettling tone, by the intense Italian of her sentences, by her skillfully controlled irony. She must have felt in Lila, I imagine, that elusive quality that seduced and at the same time alarmed, a siren power: it could happen to anyone, it happened to her, and the conversation broke off only when Gennaro slapped Marco, insulting him in dialect and grabbing a small green car. Lila got up quickly, and, seizing her son by the arm, forcefully slapped the hand that had hit the other child, and although Professor Galiani said weakly, Let it go, they're children, she rebuked him harshly, insisting that he return the toy. Marco was crying, but Gennaro didn't shed a tear; instead, he threw the toy at him with contempt. Lila hit him again, hard, on the head.

"We're going," she said, nervously.

"No, stay a little longer."

Lila sat down again.

"He's not always like that."

"He's a very handsome child. Right, Gennaro, you're a good boy?"

"He isn't good, he isn't at all good. But he's clever. Even though he's little, he can read and write all the letters, capitals and small. What do you say, Gennà, do you want to show the professor how you read?"

She picked up a magazine from a beautiful glass table, pointed to a word at random on the cover, and said: Go on, read. Gennaro refused. Lila gave him a pat on the shoulder, repeated in a threatening tone: Read, Gennà. The child reluctantly deciphered, *d-e-s-t*, then he broke off, staring angrily at Marco's little car. Marco hugged it to his chest, gave a small smile, and read confidently: *destinazione*.

Lila was disappointed, she darkened, she looked at Galiani's grandson with annoyance.

"He reads well."

"Because I devote a lot of time to him. His parents are always out."

"How old is he?"

"Three and a half."

"He seems older."

"Yes, he's sturdy. How old is your son?"

"He's five," Lila admitted reluctantly.

The professor caressed Gennaro, and said to him:

"Mamma made you read a difficult word, but you're a clever boy, I can see that you know how to read."

Just then there was a commotion, the door to the stairs opened and closed, the sound of footsteps scurrying through the house, male voices, female voices. Here are my children, Professor Galiani said, and called out: Nadia. But it wasn't Nadia who came into the room; instead a thin, very pale, very blond girl, with eyes of a blue so blue that it looked fake, burst in noisily. The girl opened wide her arms and cried to Marco: Who's going to give his mamma a kiss? The child ran to her and she embraced him, kissed him, followed by Armando, Professor Galiani's son. Lila remembered him, too, immediately, and looked at him as he practically tore Marco from his mother's arms, crying: Immediately, at least thirty kisses for papa. Marco began to kiss his father on the cheek, counting: One, two, three, four.

"Nadia," Professor Galiani called again in a suddenly irritated tone, "are you deaf? Come, there's someone here to see you."

Nadia finally looked into the room. Behind her was Pasquale.

37.

Lila's bitterness exploded again. So Pasquale, when work was over, rushed to the house of those people, amid mothers and fathers and grandmothers and aunts and happy babies, all affectionate, all well educated, all so broad-minded that they welcomed him as one of them, although he was a construction worker and still bore the dirty traces of his job?

Nadia embraced her in her emotional way. Lucky you're here, she said, leave the child with my mother, we have to talk. Lila replied aggressively that yes, they had to talk, right away, that's why she was there. And since she said emphatically that she had only a minute, Pasquale offered to take her home in the car. So they left the living room, the children, the grand-mother, and met—also Armando, also the blond girl, whose name was Isabella—in Nadia's room, a large room with a bed, a desk, shelves full of books, posters showing singers, films, and revolutionary struggles that Lila knew little about. There were three other young men, two whom she had never seen, and Dario, banged up from the beating he'd had, sprawled on Nadia's bed with his shoes on the pink quilt. All three were smoking, the room was full of smoke. Lila didn't wait, she didn't even respond to Dario's greeting. She said that they had got her in trouble, that their lack of consideration had put her at risk of being fired, that the pamphlet had caused an uproar, that they shouldn't come to the gate anymore, that because of them the fascists had showed up and everyone was now angry with both the reds and the blacks. She hissed at Dario: As for you, if you don't know how to fight stay home, you know they could kill you? Pasquale tried to interrupt her a few times, but she cut him off contemptuously, as if his mere presence in that house were a betrayal. The others instead listened in silence. Only when Lila had finished, did Armando speak. He had his mother's delicate features, and thick black eyebrows; the violet trace of his carefully shaved beard rose to his cheekbones, and he spoke in a warm, thick voice. He introduced himself, he said that he was very happy to meet her, that he regretted he hadn't been there when she spoke at the meeting, that, however, what she had told them they had discussed among themselves and since they had considered it an important contribution they had decided to put everything in writing. Don't worry, he concluded calmly, we'll support you and your comrades in every way.

Lila coughed, the smoke in the room irritated her throat.

"You should have informed me."

"It's true, but there wasn't time."

"If you really want the time you find it."

"We are few and our initiatives are more every day."

"What work do you do?"

"In what sense?"

"What do you do for a living?"

"I'm a doctor."

"Like your father?"

"Yes."

"And at this moment are you risking your job? Could you end up in the street at any moment along with your son?"

Armando shook his head unhappily and said:

"Competing for who is risking the most is wrong, Lina."

And Pasquale:

"He's been arrested twice and I have eight charges against me. Nobody here risks more or less than anyone else."

"Oh, no?"

"No," said Nadia, "we're all in the front lines and ready to assume our responsibilities."

Then Lila, forgetting that she was in someone else's house, cried:

"So if I should lose my job, I'll come and live here, you'll feed me, you'll assume responsibility for my life?"

Nadia answered placidly:

"If you like, yes."

Four words only. Lila understood that it wasn't a joke, that Nadia was serious, that even if Bruno Soccavo fired his entire work force she, with that sickly-sweet voice of hers, would give the same senseless answer. She claimed that she was in the service of the workers, and yet, from her room in a house full of books and with a view of the sea, she wanted to command you, she wanted to tell you what you should do with your work, she decided for you, she had the solution ready even if you ended up in the street. I—it was on the tip of Lila's tongue—if I want, can smash everything much better than you: I don't need you to tell me, in that sanctimonious tone, how I should think, what I should do. But she restrained herself, and said abruptly to Pasquale:

"I'm in a hurry, are you going to take me or are you staying here?"

Silence. Pasquale glanced at Nadia, muttered, I'll take you, and Lila started to leave the room, without saying goodbye. The girl rushed to lead the way, saying to her how unacceptable it was to work in the conditions that Lila herself had described so well, how urgent it was to kindle the spark of the struggle, and other phrases like that. Don't pull back, she urged, finally, before they went into the living room. But she got no response.

Professor Galiani, sitting in the armchair, was reading, a frown on her face. When she looked up she spoke to Lila, ignoring her daughter, ignoring Pasquale, who had just arrived, embarrassed.

"You're leaving?"

"Yes, it's late. Let's go, Gennaro, leave Marco his car and put your coat on."

Professor Galiani smiled at her grandson, who was pouting. "Marco gave it to him."

Lila narrowed her eyes, reduced them to cracks.

"You're all so generous in this house, thank you."

The professor watched as she struggled with her son to get his coat on.

"May I ask you something?"

"Go ahead."

"What did you study?"

The question seemed to irritate Nadia, who broke in:

"Mamma, Lina has to go."

For the first time Lila noticed some nervousness in the child's voice, and it pleased her.

"Will you let me have two words?" Professor Galiani snapped, in a tone no less nervous. Then she repeated to Lila, but kindly: "What did you study?"

"Nothing."

"To hear you speak—and shout—it doesn't seem so."

"It's true, I stopped after fifth grade."

"Why?"

"I didn't have the ability."

"How did you know?"

"Greco had it, I didn't."

Professor Galiani shook her head in a sign of disagreement, and said:

"If you had studied you would have been as successful as Greco."

"How can you say that?"

"It's my job."

"You professors insist so much on education because that's how you earn a living, but studying is of no use, it doesn't even improve you—in fact it makes you even more wicked."

"Has Elena become more wicked?"

"No, not her."

"Why not?"

Lila stuck the wool cap on her son's head. "We made a pact when we were children: I'm the wicked one."

38.

In the car she got mad at Pasquale (*Have you become the servant of those people?*) and he let her vent. Only when it seemed to him that she had come to the end of her recriminations did he start off with his political formulas: the condition of workers in the South, the condition of slavery in which they lived, the permanent blackmail, the weakness if not absence of unions, the need to force situations and reach the point of struggle. Lina, he said in dialect, his tone heartfelt, you're afraid of losing the few cents they give you and you're right, Gennaro has to grow up. But I know that you are a true comrade, I know that you understand: here we workers have never even been within the regular wage scales, we're outside all the rules, we're less than zero. So, it's blasphemy to say: leave me alone, I have my own problems and I want to mind my own business. Each of us, in the place assigned to us, has to do what he can.

Lila was exhausted; fortunately Gennaro was sleeping on the back seat with the little car clutched in his right hand. Pasquale's speech came to her in waves. Every so often the beautiful apartment on Corso Vittorio Emanuele came into her mind, along with the professor and Armando and Isabella and Nino, who had gone off to find a wife somewhere of Nadia's type, and Marco, who was three and could read much better than her son. What a useless struggle to make Gennaro become smart. The child was already losing, he was being pulled back and she couldn't hold on to him. When they reached the house and she saw that she had to invite Pasquale in she said: I don't know what Enzo's made, he's a terrible cook, maybe you don't feel like it, and hoped he would leave. But he answered: I'll stay ten minutes, then go, so she touched his arm with her fingertips and murmured:

"Don't tell him anything."

"Anything about what?"

"About the fascists. If he knows, he'll go and beat up Gino tonight."

"Do you love him?"

"I don't want to hurt him."

"Ah."

"That's the way it is."

"Remember that Enzo knows better than you and me what needs to be done."

"Yes, but don't say anything to him just the same."

Pasquale agreed with a scowl. He picked up Gennaro, who wouldn't wake up, and carried him up the stairs, followed by Lila, who was mumbling unhappily: What a day, I'm dead tired, you and your friends have got me in huge trouble. They told Enzo that they had gone to Nadia's house for a meeting, and Pasquale gave him no chance to ask questions, he talked without stopping until midnight. He said that Naples, like the whole world, was churning with new life, he praised Armando, who, good doctor that he was, instead of thinking of his career treated the poor for nothing, he took care of the children in the Quartieri and with Nadia and Isabella was involved in countless projects that served the people—a nursery school, a clinic. He said that no one was alone any longer, comrades helped comrades, the city was going through a wonderful time. You two, he said, shouldn't stay shut up here in the house, you should go out, we should be together more. And finally he announced that he was finished with the Communist Party: too many ugly things, too many compromises, national and international, he couldn't stand that dreariness anymore. Enzo was deeply disturbed by his decision, they argued about it for a long time: the party is the party, no, yes, no, enough with the politics of stabilization, we need to attack the institutional structures of the system. Lila quickly became bored, and she went to put Gennaro to bed—he was sleepy, whining as he ate his supper—and didn't return.

But she stayed awake even when Pasquale left and the evidence of Enzo's presence in the house had been extinguished. She took her temperature, it was 100. She recalled the moment when Gennaro had struggled to read. What sort of word had she put in front of him: destination. Certainly it was a word that Gennaro had never heard. It's not enough to know the alphabet, she thought, there are so many difficulties. If Nino had had him with Nadia, that child would have had a completely different destiny. She felt she was the wrong mother. And yet I wanted him, she thought, it was with Stefano that I didn't want children, with Nino yes. She had truly loved Nino. She had desired him deeply, she had desired to please him and for his pleasure had done willingly everything that with her husband she had had to do by force, overcoming disgust, in order not to be killed. But she had never felt what it was said she was supposed to feel when she was penetrated, that she was sure of, and not only with Stefano but also with Nino. Males were so attached to their penis, they were so proud of it, and they were convinced that you should be even more attached to it than they were. Even Gennaro was always playing with his; sometimes it was embarrassing how much he jiggled it in his hands, how much he pulled it. Lila was afraid he would hurt himself; and even to wash it, or get him to pee, she had had to make an effort, get used to it. Enzo was so discreet, never in his underwear in the house, never a vulgar word. For that reason she felt an intense affection for him, and was grateful to him for his devoted wait in the other room, which had never been interrupted by a wrong move. The control he exercised over things and himself seemed to her the only consolation. But then a sense of guilt emerged: what consoled her surely made him suffer. And the thought that Enzo was suffering because of her was added to all the terrible things of that day. Events and conversations whirled chaotically in her head for a long time. Tones of voice, single words. How should she act the next day in the factory? Was there really all that fervor in Naples and the world, or were Pasquale and Nadia and Armando imagining it to allay their anxieties, out of boredom, to give themselves courage? Should she trust them, with the risk of becoming captive to fantasies? Or was it better to look for Bruno again to get her out of trouble? But would it really be any use trying to placate him, with the risk that he might jump on her again? Would it help to give in to the abuses of Filippo and the supervisors? She didn't make much progress. In the end, in a waking sleep, she landed on an old principle that we two had assimilated since we were little. It seemed to her that to save herself, to save Gennaro, she had to intimidate those who wished to intimidate her, she had to inspire fear in those who wished to make her fear. She fell asleep with the intention of doing harm, to Nadia by showing her that she was just a girl from a good family, all sugary chatter, to Soccavo by ruining the pleasure he got in sniffing salamis and women in the drying room.

39.

She woke at five in the morning, in a sweat; she no longer had a fever. At the factory gate she found not the students but the fascists. Same automobiles, same faces as the day before:

they were shouting slogans, handing out leaflets. Lila felt that more violence was planned and she walked with her head down, hands in pockets, hoping to get into the factory before the fighting started. But Gino appeared in front of her.

"You still know how to read?" he asked in dialect, holding out a leaflet. Keeping her hands in her pockets, she replied:

"I do, yes, but when did you learn?"

Then she tried to go by, in vain. Gino obstructed her, he jammed the leaflet into her pocket with a gesture so violent that he scratched her hand with his nail. Lila crumpled it up calmly.

"It's not even good for wiping your ass," she said and threw it away.

"Pick it up," the pharmacist's son ordered her, grabbing her by the arm. "Pick it up now and you listen to me: yesterday afternoon I asked that cuckold your husband for permission to beat you up and he said yes."

Lila looked him straight in the eye:

"You went to ask my husband for permission to beat me up? Let go of my arm right now, you shit."

At that moment Edo arrived, and instead of pretending not to notice, as was to be expected, he stopped.

"Is he bothering you, Cerù?"

It was an instant. Gino punched him in the face, Edo ended up on the ground. Lila's heart jumped to her throat, and everything began to speed up. She picked up a rock and gripping it solidly struck the pharmacist's son right in the chest. There was a long moment. While Gino shoved her back against a light pole, while Edo tried to get up, another car appeared on the unpaved road, raising dust. Lila recognized Pasquale's broken-down car. Here, she thought, Armando listened to me, maybe Nadia, too, they're well-brought-up people, but Pasquale couldn't resist, he's coming to make war. In fact the doors opened, and five men got out, including him. They were men from the construction sites, carrying knotty clubs, and they began hitting the fascists with a methodical ferocity; they didn't get angry, they planted a single, precise blow intended to knock down the adversary. Lila immediately saw that Pasquale was heading toward Gino, and since Gino was still a few steps away from her she grabbed one of his arms with both hands and said, laughing: You'd better go or they'll kill you. But he didn't go; rather, he pushed her away again and rushed at Pasquale. Lila helped Edo get up, and tried to drag him into the courtyard, but it was difficult; he was heavy, and he was writhing, shouting insults, bleeding. He calmed down a little only when he saw Pasquale hit Gino with his stick and knock him to the ground. The confusion increased: debris the men picked up along the side of the street flew like bullets, men were spitting and screaming insults. Pasquale, leaving Gino unconscious, had rushed into the courtyard, with a man wearing only an undershirt and loose blue pants streaked with cement. Both were now bludgeoning Filippo's booth; he was locked inside, terrorized. Shouting obscenities, they smashed the windows, while the wail of a police siren grew louder. Lila noticed yet again the anxious pleasure of violence. Yes, she thought, you have to strike fear into those who wish to strike fear into you, there is no other way, blow for blow, what you take from me I take back, what you do to me I do to you. But while Pasquale and his people were getting back in the car, while the fascists did the same, carrying off Gino bodily, while the police siren got closer, she felt, terrified, that her heart was becoming like the too tightly wound spring of a toy, and she knew that she had to find a place to sit down as soon as possible. Once she was inside, she collapsed in the hallway, her back against the wall, and tried to calm down. Teresa, the large woman in her forties who worked in the gutting room, was looking after Edo, wiping the blood off his face, and she teased Lila.

"First you pull off his ear, then you help him? You should have left him outside."

"He helped me and I helped him."

Teresa turned to Edo, incredulous:

"*You* helped her?"

He stammered:

"I didn't like to see a stranger beating her up, I want to do it myself."

The woman said:

"Did you see how Filippo shat himself?"

"Serves him right," Edo muttered, "too bad all they broke was the booth."

Teresa turned to Lila and asked her, with a hint of malice:

"Did you call the Communists? Tell the truth."

Is she joking, Lila wondered, or is she a spy, who'll go running to the owner.

"No," she answered, "but I know who called the fascists."

"Who?"

"Soccavo."

40.

Pasquale appeared that evening, after dinner, with a grim expression, and invited Enzo to a meeting at the San Giovanni a Teduccio section. Lila, alone with him for a few minutes, said:

"That was a shitty thing to do, this morning."

"I do what's necessary."

"Did your friends agree with you?"

"Who are my friends?"

"Nadia and her brother."

"Of course they agreed."

"But they stayed home."

Pasquale muttered:

"And who says they stayed home?"

He wasn't in a good mood, in fact he seemed emptied of energy, as if the practice of violence had swallowed up his craving for action. Further, he hadn't asked her to go to the meeting, he had invited only Enzo, something that never happened, even when it was late, and cold, and unlikely that she would take Gennaro out. Maybe they had other male wars to fight. Maybe he was angry with her because, with her resistance to the struggle, she had caused him to look bad in front of Nadia and Armando. Certainly he was bothered by the critical tone she had used in alluding to the morning's expedition. He's convinced, Lila thought, that I don't understand why he hit Gino like that, why he wanted to beat up the guard. Good or bad, all men believe that after every one of their undertakings you have to put them on an altar as if they were St. George slaying the dragon. He considers me ungrateful, he did it to avenge me, he would like me to at least say thank you.

When the two left, she got in bed and read the pamphlets on work and unions that Pasquale had given her long ago. They helped to keep her anchored to the dull things of every day, she was afraid of the silence of the house, of sleep, of her unruly heartbeats, of the shapes that threatened to break apart at any moment. In spite of her weariness, she read for a long time, and in her usual way became excited, and learned a lot of things quickly. To feel safe, she made an effort to wait for Enzo to return. But he didn't, and finally the sound of Gennaro's regular breathing became hypnotic and she fell asleep.

The next morning Edo and the woman from the gutting room, Teresa, began to hang around her with timid, friendly words and gestures. And Lila not only didn't rebuff them but treated the other workers courteously as well. She showed herself available to those who were complaining, understanding to those who were angry, sympathetic toward those who cursed the abuses. She steered the trouble of one toward the trouble of another, joining all together with eloquent words. Above all, in the following days, she let Edo and Teresa and their tiny group talk, transforming the lunch break into a time for secret meeting. Since she could, when she wanted, give the impression that it wasn't she who was proposing and disposing but the others, she found more and more people happy to hear themselves say that their general complaints were just and urgent necessities. She added the claims of the gutting room to those of the refrigerated rooms, and those of the vats, and discovered to her surprise that the troubles of one department depended on the troubles of another, and that all together were links in the same chain of exploitation. She made a detailed list of the illnesses caused by the working conditions: damage to the hands, the bones, the lungs. She gathered enough information to demonstrate that the entire factory was in terrible shape, that the hygienic conditions were deplorable, that the raw material they handled was sometimes spoiled or of uncertain origin. When she was able to talk to Pasquale in private she explained to him what in a very short time she had started up, and he, in his peevish way, was astonished, then said beaming: I would have sworn that you would do it, and he set up an appointment with a man named Capone, who was secretary of the union local.

Lila copied down on paper in her fine handwriting everything she had done and brought the copy to Capone. The secretary examined the pages, and he, too, was enthusiastic. He said to her things like: Where did you come from, Comrade, you've done really great work, bravo. And besides, we've never managed to get into the Soccavo plant; they're all fascists in there, but now that you've arrived things have changed.

"How should we start?" she asked.

"Form a committee."

"We already are a committee."

"Good: the first thing is to organize all this."

"In what sense *organize*?"

Capone looked at Pasquale, Pasquale said nothing.

"You're asking for too many things at once, including things that have never been asked for anywhere—you have to establish priorities."

"In that place everything is a priority."

"I know, but it's a question of tactics: if you want everything at once you risk defeat."

Lila narrowed her eyes to cracks; there was some bickering. It emerged that, among other things, the committee couldn't go and negotiate directly with the owner, the union had to mediate.

"And am I not the union?" she flared up.

"Of course, but there are times and ways."

They quarreled again. Capone said: You look around a little, open the discussion, I don't know, about the shifts, about holidays, about overtime, and we'll take it from there. Anyway—he concluded—you don't know how happy I am to have a comrade like you, it's a rare thing; let's coordinate, and we'll make great strides in the food industry—there aren't many women who get involved. At that point he put his hand on his wallet, which was in his back pocket, and asked:

"Do you want some money for expenses?"

"What expenses?"

"Mimeographing, paper, the time you lose, things like that."

"No."

Capone put the wallet back in his pocket.

"But don't get discouraged and disappear, Lina, let's keep in touch. Look, I'm writing down here your name and surname, I want to talk about you at the union, we have to use you."

Lila left dissatisfied, she said to Pasquale: Who did you bring me to? But he calmed her, assured her that Capone was

154 · ELENA FERRANTE

an excellent person, said he was right, you had to understand,
there was strategy and there were tactics. Then he became
excited, almost moved, he was about to embrace her, had second thoughts, said: Move ahead, Lina, screw the bureaucracy,
meanwhile I'll inform the committee.

Lila didn't choose among the objectives. She confined herself to compressing the first draft, which was very long, into
one densely written sheet, which she handed over to Edo: a list
of requests that had to do with the organization of the work,
the pace, the general condition of the factory, the quality of the
product, the permanent risk of being injured or sick, the
wretched compensations, wage increases. At that point the
problem arose of who was to carry that list to Bruno.

"You go," Lila said to Edo.

"I get angry easily."

"Better."

"I'm not suitable."

"You're very suitable."

"No, you go, you're a member of the union. And then
you're a good speaker, you'll put him in his place right away."

41.

Lila had known from the start that it would be up to her.
She took her time; she left Gennaro at the neighbor's, and went
with Pasquale to a meeting of the committee on Via dei
Tribunali, called to discuss *also* the Soccavo situation. There
were twelve this time, including Nadia, Armando, Isabella, and
Pasquale. Lila circulated the paper she had prepared for
Capone; in that first version all the demands were more care-
fully argued. Nadia read it attentively. In the end she said:
Pasquale was right, you're one of those people who don't hold
anything back, you've done a great job in a very short time.

And in a tone of sincere admiration she praised not only the political and union substance of the document but the writing: You're so clever, she said, I've never seen this kind of material written about in this way! Still, after that beginning, she advised her not to move to an immediate confrontation with Soccavo. And Armando was of the same opinion.

"Let's wait to get stronger and grow," he said. "The situation concerning the Soccavo factory needs to develop. We've got a foot in there, which is already a great result, we can't risk getting swept away out of pure recklessness."

Dario asked:

"What do you propose?"

Nadia answered, addressing Lila: "Let's have a wider meeting. Let's meet as soon as possible with your comrades, let's consolidate your structure, and maybe with your material prepare another pamphlet."

Lila, in the face of that sudden cautiousness, felt a great, aggressive satisfaction. She said mockingly: "So in your view I've done this work and am putting my job at risk to allow *all of you* to have a bigger meeting and another pamphlet?"

But she was unable to enjoy that feeling of revenge. Suddenly Nadia, who was right opposite her, began to vibrate like a window loose in its frame, and dissolved. For no evident reason, Lila's throat tightened, and the slightest gestures of those present, even a blink, accelerated. She closed her eyes, leaned against the back of the broken chair she was sitting on, felt she was suffocating.

"Is something wrong?" asked Armando.

Pasquale became upset.

"She gets overtired," he said. "Lina, what's wrong, do you want a glass of water?"

Dario hurried to get some water, while Armando checked her pulse and Pasquale, nervous, pressed her:

"What do you feel, stretch your legs, breathe."

156 - ELENA FERRANTE

Lila whispered that she was fine and abruptly pulled her wrist away from Armando, saying she wanted to be left in peace for a minute. But when Dario returned with the water she drank a small mouthful, murmured it was nothing, just a little flu.

"Do you have a fever?" Armando asked calmly.

"Today, no."

"Cough, difficulty breathing?"

"A little, I can feel my heart beating in my throat."

"Is it a little better now?"

"Yes."

"Come into the other room."

Lila didn't want to, and yet she felt a vast sense of anguish. She obeyed, she struggled to get up, she followed Armando, who had picked up a black leather bag with gold clasps. They went into a large, cold room that Lila hadn't seen before, with three cots covered by dirty-looking old mattresses, a wardrobe with a corroded mirror, a chest of drawers. She sat down on one of the beds, exhausted: she hadn't had a medical examination since she was pregnant. When Armando asked about her symptoms, she mentioned only the weight in her chest, but added: It's nothing.

He examined her in silence and she immediately hated that silence, it seemed a treacherous silence. That detached, clean man, although he was asking questions, did not seem to trust the answers. He examined her as if only her body, aided by instruments and expertise, were a reliable mechanism. He listened to her chest, he touched her, he peered at her, and meanwhile he forced her to wait for a conclusive opinion on what was happening in her chest, in her stomach, in her throat, places apparently well known that now seemed completely unknown. Finally Armando asked her:

"Do you sleep well?"

"Very well."

"How much?"

"It depends."

"On what?"

"On my thoughts."

"Do you eat enough?"

"When I feel like it."

"Do you ever have difficulty breathing?"

"No."

"Pain in your chest?"

"A weight, but light."

"Cold sweats?"

"No."

"Have you ever fainted or felt like fainting?"

"No."

"Are you regular?"

"In what?"

"Menstruation."

"No."

"When did you last have a period?"

"I don't know."

"You don't keep track?"

"Should I keep track?"

"It's better. Do you use contraceptives?"

"What do you mean?"

"Condoms, coil, the Pill."

"What Pill?"

"A new medicine: you take it and you can't get pregnant."

"Is that true?"

"Absolutely true. Your husband has never used a condom?"

"I don't have a husband anymore."

"He left you?"

"I left him."

"When you were together did he use one?"

"I don't even know how a condom is made."

"Do you have a regular sex life?"

"What's the use of talking about these things?"

"If you don't want to we won't."

"I don't want to."

Armando put his instruments back in the case, sat down on a half-broken chair, sighed.

"You should slow down, Lina: you've pushed your body too far."

"What does that mean?"

"You're undernourished, anxious, you've seriously neglected yourself."

"And so?"

"You have a little catarrh, I'll give you a syrup."

"And so?"

"You should have a series of tests, your liver is a little enlarged."

"I don't have time for tests, give me some medicine."

Armando shook his head discontentedly.

"Listen," he said. "I understand that with you it's better not to beat around the bush: you have a murmur."

"What's that?"

"A problem with the heart, and it could be something that's not benign."

Lila made a grimace of anxiety.

"What do you mean? I might die?"

He smiled and said:

"No, only you should get checked by a cardiologist. Come see me in the hospital tomorrow, and I'll send you to someone good."

Lila furrowed her brow, got up, said coldly: "I have a lot to do tomorrow, I'm going to see Soccavo."

42.

Pasquale's worried tone exasperated her. As he was driving home he asked her:

"What did Armando say, how are you?"

"Fine, I should eat more."

"You see, you don't take care of yourself."

Lila burst out: "Pasquà, you're not my father, you're not my brother, you're no one. Leave me alone, get it?"

"I can't be worried about you?"

"No, and be careful what you do and say, especially with Enzo. If you tell him I was ill—and it's not true, I was only dizzy—you risk ruining our friendship."

"Take two sick days and don't go to Soccavo: Capone advised you against it and the committee advised against it, it's a matter of political expediency."

"I don't give a damn about political expediency: you're the one who got me in trouble and now I'll do as I like."

She didn't invite him to come in and he went away angry. Once at home, Lila cuddled Gennaro, made dinner, waited for Enzo. Now it seemed to her that she was constantly short of breath. Since Enzo was late, she fed Gennaro; she was afraid it was one of those evenings when he was seeing women and would return in the middle of the night. When the child spilled a glass of water, the caresses stopped, and she yelled at him as if he were an adult, in dialect: Will you hold still a moment, I'll hit you, why do you want to ruin my life?

Just then Enzo returned, and she tried to be nice. They ate, but Lila had the impression that the food was struggling to get to her stomach, that it was scratching her chest. As soon as Gennaro fell asleep, they turned to the installments of the Zurich course, but Enzo soon got tired, and tried, politely, to go to bed. His attempts were vain, Lila kept going until it was late, she was afraid of shutting herself in her room, she feared that as soon as she was alone in the dark the symptoms she hadn't admitted to Armando would appear, all together, and kill her. He asked her softly:

"Will you tell me what's wrong?"

"Nothing."

"You come and go with Pasquale, why, what secrets do you have?"

"It's things to do with the union, he made me join and now I have to take care of them."

Enzo looked disheartened, and she asked:

"What's wrong?"

"Pasquale told me what you're doing in the factory. You told him and you told the people on the committee. Why am I the only one who doesn't deserve to know?"

Lila became agitated, she got up, she went to the bathroom. Pasquale hadn't held out. What had he told? Only about the union seed that she wanted to plant at Soccavo or also about Gino, about her not feeling well at Via dei Tribunali? He hadn't been able to stay silent—friendship between men had its unwritten but inviolable pacts, not like that between women. She flushed the toilet, returned to Enzo and said:

"Pasquale is a spy."

"Pasquale is a friend. Whereas you, what are you?"

His tone hurt, she gave in unexpectedly, suddenly. Her eyes filled with tears and she tried in vain to push them back, humiliated by her own weakness.

"I don't want to make more trouble for you than I already have," she sobbed, "I'm afraid you'll send me away." Then she blew her nose and added in a whisper: "Can I sleep with you?"

Enzo stared at her, in disbelief.

"Sleep how?"

"However you want."

"And do you want it?"

Lila gazed at the water pitcher in the middle of the table, with its comical rooster's head: Gennaro liked it. She whispered:

"The crucial thing is for you to hold me close."

Enzo shook his head unhappily.

"You don't want me."

"I want you, but I don't feel anything."

"You don't feel anything *for me*?"

"What do you mean, I love you, and every night I wish you would call me and hold me close. *But beyond that I don't want anything.*"

Enzo turned pale, his handsome face was contorted as if by an intolerable grief, and he observed:

"I disgust you."

"No, no, no, let's do what you want, right away, I'm ready."

He had a desolate smile, and was silent for a while. Then he couldn't bear her anxiety, he muttered: "Let's go to bed."

"Each in our own room?"

"No, in my bed."

Lila, relieved, went to get undressed. She put on her nightgown, went to him trembling with cold. He was already in bed.

"I'll go here?"

"All right."

She slid under the covers, rested her head on his shoulder, put an arm around his chest. Enzo remained motionless; she felt immediately that he gave off a violent heat.

"My feet are cold," she whispered, "can I put them near yours?"

"Yes."

"Can I caress you a little?"

"Leave me alone."

Slowly the cold disappeared. The pain in her chest dissolved, she forgot the grip on her throat, she gave in to the respite of his warmth.

"Can I sleep?" she asked, dazed by weariness.

"Sleep."

43.

At dawn she started: her body reminded her that she had to wake up. Immediately, the terrible thoughts arrived, all very clear: her sick heart, Gennaro's regressions, the fascists from the neighborhood, Nadia's self-importance, Pasquale's untrustworthiness, the list of demands. Only afterward did she realize that she had slept with Enzo, but that he was no longer in the bed. She rose quickly, in time to hear the door closing. Had he arisen as soon as she fell asleep? Had he been awake all night? Had he slept in the other room with the child? Or had he fallen asleep with her, forgetting every desire? Certainly he had had breakfast alone and had left the table set for her and Gennaro. He had gone to work, without a word, keeping his thoughts to himself.

Lila, too, after taking her son to the neighbor, hurried to the factory.

"So did you make up your mind?" Edo asked, a little sulkily.

"I'll make up my mind when I like," Lila answered, returning to her old tone of voice.

"We're a committee, you have to inform us."

"Did you circulate the list?"

"Yes."

"What do the others say?"

"Silence means consent."

"No," she said, "silence means they're shitting in their pants."

Capone was right, also Nadia and Armando. It was a weak initiative, a forced effort. Lila worked at cutting the meat furi-

ously, she had a desire to hurt and be hurt. To jab her hand
with the knife, let it slip, now, from the dead flesh to her own
living flesh. To shout, hurl herself at the others, make them all
pay for her inability to find an equilibrium. Ah, Lina Cerullo,
you are beyond correction. Why did you make that list? You
don't want to be exploited? You want to improve your condition and the condition of these people? You're convinced that
you, and they, starting from here, from what you are now, will
join the victorious march of the proletariat of the whole world?
No way. March to become what? Now and forever workers?
Workers who slave from morning to night but are empow-
ered? Nonsense. Hot air to sweeten the pill of toil. You know
that it's a terrible condition, it shouldn't be improved but eliminated, you've known it since you were a child. Improve,
improve yourself? You, for example, are you improved, have
you become like Nadia or Isabella? Is your brother improved,
has he become like Armando? And your son, is he like Marco?
No, we remain us and they are they. So why don't you resign
yourself? Blame the mind that can't settle down, that is constantly seeking a way to function. Designing shoes. Getting
busy setting up a shoe factory. Rewriting Nino's articles, tor-
menting him until he did as you said. Using for your own purposes the installments from Zurich, with Enzo. And now
demonstrating to Nadia that if she is making the revolution,
you are even more. The mind, ah yes, the evil is there, it's the
mind's discontent that causes the body to get sick. I've had it
with myself, with everything. I've even had it with Gennaro:
his fate, if all goes well, is to end up in a place like this, crawl-
ing to some boss for another five lire. So? So, Cerullo, take up
your responsibilities and do what you have always had in mind:
frighten Soccavo, eliminate his habit of fucking the workers in
the drying room. Show the student with the wolf face what
you've prepared. That summer on Ischia. The drinks, the
house in Forio, the luxurious bed where I was with Nino. The

money came from this place, from this evil smell, from these days spent in disgust, from this poorly paid labor. What did I cut, here? A revolting yellowish pulp spurted out. The world turns but, luckily, if it falls it breaks.

Right before the lunch break she made up her mind, she said to Edo: I'm going. But she didn't have time to take off her apron, the owner's secretary appeared in the gutting room to tell her:

"Dottor Soccavo wants you urgently in the office."

Lila thought that some spy had told Bruno what was coming. She stopped work, took the sheet of demands from the closet and went up. She knocked on the door of the office, and went in. Bruno was not alone in the room. Sitting in a chair, cigarette in his mouth, was Michele Solara.

44.

She had always known that Michele would sooner or later reappear in her life, but finding him in Bruno's office frightened her like the spirits in the dark corners of the house of her childhood. What is he doing here, I have to get out of here. But Solara, seeing her, stood up, spread his arms wide, seemed genuinely moved. He said in Italian: Lina, what a pleasure, how happy I am. He wanted to embrace her, and would have if she hadn't stopped him with an unconscious gesture of revulsion. Michele stood for some instants with his arms outstretched, therefore, in confusion, with one hand he caressed his cheekbone, his neck, with the other he pointed to Lila, this time speaking in an artificial tone:

"But really, I can't believe it: right in the middle of the salamis, you were hiding Signora Carracci?"

Lila turned to Bruno abruptly: "I'll come back later."

"Sit down," he said, darkly.

"I prefer to stand."

"Sit, you'll get tired."

She shook her head, remained standing, and Michele gave Bruno a smile of understanding:

"She's made like that, resign yourself, she never obeys."

To Lila it seemed that Solara's voice had more power than in the past, he stressed the end of every word as if he had been practicing his pronunciation. Maybe to save her strength, maybe just to contradict him, she changed her mind and sat down. Michele also changed position, but so that he was turned completely toward her, as if Bruno were no longer in the room. He observed her carefully, affectionately, and said, in a tone of regret: your hands are ruined, too bad, as a girl you had such nice ones. Then he began to talk about the shop in Piazza dei Martiri in the manner of one imparting information, as if Lila were still his employee and they were having a work meeting. He mentioned new shelves, new light fixtures, and how he had had the bathroom door that opened onto the courtyard walled up again. Lila remembered that door and said softly, in dialect:

"I don't give a fuck about your shop."

"You mean *our:* we invented it together."

"Together with you I never invented anything."

Michele smiled again, shaking his head in a sign of mild dissent. Those who put in the money, he said, do and undo just the way those who work with their hands and their head do. Money invents scenarios, situations, people's lives. You don't know how many people I can make happy or ruin just by signing a check. And then he began chatting again, placidly; he seemed eager to tell her the latest news, as if they were two friends catching up. He began with Alfonso, who had done his job in Piazza dei Martiri well and now earned enough to start a family. But he had no wish to marry, he preferred to keep poor Marisa in the condition of fiancée for life and continued to do as he liked. So he, as his employer, had encouraged him, a regular life is good for one's employees, and had offered to pay for the wedding celebration; thus, finally, in June the marriage would take place. You see, he said, if you had continued to work for me, rather than Alfonso, I would have given you everything you asked for, you would have been a queen. Then, without giving her time to answer, he tapped the ashes of his cigarette into an old bronze ashtray and announced that he, too, was getting married, also in June, and to Gigliola, naturally, the great love of his life. Too bad I can't invite you, he complained, I would have liked to, but I don't want to embarrass your husband. And he began to talk about Stefano, Ada, and their child, first saying nice things about all three, then pointing out that the two grocery stores weren't doing as well as they used to. As long as his father's money lasted, he explained, Carracci kept afloat, but commerce is a rough sea now, Stefano's been shipping water for quite some time, he can't manage things anymore. Competition, he said, had increased, new stores were constantly opening. Marcello himself, for example, had got it into his head to expand the late Don Carlo's old store and transform it into one of those places where you can get anything, from soap to light bulbs, mortadella, and candy. And he had done it, the business was booming, it was called Everything for Everyone.

"You're saying that you and your brother have managed to ruin Stefano, too?"

"What do you mean ruin, Lina, we do our job and that's all, in fact, when we can help our friends we help them happily. Guess who Marcello has working in the new store?"

"I don't know."

"Your brother."

"You've reduced Rino to being your clerk?"

"Well, you abandoned him, and that fellow is carrying all of them on his shoulders: your father, your mother, a child,

Pinuccia, who's pregnant again. What could he do? He turned to Marcello for help and Marcello helped him. Doesn't that please you?"

Lila responded coldly:

"No, it doesn't please me, nothing you do pleases me."

Michele appeared dissatisfied, and he remembered Bruno:

"You see, as I was telling you, her problem is that she has a bad character."

Bruno gave an embarrassed smile that was meant to be conspiratorial.

"It's true."

"Did she hurt you, too?"

"A little."

"You know that she was still a child when she held a shoemaker's knife to my brother's throat, and he was twice her size? And not as a joke, it was clear that she was ready to use it."

"Seriously?"

"Yes. That girl has courage, she's determined."

Lila clenched her fists tightly. She detested the weakness she felt in her body. The room was undulating, the bodies of the dead objects and the living people were expanding. She looked at Michele, who was extinguishing the cigarette in the ashtray. He was putting too much energy into it, as if he, too, in spite of his placid tone, were giving vent to an uneasiness. Lila stared at his fingers, which went on squashing the butt, the nails were white. Once, she thought, he asked me to become his lover. But that's not what he really wants, there's something else, something that doesn't have to do with sex and that not even he can explain. He's obsessed, it's like a superstition. Maybe he thinks that I have a power and that that power is indispensable to him. He wants it but he can't get it, and it makes him suffer, it's a thing he can't take from me by force. Yes, maybe that's it. Otherwise he would have crushed me by now. But why me? What has he recognized in me that's useful to him? I mustn't stay here, under his eyes, I mustn't listen to him, what he sees and what he wants scares me. Lila said to Soccavo:

"I've got something to leave for you and then I'll go."

She got up, ready to give him the list of demands, a gesture that seemed to her increasingly pointless and yet necessary. She wished to place the piece of paper on the table, next to the ashtray, and leave that room. But Michele's voice stopped her. Now it was definitely affectionate, almost caressing, as if he had intuited that she was trying to get away from him and wanted to do everything possible to charm her and keep her. He continued speaking to Soccavo:

"You see, she really has a bad character. I'm speaking, but she doesn't give a damn, she pulls out a piece of paper, says she wants to leave. But you forgive her, because she has many good qualities that make up for her bad character. You think you hired a worker? It's not true. This woman is much, much more. If you let her, she'll change shit into gold for you, she's capable of reorganizing this whole enterprise, taking it to levels you can't even imagine. Why? Because she has the type of mind that normally no woman has but also that not even we men have. I've had an eye on her since she was a child and it's true. She designed shoes that I still sell today in Naples and outside, and I make a lot of money. And she renovated a shop in Piazza dei Martiri with such imagination that it became a salon for the rich people from Via Chiaia, from Posillipo, from the Vomero. And there are many—very many—other things she could do. But she has a crazy streak, she thinks she can always do what she wants. Come, go, fix, break. You think I fired her? No, one day, as if it were nothing, she didn't come to work. Just like that, vanished. And if you catch her again, she'll slip away again, she's an eel. This is her problem: even though she's extremely intelligent, she can't understand what she can do and what she can't. That's because she hasn't yet found a real man. A real man puts the woman in her place. She's not capable of cooking? She learns. The house is dirty? She cleans it. A real man can make a woman do everything. For example: I met a woman a while ago who didn't know how to whistle. Well, we were together for two hours only—hours of fire—and afterward I said to her: Now whistle. She—you won't believe it—whistled. If you know how to train a woman, good. If you don't know how to train her, forget about her, you'll get hurt." He uttered these last words in a very serious tone, as if they summed up an irrefutable commandment. But even as he was speaking, he must have realized that he hadn't been able, and was still unable, to respect his own law. So suddenly his expression changed, his voice changed, he felt an urgent need to humiliate her. He turned toward Lila with a jolt of impatience and said emphatically, in a crescendo of obscenities in dialect: "But with her it's difficult, it's not so easy to kiss her off. And yet you see what she looks like, she has small eyes, small tits, a small ass, she's just a broomstick. With someone like that what can you do, you can't even get it up. But an instant is enough, a single instant: you look at her and you want to fuck her."

It was at that point that Lila felt a violent bump inside her head, as if her heart, instead of hammering in her throat, had exploded in her skull. She yelled an insult at him no less obscene than the words he had uttered, she grabbed from the desk the bronze ashtray, spilling out butts and ashes, and tried to hit him. But the gesture, in spite of her fury, was slow, powerless. And even Bruno's voice—*Lina, please, what are you doing*—passed through her slowly. So maybe for that reason Solara stopped her easily and easily took away the ashtray, saying to her angrily:

"You think you work for Dottor Soccavo? You think I'm no one here? You are mistaken. Dottor Soccavo has been in my mother's red book for quite some time, and that book is a lot more important than Mao's little book. So you don't work for him, you work for me, you work for me and only me. And so far I've let you, I wanted to see what the fuck you were driving at, you and that shit you sleep with. But from now on remember that I have my eyes on you and if I need you, you better come running, got that?"

Only then Bruno jumped to his feet nervously and exclaimed: "Leave her, Michè, you're going too far."

Solara let go of Lila's wrist, then he muttered, addressing Soccavo, again in Italian:

"You're right, sorry. But Signora Carracci has this ability: one way or another she always compels you to go too far."

Lina repressed her fury, she rubbed her wrist carefully, with the tip of her finger she wiped off some ash that had fallen on it. Then she unfolded the piece of paper with the demands, she placed it in front of Bruno, and as she was going to the door she turned to Solara, saying:

"I've known how to whistle since I was five years old."

45.

When she came back down, her face very pale, Edo asked her how it went, but Lila didn't answer, she pushed him away with one hand and shut herself in the bathroom. She was afraid that Bruno would call her back, she was afraid of being forced to have a confrontation in Michele's presence, she was afraid of the unaccustomed fragility of her body—she couldn't get used to it. From the little window she spied on the courtyard and drew a sigh of relief when she saw Michele, tall, in a black leather jacket and dark pants, going bald at the temples, his handsome face carefully shaved, walk nervously to his car, and leave. Then she returned to the gutting room and Edo asked her again:

"So?"

"I did it. But from now on the rest of you have to take care of it."

"In what sense?"

She couldn't answer: Bruno's secretary had appeared, breathless, the owner wanted her right away. She went like that saint who, although she still has her head on her shoulders, is carrying it in her hands, as if it had already been cut off. Bruno, as soon as he saw her, almost screamed:

"You people want to have coffee in bed in the morning? What is this latest thing, Lina? Do you have any idea? Sit down and explain. I can't believe it."

Lila explained to him, demand by demand, in the tone she used with Gennaro when he refused to understand. She said emphatically that he had better take that piece of paper seriously and deal with the various points in a constructive spirit, because if he behaved unreasonably, the office of the labor inspector would soon come down on him. Finally she asked him what sort of trouble he'd got into, to end up in the hands of dangerous people like the Solaras. At that point Bruno lost control completely. His red complexion turned purple, his eyes grew bloodshot, he yelled that he would ruin her, that a few extra lire for the four dickheads she had set against him would be enough to settle everything. He shouted that for years his father had been bribing the inspector's office and she was dreaming if she thought he was afraid of an inspection. He cried that the Solaras would eliminate her desire to be a union member, and finally, in a choked voice, he said: Out, get out immediately, out.

Lila went to the door. On the threshold she said:

"This is the last time you'll see me. I'm done working here, starting now."

At those words Soccavo abruptly returned to himself. He had an expression of alarm, he must have promised Michele that he wouldn't fire her. He said: "Now you're insulted? Now

you're being difficult? What do you say, come here, let's discuss it, I'll decide if I should fire you or not. Bitch, I said come
here."

For a fraction of a second Ischia came to mind, the morning
we waited for Nino and his rich friend, the boy who had a house
in Forio, who was always so polite and patient, to arrive. She
went out and closed the door behind her. Immediately afterward
she began to tremble violently, she was covered with sweat. She
didn't go to the gutting room, she didn't say goodbye to Edo and
Teresa, she passed by Filippo, who looked at her in bewilderment and called to her: Cerù, where are you going, come back
inside. But she ran along the unpaved road, took the first bus for
the Marina, reached the sea. She walked for a long time. There
was a cold wind, and she went up to the Vomero in the funicular, walked through Piazza Vanvitelli, along Via Scarlatti, Via
Cimarosa, took the funicular again to go down. It was late when
she realized that she had forgotten about Gennaro. She got
home at nine, and asked Enzo and Pasquale, who were anxiously questioning her to find out what had happened to her, to
come and look for me in the neighborhood.

And now here we are, in the middle of the night, in this
bare room in San Giovanni a Teduccio. Gennaro is sleeping,
Lila talks on and on in a low voice, Enzo and Pasquale are
waiting in the kitchen. I feel like the knight in an ancient
romance as, wrapped in his shining armor, after performing a
thousand astonishing feats throughout the world, he meets a
ragged, starving herdsman, who, never leaving his pasture,
subdues and controls horrible beasts with his bare hands, and
with prodigious courage.

46.

I was a tranquil listener, and I let her talk. Some moments

of the story, especially when the expression of Lila's face and the pace of her sentences underwent a sudden, painful nervous contraction, disturbed me deeply. I felt a powerful sense of guilt, I thought: this is the life that could have been mine, and if it isn't it's partly thanks to her. Sometimes I almost hugged her, more often I wanted to ask questions, comment. But in general I held back, I interrupted two or three times at most.

For example, I certainly interrupted when she talked about Professor Galiani and her children. I would have liked her to explain better what the professor had said, what precise words she had used, if my name had ever come up with Nadia and Armando. But I realized in time the pettiness of the questions and restrained myself, even though a part of me considered the curiosity legitimate—they were acquaintances of mine, after all, who were important to me.

"Before I go to Florence for good, I should pay a visit to Professor Galiani. Maybe you'd come with me, do you want to?" and I added: "My relationship with her cooled a little, after Ischia, she blamed me for Nino's leaving Nadia." Since Lila looked at me as if she didn't see me, I said again: "The Galianis are good people, a little stuck up, but this business of the murmur should be checked."

This time she reacted.

"The murmur is there."

"All right," I said, "but even Armando said you'd need a cardiologist."

She replied:

"He heard it, anyway."

But I felt involved above all when it came to sexual matters. When she told me about the drying room, I almost said: an old intellectual jumped on me, in Turin, and in Milan a Venezuelan painter I'd known for only a few hours came to my room to get in bed as if it were a favor I owed him. Yet I held back, even with that. What sense was there in speaking of my affairs at that moment? And then really what could I have told her that had any resemblance to what she was telling me?

That last question presented itself clearly when, from a simple recitation of the facts—years before, when she told me about her wedding night, we had talked only of the most brutal facts—Lila proceeded to talk generally about her sexuality. It was a subject completely new for us. The coarse language of the environment we came from was useful for attack or self-defense, but, precisely because it was the language of violence, it hindered, rather than encouraged, intimate confidences. So I was embarrassed, I stared at the floor, when she said, in the crude vocabulary of the neighborhood, that fucking had never given her the pleasure she had expected as a girl, that in fact she had almost never felt anything, that after Stefano, after Nino, to do it really annoyed her, so that she had been unable to accept inside herself even a man as gentle as Enzo. Not only that: using an even more brutal vocabulary, she added that sometimes out of necessity, sometimes out of curiosity, sometimes out of passion, she had done everything that a man could want from a woman, and that even when she had wanted to conceive a child with Nino, and had become pregnant, the pleasure you were supposed to feel, particularly at that moment of great love, had been missing.

Before such frankness I understood that I could not be silent, that I had to let her feel how close I was, that I had to react to her confidences with equal confidences. But at the idea of having to speak about myself—the dialect disgusted me, and although I passed for an author of racy pages, the Italian I had acquired seemed to me too precious for the sticky material of sexual experiences—my uneasiness grew, I forgot how difficult her confession had been, that every word, however vulgar, was set in the weariness in her face, in the trembling of her hands, and I was brief.

"For me it's not like that," I said.

I wasn't lying, and yet it wasn't the truth. The truth was more complicated and to give it a form I would have needed practiced words. I would have had to explain that, in the time of Antonio, rubbing against him, letting him touch me had always been very pleasurable, and that I still desired that pleasure. I would have had to admit that being penetrated had disappointed me, too, that the experience was spoiled by the sense of guilt, by the discomfort of the conditions, by the fear of being caught, by the haste arising from that, by the terror of getting pregnant. But I would have had to add that Franco—the little I knew of sex was largely from him—before entering me and afterward let me rub against one of his legs, against his stomach, and that this was nice and sometimes made the penetration nice, too. As a result, I would have had to tell her, I was now waiting for marriage, Pietro was a very gentle man, I hoped that in the tranquility and the legitimacy of marriage I would have the time and the comfort to discover the pleasure of coitus. There, if I had expressed myself like that, I would have been honest. But the two of us, at nearly twenty-five, did not have a tradition of such articulate confidences. There had been only small general allusions when she was engaged to Stefano and I was with Antonio, bashful phrases, hints. As for Donato Sarratore, as for Franco, I had never talked about either one. So I kept to those few words— *For me it's not like that*—which must have sounded to her as if I were saying: *Maybe you're not normal.* And in fact she looked at me in bewilderment, and said as if to protect herself:

"In the book you wrote something else."

So she had read it. I murmured defensively:

"I don't even know anymore what ended up in there."

"Dirty stuff ended up in there," she said, "stuff that men don't want to hear and women know but are afraid to say. But now what—are you hiding?"

She used more or less those words, certainly she said *dirty*.

She, too, then, cited the risqué pages and did it like Gigliola, who had used the word *dirt*. I expected that she would offer an evaluation of the book as a whole, but she didn't, she used it only as a bridge to go back and repeat what she called several times, insistently, *the bother of fucking*. That is in your novel, she exclaimed, and if you told it you know it, it's pointless for you to say: For me it's not like that. And I mumbled Yes, maybe it's true, but I don't know. And while she with a tortured lack of shame went on with her confidences—the great excitement, the lack of satisfaction, the sense of disgust—I thought of Nino, and the questions I had so often turned over and over reappeared. Was that long night full of tales a good moment to tell her I had seen him? Should I warn her that for Gennaro she couldn't count on Nino, that he already had another child, that he left children behind him heedlessly? Should I take advantage of that moment, of those admissions of his, to let her know that in Milan he had said an unpleasant thing about her: *Lila is made badly even when it comes to sex*? Should I go so far as to tell her that in those agitated confidences of hers, even in that way of reading the *dirty* pages of my book, now, while she was speaking I seemed to find confirmation that Nino was, in essence, right? What in fact had Sarratore's son intended if not what she herself was admitting? Had he realized that for Lila being penetrated was only a duty, that she couldn't enjoy the union? He, I said to myself, is experienced. He has known many women, he knows what good female sexual behavior is and so he recognizes when it's bad. *To be made badly when it comes to sex* means, evidently, not to be able to feel pleasure in the male's thrusting; it means twisting with desire and rubbing yourself to quiet that desire, it means grabbing his hands and placing them against your sex as I sometimes did with Franco, ignoring his annoyance, the boredom of the one who has already had his orgasm and now would like to go to sleep. My uneasiness increased, I thought: I wrote *that* in my novel, is *that* what Gigliola and Lila recognized, was *that* what Nino recognized, perhaps, and the reason he wanted to talk about it? I let everything go and whispered somewhat randomly:

"I'm sorry."

"What?"

"That your pregnancy was without joy."

She responded with a flash of sarcasm:

"Imagine how I felt."

My last interruption came when it had begun to get light, and she had just finished telling me about the encounter with Michele. I said: That's enough, calm down, take your temperature. It was 101. I hugged her tight, I whispered: now I'll take care of you, and until you're better we'll stay together, and if I have to go to Florence you and the child will come with me. She refused energetically, she made the final confession of that night. She said she had been wrong to follow Enzo to San Giovanni a Teduccio, she wanted to go back to the neighborhood.

"To the neighborhood?"

"Yes."

"You're crazy."

"As soon as I feel better I'll do it."

I rebuked her, I told her it was a thought induced by the fever, that the neighborhood would exhaust her, that to set foot there was stupid.

"I can't wait to leave," I exclaimed.

"You're strong," she answered, to my astonishment. "I have never been. The better and truer you feel, the farther away you go. If I merely pass through the tunnel of the *stradone*, I'm scared. Remember when we tried to get to the sea but it started raining? Which of us wanted to keep going and which of us made an about-face, you or me?"

"I don't remember. But, anyway, don't go back to the neighborhood."

I tried in vain to make her change her mind. We discussed it for a long time.

"Go," she said finally, "talk to the two of them, they've been waiting for hours. They haven't closed their eyes and they have to go to work."

"What shall I tell them?"

"Whatever you want."

I pulled the covers up, I also covered Gennaro, who had been tossing in his sleep all night. I realized that Lila was already falling asleep. I whispered:

"I'll be back soon."

She said: "Remember what you promised."

"What?"

"You've already forgotten? If something happens to me, you've got to take Gennaro."

"Nothing will happen to you."

As I went out of the room Lila started in her half-sleep, she whispered: "Watch me until I fall asleep. Watch me always, even when you leave Naples. That way I'll know that you see me and I'm at peace."

47.

In the time that passed between that night and the day of my wedding—I was married on May 17, 1969, in Florence, and, after a honeymoon of just three days in Venice, enthusiastically began my life as a wife—I tried to do all I could for Lila. At first, in fact, I thought simply that I would help her until she got over the flu. I had things to do about the house in Florence, I had a lot of engagements because of the book—the telephone rang constantly, and my mother grumbled that she had given the number to half the neighborhood but no one called her, to have that thingamajig in the house, she said, is just a bother, since the calls were almost always for me—I wrote notes for hypothetical new novels, I tried to fill the gaps in my literary and political education. But my friend's general state of weakness soon led me to neglect my own affairs and occupy myself with her. My mother realized right away that we had resumed our friendship: she found it shameful, she flew into a rage, she was full of insults for both of us. She continued to believe that she could tell me what to do and what not to, she limped after me, criticizing me. Sometimes she seemed determined to insert herself into my body, simply to keep me from being my own master. What do you have in common with her anymore, she insisted, think of what you are and of what she is, isn't that disgusting book you wrote enough, you want to go on being friends with a whore? But I behaved as if I were deaf. I saw Lila every day and from the moment I left her sleeping in her room and went to face the two men who had waited all night in the kitchen I devoted myself to reorganizing her life.

I told Enzo and Pasquale that Lila was ill, she couldn't work at the Soccavo factory anymore, she had quit. With Enzo I didn't have to waste words, he had understood for a while that she couldn't go on at the factory, that she had gotten into a difficult situation, that something inside her was giving in. Pasquale, instead, driving back to the neighborhood on the early-morning streets, still free of traffic, objected. Let's not overdo it, he said, it's true that Lila has a hard life, but that's what happens to all the exploited of the world. Then, following a tendency he had had since he was a boy, he went on to speak about the peasants of the south, the workers of the north, the populations of Latin America, of northeastern Brazil, of Africa, about the Negroes, the Vietnamese, American imperialism. I soon stopped him, saying: Pasquale, if Lina goes on as she has she'll die. He wouldn't concede, he continued to object, and not because he didn't care about Lila but because the struggle at Soccavo seemed to him important, he considered our friend's role crucial, and deep down he was convinced that all those stories about a little flu came not so much from her as from me, a bourgeois intellectual more worried about a slight fever than about the nasty political consequences of a workers' defeat. Since he couldn't make up his mind to say these things to me explicitly but spoke in sentence fragments, I summed it up for him with soothing clarity, to show him I had understood. That made him even more anxious and as he left me at the gate he said: I have to go to work now, Lenù, but we'll talk about it again. As soon as I returned to the house in San Giovanni a Teduccio I took Enzo aside and said: Keep Pasquale away from Lina if you love her, she mustn't hear any talk of the factory.

In that period I always carried in my purse a book and a notebook: I read on the bus or when Lila was sleeping. Sometimes I discovered her with her eyes open, staring at me, maybe she was peeking to see what I was reading, but she never asked me the title of the book, and when I tried to read her some passages—from scenes at the Upton Inn, I remember—she closed her eyes as if I were boring her. The fever passed in a few days, but the cough didn't, so I forced her to stay in bed. I cleaned the house, I cooked, I took care of Gennaro. Maybe because he was already big, somewhat aggressive, willful, he didn't have the defenseless charm of Mirko, Nino's other child. But sometimes in the midst of violent games he would turn unexpectedly sad, and fall asleep on the floor; that softened me, and I grew fond of him, and when that became clear to him he attached himself to me, keeping me from doing chores or reading.

Meanwhile I tried to get a better understanding of Lila's situation. Did she have money? No. I lent her some and she accepted it after swearing endlessly that she would pay me back. How much did Bruno owe her? Two months' salary. And severance pay? She didn't know. What was Enzo's job, how much did he earn? No idea. And that correspondence course in Zurich—what concrete possibilities did it offer? Who knows. She coughed constantly, she had pains in her chest, sweats, a vise in her throat, her heart would suddenly go crazy. I wrote down punctiliously all the symptoms and tried to convince her that another medical examination was necessary, more thorough than the one Armando had done. She didn't say yes but she didn't oppose it. One evening before Enzo returned, Pasquale looked in, he said very politely that he, his comrades on the committee, and some workers at the Soccavo factory wanted to know how she was. I replied that she wasn't well, she needed rest, but he asked to see her just the same, to say hello. I left him in the kitchen, I went to Lila, I advised her not to see him. She made a face that meant: I'll do as you want. I was moved by the fact that she gave in to me—she who had always commanded, done and undone—without arguing.

48.

At home that same night I made a long call to Pietro, telling him in detail all Lila's troubles and how important it was to me to help her. He listened patiently. At a certain point he even exhibited a spirit of collaboration: he remembered a young Pisan Greek scholar who was obsessed with computers and imagined that they would revolutionize philology. I was touched by the fact that, although he was a person who was always buried in his work, on this occasion, for love of me, he made an effort to be useful.

"Find him," I begged him, "tell him about Enzo, you never know, maybe some job prospects might turn up."

He promised he would and added that, if he remembered correctly, Mariarosa had had a brief romance with a young

Neapolitan lawyer: maybe he could find him and ask if he could help.

"To do what?"

"To get your friend's money back."

I was excited.

"Call Mariarosa."

"All right."

I insisted: "Don't just promise, call her, please."

He was silent for a moment, then he said: "Just then you sounded like my mother."

"In what sense?"

"You sounded like her when something is very important to her."

"I'm very different, unfortunately."

He was silent again.

"You're different, fortunately. But in these types of things there's no one like her. Tell her about that girl and you'll see, she'll help you."

I telephoned Adele. I did it with some embarrassment, which I overcame by reminding myself of all the times I had seen her at work, for my book, in the search for the apartment in Florence. She was a woman who liked to be busy. If she needed something, she picked up the telephone and, link by link, put together the chain that led to her goal. She knew how to ask in such a way that saying no was impossible. And she crossed ideological borders confidently, she respected no hierarchies, she tracked down cleaning women, bureaucrats, industrialists, intellectuals, ministers, and she addressed all with cordial detachment, as if the favor she was about to ask she was in fact already doing for them. Amid a thousand awkward apologies for disturbing her, I told Adele in detail about my friend, and she became curious, interested, angry. At the end she said:

"Let me think."

"Of course."

"Meanwhile, can I give you some advice?"

"Of course."

"Don't be timid. You're a writer, use your role, test it, make something of it. These are decisive times, everything is turning upside down. Participate, be present. And begin with the scum in your area, put their backs to the wall."

"How?"

"By writing. Frighten Soccavo to death, and others like him. Promise you'll do it?"

"I'll try."

She gave me the name of an editor at *l'Unità*.

49.

The telephone call to Pietro and, especially, the one to my mother-in-law released a feeling that until that moment I had kept at bay, that in fact I had repressed, but that was alive and ready to advance. It had to do with my changed status. It was likely that the Airotas, especially Guido but perhaps Adele herself, considered me a girl who, although very eager, was far from the person they would have chosen for their son. It was just as likely that my origin, my dialectal cadence, my lack of sophistication in everything, had put the breadth of their views to a hard test. With just a slight exaggeration I could hypothesize that even the publication of my book was part of an emergency plan intended to make me presentable in their world. But the fact remained, incontrovertible, that they had accepted me, that I was about to marry Pietro, with their consent, that I was about to enter a protective family, a sort of well-fortified castle from which I could proceed without fear or to which I could retreat if I were in danger. So it was urgent that I get used to that new membership, and above all I had to be conscious of it. I was no longer a small match-seller almost down to the last match; I had won for myself a large supply of matches. And so—I suddenly understood—I could do for Lila much more than I had calculated on doing.

It was with this perspective that I had my friend give me the documentation she had collected against Soccavo. She handed it over passively, without even asking what I wanted to do with it. I read with increasing absorption. How many terrible things she had been able to say precisely and effectively. How many intolerable experiences could be perceived behind the descrip- tion of the factory. I turned the pages in my hands for a long time, then suddenly, almost without coming to a decision, I looked in the telephone book, I called Soccavo. I subdued my voice to the right tone, I asked for Bruno. He was cordial— *What a pleasure to talk to you*—I cold. He said: You've done so many great things, Elena, I saw a picture of you in *Roma*, bravo, what a wonderful time we had on Ischia. I answered that it was a pleasure to talk to him, too, but that Ischia was far away, and for better and worse we had all changed, that in his case, for example, I had heard some nasty rumors that I hoped were not true. He understood immediately and protested. He spoke harshly of Lila, of her ungratefulness, of the trouble she had caused him. I changed my tone, I said that I believed Lila more than him. Take a pencil and paper, I said, write down my number, got it? Now give instructions for her to be paid down to the last lira you owe her, and let me know when I can come and get the money: I wouldn't like to see your picture in the papers, too.

I hung up before he could object, feeling proud of myself. I hadn't shown the least emotion, I had been curt, a few remarks in Italian, polite first, then aloof. I hoped that Pietro was right: was I really acquiring Adele's tone, was I learning, without real- izing it, her way of being in the world? I decided to find out whether I was capable, if I wanted, of carrying out the threat I had ended the phone call with. Agitated—as I had not been when I called Bruno, still the boring boy who had tried to kiss me on the beach of Citara—I dialed the number of the editorial offices of *l'Unità*. While the telephone rang, I hoped that the voice of my mother yelling at Elisa in dialect in the background wouldn't be heard. My name is Elena Greco, I said to the switchboard operator, and I didn't have time to explain what I wanted before the woman exclaimed: Elena Greco the writer? She had read my book, and was full of compliments. I thanked her, I felt happy, strong, I explained, unnecessarily, that I had in mind an article about a factory on the outskirts, and I gave the name of the editor Adele had suggested. The operator congratulated me again, then she resumed a professional tone. Hold on, she said. A moment later a very hoarse male voice asked me in a teasing tone since when practitioners of literature had been willing to dirty their pens on the subject of piece work, shifts, and overtime, very boring subjects that young, successful novelists in particular stayed away from.

"What's the angle?" he asked. "Construction, longshoremen, miners?"

"It's a sausage factory," I said. "Not a big deal."

The man continued to make fun of me: "You don't have to apologize, it's fine. If Elena Greco, to whom this newspaper devoted no less than half a page of profuse praise, decides to write about sausages, can we poor editors possibly say: that it doesn't interest us? Are thirty lines enough? Too few? Let's be generous, make it sixty. When you've finished, will you bring it to me in person or dictate it?"

I began working on the article right away. I had to squeeze out of Lila's pages my sixty lines, and for love of her I wanted to do a good job. But I had no experience of newspaper writing, apart from when, at the age of fifteen, I had tried to write about the conflict with the religion teacher for Nino's journal: with terrible results. I don't know, maybe it was that memory that complicated things. Or maybe it was the editor's sarcastic tone that rang in my ears, especially when, at the end of the call, he asked me to give his best to my mother-in-law. Certainly I took a lot of time, I wrote and rewrote stubbornly. But even when the article seemed to be finished I wasn't satisfied and I didn't take it to the newspaper. I have to talk to Lila first, I said to myself, it's a thing that should be decided together; I'll turn it in tomorrow.

The next day I went to see Lila; she seemed particularly unwell. She complained that when I wasn't there certain presences took advantage of my absence and emerged from objects to bother her and Gennaro. Then she realized that I was alarmed and, in a tone of amusement, said it was all nonsense, she just wanted me to be with her more. We talked a lot, I soothed her, but I didn't give her the article to read. What held me back was the idea that if *l'Unità* rejected the piece I would be forced to tell her that they hadn't found it good, and I would feel humiliated. It took a phone call from Adele that night to give me a solid dose of optimism and make up my mind. She had consulted her husband and also Mariarosa. She had moved half the world in a few hours: luminaries of medicine, socialist professors who knew about the union, a Christian Democrat whom she called a bit foolish but a good person and an expert in workers' rights. The result was that I had an appointment the next day with the best cardiologist in Naples—a friend of friends, I wouldn't have to pay—and that the labor inspector would immediately pay a visit to the Soccavo factory, and that to get Lila's money I could go to that friend of Mariarosa's whom Pietro had mentioned, a young socialist lawyer who had an office in Piazza Nicola Amore and had already been informed.

"Happy?"

"Yes."

"Did you write your article?"

"Yes."

"You see? I was sure you wouldn't do it."

"In fact it's ready, I'll take it to *l'Unità* tomorrow."

"Good. I run the risk of underestimating you."

"It's a risk?"

"Underestimating always is. How's it going with that poor little creature my son?"

50.

From then on everything became fluid, almost as if I possessed the art of making events flow like water from a spring. Even Pietro had worked for Lila. His colleague the Greek scholar turned out to be extremely talkative but useful just the same: he knew someone in Bologna who really was a computer expert—the reliable source of his philological fantasies—and he had given him the number of an acquaintance in Naples, judged to be equally reliable. He gave me the name, address, and telephone number of the Neapolitan, and I thanked him warmly, commenting with affectionate irony on his forced entrepreneurship—I even sent him a kiss over the phone.

I went to see Lila immediately. She had a cavernous cough, her face was strained and pale, her gaze excessively watchful. But I was bringing good news and was happy. I shook her, hugged her, held both her hands tight, and meanwhile told her about the phone call I had made to Bruno, read her the article I had written, enumerated the results of the painstaking efforts of Pietro, of my mother-in-law, of my sister-in-law. She listened as if I were speaking from far away—from another world into which I had ventured—and could hear clearly only half the things I was saying. Besides, Gennaro was constantly tugging on her to play with him, and, as I spoke, she was attending to him, but without warmth. I felt content just the same. In the past Lila had opened the miraculous drawer of the grocery store and had bought me everything, especially books. Now I opened my drawers and paid her back, hoping that she would feel safe, as I now did.

"So," I asked her finally, "tomorrow morning you'll go to the cardiologist?"

She reacted to my question in an incongruous way, saying with a small laugh: "Nadia won't like this way of doing things. And her brother won't, either."

"What way, I don't understand."

"Nothing."

"Lila," I said, "please, what does Nadia have to do with it, don't give her more importance than she already gives herself. And forget Armando, he's always been superficial."

I surprised myself with those judgments, after all I knew very little about Professor Galiani's children. And for a few seconds I had the impression that Lila didn't recognize me but saw before her a spirit who was exploiting her weakness. In fact, rather than criticizing Nadia and Armando, I only wanted her to understand that the hierarchies of power were different, that compared to the Airotas the Galianis didn't count, that people like Bruno Soccavo or that thug Michele counted even less, that in other words she should do as I said and not worry. But as I was speaking I realized I was in danger of boasting and I caressed her cheek, saying that, of course, I admired Armando and Nadia's political engagement, and then I added, laughing: but trust me. She muttered:

"O.K., we'll go to the cardiologist."

I persisted:

"And for Enzo what appointment should I make, what time, what day?"

"Whenever you want, but after five."

As soon as I got home I went back to the telephone. I called the lawyer, I explained Lila's situation in detail. I called the cardiologist, I confirmed the appointment. I telephoned the computer expert, he worked at the Department of Public Works: he said that the Zurich courses were useless, but that I could send Enzo to see him on such and such a day at such an address. I called *l'Unità*, the editor said: You're certainly taking your sweet time—are you bringing me this article, or are we waiting for Christmas? I called Soccavo's secretary and asked her to tell her boss that, since I hadn't heard from him, my article would be out soon in *l'Unità*.

That last phone call provoked an immediate, violent reaction. Soccavo called me two minutes later and this time he wasn't friendly; he threatened me. I answered that, momentarily, he would have the inspector on his back and a lawyer who would take care of Lila's interests. Then, that evening, pleasantly overexcited—I was proud of fighting against injustice, out of affection and conviction, in spite of Pasquale and Franco, who thought they could still give me lessons—I hurried to *l'Unità* to deliver my article.

The man I had talked to was middle-aged, short, and fat, with small, lively eyes that permanently sparkled with a benevolent irony. He invited me to sit down on a dilapidated chair and he read the article carefully.

"And this is sixty lines? To me it seems like a hundred and fifty."

I reddened, I said softly: "I counted several times, it's sixty."

"Yes, but written by hand and in a script that couldn't be read with a magnifying glass. But the piece is very good, Comrade. Find a typewriter somewhere and cut what you can."

"Now?"

"And when? For once I've got something people will actually look at if I put it on the page, and you want to make me wait for doomsday?"

51.

What energy I had in those days. We went to the cardiologist, a big-name professor who had a house and office in Via
Crispi. I took great care with my appearance for the occasion.
Although the doctor was from Naples, he was connected with
Adele's world and I didn't want to make a bad impression. I
brushed my hair, wore a dress that she had given me, used a
subtle perfume that resembled hers, put on light makeup. I
wanted the professor, if he spoke to my mother-in-law on the
telephone, or if by chance they met, to speak well of me. Lila
instead looked as she did every day at home, careless of her
appearance. We sat in a grand waiting room, with nineteenth-
century paintings on the walls: a noblewoman in an armchair
with a Negro servant in the background, a portrait of an old
lady, and a large, lively hunting scene. There were two other
people waiting, a man and a woman, both old, both with the
tidy, elegant look of prosperity. We waited in silence. Lila, who
on the way had repeatedly praised my appearance, said only, in
a low voice: You look like you came out of one of these paintings—you're the lady and I'm the maid.

We didn't wait long. A nurse called us; for no obvious reason, we went ahead of the patients who were waiting. Now Lila
became agitated, she wanted me to be present at the examination, she swore that alone she would never go in, and she
pushed me forward as if I were the one being examined. The
doctor was a bony man in his sixties, with thick gray hair. He
greeted me politely, he knew everything about me, and chatted
for ten minutes as if Lila weren't there. He said that his son had
also graduated from the Normale, but six years before me. He
noted that his brother was a writer and had a certain reputation, but only in Naples. He was full of praise for the Airotas,
he knew a cousin of Adele's very well, a famous physicist. He
asked me:

"When is the wedding?"

"May 17th."

"The seventeenth? That's bad luck, please change the date."

"It's not possible."

Lila was silent the whole time. She paid no attention to the professor, I felt her curiosity on me, she seemed amazed by my every gesture and word. When, finally, the doctor turned to her, questioning her at length, she answered unwillingly, in dialect or in an ugly Italian that imitated dialect patterns. Often I had to interrupt to remind her of symptoms that she had reported to me or to stress those which she minimized. Finally she submitted to a thorough examination and exhaustive tests, with a sullen expression, as if the cardiologist and I were doing her a wrong. I looked at her thin body in a threadbare pale blue slip that was too big for her. Her long neck seemed to be struggling to hold up her head, the skin was stretched over her bones like tissue paper that might tear at any moment. I realized that the thumb of her left hand every so often had a small, reflexive twitch. It was a good half hour before the professor told her to get dressed. She kept her eyes on him as she did so; now she seemed frightened. The cardiologist went to the desk, sat down, and finally announced that everything was in order, he hadn't found a murmur. Signora, he said, you have a perfect heart. But the effect of the verdict on Lila was apparently dubious, she didn't seem pleased, in fact she seemed irritated. It was I who felt relieved, as if it were my heart, and it was I who showed signs of worry when the professor, again addressing me and not Lila, as if her lack of reaction had offended him, added, with a frown, that, however, given the general state of my friend, urgent measures were necessary. The problem, he said, isn't the cough: the signora has a cold, has had a slight flu, and I'll give her some cough syrup. The problem, according to him, was that she was exhausted, run down. Lila had to take better care of herself, eat regularly, have a tonic treatment, get at least eight hours of sleep a night. The majority of your friend's symptoms, he said, will vanish when she regains her strength. In any case, he concluded, I would advise a neurological examination.

It was the penultimate word that roused Lila. She scowled, leaned forward, said in Italian: "Are you saying that I have a nervous illness?"

The doctor looked at her in surprise, as if the patient he had just finished examining had been magically replaced by another person.

"Not at all: I'm only advising an examination."

"Did I say or do something I shouldn't have?"

"No, madam, there's no need to worry. The examination serves only to get a clear picture of your situation."

"A relative of mine," said Lila, "a cousin of my mother's, was unhappy, she'd been unhappy her whole life. In the summer, when I was little, I would hear her through the open window, shouting, laughing. Or I would see her on the street doing slightly crazy things. But it was unhappiness, and so she never went to a neurologist, in fact she never went to any doctor."

"It would have been useful to go."

"Nervous illnesses are for ladies."

"Your mother's cousin isn't a lady?"

"No."

"And you?"

"Even less so."

"Do you feel unhappy?"

"I'm very well."

The doctor turned to me again, irritably: "Absolute rest. Have her do this treatment, regularly. If you have some way of taking her to the country, it would be better."

Lila burst out laughing, she returned to dialect: "The last

time I went to a doctor he sent me to the beach and it brought
me a lot of grief."

The professor pretended not to hear, he smiled at me as if
to elicit a conspiratorial smile, gave me the name of a friend
who was a neurologist, and telephoned himself so that the man
would see us as soon as possible. It wasn't easy to drag Lila to
the new doctor's office. She said she didn't have time to waste,
she was already bored enough by the cardiologist, she had to
get back to Gennaro, and above all she didn't have money to
throw away nor did she want me to throw away mine. I assured
her that the examination would be free and in the end, reluctantly, she gave in.

The neurologist was a small lively man, completely bald,
who had an office in an old building in Toledo and displayed in
his waiting room an orderly collection of philosophy books. He
liked to hear himself talk, and he talked so much that, it seemed
to me, he paid more attention to the thread of his own discourse than to the patient. He examined her and addressed me,
he asked her questions and propounded to me his observations,
taking no notice of the responses she gave. In the end, he concluded abstractedly that Lila's nervous system was in order, just
like her cardiac muscle. But—he said, continuing to address
me—my colleague is right, dear Dottoressa Greco, the body is
weakened, and as a result both the irascible and the concupis-
cible passions have taken advantage of it to get the upper hand
over reason: let's restore well-being to the body and we'll
restore health to the mind. Then he wrote out a prescription, in
indecipherable marks, but pronouncing aloud the names of the
medicines, the doses. Then he moved on to advice. He advised,
for relaxation, long walks, but avoiding the sea: better, he said,
the woods of Capodimonte or Camaldoli. He advised reading,
but only during the day, never at night. He advised keeping the
hands employed, even though a careful glance at Lila's would
have been enough to realize that they had been too much

employed. When he began to insist on the neurological benefits
of crochet work, Lila became restless in her chair, and without
waiting for the doctor to finish speaking, she asked him, following the course of her own secret thoughts:

"As long as we're here, could you give me the pills that pre-
vent you from having children?"

The doctor frowned, and so, I think, did I. The request
seemed out of place.

"Are you married?"

"I was, not now."

"In what sense not now?"

"I'm separated."

"You're still married."

"Well."

"Have you had children?"

"I have one."

"One isn't much."

"It's enough for me."

"In your condition pregnancy would help, there is no better medicine for a woman."

"I know women who were destroyed by pregnancy. Better
to have the pills."

"For that problem of yours you'll have to consult a gynecologist."

"You only know about nerves, you don't know about
pills?"

The doctor was irritated. He chatted a little more and then,
in the doorway, gave me the address and telephone number of
a doctor who worked in a clinic in Ponte di Tappia. Go to her,
he said, as if it were I who had asked for the contraceptives,
and he said goodbye. On the way out the secretary asked us to
pay. The neurologist, I gathered, was outside the chain of
favors that Adele had set in motion. I paid.

Once we were in the street Lila almost shouted, irately: I

will not take a single one of the medicines that shit gave me, since my head is falling off just the same, I already know it. I answered: I disagree, but do as you like. Then she was confused, she said quietly: I'm not angry with you, I'm angry with the doctors, and we walked in the direction of Ponte di Tappia, but without saying so, as if we were strolling aimlessly, just to stretch our legs. First she was silent, then she imitated in annoyance the neurologist's tone and his babble. It seemed to me that her impatience signaled a return of vitality. I asked her:

"Is it going a little better with Enzo?"

"It's the same as always."

"Then what do you want with the pills?"

"Do you know about them?"

"Yes."

"Do you take them?"

"No, but I will as soon as I'm married."

"You don't want children?"

"I do, but I have to write another book first."

"Does your husband know you don't want them right away?"

"I'll tell him."

"Shall we go see this woman and have her give both of us pills?"

"Lila, it's not candy you can take whenever you like. If you're not doing anything with Enzo forget it."

She looked at me with narrowed eyes, cracks in which her pupils were scarcely visible: "I'm not doing anything now but later who knows."

"Seriously?"

"I shouldn't, in your opinion?"

"Yes, of course."

At Ponte di Tappia we looked for a phone booth and called the doctor, who said she could see us right away. On the way to the clinic I made it clear to Lila that I was glad she was getting close to Enzo, and she seemed encouraged by my approval. We went back to being the girls of long ago, we began joking, partly serious, partly pretending, saying to each other: You do the talking, you're bolder, no you, you're dressed like a lady, I'm not in a hurry, I'm not, either, then why are we going.

The doctor was waiting for us at the entrance, in a white coat. She was a cordial woman, with a shrill voice. She invited us to the café and treated us like old friends. She emphasized repeatedly that she wasn't a gynecologist, but she was so full of explanations and advice that, while I kept to myself, somewhat bored, Lila asked increasingly explicit questions, made objections, asked new questions, offered ironic observations. They became very friendly. Finally, along with many recommendations, she gave each of us a prescription. The doctor refused to be paid because, she said, it was a mission she and her friends had. As she left—she had to go back to work—instead of shaking hands she embraced us. Lila, once we were in the street, said seriously: Finally a good person. She was cheerful then— I hadn't seen her like that for a long time.

52.

In spite of the editor's enthusiasm, *l'Unità* put off publishing my article. I was anxious, afraid that it wouldn't come out at all. But the day after the neurological exam I went out early to the newsstand and scanned the paper, jumping rapidly from page to page, until, at last, I found it. I expected that it would run, heavily cut, amid the local items, but instead it was in the national news, complete, with my byline, which pierced me like a long needle when I saw it in print. Pietro called me, happy about it, and Adele, too, was pleased; she said that her husband had liked the article very much and so had Mariarosa. But the surprising thing was that the head of my publishing house, along with two well-known intellectuals who had been connected to the firm for years, and Franco, Franco Mari, telephoned to congratulate me. Franco had asked Mariarosa for my number, and he spoke with respect, he said that he was pleased, that I had provided an example of a thorough investigation into the condition of workers, that he hoped to see me soon to talk about it. I expected at that point that through some unforeseen channel Nino would communicate his approval. But in vain—I was disappointed. There was no word from Pasquale, either, but then out of political disgust he had long ago stopped reading the party newspaper. The editor from *l'Unità,* however, consoled me, seeking me out to tell me how much the editorial office had liked the piece, and encouraging me, in his usual teasing way, to buy a typewriter and write more good articles.

I have to say that the most disorienting phone call was from Bruno Soccavo. He had his secretary call me, then he got on the phone. He spoke in a melancholy tone, as if the article, which he didn't even mention at first, had hit him so hard that it had sapped his energy. He said that in our time on Ischia, and our beautiful walks on the beach, he had loved me as he had never loved. He declared his utter admiration for the direction that, although I was very young, I had given to my life. He swore that his father had handed over to him a business in a lot of trouble, beset by evil practices, and that he was merely the blameless inheritor of a situation that in his eyes was deplorable. He stated that my article—finally he mentioned it—had been illuminating and that he wished to correct as soon as possible the many defects inherited from the past. He was sorry about the misunderstandings with Lila and told me that the administration was arranging everything with my lawyer. He concluded softly: you know the Solaras, in this difficult situation they're helping me give the Soccavo factory a new face. And he added: Michele sends you warm greetings. I exchanged the greetings, I took note of his good intentions, and I hung up. But right away I called Mariarosa's lawyer friend to tell him about that phone call. He confirmed that the money question had been resolved, and I met him a few days later in the office where he worked. He wasn't much older than me, well dressed, and likable, except for unpleasantly thin lips. He wanted to take me out for coffee. He was full of admiration for Guido Airota, he remembered Pietro well. He gave me the sum that Soccavo had paid for Lila, he urged me to be careful not to have my purse snatched. He described the chaos of students and union members and police he had found at the gates, he said that the labor inspector had also showed up at the factory. And yet he didn't seem satisfied. Only when we were saying goodbye, he asked me at the door:

"You know the Solaras?"

"They're from the neighborhood where I grew up."

"You know that they are behind Soccavo?"

"Yes."

"And you're not worried?"

"I don't understand."

"I mean: the fact that you've known them forever and that you studied outside Naples—maybe you can't see the situation clearly."

"It's very clear."

"In recent years the Solaras have expanded, in this city they're important."

"And so?"

He pressed his lips together, shook my hand.

"And so nothing: we've got the money, everything's in order. Say hello to Mariarosa and Pietro. When's the wedding? Do you like Florence?"

53.

I gave the money to Lila, who counted it twice with satisfaction and wanted to give me back immediately the amount I had lent her. Enzo arrived soon afterward, he had just been to see the person who knew about computers. He seemed pleased, naturally within the bounds of his impassiveness, which, maybe even against his own wishes, choked off emotions and words. Lila and I struggled to get the information out of him, but finally a fairly clear picture emerged. The expert had been extremely kind. At first he had repeated that the Zurich course was a waste of money, but then he had realized that Enzo, in spite of the uselessness of the course, was smart. He had told him that IBM was about to start producing a new computer in Italy, in the Vimercate factory, and that the Naples branch had an urgent need for operators, keypunch operators, programmer-analysts. He had assured him that, as soon as the company started training courses, he would let Enzo know. He had written down all his information.

"Did he seem serious?" Lila asked.

Enzo, to give proof of the man's seriousness, nodded at me, said: "He knew all about Lenuccia's fiancé."

"Meaning?"

"He told me he's the son of an important person."

Annoyance showed in Lila's face. She knew, obviously, that the appointment had been arranged by Pietro and that the name Airota counted in the positive outcome of the meeting, but she seemed put out by the fact that Enzo should notice it. I thought she was bothered by the idea that he, too, owed me something, as if that debt, which between her and me could have no consequence, not even the subordination of gratitude, might instead be harmful to Enzo. I said quickly that the prestige of my father-in-law didn't count that much, that the computer expert had explained even to me that he would help only if Enzo was good. And Lila, making a slightly excessive gesture of approval, said emphatically:

"He's really good."

"I've never seen a computer," Enzo said.

"So? That guy must have understood anyway that you know what you're doing."

He thought about it, and turned to Lila with an admiration that for an instant made me jealous: "He was impressed by the exercises you made me do."

"Really?"

"Yes. Especially diagramming things like ironing, and hammering a nail."

Then they began joking with one another, resorting to a jargon that I didn't understand and that excluded me. And suddenly they seemed to me a couple in love, very happy, with a secret so secret that it was unknown even to them. I saw again the courtyard when we were children. I saw her and Enzo competing to be first in arithmetic as the principal and Maestra Olivieri looked on. I saw Lila, who never cried, in despair because she had thrown a rock and injured him. I thought: their way of being together comes from something better in the neighborhood. Maybe Lila is right to want to go back.

54.

I began to pay attention to the "For rent" signs fixed to the building entrances, indicating apartments available. Meanwhile, an invitation to the wedding of Gigliola Spagnuolo and Michele Solara arrived, not for my family but for me. And a few hours later, by hand, came another invitation: Marisa Sarratore and Alfonso Carracci were getting married, and both the Solara family and the Carracci family addressed me with deference: *egregia dottoressa* Elena Greco. Almost immediately, I considered the two wedding invitations an opportunity to find out if it was a good idea to encourage Lila's return to the neighborhood. I planned to go and see Michele, Alfonso, Gigliola, and Marisa, apparently to offer congratulations and to explain that I would not be in Naples when the weddings took place but in fact to discover if the Solaras and the Carraccis still wanted to torture Lila. It seemed to me that Alfonso was the only person capable of telling me in a dispassionate way how resentful Stefano still was. And with Michele, even though I hated him—perhaps above all because I hated him—I thought I could speak with composure about Lila's health problems, letting him know that, even though he thought he was a big shot and teased me as if I were still a little girl, I now had sufficient power to complicate his life, and his affairs, if he continued to persecute my friend. I put both cards in my purse, I didn't want my mother to see them and be offended at the respect shown to me and not to my father and her. I set aside a day to devote to these visits.

The weather wasn't promising, so I carried an umbrella, but I was in a good mood, I wanted to walk, reflect, give a sort of farewell to the neighborhood and the city. Out of the habit of a diligent student, I started with the more difficult meeting, the one with Solara. I went to the bar, but neither he nor Gigliola nor even Marcello was there; someone said that they might be at the new place on the *stradone*. I stopped in and looked around with the attitude of someone with nothing better to do. Any memory of Don Carlo's shop had been utterly erased—the dark, deep cave where as a child I had gone to buy liquid soap and other household things. From the windows of the building's third floor an enormous vertical sign hung down over the wide entrance: Everything for Everyone. The store was brightly lit, even though it was day, and offered merchandise of every type, the triumph of abundance. I saw Lila's brother, Rino, who had grown very fat. He treated me coldly, saying that he was the boss there, he didn't know anything about the Solaras. If you're looking for Michele, go to his house, he said bitterly, and turned his back as if he had something urgent to do.

I started walking again, and reached the new neighborhood, where I knew that the entire Solara family had, years earlier, bought an enormous apartment. The mother, Manuela, the loan shark, opened the door; I hadn't seen her since the time of Lila's wedding. I felt that she had been observing me through the spyhole. She looked for a long time, then she drew back the bolt and appeared in the frame of the door, her figure partly contained by the darkness of the apartment, partly eroded by the light coming from the large window on the stairs. She was as if dried up. The skin was stretched over her large bones, one of her pupils was very bright and the other as if dead. In her ears, around her neck, against the dark dress that hung loosely, gold sparkled, as if she were getting ready for a party. She treated me politely, inviting me to come in, have coffee. Michele wasn't there, did I know that he had another house, on Posillipo, where he was to go and live after his marriage. He was furnishing it with Gigliola.

"They're going to leave the neighborhood?" I asked.

"Yes, certainly."

"For Posillipo?"

"Six rooms, Lenù, three facing the sea. I would have preferred the Vomero, but Michele does as he likes. Anyway, there's a breeze, in the morning, and a light that you can't imagine."

I was surprised. I would never have believed that the Solaras would move away from the area of their trafficking, from the den where they hid their booty. But here was Michele, the shrewdest, the greediest of the family, going to live somewhere else, up, on the Posillipo, facing the sea and Vesuvio. The brothers' craving for greatness really had increased, the lawyer was right. But at the moment the fact cheered me, I was glad that Michele was leaving the neighborhood. I found that this favored Lila's possible return.

55.

I asked Signora Manuela for the address, said goodbye, and crossed the city, first by subway to Mergellina, then on foot, and by bus up Posillipo. I was curious. I now felt that I belonged to a legitimate power, universally admired, haloed by a high level of culture, and I wanted to see what garish guise was being given to the power I had had before my eyes since childhood—the vulgar pleasure of bullying, the unpunished practice of crime, the smiling tricks of obedience to the law, the display of profligacy—as embodied by the Solara brothers. But Michele escaped me again. On the top floor of a recent structure I found only Gigliola, who greeted me with obvious amazement and an equally obvious bitterness. I realized that as long as I had used her mother's telephone at all hours I had been cordial, but ever since I'd had the phone installed at home the entire Spagnuolo family had gone out of my life, and I'd scarcely noticed. And now without warning, at noon, on a dark day that threatened rain, I showed up here, in Posillipo, bursting into the house of a bride where everything was still topsy-turvy? I was ashamed, and greeted her with artificial warmth so that she would forgive me. For a while Gigliola remained sullen, and perhaps also alarmed, then her need to boast prevailed. She wanted me to envy her, she wanted to feel in a tangible way that I considered her the most fortunate of us all. And so, observing my reactions, enjoying my enthusiasm, she showed me the rooms, one by one, the expensive furniture, the gaudy lamps, two big bathrooms, the huge hot-water heater, the refrigerator, the washing machine, three telephones, unfortunately not yet hooked up, the I don't know how many-inch television, and finally the terrace, which wasn't a terrace but a hanging garden filled with flowers, whose multicolored variety the ugly day kept me from appreciating.

"Look, have you ever seen the sea like that? And Naples? And Vesuvius? And the sky? In the neighborhood was there ever all that sky?"

Never. The sea was of lead and the gulf clasped it like the rim of a crucible. A dense churning mass of black clouds was rolling toward us. But in the distance, between sea and clouds, there was a long gash that collided with the violet shadow of Vesuvius, a wound from which a dazzling whiteness dripped. We stood looking at it for a long time, our clothes pasted to us by the wind. I was as if hypnotized by the beauty of Naples; not even from the terrace of the Galianis, years before, had I seen it like this. The defacement of the city provided high-cost observatories of concrete from which to view an extraordinary landscape; Michele had acquired a memorable one.

"Don't you like it?"

"Marvelous."

"There's no comparison with Lina's house in the neighborhood, is there?"

"No, no comparison."

"I said Lina, but now Ada's there."

"Yes."

"Here it's much more upper-class."

"Yes."

"But you made a face."

"No, I'm happy for you."

"To each his own. You're educated, you write books, and I have this."

"Yes."

"You're not sure."

"I'm very sure."

"If you look at the nameplates in this building, you'll see, only professionals, lawyers, big professors. The view and the luxuries are expensive. If you and your husband save, in my opinion you could buy a house like this."

"I don't think so."

"He doesn't want to come and live in Naples?"

"I doubt it."

"You never know. You're lucky: I've heard Pietro's voice on the telephone quite a few times, and I saw him from the window—it's obvious that he's a clever man. He's not like Michele, he'll do what you want."

At that point she dragged me inside, she wanted us to eat something. She unwrapped prosciutto and provolone, she cut slices of bread. It's still camping, she apologized, but sometime when you're in Naples with your husband come and see me, I'll show you how I've arranged everything. Her eyes were big and shining, she was excited by the effort of leaving no doubts about her prosperity. But that improbable future—Pietro and I coming to Naples and visiting her and Michele—must have appeared perilous. For a moment she was distracted, she had bad thoughts, and when she resumed her boasting she had lost faith in what she was saying, she began to change. I've been lucky, too, she repeated, yet she spoke without satisfaction—rather, with a kind of sarcasm addressed to herself. Carmen, she enumerated, ended up with the gas pump attendant on the *stradone*, Pinuccia is poisoned by that idiot Rino, Ada is Stefano's whore. Instead, I have Michele, lucky me, who is handsome, intelligent, bosses everybody, is finally making up his mind to marry me and you see where he's put me, you don't know what a celebration he's prepared—not even the Shah of Persia when he married Soraya had a wedding like ours. Yes, lucky I grabbed him as a child, I was the sly one. And she went on, but taking a self-mocking turn. She wove the praises of her own cleverness, slipping slowly from the luxuries that she had acquired by winning Solara to the solitude of her duties as a bride. Michele, she said, is never here, it's as if I were getting married by myself. And she suddenly asked me, as if she really wanted an opinion: Do you think I exist? Look at me, in your view do I exist? She hit her full breasts with her open hand, but she did it as if to demonstrate physically that the hand went right through her, that her body, because of Michele, wasn't there. He had taken everything of her, immediately, when she was almost a child. He had consumed her, crumpled her, and now that she was twenty-five he was used to her, he didn't even look at her anymore. He fucks here and there as he likes. The revulsion I feel, when someone asks how many children do you want and he brags, he says: Ask Gigliola, I already have children, I don't even know how many. Does your husband say such things? Does your husband say: With Lenuccia I want three, with the others I don't know? In front of everyone he treats me like a rag for wiping the floor. And I know why. He's never loved me. He's marrying me to have a faithful servant, that's the reason all men get married. And he keeps saying to me: What the fuck am I doing with you, you don't know anything, you have no intelligence, you have no taste, this beautiful house is wasted, with you everything becomes disgusting. She began to cry, saying between her sobs:

"I'm sorry, I'm talking like this because you wrote that book I liked, and I know you've suffered."

"Why do you let him say those things to you?"

"Because otherwise he won't marry me."

"But after the wedding make him pay for it."

"How? He doesn't give a damn about me: even now I never see him, imagine afterward."

"Then I don't understand you."

"You don't understand me because you're not me. Would you take someone if you knew very well that he was in love with someone else?"

I looked at her in bewilderment: "Michele has a lover?"

"Lots of them, he's a man, he sticks it in wherever he can. But that's not the point."

"What is?"

"Lenù, if I tell you you mustn't repeat it to anyone, otherwise Michele will kill me."

I promised, and I kept the promise: I write it here, now, only because she's dead. She said:

"He loves Lina. And he loves her in a way he never loved me, in a way he'll never love anyone."

"Nonsense."

"You mustn't say it's nonsense, Lenù, otherwise it's better that you go. It's true. He's loved Lina since the terrible day when she put the shoemaker's knife to Marcello's throat. I'm not making it up, he told me."

And she told me things that disturbed me profoundly. She told me that not long before, in that very house, Michele had gotten drunk one night and told her how many women he had been with, the precise number: a hundred and twenty-two, paying and free. You're on that list, he said emphatically, but you're certainly not among those who gave me the most pleasure. You know why? Because you're an idiot, and even to fuck well it takes a little intelligence. For example you don't know how to give a blow job, you're hopeless, and it's pointless to explain it to you, you can't do it, it's too obvious that it disgusts you. And he went on like that for a while, making speeches that became increasingly crude; with him vulgarity was normal. Then he wanted to explain clearly how things stood: he was marrying her because of the respect he felt for her father, a skilled pastry maker he was fond of; he was marrying her because one had to have a wife and even children and even an official house. But there should be no mistake: she was nothing to him, he hadn't put her on a pedestal, she wasn't the one he loved best, so she had better not be a pain in the ass, believing she had some rights. Brutal words. At a certain point Michele himself must have realized it, and he became gripped by a kind of melancholy. He had murmured that women for him were all games with a few holes for playing in. All. All except one. Lina was the only woman in the world he loved—love, yes, as in the films—and respected. He told me, Gigliola sobbed, that she would have known how to furnish this house. He told me that giving her money to spend, yes, that would be a pleasure. He told me that with her he could have become truly important, in Naples. He said to me: You remember what she did with the wedding photo, you remember how she fixed up the shop? And you, and Pinuccia, and all the others, what the fuck are you, what the fuck do you know how to do? He had said those things to her and not only those. He had told her that he thought about Lila night and day, but not with normal desire, his desire for her didn't resemble what he knew. *In reality he didn't want her.* That is, he didn't want her the way he generally wanted women, to feel them under him, to turn them over, turn them again, open them up, break them, step on them, and crush them. He didn't want her in order to have sex and then forget her. He wanted the subtlety of her mind with all its ideas. He wanted her imagination. And he wanted her without ruining her, to make her last. He wanted her not to screw her—that word applied to Lila disturbed him. He wanted to kiss her and caress her. He wanted to be caressed, helped, guided, commanded. He wanted to see how she changed with the passage of time, how she aged. He wanted to talk with her and be helped to talk. You understand? He spoke of her in way that to me, to me—when we are about to get married—he has never spoken. I swear it's true. He whispered: My brother Marcello, and that dickhead Stefano, and Enzo with his cheeky face, what have they understood of Lina? Do they know what they've lost, what they might lose? No, they don't have the intelligence. I alone know what she is, who she is. *I recognized her.* And I suffer thinking of how she's wasted. He was raving, just like that, unburdening himself. And I listened to him without saying a word, until he fell asleep. I looked at him and I said: how is it possible that Michele is capable of that feeling—it's not him speaking, it's someone else. And I hated that someone else, I thought: Now I'll stab him in his sleep and take back my Michele. Lila no, I'm not angry with her. I wanted to kill her years ago, when Michele took the shop on Piazza dei Martiri away from me and sent me back behind the counter in the pastry shop. Then I felt like shit. But I don't hate her anymore, she has nothing to do with it. She always wanted to get out of it. She's not a fool like me, I'm the one marrying him, she'll never take him. In fact, since Michele will grab everything there is to grab, but not her, I've loved her for quite a while: at least there's someone who can make him shit blood.

I listened, now and then I tried to play it down, to console her. I said: If he's marrying you it means that, whatever he says, you're important to him, don't feel hopeless. Gigliola shook her head energetically, she dried her cheeks with her fingers. You don't know him, she said, no one knows him like me. I asked:

"Could he lose his head, do you think, and hurt Lina?"

She uttered a kind exclamation, between a laugh and a cry.

"Him? Lina? Haven't you seen how he's behaved all these years? He could hurt me, you, anyone, even his father, his mother, his brother. He could hurt all the people Lina is attached to, her son, Enzo. And he could do it without a qualm, coldly. But to her, her person, he will never do anything."

56.

I decided to complete my exploratory tour. I walked to Mergellina and when I reached Piazza dei Martiri the black sky was so low that it seemed to be resting on the buildings. I hurried into the elegant Solara shoe store certain that the storm would burst at any moment. Alfonso was even more handsome than I remembered, with his big eyes and long lashes, his sharply drawn lips, his slender yet strong body, his Italian made slightly artificial by the study of Latin and Greek. He was genuinely happy to see me. The arduous years of middle school and high school we'd spent together had created an affectionate bond, and even though we hadn't seen each other for a long time, we picked up again right away. We started joking. We talked easily, the words tumbling out, about our academic past, the teachers, the book I had published, his marriage, mine. It was I, naturally, who brought up Lila, and he became flustered, he didn't want to speak ill of her, or of his brother, or Ada. He said only:

"It was predictable that it would end like this."

"Why?"

"You remember when I told you that Lina scared me?"

"Yes."

"It wasn't fear, I understood much later."

"What was it?"

"Estrangement and belonging, an effect of distance and closeness at the same time."

"Meaning what?"

"It's hard to say: you and I became friends immediately, you I love. With her that always seemed impossible. There was something tremendous about her that made me want to go down on my knees and confess my most secret thoughts."

I said ironically: "Great, an almost religious experience."

He remained serious: "No, only an admission of inferiority. But when she helped me study, that was great, yes. She would read the textbook and immediately understand it, then she'd summarize it for me in a simple way. There have been, and still are today, moments when I think: If I had been born a woman

I would have wanted to be like her. In fact, in the Carracci family we were both alien bodies, neither she nor I could endure. So her faults never mattered to me, I always felt on her side."

"Is Stefano still angry with her?"

"I don't know. Even if he hates her, he has too many problems to be aware of it. Lina is the least of his troubles at the moment."

The statement seemed sincere and, above all, well founded. I put Lina aside. I went back instead to asking him about Marisa, the Sarratore family, finally Nino. He was vague about all of them, especially Nino, whom no one—by Donato's wishes, he said—had dared to invite to the intolerable wedding that was in store for him.

"You're not happy to be getting married?" I ventured.

He looked out the window: there was lightning and thunder but still no rain. He said: "I was fine the way I was."

"And Marisa?"

"No, she wasn't fine."

"You wanted her to be your fiancée for life?"

"I don't know."

"So finally you've satisfied her."

"She went to Michele."

I looked at him uncertainly. "In what sense?"

He laughed, a nervous laugh.

"She went to him, she set him against me."

I was sitting on a pouf, he was standing, against the light. He had a tense, compact figure, like the toreador in a bull-fighting film.

"I don't understand: you're marrying Marisa because she asked Solara to tell you that you had to do it?"

"I'm marrying Marisa in order not to upset Michele. He put me in here, he trusted my abilities, I'm fond of him."

"You're crazy."

"You say that because you all have the wrong idea about Michele, you don't know what he's like." His face contracted, he tried vainly to hold back tears. He added, "Marisa is pregnant."

"Ah."

So that was the real reason. I took his hand, in great embarrassment I tried to soothe him. He became quiet with a great effort, and said:

"Life is a very ugly business, Lenù."

"It's not true: Marisa will be a good wife and a fine mother."

"I don't give a damn about Marisa."

"Now don't overdo it."

He fixed his eyes on me, I felt he was examining me as if to understand something about me that left him bewildered. He asked: "Lina never said anything even to you?"

"What should she have said?"

He shook his head, suddenly amused.

"You see I'm right? She is an unusual person. Once I told her a secret. I was afraid and I needed to tell someone the reason for my fear. I told her and she listened attentively, and I calmed down. It was important for me to talk to her, it seemed to me that she listened not with her ears but with an organ that she alone had and that made the words acceptable. At the end I didn't ask her, as one usually does: swear, please, not to betray me. But it's clear that if she hasn't told you she hasn't told anyone, not even out of spite, not even in the period that was hardest for her, when my brother hated her and beat her."

I didn't interrupt him. I felt only that I was sorry because he had confided something to Lila and not to me, although I had been his friend forever. He must have realized that and he decided to make up for it. He hugged me tight, and whispered in my ear:

"Lenù, I'm a queer, I don't like girls."

When I was about to leave, he said softly, embarrassed: I'm

sure you already knew. This increased my unhappiness; in fact it had never occurred to me.

<h2 style="text-align:center">57.</h2>

The long day passed in that way, without rain but dark. And then began a reversal that rapidly changed a phase of apparent growth in the relationship between Lila and me into a desire to cut it off and return to taking care of my own life. Or maybe it had begun before that, in tiny details that I scarcely noticed as they struck me, and now instead were starting to add up. The trip had been useful, and yet I came home unhappy. What sort of friendship was mine and Lila's, if she had been silent about Alfonso for years, though she knew I had a close relationship with him? Was it possible that she hadn't realized Michele's absolute dependence on her, or for her own reasons had she decided not to say anything? On the other hand, I—how many things had I kept hidden from her?

For the rest of the day I inhabited a chaos of places, times, various people: the haunted Signora Manuela, the vacuous Rino, Gigliola in elementary school, Gigliola in middle school, Gigliola seduced by the potent good looks of the Solara boys, Gigliola dazzled by the Fiat 1100, and Michele who attracted women like Nino but, unlike him, was capable of an absolute passion, and Lila, Lila who had aroused that passion, a rapture that was fed not only by a craving for possession, by thuggish bragging, by revenge, by low-level desire, as she might say, but was an obsessive form of appreciation of a woman, not devotion, not subservience, but rather a sought-after form of male love, a complex feeling that was capable—with determination, with a kind of ferocity—of making a woman the chosen among women. I felt close to Gigliola, I understood her humiliation.

That night I went to see Lila and Enzo. I didn't say anything about that exploration I had made for love of her and also to protect the man she lived with. I took advantage instead of a moment when Lila was in the kitchen feeding the child to tell Enzo that she wanted to go back to the neighborhood. I decided not to hide my opinion. I said it didn't seem like a good idea to me, but that anything that could help stabilize her—she was healthy, she had only to regain some equilibrium—or that she considered such, should be encouraged. All the more since time had passed and, as far as I knew, in the neighborhood they wouldn't be worse off than in San Giovanni a Teduccio. Enzo shrugged.

"I have nothing against it. I'll have to get up earlier in the morning, return a little later in the evening."

"I saw that Don Carlo's old apartment is for rent. The children have gone to Caserta and the widow wants to join them."

"What's the rent?"

I told him: in the neighborhood the rents were lower than in San Giovanni a Teduccio.

"All right," Enzo agreed.

"You realize you'll have some problems anyway."

"There are problems here, too."

"The irritations will increase, and also the claims."

"We'll see."

"You'll stay with her?"

"As long as she wants, yes."

We joined Lila in the kitchen. She had just had a fight with Gennaro. Now that the child spent more time with his mother and less with the neighbor he was disoriented. He had less freedom, he was forced to give up a set of habits, and he rebelled by insisting, at the age of five, on being fed with a spoon. Lila had started yelling, he had thrown the plate, which shattered on the floor. When we went into the kitchen she had just slapped him. She said to me aggressively:

"Was it you who pretended the spoon was an airplane?"

"Just once."

"You shouldn't."

I said: "It won't happen again."

"No, never again, because you're going to be a writer and I have to waste my time like this."

Slowly she grew calmer, I wiped up the floor. Enzo told her that looking for a place in the neighborhood was fine with him, and I told her about Don Carlo's apartment, smothering my resentment. She listened unwillingly as she comforted the child, then she reacted as if it were Enzo who wanted to move, as if I were the one encouraging that choice. She said: All right, I'll do as you like.

The next day we all went to see the apartment. It was in poor condition, but Lila was enthusiastic: she liked that it was on the edge of the neighborhood, almost near the tunnel, and that from the windows you could see the gas pump of Carmen's fiancé. Enzo observed that at night they would be disturbed by the trucks that passed on the *stradone* and by the trains at the shunting yard. But since she found pleasure even in the sounds that had been part of our childhood, they came to an agreement with the widow for a suitable rent. From then on, every evening Enzo, instead of returning to San Giovanni a Teduccio, went to the neighborhood to carry out a series of improvements that would transform the apartment into a worthy home.

It was now almost May, the date of my wedding was approaching, and I was going back and forth to Florence. But Lila, as if she considered that deadline irrelevant, drew me into shopping for the finishing touches for the apartment. We bought a double bed, a cot for Gennaro, we went together to apply for a telephone line. People saw us on the street, some greeted only me, some both, others pretended not to have seen either of us. Lila seemed in any case relaxed. Once we ran into Ada; she was alone, she nodded cordially, and kept going as if she were in a hurry. Once we met Maria, Stefano's mother, Lila and I greeted her, she turned her head. Once Stefano himself passed in the car and stopped of his own initiative; he got out of the car, spoke only to me, cheerfully, asked about my wedding, praised Florence, where he had been recently with Ada and the child; finally patted Gennaro, gave a nod to Lila, and left. Once we saw Fernando, Lila's father: bent and very aged, he was standing in front of the elementary school, and Lila became agitated, she told Gennaro that she wanted him to meet his grandfather. I tried to restrain her, but she wanted to go anyway, and Fernando, behaving as if his daughter weren't present, looked at his grandson for a few seconds and said plainly, If you see your mother, tell her she's a whore, and went off.

But the most disturbing encounter, even if at the time it seemed the least significant, was a few days before she finally moved to the new apartment. Just as we came out of the house, we ran into Melina, who was holding by the hand her granddaughter Maria, the child of Stefano and Ada. She had her usual absent-minded air but she was nicely dressed, she had peroxided her hair, her face was heavily made up. She recognized me but not Lila, or maybe at first she chose to speak only to me. She talked to me as if I were still the girlfriend of her son, Antonio: she said that he would be back soon from Germany and that in his letters he always asked about me. I complimented her warmly on her dress and her hair, she seemed pleased. But she was even more pleased when I praised her granddaughter, who timidly clung to her grandmother's skirt. At that point she must have felt obliged to say something nice about Gennaro, and she turned to Lila: Is he your son? Only then did she seem to remember her. Until that moment she had stared at her without saying a word, and it must have occurred to her that here was the woman whose husband her own daughter Ada had taken. Her eyes were sunk deep in the large sockets, she said seriously: Lina, you've gotten ugly and thin, of course Stefano left you, men like flesh, otherwise they don't know where to put their hands and they leave. Then with a rapid jerk of her head she turned to Gennaro, and pointing to the little girl almost screamed: You know that's your sister? Give each other a kiss, come on, my goodness how cute you are. Gennaro immediately kissed the girl, who let herself be kissed without protesting, and Melina, seeing the two faces next to each other, exclaimed: They both take after their father, they're identical. After that statement, as if she had urgent things to do, she tugged her granddaughter and left without another word.

Lila had stood mute the whole time. But I understood that something extremely violent had happened to her, like the time when, as a child, she had seen Melina walking on the *stradone* eating soap flakes. As soon as the woman and the child were some distance away, she started, she ruffled her hair with one hand, she blinked, she said: I'll become like that. Then she tried to smooth her hair, saying:

"Did you hear what she said?"

"It's not true that you're ugly and skinny."

"Who gives a damn if I'm ugly and skinny, I'm talking about the resemblance."

"What resemblance?"

"Between the two children. Melina's right, they're both identical to Stefano."

"Come on, the girl is, but Gennaro is different."

She burst out laughing: after a long time her old, mean laugh was back.

She repeated: "They're two peas in a pod."

58.

I absolutely had to go. What I could do for her I had done, now I was in danger of getting caught up in useless reflections

on who the real father of Gennaro was, on how far-seeing
Melina was, on the secret motions of Lila's mind, on what she
knew or didn't know or supposed and didn't say, or was con-
venient for her to believe, and so on, in a spiral that was dam-
aging to me. We discussed that encounter, taking advantage of
the fact that Enzo was at work. I used clichés like: A woman
always knows who the father of her children is. I said: You
always felt that child was Nino's, in fact you wanted him for
that reason, and now you're sure it's Stefano's just because
crazy Melina said so? But she sneered, she said: What an idiot,
how could I not have known, and—something incomprehensible to me—she seemed pleased. So in the end I was silent. If
that new conviction helped her to feel better, good. And if it
was another sign of her instability, what could I do? Enough.
My book had been bought in France, Spain, and Germany, it
would be translated. I had published two more articles on
women working in factories in Campania, and *l'Unità* was content. From the publisher came solicitations for a new novel. In
other words, I had to take care of countless things of my own;
for Lila I had done all I could, and I couldn't continue to get
lost in the tangles of her life. In Milan, encouraged by Adele, I
bought a cream-colored suit for the wedding, it looked good
on me, the jacket was fitted, the skirt short. When I tried it on
I thought of Lila, of her gaudy wedding dress, of the photograph that the dressmaker had displayed in the shop window
on the Rettifilo, and the contrast made me feel definitively different. Her wedding, mine: worlds now far apart. I had told
her earlier that I wasn't getting married in a church, that I
wouldn't wear a traditional wedding dress, that Pietro had
barely agreed to the presence of close relatives.

"Why?" she had asked, but without particular interest.

"Why what?"

"Why aren't you getting married in church."

"We aren't believers."

"And the finger of God, the Holy Spirit?" she had quoted, reminding me of the article we had written together as girls.

"I'm grown up."

"But at least have a party, invite your friends."

"Pietro doesn't want to."

"You wouldn't invite even me?"

"Would you come?"

She laughed, shaking her head.

"No."

That was it. But in early May, when I had decided on a final venture before leaving the city for good, things took an unpleasant turn concerning my wedding, but not only that. I decided to go and see Professor Galiani. I looked for her number, I called. I said I was about to get married, I was going to live in Florence, I wanted to come and say goodbye to her. She, without surprise, without joy, but politely, invited me for five o'clock the next day. Before hanging up she said: Bring your friend, Lina, if you want.

Lila in that case didn't have to be asked twice, and she left Gennaro with Enzo. I put on makeup, I fixed my hair, I dressed according to the taste I had developed from Adele, and helped Lila to at least look respectable, since it was difficult to persuade her to dress up. She wanted to bring pastries, I said it wasn't suitable. Instead I bought a copy of my book, although I assumed that Professor Galiani had read it: I did it so that I would have a way of inscribing it to her.

We arrived punctually, rang the bell, silence. We rang again. Nadia opened the door, breathless, half dressed, without her usual courtesy, as if we had introduced disorder not only into her appearance but also into her manners. I explained that I had an appointment with her mother. She's not here, she said, but make yourselves comfortable in the living room. She disappeared. We remained mute, but exchanged little smiles of uneasiness in the silent house. Perhaps five minutes passed, finally steps could be heard in the hall. Pasquale appeared, slightly disheveled. Lila didn't show the least surprise, but I exclaimed, in real astonishment: What are you doing here? He answered seriously, unfriendly: What are *you two* doing here. And the phrase reversed the situation, I had to explain to him, as if that were his house, that I had an appointment with my professor.

"Ah," he said, and asked Lila, teasingly, "Are you recovered?"

"Pretty much."

"I'm glad."

I got angry, I answered for her, I said that Lila was only now beginning to get better and that anyway the Soccavo factory had been taught a lesson—the inspectors had paid a visit, the business had had to pay Lila everything she was owed.

"Yes?" he said just as Nadia reappeared, now immaculate, as if she were going out. "You understand, Nadia? Dottoressa Greco says she taught Soccavo a lesson."

I exclaimed: "Not me."

"Not her, God Almighty taught Soccavo a lesson."

Nadia gave a slight smile, crossed the room and although there was a sofa free she sat on Pasquale's lap. I felt ill at ease.

"I only tried to help Lina."

Pasquale put his arm around Nadia's waist, leaned toward me, said:

"Excellent. You mean that in all the factories, at all the construction sites, in every corner of Italy and the world, as soon as the owner kicks up a fuss and the workers are in danger, we'll call Elena Greco: she telephones her friends, the labor authority, her connections in high places, and resolves the situation."

He had never spoken to me like that, not even when I was a girl and he seemed to me already adult, and acted like a political expert. I was offended, and was about to answer, but Nadia interrupted, ignoring me. She spoke to Lila, in her slow little voice, as if it were not worth the trouble to speak to me.

"The labor inspectors don't count for anything, Lina. They went to Soccavo, they filled out their forms, but then? In the factory everything is the same as before. And meanwhile those who spoke out are in trouble, those who were silent got a few lire under the counter, the police charged us, and the fascists came right here and beat up Armando."

She hadn't finished speaking when Pasquale started talking to me more harshly than before, this time raising his voice:

"Explain to us what the fuck you thought you resolved," he said, with genuine pain and disappointment. "You know what the situation is in Italy? Do you have any idea what the class struggle is?"

"Don't shout, please," Nadia asked him, then she turned again to Lila, almost whispering: "Comrades do not abandon one another."

She answered: "It would have failed anyway."

"What do you mean?"

"In that place you don't win with leaflets or even by fighting with the fascists."

"How do you win?"

Lila was silent, and Pasquale, now turning to her, hissed:

"You win by mobilizing the good friends of the owners? You win by getting a little money and screwing everyone else?"

Then I burst out: "Pasquale, stop it." Involuntarily I, too, raised my voice. "What kind of tone is that? It wasn't like that."

I wanted to explain, silence him, even though I felt an emptiness in my head, I didn't know what arguments to resort to, and the only concept that occurred to me readily was malicious and politically useless: You treat me like this because, now that you've got your hands on this young lady from a good family, you're full of yourself? But Lila, here, stopped me with a completely unexpected gesture of irritation, which confused me. She said:

"That's enough, Lenù, they're right."

I was upset. They were right? I wanted to respond, to get angry at her. What did she mean? But just then Professor Galiani arrived: her footsteps could be heard in the hall.

59.

I hoped that the professor hadn't heard me shouting. But at the same time I wanted to see Nadia jump off Pasquale's lap and hurry over to the sofa, I wished to see both of them humiliated by the need to pretend an absence of intimacy. I noticed that Lila, too, looked at them sardonically. But they stayed where they were; Nadia, in fact, put an arm around Pasquale's neck, as if she were afraid of falling, and said to her mother, who had just appeared in the doorway: Next time, tell me if you're having visitors. The professor didn't answer, she turned to us coldly: I'm sorry I was late, let's sit in my study. We followed her, while Pasquale moved Nadia off him, saying in a tone that seemed to me suddenly depressed: Come on, let's go.

Professor Galiani led us along the hall muttering irritably: What really bothers me is the boorishness. We entered an airy room with an old desk, a lot of books, sober, cushioned chairs. She assumed a polite tone, but it was clear that she was struggling with a bad mood. She said she was happy to see me and to see Lila again; yet at every word, and between the words, I felt her rage increasing, and I wanted to leave as quickly as possible. I apologized for not having come to see her, and went on somewhat breathlessly about studying, the book, the innumerable things that had overwhelmed me, my engagement, my approaching marriage.

"Are you getting married in church or only in a civil service?"

"Only a civil service."

"Good for you."

She turned to Lila, to draw her into the conversation: "You were married in church?"

"Yes."

"Are you a believer?"

"No."

"Then why did you get married in church?"

"That's what's done."

"You don't always have to do things just because they're done."

"We do a lot of them."

"Will you go to Elena's wedding?"

"She didn't invite me."

I was startled, I said right away:

"It's not true."

Lila laughed harshly: "It's true, she's ashamed of me."

Her tone was ironic, but I felt wounded anyway. What was happening to her? Why had she said earlier, in front of Nadia and Pasquale, that I was wrong, and now was making that hostile remark in front of the professor?

"Nonsense," I said, and to calm down I took the book out of my bag and handed it to Professor Galiani, saying: I wanted to give you this. She looked at it for a moment without seeing it, perhaps following her own thoughts, then she thanked me, and saying that she already had a copy, gave it back:

"What does your husband do?"

"He's a professor of Latin literature in Florence."

"Is he a lot older than you?"

"He's twenty-seven."

"So young, already a professor?"

"He's very smart."

"What's his name?"

"Pietro Airota."

Professor Galiani looked at me attentively, like when I was at school and I gave an answer that she considered incomplete.

"Relative of Guido Airota?"

"He's his son."

She smiled with explicit malice.

"Good marriage."

"We love each other."

"Have you already started another book?"

"I'm trying."

"I saw that you're writing for *l'Unità*."

"A bit."

"I don't write for it anymore, it's a newspaper of bureaucrats."

She turned again to Lila, she seemed to want to let her know how much she liked her. She said to her:

"It's remarkable what you did in the factory."

Lila grimaced in annoyance.

"I didn't do anything."

"That's not true."

The professor got up, rummaged through the papers on the desk, and showed her some pages as if they were an incontrovertible truth.

"Nadia left this around the house and I took the liberty of reading it. It's a courageous, new work, very well written. I wanted to see you so that I could tell you that."

She was holding in her hand the pages that Lila had written, and from which I had taken my first article for *l'Unità*.

60.

Oh yes, it was really time to get out. I left the Galiani house embittered, my mouth dry, without the courage to say to the professor that she didn't have the right to treat me like that. She hadn't said anything about my book, although she'd had it for some time and surely had read it or at least skimmed it. She hadn't asked for a dedication in the copy I had brought for that reason and when, before leaving—out of weakness, out of a need to end that relationship affectionately—I had offered anyway, she hadn't answered, she had smiled, and continued to talk to Lila. Above all, she had said nothing about my articles, rather she had mentioned them only to include them in her negative opinion of *l'Unità*, and then pulled out Lila's pages and began to talk to her as if my opinion on the subject didn't count, as if I were no longer in the room. I would have liked to yell: Yes, it's true, Lila has a tremendous intelligence, an intelligence that I've always recognized, that I love, that's influenced everything I've done; but I've worked hard to develop mine and I've been successful, I'm valued everywhere, I'm not a pretentious nobody like your daughter. Instead, I listened silently while they talked about work and the factory and the workers demands. They kept talking, even on the landing, until Professor Galiani absently said goodbye to me, while to Lila she said, now using the familiar *tu*, Stay in touch, and embraced her. I felt humiliated. Moreover, Pasquale and Nadia hadn't returned, I hadn't had a chance to refute them and my anger at them was still raging inside me: why was it wrong to help a friend, to do it I had taken a risk, how could they dare to criticize what I'd done. Now, on the stairs, in the lobby, on the sidewalk of Corso Vittorio Emanuele, it was only Lila and me. I was ready to shout at her: Do you really think I'm ashamed of you, what were you thinking, why did you say those two were right, you're ungrateful, I did all I could to stay close to you, to be useful to you, and you treat me like that, you really have a sick mind. But as soon as we were outside, even before I could open my mouth (and on the other hand what would have changed if I had?), she took me by the arm and began to defend me against Professor Galiani.

I couldn't find a single opening in order to reproach her for aligning herself with Pasquale and Nadia, or for the senseless accusation that I didn't want her at my wedding. She behaved as if it had been another Lila who said those things, a Lila of whom she herself knew nothing and whom it was pointless to ask for explanations. What terrible people—she began, and spoke without stopping all the way to the subway at Piazza Amedeo—did you see how the old woman treated you, she wanted to get revenge, she can't bear that you write books and articles, she can't bear that you're about to marry well, she especially can't bear that Nadia, brought up precisely to be the best of all, Nadia who was to give her so much satisfaction, isn't up to anything good, is sleeping with a construction worker and acting like a whore right in front of her: no, she can't bear it, but you're wrong to be upset, forget about it, you shouldn't have left her your book, you shouldn't have asked if she wanted it inscribed, you especially shouldn't have done that, those are people who should be treated with a kick in the ass, your weakness is that you're too good, you swallow every- thing that educated people say as if they're the only ones who had a mind, but it's not true, relax, go, get married, have a hon- eymoon, you were too worried about me, write another novel, you know that I expect great things from you, I love you.

I simply listened, overwhelmed. With her, there was no way to feel that things were settled; every fixed point of our relation- ship sooner or later turned out to be provisional; something shifted in her head that unbalanced her and unbalanced me. I couldn't understand if those words were in fact intended to apologize to me, or if she was lying, concealing feelings that she had no intention of confiding to me, or if she was aiming at a final farewell. Certainly she was false, and she was ungrateful, and I, in spite of all that had changed for me, continued to feel inferior. I felt that I would never free myself from that inferior- ity, and that seemed to me intolerable. I wished—and I couldn't keep the wish at bay—that the cardiologist had been wrong, that Armando had been right, that she really was ill and would die.

For years after that, we didn't see each other, we only talked on the phone. We became for each other fragments of a voice, without any visual corroboration. But the wish that she would die remained in a far corner, I tried to get rid of it but it would- n't go away.

61.

The night before I left for Florence I couldn't sleep. Of all the painful thoughts the most persistent had to do with Pasquale. His criticisms burned me. At first I had rejected them altogether, now I was wavering between the conviction that they were undeserved and the idea that if Lila said he was right maybe I really had been mistaken. Finally I did some- thing I had never done: I got out of bed at four in the morning and left the house by myself, before dawn. I felt very unhappy; I wished something terrible would happen to me, an event that, punishing me for my mistaken actions and my wicked thoughts, would as a result punish Lila, too. But nothing hap- pened. I walked for a long time on the deserted streets, which were much safer than when they were crowded. The sky turned violet. I reached the sea, a gray sheet under a pale sky with scattered pink-edged clouds. The mass of Castel dell'Ovo was cut sharply in two by the light, a shining ochre shape on the Vesuvius side, a brown stain on the Mergellina and Posillipo side. The road along the cliff was empty, the sea made no sound but gave off an intense odor. Who knows what feel- ing I would have had about Naples, about myself, if I had waked every morning not in my neighborhood but in one of those buildings along the shore. What am I seeking? To change my origins? To change, along with myself, others, too? Repopulate this now deserted city with citizens not assailed by poverty or greed, not bitter or angry, who could delight in the splendor of the landscape like the divinities who once inhabited it? Indulge my demon, give him a good life and feel happy? I had used the power of the Airotas, people who for generations had been fighting for socialism, people who were on the side of men and women like Pasquale and Lila, not because I thought I would be fixing all the broken things of the world but because I was in a position to help a person I loved, and it seemed wrong not to do so. Had I acted badly? Should I have left Lila in trouble? Never again, never again would I lift a finger for anyone. I departed, I went to get married.

62.

I don't remember anything about my wedding. A few photographs, acting as props, rather than inspiring memory, have frozen it around a few images: Pietro with an absent-minded expression, me looking angry, my mother, who is out of focus but manages nevertheless to appear unhappy. Or not. It's the ceremony itself that I can't remember, but I have in mind the long discussion I had with Pietro a few days before we got married. I told him that I intended to take the Pill in order not to have children, that it seemed to me urgent to try first of all to write another book. I was sure that he would immediately agree. Instead, surprisingly, he was opposed. First he made it a problem of legality, the Pill was not yet officially for sale; then he said there were rumors that it ruined one's health; then he made a complicated speech about sex, love, and reproduction; finally he stammered that someone who really has to write will write anyway, even if she is expecting a baby. I was unhappy, I was angry, that reaction seemed to me not consistent with the educated youth who wanted only a civil marriage, and I told him so. We quarreled. Our wedding day arrived and we were not reconciled: he was mute, I cold.

There was another surprise, too, that hasn't faded: the

reception. We had decided to get married, greet our relatives, and go home without any sort of celebration. That decision had developed through the combination of Pietro's ascetic tendency and my intention to demonstrate that I no longer belonged to the world of my mother. But our line of conduct was secretly undone by Adele. She dragged us to the house of a friend of hers, for a toast, she said; and there, instead, Pietro and I found ourselves at the center of a big reception, in a very aristocratic Florentine dwelling, among a large number of relatives of the Airotas and famous and very famous people who lingered until evening. My husband became taciturn, I wondered, bewildered, why, since in fact it was a celebration for *my* wedding, I had had to be limited to inviting only my immediate family. I said to Pietro:

"Did you know this was happening?"

"No."

For a while we confronted the situation together. But soon he evaded the attempts of his mother and sister to introduce him to this man, to that woman; he entrenched himself in a corner with my relatives and talked to them the whole time. At first I resigned myself, somewhat uneasily, to inhabiting the trap we had fallen into, then I began to find it exciting that well-known politicians, prestigious intellectuals, young revolutionaries, even a well-known poet and a famous novelist showed interest in me, in my book, and spoke admiringly of my articles in *l'Unità*. The time flew by, I felt more and more accepted in the world of the Airotas. Even my father-in-law wanted to detain me, questioning me kindly on my knowledge of labor matters. A small group formed, of people engaged in the debate, in newspapers and journals, over the tide of demands that was rising in Italy. And me, here I was, with them, and it was my celebration, and I was at the center of the conversation.

At some point, my father-in-law warmly praised an essay,

published in *Mondo Operaio,* that in his view laid out the problem of democracy in Italy with crystalline intelligence. Drawing on a large number of facts, the piece demonstrated that, as long as the state television, the big papers, the schools, the universities, the judiciary worked day after day to solidify the dominant ideology, the electoral system would in fact be rigged, and the workers' parties would never have enough votes to govern. Nods of assent, supporting citations, references to this article and that one. Finally, Professor Airota, with all his authority, mentioned the name of the author of the article, and I knew even before he uttered it—Giovanni Sarratore—that it was Nino. I was so happy that I couldn't contain myself, I said I knew him, I called Adele over to confirm to her husband and the others how brilliant my Neapolitan friend was.

Nino was present at my wedding even if he wasn't present, and speaking of him I felt authorized to talk also about myself, about the reasons I had become involved in the workers' struggle, about the need to provide the parties and parliamentary representatives on the left with hard data so that they could address the delays in their understanding of the current political and economic period, and so on with other stock phrases I had learned only recently but used with assurance. I felt clever. My mood brightened; I enjoyed being with my in-laws and feeling admired by their friends. At the end, when my relatives timidly said goodbye and hurried off somewhere to wait for the first train to take them back to Naples, I no longer felt irritated with Pietro. He must have realized it, because he, in turn, softened, and the tension vanished.

As soon as we got to our apartment and closed the door we began to make love. At first it was very pleasurable, but the day reserved for me yet another surprising fact. Antonio, my first boyfriend, when he rubbed against me was quick and intense; Franco made great efforts to contain himself but at a certain point he pulled away with a gasp, or when he had a condom stopped suddenly and seemed to become heavier, crushing me under his weight and laughing in my ear. Pietro, on the other hand, strained for a time that seemed endless. His thrusting was deliberate, violent, so that the initial pleasure slowly diminished, overwhelmed by the monotonous insistence and the hurt I felt in my stomach. He was covered with sweat from his long exertions, maybe from suffering, and when I saw his damp face and neck, touched his wet back, desire disappeared completely. But he didn't realize it, he continued to withdraw and then sink into me forcefully, rhythmically, without stopping. I didn't know what to do. I caressed him, I whispered words of love, and yet I hoped that he would stop. When he exploded with a roar and collapsed, finally exhausted, I was content, even though I was hurting and unsatisfied.

He didn't stay in bed long; he got up and went to the bathroom. I waited for him for a few minutes, but I was tired, I fell asleep. I woke with a start after an hour and realized that he hadn't come back to bed. I found him in his study, at the desk.

"What are you doing?"

He smiled at me.

"I'm working."

"Come to bed."

"You go, I'll join you later."

I'm sure that I became pregnant that night.

63.

As soon as I discovered that I was expecting a child I was overwhelmed by anxiety and I called my mother. Although our relationship had always been contentious, in that situation the need to talk to her prevailed. It was a mistake: she immediately started nagging. She wanted to leave Naples, settle in with me, help me, guide me, or, vice versa, bring me to the neighborhood, have me back in her house, entrust me to the old midwife who had delivered all her children. I had a hard time putting her off, I said that a gynecologist friend of my mother-in-law was looking after me, a great professor, and I would give birth in his clinic. She was offended. She hissed: you prefer your mother-in-law to me. She didn't call again.

After a few days, on the other hand, I heard from Lila. We had had some telephone conversations after I left, but brief, a few minutes, we didn't want to spend too much, she cheerful, I aloof, she asking ironically about my life as a newlywed, I inquiring seriously about her health. This time I realized that something wasn't right.

"Are you angry with me?" she asked.

"No, why should I be?"

"You don't tell me anything. I got the news only because your mother is bragging to everyone that you're pregnant."

"I just got the confirmation."

"I thought you were taking the Pill."

I was embarrassed.

"Yes, but then I decided not to."

"Why?"

"The years are passing."

"And the book you're supposed to write?"

"I'll see later."

"You'd better."

"I'll do what I can."

"You have to do the maximum."

"I'll try."

"I'm taking the Pill."

"So with Enzo it's going well?"

"Pretty well, but I don't ever want to be pregnant again."

She was silent, and I didn't say anything, either. When she began talking once more, she told me about the first time she had realized she was expecting a baby, and the second. She described both as terrible experiences: the second time, she said, I was sure the baby was Nino's and even though I felt sick I was happy. But, happy or not, you'll see, the body suffers, it doesn't like losing its shape, there's too much pain. From there she went on in a crescendo that got darker and darker, telling me things she had told me before but never with the same desire to pull me into her suffering, so that I, too, would feel it. She seemed to want to prepare me for what awaited me, she was very worried about me and my future. This life of another, she said, clings to you in the womb first and then, when it finally comes out, it takes you prisoner, keeps you on a leash, you're no longer your own master. With great animation she sketched every phase of my maternity, tracing it over hers, expressing herself with her habitual effectiveness. It's as if you fabricated your very own torture, she exclaimed, and I realized then that she wasn't capable of thinking that she was her self and I was my self; it seemed to her inconceivable that I could have a pregnancy different from hers, and a different feeling about children. She so took it for granted that I would have the same troubles that she seemed ready to consider any possible joy I found in motherhood a betrayal.

I didn't want to listen to her anymore, I held the receiver away from my ear, she was scaring me. We said goodbye coolly.

"If you need me," she said, "let me know."

"All right."

"You helped me, now I want to help you."

"All right."

That phone call didn't help me at all; rather, it left me unsettled. I lived in a city I knew nothing about, even if thanks to Pietro I now was acquainted with every corner of it, which I could not say of Naples. I loved the path along the river, I took beautiful walks, but I didn't like the color of the houses, it put me in a bad mood. The teasing tone of the inhabitants—the porter in our building, the butcher, the baker, the mailman—incited me to become teasing, too, and a hostility with no motivation emerged from it. And then the many friends of my in-laws, so available on the day of the wedding, had never showed up again, nor did Pietro have any intention of seeing them. I felt alone and fragile. I bought some books on how to become a perfect mother and prepared with my usual diligence.

Days passed, weeks, but, surprisingly, the pregnancy didn't weigh on me at all; in fact it made me feel light. The nausea was negligible, I felt no breakdown in my body, in my mood, in the wish to be active. I was in the fourth month when my book received an important prize that brought me greater fame and a little more money. I went to the prize ceremony in spite of the political climate, which was hostile to that type of recognition, feeling that I was in a state of grace; I was proud of myself, with a sense of physical and intellectual fullness that made me bold, expansive. In the thank-you speech I went overboard, I said I felt as happy as the astronauts on the white expanse of the moon. A couple of days later, since I felt strong, I telephoned Lila to tell her about the prize. I wanted to let her know that things were not going as she had predicted, that in fact they were going smoothly, that I was satisfied. I felt so pleased with myself that I wanted to skip over the unhappiness she had caused me. But Lila had read in *Il Mattino*—only the Naples papers had devoted a few lines to the prize—that phrase of mine about the astronauts, and, without giving me time to speak, she criticized me harshly. The white expanse of the moon, she said ironically, sometimes it's better to say nothing than to talk nonsense. And she added that the moon was a rock among billions of other rocks, and that, as far as rocks go, the best thing was to stand with your feet planted firmly in the troubles of the earth.

I felt a viselike grip in my stomach. Why did she continue to wound me? Didn't she want me to be happy? Or maybe she hadn't recovered and her illness had heightened her mean side? Bitter words came to me, but I couldn't utter them. As if she didn't even realize she had hurt me, or as if she felt she had the right, she went on to tell me what was happening to her, in a very friendly tone. She had made peace with her brother, with her mother, even with her father; she had quarreled with Michele Solara on the old matter of the label on the shoes and the money he owed Rino; she had been in touch with Stefano to claim that, at least from the economic point of view, he should act as Gennaro's father, too, and not just Maria's. Her remarks were irascible, sometimes vulgar: against Rino, the Solaras, Stefano. And at the end she asked, as if she had an urgent need for my opinion: Did I do the right thing? I didn't answer. I had won an important prize and she had mentioned only that phrase about the astronauts. I asked her, maybe to offend her, if she still had those symptoms that unglued her head from her body. She said no, she repeated a couple of times that she was very well, she said with a mocking laugh: Only, sometimes out of the corner of my eye I see people coming out of the furniture. Then she asked me: Is everything all right with the pregnancy? Good, very good, I said, never felt better.

I traveled a lot in those months. I was invited here and there not only because of my book but also because of the articles I was writing, which in turn forced me to travel to see close up the new kinds of strike, the reactions of the owners. I never thought of trying to become a freelance journalist. I did it because doing it I was happy. I felt disobedient, in revolt and inflated with such power that my meekness seemed a disguise. In fact it enabled me to join the pickets in front of the factories, to talk to workers, both men and women, and to union officials, to slip out among the policemen. Nothing frightened me. When the Banca di Agricoltura in Milan was bombed I was in the city, at the publisher's, but I wasn't alarmed, I didn't have dark presentiments. I thought of myself as part of an unstoppable force,

I thought I was invulnerable. No one could hurt me and my child. We two were the only enduring reality, I visible and he (or she: but Pietro wanted a boy) for now invisible. The rest was a flow of air, an immaterial wave of images and sounds that, whether disastrous or beneficial, constituted material for my work. It passed by or it loomed so that I could put it into magic words in a story, an article, a speech, taking care that nothing ended up outside the frame, and that every concept pleased the Airotas, the publishing house, Nino, who surely somewhere was reading me, even Pasquale, why not, and Nadia, and Lila, all of whom would finally have to think: Look, we were wrong about Lena, she's on our side, see what she's writing.

It was a particularly intense time, that period of the pregnancy. It surprised me that being pregnant made me more eager to make love. It was I who initiated it, embraced Pietro, kissing him, even though he had no interest in kissing and began almost immediately to make love in that prolonged, painful way of his. Afterward he got up and worked until late. I slept for an hour or two, then I woke up, found him gone, turned on the light, and read until I was tired. Then I went to his room, insisted that he come to bed. He obeyed, but he got up early: sleep seemed to frighten him. Whereas I slept until midday.

There was only one event that distressed me. I was in my seventh month and my belly was heavy. I was outside the Nuovo Pignone factory when scuffles broke out, and I hurried away. Maybe I made a wrong movement, I don't know, I felt a painful spasm in the center of my right buttock that extended along my leg like a hot wire. I limped home, went to bed, and it passed. But every so often the pain reappeared, radiating through my thigh toward my groin. I learned to respond by finding positions that alleviated it, but when I realized that I was starting to limp all the time I was terrified, and I went to the gynecologist. He reassured me, saying that everything was in order, the weight I was carrying in my womb tired me out, causing this slight sciatica. Why are you so worried, he asked in an affectionate tone, you're such a serene person. I lied, I said I didn't know. In reality I knew perfectly well: I was afraid that my mother's gait had caught up with me, that she had settled in my body, that I would limp forever, like her.

I was soothed by the reassurances of the gynecologist; the pain lasted for a while longer, then disappeared. Pietro forbade me to do other foolish things, no more running around. I admitted that he was right, and spent the last weeks of my pregnancy reading; I wrote almost nothing. Our daughter was born on February 12, 1970, at five-twenty in the morning. We called her Adele, even though my mother-in-law kept repeating, poor child, Adele is a terrible name, give her any other name, but not that. I had atrocious labor pains, but they didn't last long. When the baby emerged and I saw her, black-haired, a violet organism that, full of energy, writhed and wailed, I felt a physical pleasure so piercing that I still know no other pleasure that compares to it. We didn't baptize her; my mother screamed terrible things on the telephone, she swore she would never come to see her. She'll calm down, I thought, sadly, and anyway if she doesn't it's her loss.

As soon as I was back on my feet I telephoned Lila, I didn't want her to be angry that I hadn't told her anything.

"It was a wonderful experience," I told her.

"What?"

"The pregnancy, the birth. Adele is beautiful, and very good."

She answered: "Each of us narrates our life as it suits us."

64.

What a tangle of threads with untraceable origins I discovered in myself in that period. They were old and faded, very new, sometimes bright-colored, sometimes colorless, extremely thin, almost invisible. That state of well-being ended suddenly, just when it seemed to me that I had escaped Lila's prophecies. The baby became troublesome, and the oldest parts of that jumble surfaced as if stirred by a distracted gesture. At first, when we were still in the clinic, she attached herself easily to my breast, but once we were home something went wrong and she didn't want me anymore. She sucked for a few seconds, then shrieked like a furious little animal. I felt weak, vulnerable to old superstitions. What was happening to her? Were my nipples too small, did they slip out? Did she not like my milk? Or was it an aversion toward me, her mother, had she been inoculated remotely with an evil spell?

An ordeal began, as we went from doctor to doctor, she and I alone; Pietro was always busy at the university. My bosom, swollen uselessly, hurt; I had burning stones in my breasts; I imagined infections, amputations. To empty them, to get enough milk to nourish the baby with a bottle, to alleviate the pain, I tortured myself with a breast pump. I whispered, coaxing her: come on, sweetie, suck, such a good baby, so sweet, what a dear little mouth, what dear little eyes, what's the matter. In vain. First I decided, regretfully, to try mixed feeding, then I gave up on that, too. I tried artificial milk, which required lengthy preparations night and day, a tiresome system of sterilizing nipples and bottles, an obsessive check of her weight before and after feeding, a sense of guilt every time she had diarrhea. Sometimes I thought of Silvia, who, in the turbulent atmosphere of the student gathering in Milan, breast-fed Nino's child, Mirko, so easily. Why not me? I suffered long secret crying spells.

For a few days the baby settled down. I was relieved, hoping the moment had arrived to get my life back in order. But the reprieve lasted less than a week. In her first year of life the baby barely closed her eyes; her tiny body writhed and screamed for hours, with an unsuspected energy and endurance. She was quiet only if I carried her around the house, holding her tight in my arms, speaking to her: Now mamma's splendid creature is good, now she's quiet, now she's resting, now she's sleeping. But the splendid creature wouldn't sleep, she seemed to fear sleep, like her father. What was wrong: a stomach ache, hunger, fear of abandonment because I hadn't breast-fed her, the evil eye, a demon that had entered her body? And what was wrong with me? What poison had polluted my milk? And the leg? Was it imagination or was the pain returning? My mother's fault? Did she want to punish me because I had been trying all my life not to be like her? Or was there something else?

One night I seemed to hear the sound of Gigliola's voice, faint, repeating throughout the neighborhood that Lila had a tremendous power, that she could cast an evil spell by fire, that she smothered the creatures in her belly. I was ashamed of myself, I tried to resist, I needed rest. So I tried leaving the baby to Pietro, who thanks to his habit of studying at night wasn't so tired. I said: I'm exhausted, call me in a couple of hours, and I went to bed and fell asleep as if I had lost consciousness. But once I was wakened by the baby's desperate wailing, I waited; it didn't stop. I got up. I discovered that Pietro had dragged the crib into his study and, paying no attention to his daughter's cries, was bent over his books, taking notes as if he were deaf. I lost all my manners, and regressed, insulting him in my dialect. You don't give a damn about anything, that stuff is more important than your daughter? My husband, distant, cool, asked me to leave the room, take away the crib. He had an important article to finish for an English journal, the deadline was very near. From then on I stopped asking him for help and if he offered I said: Go on, thanks, I know you have things to do. After dinner he hung around me uncertain, awkward, then he closed himself in his study and worked until late at night.

65.

I felt abandoned but with the impression that I deserved it: I wasn't capable of providing tranquility for my daughter. Yet I kept going, doggedly, even though I was more and more frightened. My organism was rejecting the role of mother. And no matter how I denied the pain in my leg by doing everything possible to ignore it, it had returned, and was getting worse. But I persisted, I wore myself out taking charge of everything. Since the building had no elevator, I carried the stroller with the baby in it up and down, I did the shopping, came home loaded down with bags, I cleaned the house, I cooked, I thought: I'm becoming ugly and old before my time, like the women of the neighborhood. And naturally, just when I was particularly desperate, Lila telephoned.

As soon as I heard her voice I felt like yelling at her: What have you done to me, everything was going smoothly and now, suddenly, what you said is happening, the baby is sick, I'm limping, it's impossible, I can't bear it anymore. But I managed to restrain myself in time, I said quietly, everything's fine, the baby's a little fussy and right now she's not growing much, but she's wonderful, I'm happy. Then, with feigned interest, I asked about Enzo, Gennaro, her relations with Stefano, her brother, the neighborhood, if she had had other problems with Bruno Soccavo and Michele. She answered in an ugly, obscene, aggressive dialect, but mostly without rage. Soccavo, she said, has to bleed. And when I run into Michele I spit in his face. As for Gennaro, she now referred to him explicitly as Stefano's son, saying, he's stocky like his father, and she laughed when I said he's such a nice little boy. She said: You're such a good little mamma, you take him. In those phrases I heard the sarcasm of someone who knew, thanks to some mysterious secret power, what was really happening to me, and I felt rancor, but I became even more insistent with my charade—listen to what a sweet voice Dede has, it's really pleasant here in Florence, I'm reading an interesting book by Baran—and I kept going until she forced me to end it by telling me about the IBM course that Enzo had started.

Only of him did she speak with respect, at length, and right afterward she asked about Pietro.

"Everything's going well with your husband?"

"Very well."

"And for me with Enzo."

When she hung up, her voice left a trail of images and sounds of the past that stayed in my mind for hours: the court-yard, the dangerous games, the doll she had thrown into the cellar, the dark stairs we climbed to Don Achille's to retrieve it, her wedding, her generosity and her meanness, how she had taken Nino. She can't tolerate my good fortune, I thought fearfully, she wants me with her again, under her, supporting her in her affairs, in her wretched neighborhood wars. Then I said to myself: How stupid I've been, what use has my education been, and I pretended everything was under control. To my sister Elisa, who called frequently, I said that being a mother was wonderful. To Carmen Peluso, who told me about her marriage to the gas-pump owner on the *stradone*, I responded: What good news, I wish you every happiness, say hello to Pasquale, what's he up to. With my mother, the rare times she called, I pretended I was ecstatic, but once I broke down and asked her: What happened to your leg, why do you limp. She answered: What does it matter to you, mind your own business.

I struggled for months, trying to keep at bay the more opaque parts of myself. Occasionally I surprised myself by praying to the Madonna, even though I considered myself an atheist, and was ashamed. More often, when I was alone in the house with the baby, I let out terrible cries, not words, only breath spilling out along with despair. But that difficult period wouldn't end; it was a grueling, tormented time. At night, I carried the baby up and down the hall, limping. I no longer whispered sweet nonsense phrases, I ignored her and tried to think of myself. I was always holding a book, a journal, even though I hardly managed to read anything. During the day, when Adele slept peacefully—at first I called her Ade, without realizing how it sounded like Hades, a hell summed up in two syllables, so that when Pietro pointed it out I was embarrassed and began calling her Dede—I tried to write for the newspaper. But I no longer had time—and certainly not the desire—to travel around on behalf of *l'Unità*. So the things I wrote had no energy, they were merely demonstrations of my formal skill, flourishes lacking substance. Once, having written an article, I had Pietro read it before dictating it to the editorial office. He said: "It's empty."

"In what sense?"

"It's just words."

I felt offended, and dictated it just the same. It wasn't published. And from then on, with a certain embarrassment, both the local and the national editorial offices began to reject my texts, citing problems of space. I suffered, I felt that everything that up to a short time earlier I had taken as an unquestioned condition of life and work was rapidly collapsing around me, as if violently jolted from inaccessible depths. I read just to keep my eyes on a book or a newspaper, but it was as if I had stopped at the signs and no longer had access to the meanings. Two or three times I came across articles by Nino, but reading them didn't give me the usual pleasure of imagining him, of hearing his voice, of enjoying his thoughts. I was happy for him, certainly: if he was writing it meant that he was well, he was living his life who knows where, with who knows whom.

But I stared at the signature, I read a few lines, I retreated, as if every one of his sentences, black on white, made my situation even more unbearable. I lost interest in things, I couldn't even bother with my appearance. And besides, for whom would I bother? I saw no one, only Pietro, who treated me courteously, but I perceived that for him I was a shadow. At times I seemed to think with his mind and I imagined I felt his unhappiness. Marrying me had only complicated his existence as a scholar, and just when his fame was growing, especially in England and the United States. I admired him, and yet he irritated me. I always spoke to him with a mixture of resentment and inferiority.

Stop it, I ordered myself one day, forget *l'Unità*, it will be enough if I can find the right approach for a new book: as soon as it's done, everything will be in order. But what book? To my mother-in law, to the publisher, I claimed that I was at a good point, but I was lying, I lied on every occasion in the friendliest tones. In fact all I had was notebooks crammed with idle notes, nothing else. And when I opened them, at night or during the day, according to the schedule that Dede imposed on me, I fell asleep without realizing it. One late afternoon Pietro returned from the university and found me in a condition worse than the one I had surprised him in some time earlier: I was in the kitchen, fast sleep, with my head resting on the table; the baby had missed her feeding and was screaming, off in the bedroom. Her father found her in the crib, half naked, forgotten. When Dede calmed down, greedily attached to the bottle, Pietro said in despair: "Is it possible that you don't have anyone who could help you?"

"Not in this city, and you know that perfectly well."

"Have your mother come, your sister."

"I don't want to."

"Then ask your friend in Naples: you did so much for her, she'll do the same for you."

I started. For a fraction of a second, part of me had the clear sensation that Lila was in the house already, present: if once she had been hiding inside me, now, with her narrow eyes, her furrowed brow, she had slipped into Dede. I shook my head energetically. Get rid of that image, that possibility, what was I looking onto?

Pietro resigned himself to calling his mother. Reluctantly he asked her if she could come and stay with us for a little while.

66.

I entrusted myself to my mother-in-law with an immediate sense of relief, and here, too, she showed herself to be the woman I would have liked to resemble. In the space of a few days she found a big girl named Clelia, barely twenty, and originally from the Maremma, to whom she gave detailed instructions about taking care of the house, the shopping, the cooking. When Pietro found Clelia in the house without even having been consulted he made a gesture of annoyance.

"I don't want slaves in my house," he said.

Adele answered calmly: "She's not a slave, she's a salaried employee."

And I, fortified by the presence of my mother-in-law, stammered: "Do you think I should be a slave?"

"You're a mother, not a slave."

"I wash and iron your clothes, I clean the house, I cook for you, I've given you a daughter, I bring her up in the midst of endless difficulties, I'm worn out."

"And who makes you do that, have I ever asked you for anything?"

I couldn't bear to argue, but Adele did, she crushed her son with a sometimes ferocious sarcasm, and Clelia remained. Then she took the child away from me, carried the crib into the

room I had given her, managed with great precision the schedule of bottles both at night and during the day. When she
noticed that I was limping, she took me to a doctor, a friend of
hers, who prescribed various injections. She herself appeared
every morning and every evening with the syringe and the vials,
to blithely stick the needle into my buttocks. I felt better right
away, the pain in my leg disappeared, my mood improved, I
was happier. But Adele didn't stop there. She politely insisted
that I attend to myself, she sent me to the hairdresser, made me
go back to the dentist. And above all she talked to me constantly about the theater, the cinema, a book she was translat-
ing, another she was editing, what her husband or other
famous people whom she called familiarly by name had written in this or that journal. From her I heard for the first time
about the new radical feminist tracts. Mariarosa knew the
women who were writing them; she was infatuated with them,
admired them. Not Adele. She said with her usual ironic attitude that they went on and on about the feminist question as if
it could be dealt with separately from the class conflict. Read
them anyway, she advised me, and left me a couple of those little volumes with a final cryptic phrase: Don't miss anything, if
you want to be a writer. I put them aside, I didn't want to waste
time with writings that Adele herself disparaged. But I also felt,
just then, that in no way did my mother-in-law's cultivated conversation arise from a true need to exchange ideas with me.
Adele intended to systematically pull me out of the desperate
state of an incompetent mother, she was rubbing words
together to strike a spark and rekindle my frozen mind, my
frozen gaze. But the truth was that she liked saving me more
than listening to me.

And yet. Yet Dede, in spite of everything, continued to cry
at night, I heard her and became agitated, she gave off a sense
of unhappiness that undid the beneficial action of my mother-
in-law. And though I had more time I still couldn't write. And

Pietro, who was usually controlled, in the presence of his mother became uninhibited to the point of rudeness; his return home was almost always followed by an aggressive exchange of sarcastic remarks, and this only increased the sense of breakdown I felt around me. My husband—I soon realized—found it natural to consider Adele ultimately responsible for all his problems. He got angry with her for everything, even what happened to him at work. I knew almost nothing about the wearing tensions that he was experiencing at the university; in general to my *how are things* he responded *fine*, he tended to spare me. But with his mother the barriers broke down; he assumed the recriminatory tone of the child who feels neglected. He poured out onto Adele everything he hid from me, and if I was present he acted as if I weren't, as if I, his wife, were to act only as silent witness.

Thus many things became clear to me. His colleagues, all older than him, attributed his dazzling career, as well as the small reputation that he was starting to develop abroad, to the name he bore, and had isolated him. The students considered him unnecessarily rigid, a pedantic bourgeois who tended his own plot without making any concession to the chaos of the present, in other words a class enemy. And he, as usual, neither defended himself nor attacked, but kept straight on his path, offering—of this I was sure—lectures of acute intelligence, assessing students' abilities with equal acuity, failing them. But it's hard, he almost shouted at Adele, one evening, in a tone of complaint. Then he immediately lowered his voice, said that he needed tranquility, that the job was a struggle, that no small number of his colleagues set the students against him, that groups of youths often erupted into the classroom where he was teaching and forced him to break off the classes, that despicable slogans had appeared on the walls. At that point, even before Adele could speak, I lost control. If you were a little less reactionary, I said, those things wouldn't happen to you. And he, for the first time since I'd known him, answered rudely, hissing: Shut up, you always speak in clichés.

I locked myself in the bathroom and I suddenly realized that I scarcely knew him. What *did* I know about him? He was a peaceful man but determined to the point of stubbornness. He was on the side of the working class and the students, but he taught and gave exams in the most traditional way. He was an atheist, he hadn't wanted to get married in a church, he had insisted that Dede not be baptized, but he admired the early Christian communities of the Oltrarno and he spoke on religious matters with great expertise. He was an Airota, but he couldn't bear the privileges and comforts that came from that. I calmed down, I tried to be closer to him, more affectionate. He's my husband, I said to myself, we ought to talk more. But Adele's presence became increasingly problematic. There was something unexpressed between them that drove Pietro to set aside manners and Adele to speak to him as if he were a fool with no hope of redemption.

We lived now like that, amid constant battles: he quarreled with his mother, he ended up saying something that made me angry, I attacked him. Until the point came when my mother-in-law, at dinner, in my presence, asked him why he was sleeping on the sofa. He answered: It's better if you leave tomorrow. I didn't intervene, and yet I knew why he slept on the sofa: he did it for me, so that he wouldn't disturb me when, around three, he stopped working and allowed himself some rest. The next day Adele returned to Genoa. I felt lost.

67.

Nevertheless, the months passed and both the baby and I made it. Dede started walking by herself the day of her first birthday: her father squatted in front of her, encouraged her warmly, she smiled, left me, and moved unsteadily toward him, arms outstretched, mouth half open, as if it were the happy goal of her year of crying. From then on, her nights became tranquil, and so did mine. She spent more time with Clelia, her anxieties diminished, I carved out some space for myself. But I discovered that I had no desire for demanding activities. As after a long illness, I couldn't wait to go outside, enjoy the sun and the colors, walk on the crowded streets, look in the shop windows. And since I had some money of my own, in that period I bought clothes for myself, for the baby, and for Pietro, I crowded the house with furniture and knickknacks, I squandered money as I never had before. I felt the need to be pretty, to meet interesting people, have conversations, but I hadn't made any friends, and Pietro, for his part, rarely brought guests home.

I tried gradually to resume the satisfying life I had had until a year before, and only then noticed that the telephone hardly ever rang, that the calls for me were rare. The memory of my novel was fading and, with it, interest in my name was diminishing. That period of euphoria was followed by a phase of anxiety and, occasionally, depression, as I wondered what to do; I began reading contemporary literature again, and was often ashamed of my novel, which in comparison seemed frivolous and very traditional; I put aside the notes for the new book, which tended to repeat the old one, and made an effort to think of a story with more political engagement, one that would contain the tumult of the present.

I made a few timid phone calls to *l'Unità* and tried again to write articles, but I soon realized that my pieces no longer appealed to the editors. I had lost ground, I wasn't well informed, I didn't have time to go and examine particular situations and report on them, I wrote elegant sentences of an abstract rigor to announce—in that particular newspaper, to whom I'm not sure—my support of the harshest criticisms of the Communist Party and the unions. Today it's hard to explain why I insisted on writing that stuff or, rather, why, although I scarcely took part in the city's political life, and in spite of my meekness, I felt increasingly drawn to extreme positions. Maybe I did it out of insecurity. Or maybe out of distrust in every form of mediation, a skill that, from early childhood, I associated with the intrigues of my father, who operated shrewdly in the inefficiency of the city hall. Or out of the vivid knowledge of poverty, which I felt an obligation not to forget; I wanted to be on the side of those who remained downtrodden and were fighting to turn everything upside down. Or because everyday politics, the demands that I myself had scrupulously written about, didn't matter to me, I wished that *something great*—I had used and often did use that formulation—would break out, which I could experience, and report on. Or because—and this was hard to admit—my model remained Lila, with her stubborn unreasonableness that refused to accept half measures, so that although I was now distant from her in every way, I wanted to say and do what I imagined she would say and do if she had had my tools, if she had not confined herself within the space of the neighborhood.

I stopped buying *l'Unità*, I began to read *Lotta Continua* and *Il Manifesto*. In the latter, I discovered, Nino's name sometimes appeared. His articles were, as usual, well documented, and shaped with cogent logic. As I had when I talked to him as a girl, I, too, felt the need to contain myself in a network of deliberately formulated general propositions that would keep me from breaking down. I noticed that I no longer thought of him with desire, or even with love. He had become, it seemed to me, a figure of regret, the synthesis of what I was at risk of not becoming, even though I had had the opportunity. We were born in the same environment, both had brilliantly got out of it. Why then was I sliding into despair? Because of marriage? Because of motherhood and Dede? Because I was a woman, because I had to take care of house and family and clean up shit and change diapers? Every time I came upon an article by Nino, and the article seemed well done, I was resentful. And the person who paid for it was Pietro, in fact the only person I had to talk to. I got angry at him, I accused him of abandoning me in the most terrible period of my life, of caring only about his career and forgetting me. Our relations—I had trouble admitting it because it frightened me, but that was the reality—got worse and worse. I knew that he suffered because of his problems at work, and yet I couldn't forgive him, rather I criticized him, often starting from political positions no different from those of the students who made things so hard for him. He listened to me uneasily, scarcely responding. I suspected, in those moments, that the words he had shouted before (*shut up, you speak in clichés*) hadn't been an accidental loss of temper but indicated that in general he didn't consider me capable of a serious discussion. It exasperated me, depressed me, my rancor increased, especially because I myself knew that I wavered between contradictory feelings whose essence could be summed up like this: it was inequality that made school laborious for some (me, for example), and almost a game for others (Pietro, for example); on the other hand, inequality or not, one had to study, and do well, in fact very well—I was proud of my journey, of the intelligence I had demonstrated, and I refused to believe that my labor had been in vain, if in certain ways obtuse. And yet, for obscure reasons, with Pietro I gave expression only to the injustice of inequality. I said to him: You act as if all your students were the same, but it's not like that, it's a form of sadism to insist on the same results from kids who haven't had the same opportunities. And I even criticized him when he reported that he'd had a violent discussion with a colleague some twenty years his senior, an acquaintance of his sister's, who had thought he would find in him an ally against the most conservative part of the faculty. It happened that that man had in a friendly way advised him to be less severe with the students. Pietro had replied in his polite but un-nuanced way that he didn't think he was severe but only demanding. Well, the other had said, be less demanding, especially with the ones who are generously spending a lot of their time changing the current situation. At that point things came to a head, although I don't know exactly how or based on what arguments. Pietro, whose account was as usual minimal, first maintained that he had said only, in self-defense, that it was his habit always to treat all students with the respect that they deserved; then he admitted he had accused his colleague of using a double standard, of accommodating the students who were more aggressive and ruthless and even humiliating the more fearful ones. The man had taken offense, had gone so far as to say that only the fact that he knew his sister well prevented him from telling Pietro—and meanwhile, however, he had told him—that he was a fool unworthy of the professorship he held.

"Couldn't you be more cautious?"

"I am cautious."

"It doesn't seem that way to me."

"Well, I have to say what I think."

"Maybe you should find out who are your friends and who are your enemies."

"I don't have enemies."

"Or friends, either."

One thing leads to another—I overdid it. The result of your behavior, I hissed at him, is that no one in this city, least of all the friends of your parents, invites us to dinner or a concert or for a visit to the country.

68.

It was evident to me now that Pietro, at the university, was considered a dull man, very remote from the keen activism of his family, an unsuccessful Airota. And I shared that opinion, something that did not help our life in common or our intimate relations. When Dede finally settled down and began to sleep regularly, he returned to our bed, but as soon as he approached me I felt irritated, I was afraid of getting pregnant again, I wanted him to let me sleep. So I pushed him away, wordlessly, or simply turned my back, and if he insisted and pressed his sex against my nightgown, I hit his leg gently with my heel, a signal: I don't want to, I'm sleepy. Pietro retreated unhappily, he got up and went to his study.

One night we argued yet again about Clelia. There was always some tension when we had to pay her, but on that occasion it was clear that Clelia was an excuse. He said somberly: Elena, we have to examine our relationship and take stock. I agreed immediately. I told him that I adored his intelligence and his civility, that Dede was marvelous, but I added that I didn't want more children, I found the isolation I had ended up in unbearable, I wanted to return to an active life, I hadn't slaved since childhood just to be imprisoned in the roles of wife and mother. We talked, I bitterly, he with courtesy. He stopped protesting about Clelia, he gave in. He decided to buy condoms, he began to invite friends or, rather, acquaintances—he didn't have any friends—to dinner, he resigned himself to my going sometimes with Dede to meetings and demonstrations, in spite of the increasingly frequent violence in the streets.

But that new course, rather than improving my life, complicated it. Dede became more attached to Clelia and when I took her out she was bored, she got upset, she pulled my ears, my hair, my nose, tearfully begging for her. I was convinced that she was happier with the girl from the Maremma than with me, and the suspicion returned that because I hadn't breast-fed her and her first year of life had been hard, I was now a dark figure in her eyes, the mean woman who was constantly scolding her, and who, out of jealousy, mistreated her cheerful nanny, a playmate, a storyteller. She pushed me away even when with a mechanical gesture I wiped the snot off her nose with a handkerchief or the remains of food off her mouth. She cried, she said I was hurting her.

As for Pietro, the condoms dulled his sensitivity even more, and it took him even longer to reach orgasm, which made him suffer, and made me suffer. Sometimes I made him take me from behind, I had the impression that it was less painful, and while he dealt those violent blows I grabbed his hand and brought it to my sex hoping he would understand that I wanted to be caressed. But he seemed incapable of doing both things, and since he preferred the first he almost immediately forgot the second, nor, once satisfied, did he seem to understand that I wanted some part of his body to consummate, in turn, my desire. After he had had his pleasure he caressed my hair, and whispered, I'll work a little. When he left, the solitude seemed to me a consolation prize.

Sometimes, at the demonstrations, I observed with curiosity the young men who exposed themselves fearlessly to every danger, who were charged with a joyful energy even when they felt threatened and became threatening. I felt their fascination, I was attracted by that fever heat. But I considered myself remote in every way from the bright girls who surrounded them, I was too cultured, wore glasses, was married, my time was always limited. I returned home unhappy, I treated my husband coldly, I felt I was already old. A few times I daydreamed that one of those young men—he was well known in Florence, very popular—noticed me and dragged me away, as when, in adolescence, I felt clumsy and wouldn't dance, but Antonio or Pasquale would take me by the arm and force me.

Naturally it never happened. Rather, it was the acquaintances Pietro began to bring home who created complications. I labored to prepare dinners, I played the wife who can keep the conversation interesting, and I didn't complain, I had asked my husband to invite people. But I soon perceived, uneasily, that that ritual was not complete in itself: I was attracted by any man who gave me the slightest encouragement. Tall, short, thin, fat, ugly, handsome, old, married or a bachelor, if the guest praised an observation of mine, if he had nice things to say about my book, if he grew excited by my intelligence, I looked at him cordially and in a brief exchange of phrases and glances my availability communicated itself. Then the man, bored at the start, became lively, ignoring Pietro, redoubling his attentions to me. His words grew more allusive, and his gestures, his attitude in the course of conversation gained intimacy. With his fingertips he grazed my shoulder, my hand, looked into my eyes formulating sentimental phrases, touched my knees with his, the tips of my shoes with his shoes.

At those moments I felt good, I forgot the existence of Pietro and Dede, the wake of boring obligations they trailed. I feared only the moment when the guest would leave and I would fall back into the dreariness of my house: pointless days, idleness, rage concealed behind meekness. So I went overboard: excitement goaded me to talk too much and too loudly, I crossed my legs, hiking up my skirt as far as possible, with a careless gesture I unfastened a button on my shirt. It was I who shortened the distances, as if a part of me were convinced that, if in some way I clung to that stranger, some of the well-being I felt at that moment would remain in my body, and when he had left the apartment, along with his wife or companion, I would feel the depression, the emptiness behind the display of feelings and ideas, the anguish of failure.

In reality, afterward, alone in bed while Pietro studied, I felt simply stupid and despised myself. But however I tried I couldn't change myself. Especially because those men were convinced they had made an impression and generally called the next day, invented excuses to see me again. I accepted. But as soon as I arrived at the appointment I was frightened. The simple fact that they were excited, although they were, let's say, thirty years older or were married, canceled their authority, canceled the savior role I had assigned them, and the very pleasure I had felt during the game of seduction was a shameful mistake. I asked myself in bewilderment: Why did I behave like that, what's happening to me? I paid more attention to Dede and Pietro.

But at the first chance it all started again. I fantasized, I listened at high volume to the music I had been ignorant of as a girl, I didn't read, I didn't write. And I felt increasingly regretful that, because of my self-discipline in everything, I had missed the joy of letting go that the women of my age, of the milieu I now lived in, made a show of having enjoyed and enjoying. Whenever Mariarosa, for example, appeared in Florence, sometimes for research, sometimes for political meetings, she came to stay with us, always with different men, sometimes with girlfriends, and she took drugs, and offered them to her companions and to us, and if Pietro darkened and shut himself in his study, I was fascinated, and though hesitant to try smoking or LSD—I was afraid I would feel sick—I stayed to talk to her and her friends until late into the night.

They talked about everything; often the exchanges were violent, and I had the impression that the good language I had struggled to acquire had become inadequate. Too neat, too clean. Look how Mariarosa's language has changed, I thought, she's broken with her upbringing, she's got a dirty mouth. Pietro's sister now expressed herself more vulgarly than Lila and I had as girls. She didn't utter a noun that wasn't preceded by "fucking." *Where did I put that fucking match, where are the fucking cigarettes.* Lila had never stopped talking like that; so what was I supposed to do, become like her again, go back to the starting point? Then why had I worn myself out?

I observed my sister-in-law. I liked how she displayed solidarity with me and embarrassed her brother, instead, and the men she brought home. One night she abruptly interrupted the conversation to say to the young man with her: enough, let's go fuck. *Fuck*. Pietro had invented a well-mannered child's jargon for sexual things, I had acquired it and used it in place of the vulgar dialect vocabulary I had known since early childhood. But now, if one truly wanted to feel part of the changing world, was it necessary to bring back the obscene words, to say: I want to screw, fuck me this way and that way? Unimaginable with my husband. But the few men I saw, all highly educated, willingly pretended to be lower-class, were amused by women who acted like sluts, and seemed to enjoy treating a woman like a whore. At first these men were very formal, they controlled themselves. But they couldn't wait to start a skirmish that moved from the unsaid to the said, to the more explicitly said, in a game of freedom where female shyness was considered a sign of hypocritical foolishness. Candor, rather, immediacy: these were the qualities of the liberated woman, and I made an effort to live up to them. But the more I did, the more I felt enthralled by my interlocutor. A couple of times it seemed to me that I was falling in love.

69.

It happened first with a lecturer in Greek literature, a man of my age, originally from Asti, who had in his home town a fiancée with whom he said he was unhappy; then with the husband of a temporary lecturer in papyrology, a couple with two small children, she from Catania, he from Florence, an engineer who taught mechanics, named Mario, who was seven years older than me. He had an extensive political education, a lot of authority in public, long hair, and in his spare time he played drums in a rock band. With both, the routine was the same: Pietro invited them to dinner, I began to flirt. Phone calls, carefree participation in demonstrations, many walks, sometimes with Dede, sometimes alone, and occasional movies. With the Greek lecturer I retreated as soon as he became explicit. But Mario trapped me in a tightening net and one evening, in his car, he kissed me, he kissed me for a long time and, putting his hands in my bra, caressed my breasts. I pushed him away with difficulty, I said I didn't want to see him anymore. But he called, he called again, I missed him, I gave in. Since he had kissed me and touched me, he was sure he had some rights and behaved immediately as if we were starting up again from the point where we had left off. He insisted, proposed, demanded. When I, on the one hand, led him on and, on the other, dodged him, laughing, he got offended, he offended me.

One morning I was walking with him and Dede, who, if I remember, was a little over two and was completely absorbed by a beloved doll, Tes, a name she had invented. In the circumstances, I was paying scarcely any attention to her, carried away by the verbal game, and sometimes I forgot about her completely. As for Mario, he gave no importance to the child's presence, he was interested only in keeping after me, with his uninhibited talk, and he turned to Dede to whisper playfully in her ear things like: Please, will you tell your mamma to be nice to me? The time flew, we parted, Dede and I headed home. But after a few steps the child said harshly: Tes told me she has a secret to tell Papa. My heart stopped in my chest. Tes? And what will she tell Papa? Tes knows. Something good or bad? Bad. I threatened her: You explain to Tes that if she reports that thing to Papa you will lock her up in the storeroom, in the dark. She burst into tears, and I had to carry her home: she who, to please me, would walk and walk, pretending that she never got tired. Dede understood, therefore, or at least perceived, that between that man and me there was something that her father wouldn't tolerate.

I again broke off the meetings with Mario. What was he, in the end? A middle-class man who liked pornographic wordplay. But I couldn't control my restlessness, an eagerness for violation was growing in me, I wanted to break the rules, as the entire world seemed to be breaking the rules. I wanted, even just once, to break out of marriage, or, why not, everything in my life, what I had learned, what I had written, what I was trying to write, the child I had brought into the world. Ah yes, marriage was a prison: Lila, who had courage, had escaped at risk of her very life: and what risks did I run with Pietro, so distracted, so absent? None. So? I called Mario. I left Dede to Clelia, I went to his office. We kissed, he sucked my nipples, he touched me between the legs as Antonio had at the ponds years before. But when he pulled down his pants and, with his underpants at his knees, grabbed me by the neck and tried to push me against his sex I wriggled free, said no, put myself in order, and rushed away.

I returned home in great agitation, filled with guilt. I made love with Pietro passionately, I had never felt so rapt, it was I who said no to the condom. What am I worried about, I said to myself, I'm near my period, nothing will happen. But it did happen. Within a few weeks I found that I was pregnant again.

70.

With Pietro I didn't even hint at abortion—he was very happy that I was giving him another child—and, besides, I myself was afraid of trying that route, the very word made my stomach hurt. Adele mentioned abortion on the telephone, but

I immediately avoided the subject with stock phrases like: Dede needs company, growing up alone is hard, it's better for her to have a little brother or sister.

"The book?"

"It's going well," I lied.

"Will you let me read it?"

"Of course."

"We're all waiting."

"I know."

I was panic-stricken, almost without thinking I made a move that astounded Pietro, maybe even me. I telephoned my mother, I said I was expecting another child, I asked if she wanted to come and stay in Florence for a while. She muttered that she couldn't, she had to take care of my father, of my siblings. I shouted at her: It'll be your fault if I don't write anymore. Who gives a damn, she answered, isn't it enough for you to lead the life of a lady? And she hung up. But five minutes later Elisa telephoned. I'll take care of the household, she said, Mamma will leave tomorrow.

Pietro picked up my mother at the station in the car, which made her proud, made her feel loved. As soon as she set foot in the house I listed a series of rules: Don't move anything around in Pietro's study or mine; don't spoil Dede; don't interfere between me and my husband; supervise Clelia without fighting with her; stay in the kitchen or your room if I have guests. I was resigned to the idea that she wouldn't respect any of those rules, but instead, as if the fear of being sent away had modified her nature, she became within a few days a devoted servant who provided for every necessity of the house and resolved every problem decisively and efficiently without ever disturbing me or Pietro.

From time to time she went to Naples and her absence immediately made me feel exposed to chance, I was afraid she would never return. But she always did. She told me the news of the neighborhood (Carmen was pregnant, Marisa had had a boy, Gigliola was giving Michele Solara a second child; she said nothing about Lila, to avoid conflict) and then she became a kind of invisible household spirit who insured for all of us clean, ironed clothes, meals that tasted of childhood, an apartment that was always tidy, an orderliness that, as soon as it was disturbed, was put back in order with a maniacal punctuality. Pietro thought of trying again to get rid of Clelia and my mother was in agreement. I got angry, but instead of raging at my husband I lost my temper with her, and she withdrew into her room without responding. Pietro reproached me and made an effort to reconcile us quickly. He adored her, he said she was a very intelligent woman, and he would sit in the kitchen with her after dinner, chatting. Dede called her Grandma and grew so attached to her that she was irritated when Clelia appeared. Now, I said to myself, everything is in order, now you have no excuses. And I forced myself to focus on the book.

I looked at my notes again. I was absolutely convinced that I had to change course. I wanted to leave behind me what Franco had called *petty love affairs* and write something suited to a time of demonstrations, violent deaths, police repression, fears of a coup d'état. I couldn't get beyond a dozen inert pages. What was missing, then? It was hard to say. Naples, maybe, the neighborhood. Or an image like the Blue Fairy. Or a passion. Or an authoritative voice that would direct me. I sat at the desk for hours, in vain, I leafed through novels, I never went out of the room for fear of being captured by Dede. How unhappy I was. I heard the voice of the child in the hall, Clelia's, my mother's limping step. I lifted my skirt, I looked at the belly that was already starting to grow, spreading an unde-sired well-being through my whole organism. I was for the sec-ond time pregnant and yet empty.

71.

It was then that I began telephoning Lila, not sporadically, as I had until then, but almost every day. I made the expensive intercity calls with the sole purpose of crouching in her shadow, letting my pregnancy run its course, hoping that, in line with an old habit, she would set my imagination in motion. Naturally I was careful not to say the wrong things, and I hoped that she wouldn't, either. I knew clearly, now, that our friendship was possible only if we controlled our tongues. For example, I couldn't confess to her that a dark part of me feared that she was casting an evil spell on me from afar, that that part still hoped that she was really sick and would die. For example, she couldn't tell me the real reasons that motivated the rough, often offensive, tone in which she treated me. So we confined ourselves to talking about Gennaro, who was one of the smartest children in the elementary school, about Dede, who already knew how to read, and we did it like two mothers doing the normal boasting of mothers. Or I mentioned my attempt to write, but without making a big deal of it, I said only: I'm working, it's not easy, being pregnant makes me tired. Or I tried to find out if Michele was still hanging around her, to somehow capture her and keep her. Or, sometimes, I would ask if she liked certain movie or television actors, and urge her to tell me if men unlike Enzo attracted her, and perhaps confide to her that it happened to me, too, that I was attracted to men unlike Pietro. But this last subject didn't seem to interest her. When I mentioned an actor she always said: Who's he, I've never seen him in the movies or on television. And if I merely uttered the name of Enzo she began updating me on the computer story, bewildering me with an incomprehensible jargon.

Her accounts were enthusiastic, and occasionally, on the hypothesis that they might be useful to me in the future, I took notes while she spoke. Enzo had made it, now he worked in an

underwear factory fifty kilometers from Naples. The company
had rented an IBM machine and he was the systems engineer.
You know what kind of work that is? He diagrams manual
processes by transforming them into flow charts. The central
unit of the machine is as big as a wardrobe with three doors
and it has a memory of 8 kilobytes. You can't imagine how hot
it is, Lenù: the computer is worse than a stove. Maximum
abstraction along with sweat and a terrible stink. She talked to
me about ferrite cores, rings traversed by an electrical cable
whose tension determined the rotation, 0 or 1, and a ring was
a bit, and the total of eight rings could represent a byte, that is
a character. Enzo was the singular protagonist of Lila's mono-
logues. He dominated all that material like a god, he manipu-
lated the vocabulary and the substance inside a large room
with big air-conditioners, a hero who could make the machine
do everything that people did. Is that clear? she asked me every
so often. I answered yes, weakly, but I didn't know what she
was talking about. I perceived only that she noticed that nothing was clear to me, and I was ashamed of this.

Her enthusiasm grew with every phone call. Enzo was now
earning a hundred and forty-eight thousand lire a month,
exactly, *a hundred and forty-eight*. Because he was so smart, the
most intelligent man she had ever met. So smart, so clever, that
he had soon become indispensable and had managed to get
her hired, as an assistant. Here, this was the news: Lila was
working again, and this time she liked it. He's the boss, Lenù,
and I'm the deputy. I leave Gennaro with my mother—sometimes even with Stefano—and I go to the factory every morning. Enzo and I study the company point by point. We do
everything the employees do so we know what we have to put
into the computer. We check off, I don't know, the transac-
tions, we attach the stamps to the invoices, we check the
trainees' cards, the time cards, and then we transform everything into diagrams and holes in cards. Yes, yes, I'm also a

punch-card operator: I'm there with three other women, and I'm getting eighty thousand lire. A hundred and forty-eight plus eighty is two hundred and twenty-eight, Lenù. Enzo and I are rich, and it will be even better in a few months, because the owner realized that I'm very capable and wants me to take a course. You see what sort of life I have, are you pleased?

72.

One night she was the one who telephoned, she said she had just had some bad news: Dario, the student she had told me about some time earlier, the kid from the committee who handed out leaflets in front of the Soccavo factory, had been beaten to death, right outside of school, in Piazza del Gesù.

She seemed worried. She spoke of a black cloud that lay oppressively on the neighborhood and the whole city, attacks and more attacks. Behind many of these beatings, she said, were Gino's fascists, and behind Gino was Michele Solara, names that, in uttering, she charged with old disgust, new rage, as if beneath what she said there was much else about which she was silent. I thought: How can she be so sure that they're the ones responsible? Maybe she's stayed in touch with the students of Via dei Tribunali, maybe Enzo's computers are not the only thing in her life. I listened without interrupting while she let the words flow in her usual gripping way. She told me in great detail about a number of expeditions by the fascists, who started at the party headquarters opposite the elementary school, spread up the Rettifilo, through Piazza Municipio, up the Vomero, and attacked comrades with iron bars and knives. Even Pasquale had been beaten a couple of times, his front teeth had been broken. And Enzo, one night, had fought with Gino himself right in front of their house.

Then she stopped, she changed her tone. Do you remember,

she asked, the atmosphere of the neighborhood when we were little? It's worse, or rather no, it's the same. And she mentioned her father-in-law, Don Achille Carracci, the loan shark, the Fascist, and Peluso, the carpenter, the Communist, and the war taking place right before our eyes. We slipped slowly back into those times, I remembered one detail, she another. Until Lila accentuated the visionary quality of her phrases and began to tell the story of the murder of Don Achille the way she had as a girl, with many fragments of reality and many of imagination. The knife to the neck, the spurting blood that had stained a copper pot. She ruled out, as she had at the time, that it was the carpenter who killed him. She said, with adult conviction: justice then, and today, for that matter, settled for the most obvious trail, the one that led to the Communist. Then she exclaimed: Who says it was really Carmen and Pasquale's father? And who says it was a man and not a woman? As in one of our childhood games, when it seemed to us that we were in all ways complementary, I followed her step by step, adding my voice excitedly to hers, and I had the impression that together—the girls of the past and the adults of the present—we were arriving at a truth that for two decades had been unspeakable. *Think about it*, she said, *who really gained from that murder, who ended up with the money-lending market that Don Achille controlled?* Yes, who? We found the answer in unison: the person who had gotten something out of it was the woman with the red book, Manuela Solara, the mother of Marcello and Michele. She killed Don Achille, we said excitedly, and then, turning melancholy, said softly, first I, then she: but what are we talking about, that's enough, we're still children, we'll never grow up.

73.

Finally the moment seemed auspicious, it was a long time

since we'd had our old harmony. Only this time the harmony really was confined to a tangle of vibrating breaths along the telephone wires. We hadn't seen each other for a long time. She didn't know what I looked like after two pregnancies, I didn't know if she was still pale and very thin, or had changed. For several years I had been speaking to a mental image that the voice was slowly reviving. Maybe for that reason, the murder of Don Achille suddenly seemed like an invention, the core of a possible story. And once I got off the telephone I tried to put order into our conversation, reconstructing the passages on the basis of which Lila, fusing past and present, had led me from the murder of poor Dario to that of the loan shark, up to Manuela Solara. I had trouble sleeping, I pondered for a long time. I felt with increasing lucidity that that material might be a shore from which to lean out and grasp a story. In the following days I mixed Florence with Naples, the tumults of the present with distant voices, the comfort of now and the struggle I had had to pull myself out of my origins, the anxiety of losing everything and the fascination of regression. As I thought about it I became convinced that I could make a book out of it. With great effort, with constant, painful second thoughts, I filled a graph-paper notebook, constructing a web of violence that welded together the past twenty years. Sometimes Lila telephoned, she asked:

"Why don't you call anymore, aren't you well?"

"I'm very well, I'm writing."

"And when you write I no longer exist?"

"You exist but I'm distracted."

"If I'm ill, if I need you?"

"Call."

"And if I don't telephone you stay inside your novel?"

"Yes."

"I envy you, lucky you."

I worked with growing anxiety that I wouldn't be able to

get to the end of the story before the baby was born, I was afraid I might die while I was giving birth, leaving the book unfinished. It was hard, nothing like the happy unconsciousness in which I had written the first novel. Once I had sketched out the story, I decided to give the text a more thoughtful pace. I wanted the writing to be lively, new, deliberately chaotic, and I didn't hold back. So I worked on a second, detailed draft. I went back and rewrote every line even when, thanks to a Lettera 32 that I had bought when I was expecting Dede, thanks to carbon paper, I had transformed the notebooks into a solid typescript in triplicate, almost two hundred pages, with not a single typing mistake.

It was summer, it was very hot, my belly was enormous. The pain in my buttock had reappeared, it came and went, and my mother's step in the hall got on my nerves. I stared at the pages, I discovered that I was afraid of them. For days I couldn't make up my mind, I worried about giving it to Pietro to read. Maybe, I thought, I should send it directly to Adele, this isn't the type of story for him. And besides, with the persistence that distinguished him, he continued to make life difficult for himself at the university, coming home in a state of agitation, making abstract speeches about the value of law—in other words, he wasn't in the right state of mind to read a novel about workers, bosses, struggles, blood, camorrists, loan sharks. What's more, *my* novel. He keeps me separate from the confusion inside him, he's never been interested in what I was and what I've become, what's the point of giving him the book? He'll just discuss this or that choice of word, and the punctuation, and if I insist on an opinion he'll say something vague. I sent Adele a copy of the manuscript, then I called her.

"I've finished."

"I'm so pleased. Will you let me read it?"

"I sent it to you this morning."

"Good, I can't wait to read it."

74.

I settled myself to wait, a wait that became much more anxious than that for the child who was kicking in my belly. I counted five days, one after another, no word from Adele. On the sixth day, at dinner, while Dede was making an effort to eat by herself in order not to displease me, and her grandmother was desperate to help her but didn't, Pietro asked me:

"Did you finish your book?"

"Yes."

"And why did you give it to my mother to read and not me?"

"You're busy, I didn't want to bother you. But if you want to read it, there's a copy on my desk."

He didn't answer. I waited, I asked:

"Adele told you I sent it to her?"

"Who else would it have been?"

"Did she finish it?"

"Yes."

"What does she think?"

"She'll tell you, it's between you two."

He was offended. After dinner I moved the manuscript from my desk to his, I put Dede to bed, I watched television without seeing or hearing anything, and finally I went to bed. I couldn't close my eyes: Why had Adele talked to Pietro about the book but hadn't yet called me? The next day, July 30, 1973, I went to see if my husband had started reading: the typescript was under the books he had been working on for most of the night, it was clear that he hadn't even looked through it. I became nervous, I shouted at Clelia to take care of Dede, not to sit around and let my mother to do everything. I was very harsh with her, and my mother evidently took it as a sign of affection. She touched my belly as if to calm me, she asked:

"If it's another girl what will you call her?"

I had other things on my mind, my leg hurt, I answered without thinking:

"Elsa."

She darkened, I realized too late that she was expecting me to say: We gave Dede the name of Pietro's mother, and if it's another girl this time we'll give her your name. I tried to justify it, but reluctantly. I said: Ma, try to understand, your name is Immacolata, I can't give my daughter a name like that, I don't like it. She grumbled: Why, is Elsa nicer? I replied: Elsa is like Elisa, if I give her the name of my sister you should be pleased. She didn't say another word. Oh, how tired I was of every-thing. The heat was getting worse, I was dripping with sweat, I couldn't stand my heavy belly, I couldn't stand my limping, I couldn't stand anything, not a thing.

Finally, a little before lunchtime, Adele telephoned. Her voice lacked its usual ironic inflection. She spoke slowly and seriously, I felt that every word was a struggle: she said, with a lot of euphemistic phrases and many fine distinctions, that the book wasn't good. But when I tried to defend it, she stopped looking for formulations that wouldn't hurt me and became explicit. The protagonist was unlikable. The characters were caricatures. Situations and dialogues were mannered. The writing tried to be modern and was only confused. All that hatred was unpleasant. The ending was crude, like a spaghetti Western, it was an insult to my intelligence, my education, my talent. I resigned myself to silence, I listened to her criticisms to the end. She concluded by saying: The earlier novel was vivid, innovative, this, however, is old in its contents and so pretentiously written that the words seem empty. I said quietly: Maybe at the publisher they'll be kinder. She stiffened and replied: If you want to send it, go ahead, but I would assume they'll judge it unpublishable. I didn't know what to say, I said: All right, I'll think about it, goodbye. She kept me on the line, however, and, rapidly changing her tone, began to speak affectionately of Dede, of my mother, my pregnancy, of Mariarosa, who enraged her. Then she asked:

"Why didn't you give the novel to Pietro?"

"I don't know."

"He could have advised you."

"I doubt it."

"You don't respect him?"

"No."

Afterward, shut in my study, I despaired. It had been humiliating, intolerable. I could hardly eat, I fell asleep with the window closed despite the heat. At four in the afternoon I had my first labor pains. I said nothing to my mother, I took the bag I had prepared, I got in the car, and drove to the clinic, hoping to die on the way, I and my second child. Instead everything went smoothly. The pain was excruciating, but in a few hours I had another girl. Pietro insisted the next morning that our second daughter should be given the name of my mother, it seemed to him a necessary tribute. I replied bitterly that I was tired of following tradition, I repeated that she was to be called Elsa. When I came home from the clinic, the first thing I did was call Lila. I didn't tell her I had just given birth, I asked if I could send her the novel.

I heard her breathing lightly for a few seconds, then she said: "I'll read it when it comes out."

"I need your opinion right away."

"I haven't opened a book for a long time, Lenù, I don't know how to read anymore, I'm not capable."

"I'm asking you as a favor."

"The other you just published, period; why not this one?"

"Because the other one didn't even seem like a book to me."

"I can only tell you if I like it."

"All right, that's enough."

75.

While I was waiting for Lila to read, we learned that there was a cholera outbreak in Naples. My mother became excessively agitated, then distracted, finally she broke a soup tureen I was fond of, and announced that she had to go home. I imagined that if the cholera figured heavily in that decision, my refusal to give her name to my new daughter wasn't secondary. I tried to make her stay but she abandoned me anyway, when I still hadn't recovered from the birth and my leg was hurting. She could no longer bear to sacrifice months and months of her life to me, a child of hers without respect and without gratitude, she would rather go and die of the cholera bacterium with her husband and her good children. Yet even in the doorway she maintained the impassiveness that I had imposed on her: she didn't complain, she didn't grumble, she didn't reproach me for anything. She was happy for Pietro to take her to the station in the car. She felt that her son-in-law loved her and probably—I thought—she had controlled herself not to please me so that she wouldn't make a bad impression on him. She became emotional only when she had to part from Dede. On the landing she asked the child in her effortful Italian: Are you sorry that grandma is leaving? Dede, who felt that departure as a betrayal, answered grimly: No.

I was angry with myself, more than with her. Then I was seized by a self-destructive frenzy and a few hours later I fired Clelia. Pietro was amazed, alarmed. I said to him rancorously that I was tired of fighting with Dede's Maremman accent, with my mother's Neapolitan one. I wanted to go back to being mistress of my house and my children. In reality I felt guilty and had a great need to punish myself. With desperate pleasure I surrendered to the idea of being overwhelmed by the two children, by my domestic duties, by my painful leg.

I had no doubt that Elsa would compel me to a year no less terrible than the one I'd had with Dede. But maybe because I was more experienced with newborns, maybe because I was resigned to being a bad mother and wasn't anxious about perfection, the infant attached herself to my breast with no trouble and devoted herself to feeding and sleeping. As a result I, too, slept a lot, those first days at home, and Pietro surprisingly cleaned the house, did the shopping and cooking, bathed Elsa, played with Dede, who was as if dazed by the arrival of a sister and the departure of her grandmother. The pain in my leg suddenly disappeared. And I was in a generally peaceful state when, one late afternoon, as I was napping, my husband came to wake me: Your friend from Naples is on the phone, he said. I hurried to answer.

Lila had talked to Pietro for a long time, she said she couldn't wait to meet him in person. I listened reluctantly— Pietro was always amiable with people who didn't belong to the world of his parents—and since she dragged it out in a tone that seemed to me nervously cheerful, I was ready to shout at her: I've given you the chance to hurt me as much as possible, hurry up, speak, you've had the book for thirteen days, let me know what you think. But I confined myself to breaking in abruptly:

"Did you read it or not?"

She became serious.

"I read it."

"And so?"

"It's good."

"Good how? Did it interest you, amuse you, bore you?"

"It interested me."

"How much? A little? A lot?"

"A lot."

"And why?"

"Because of the story: it makes you want to read."

"And then?"

"Then what?"

I stiffened, and said:

"Lila, I absolutely have to know how this thing that I wrote is and I have no one else who can tell me, only you."

"I'm doing that."

"No, it's not true, you're cheating me: you've never talked about anything in such a superficial way."

There was a long silence. I imagined her sitting, legs crossed, next to an ugly little table on which the telephone stood. Maybe she and Enzo had just returned from work, maybe Gennaro was playing nearby. She said:

"I told you I don't know how to read anymore."

"That's not the point: it's that I need you and you don't give a damn."

Another silence. Then she muttered something I didn't understand, maybe an insult. She said harshly, resentful: I do one job, you do another, what do you expect from me, you're the one who had an education, you're the one who knows what books should be like. Then her voice broke, she almost cried: You mustn't write those things, Lenù, you aren't that, none of what I read resembles you, it's an ugly, ugly book, and the one before it was, too.

Like that. Rapid and yet strangled phrases, as if her breath, light, a whisper, had suddenly become solid and couldn't move in and out of her throat. I felt sick to my stomach, a sharp pain above my belly, which grew sharper, but not because of what she said but rather because of *how* she said it. Was she sobbing? I exclaimed anxiously: Lila, what's wrong, calm down, come on, breathe. She didn't calm down. They were really sobs, I heard them in my ear, burdened with such suffering that I couldn't feel the wound of that *ugly, Lenù, ugly, ugly*, nor was I offended that she reduced my first book, too—the book that had sold so well, the book of my success, but of which she had never told me what she thought—to a failure. What hurt me was her weeping. I wasn't prepared, I hadn't expected it. I would have preferred the mean Lila, I would have preferred her treacherous tone. But no, she was sobbing, and she couldn't control herself.

I felt bewildered. All right, I thought, I've written two bad books, but what does it matter, this unhappiness is much more serious. And I said softly: Lila, why are you crying, I should be crying, stop it. But she shrieked: Why did you make me read it, why did you force me to tell you what I think, I should have kept it to myself. And I: No, I'm glad you told me, I swear. I wanted her to quiet down but she couldn't, she poured out on me a confusion of words: Don't make me read anything else, I'm not fit for it, I expect the best from you, I'm too certain that you can do better, I *want* you to do better, it's what I want most, because who am I if you aren't great, who am I? I whispered: Don't worry, always tell me what you think, that's the only way you can help me, you've helped me since we were children, without you I'm not capable of anything. And finally she smothered her sobs, she said, sniffling: Why did I start crying, I'm an idiot. She laughed: I didn't want to upset you, I had prepared a positive speech, imagine, I wrote it, I wanted to make a good impression. I urged her to send it, I said, it could be that you know better than I do what I should write. And at that point we forgot the book, I told her that Elsa was born, we talked about Florence, Naples, the cholera. What cholera, she said sarcastically, there's no cholera, there's only the usual mess and the fear of dying in shit, more fear than facts, we eat a bag of lemons and no one shits anymore.

Now she talked continuously, without a break, almost cheerful, a weight had been lifted. As a result I began again to feel the bind I was in—two small daughters, a husband generally absent, the disaster of the writing—and yet I didn't feel anxious; rather, I felt light, and I brought the conversation back to my failure. I had in mind phrases like: the thread is broken, that fluency of yours that had a positive effect on me is gone, now I'm truly alone. But I didn't say it. I confessed instead in a self-satirizing tone that behind the labor of that book was the desire to settle accounts with the neighborhood, that it seemed to me to represent the great changes that surrounded me, that what had in some way suggested it, encouraging me, was the story of Don Achille and the mother of the Solaras. She burst out laughing. She said that the disgusting face of things alone was not enough for writing a novel: without imagination it would seem not a true face but a mask.

76.

I don't really know what happened to me afterward. Even now, as I sort out that phone call, it's hard to relate the effects of Lila's sobs. If I look closely, I have the impression of seeing mainly a sort of incongruous gratification, as if that crying spell, in confirming her affection and the faith she had in my abilities, had ultimately cancelled out the negative judgment of both books. Only much later did it occur to me that the sobs had allowed her to destroy my work without appeal, to escape my resentment, to impose on me a purpose so high—*don't disappoint her*—that it paralyzed every other attempt to write. But I repeat: however much I try to decipher that phone call, I can't say that it was at the origin of this or that, that it was an exalted moment of our friendship or one of the most wretched. Certainly Lila reinforced her role as a mirror of my inabilities. Certainly I was more willing to accept failure, as if Lila's opinion were much more authoritative—but also more persuasive and more affectionate—than that of my mother-in-law.

In fact a few days later I called Adele and said to her: Thank you for being so frank, I realized that you're right, and it strikes me now that my first book, too, had a lot of flaws. Maybe I ought to think about it, maybe I'm not a good writer, or I simply need more time. My mother-in-law hastily drowned me in compliments, praised my capacity for self-criticism, reminded me that I had an audience and that that audience was waiting. I said yes, of course. And right afterward I put the last copy of the novel in a drawer, I also put away the notebooks full of notes, I let myself be absorbed by daily life. The irritation at that useless labor extended to my first book, too, perhaps even to the literary purposes of writing. If an image or an evocative phrase came to mind, I felt a sense of uneasiness, and moved on to something else.

I devoted myself to the house, to the children, to Pietro. Not once did I think of having Clelia back or of replacing her with someone else. Again I took on everything, and certainly I did it to put myself in a stupor. But it happened without effort, without bitterness, as if I had suddenly discovered that this was the right way of spending one's life, and a part of me whispered: Enough of those silly notions in your head. I organized the household tasks rigidly, and I took care of Elsa and Dede with an unexpected pleasure, as if besides the weight of the womb, besides the weight of the manuscript, I had rid myself of another, more hidden weight, which I myself was unable to name. Elsa proved to be a placid creature—she took long happy baths, she nursed, she slept, she smiled even in her sleep—but I had to be very attentive to Dede, who hated her sister. She woke in the morning with a wild expression, recounting how she had saved the baby from fire, from a flood, from a wolf, but mostly she pretended to be a newborn herself, and asked to suck on my nipples, imitated infant wails, refused to act as what she now was, a child of almost four with highly developed language, perfectly independent in her primary functions. I was careful to give her a lot of affection, to praise her intelligence and her ability, to persuade her that I needed her help with everything, the shopping, the cooking, keeping her sister out of trouble.

Meanwhile, since I was terrified by the possibility of getting pregnant again, I began to take the Pill. I gained weight, I felt as if I'd swelled up, yet I didn't dare stop: a new pregnancy frightened me more than any other thing. And then my body didn't matter to me the way it used to. The two children seemed to have confirmed that I was no longer young, that the signs of my labors—washing them, dressing them, the stroller, the shopping, cooking, one in my arms and one by the hand, both in my arms, wiping the nose of one, cleaning the mouth of the other—testified to my maturity as a woman, that to become like the mammas of the neighborhood wasn't a threat but the order of things. It's fine this way, I told myself.

Pietro, who had given in on the Pill after resisting for a long time, examined me, preoccupied. You're getting fat. What are those spots on your skin? He was afraid that the children, and he, and I were getting sick, but he hated doctors. I tried to reassure him. He had gotten very thin lately: he always had circles under his eyes and white strands had appeared in his hair; he complained of pain in his knee, in his right side, in his shoulder, and yet he wouldn't have an examination. I forced him to go, I went with him, along with the children, and, apart from the need for some sleeping pills, he turned out to be very healthy. That made him euphoric for a few hours, and all his symptoms vanished. But in a short time, in spite of the sedatives, he felt ill again. Once Dede wouldn't let him watch the news—it was right after the coup in Chile—and he spanked her much too hard. And as soon as I began to take the Pill he developed a desire to make love even more frequently than before, but only in the morning or the afternoon, because—he said—it was the evening orgasm that made him sleepless; then he was compelled to study for a good part of the night, which made him feel chronically tired and consequently ill.

Nonsensical talk: working at night had always been for him a habit and a necessity. Yet I said: Let's not do it at night anymore, anything was fine with me. Of course, sometimes I was exasperated. It was hard to get help from him even in small things: the shopping when he was free, washing the dishes after dinner. One evening I lost my temper: I didn't say anything terrible, I just raised my voice. And I made an important discovery: if I merely shouted, his stubbornness disappeared and he obeyed me. It was possible, by speaking harshly, to make even his unpredictable pains go away, even his neurotic wish to make love constantly. But I didn't like doing it. When I behaved like that, I was sorry, it seemed to cause a painful tremor in his brain. Besides, the results weren't lasting. He gave in, he adjusted, he took on tasks with a certain gravity, but then he really was tired, he forgot agreements, he went back to thinking only about himself. In the end I let it go, I tried to make him laugh, I kissed him. What did I gain from a few washed dishes, poorly washed at that? Better to leave him tranquil, I was glad when I could avoid tension.

In order not to upset him I also learned not to say what I thought. He didn't seem to care, anyway. If he talked, I don't know, about the government measure in response to the oil crisis, if he praised the rapprochement of the Communist Party to the Christian Democrats, he preferred me to be only an approving listener. And when I appeared to disagree he assumed an absent-minded expression, or said in a tone that he obviously used with his students: you were badly brought up, you don't know the value of democracy, of the state, of the law, of mediation between established interests, balance between nations—you like apocalypse. I was his wife, an educated wife, and he expected me to pay close attention when he spoke to me about

278 · ELENA FERRANTE

politics, about his studies, about the new book he was working on, filled with anxiety, wearing himself out, but the attention had to be affectionate; he didn't want opinions, especially if they caused doubts. It was as if he were thinking out loud, explaining to himself. And yet his mother was a completely different type of woman. And so was his sister. Evidently he didn't want me to be like them. During that period of weakness, I understood from certain vague remarks that he wasn't happy about not only the success of my first book but its very publication. As for the second, he never asked me what had happened to the manuscript and what future projects I had. The fact that I no longer mentioned writing seemed to be a relief to him.

That Pietro every day revealed himself to be worse than I had expected did not, however, drive me again toward others. At times I ran into Mario, the engineer, but I quickly discovered that the desire to seduce and be seduced had disappeared and in fact that former agitation seemed to me a rather ridiculous phase; luckily it had passed. The craving to get out of the house, participate in the public life of the city also diminished. If I decided to go to a debate or a demonstration, I always took the children, and I was proud of the bags I toted, stuffed with everything they might need, of the cautious disapproval of those who said: They're so little, it might be dangerous.

But I went out every day, in whatever weather, so that my daughters could have air and sun. I never went without taking a book. Out of a habit that I had never lost, I continued to read wherever I was, even if the ambition of making a world for myself had vanished. I generally took a short walk and then sat on a bench not far from home. I paged through complicated essays, I read the newspaper, I yelled: Dede, don't go far, stay close to Mamma. I was that, I had to accept it. Lila, whatever turn her life might take, was different.

77.

It happened that around that time Mariarosa came to Florence to present the book of a university colleague of hers on the *Madonna del Parto*. Pietro swore he wouldn't miss it, but at the last minute he made an excuse and hid somewhere. My sister-in-law arrived by car, alone this time, a bit tired but affectionate as always and loaded with presents for Dede and Elsa. She never mentioned my aborted novel, even though Adele had surely told her about it. She talked volubly about trips she'd taken, about books, with her usual enthusiasm. She pursued energetically the many novelties of the planet. She would assert one thing, get tired of it, go on to another that a little earlier, out of distraction, blindness, she had rejected. When she spoke about her colleague's book, she immediately gained the admiration of the art historians in the audience. And the evening would have run smoothly along the usual academic tracks if at a certain point, with an abrupt swerve, she hadn't uttered remarks, occasionally vulgar, of this type: children shouldn't be given to any father, least of all God the Father, children should be given to themselves; the moment has arrived to study as women and not as men; behind every discipline is the penis and when the penis feels impotent it resorts to the iron bar, the police, the prisons, the army, the concentration camps; and if you don't submit, if, rather, you continue to turn everything upside down, then comes slaughter. Shouts of discontent, of agreement: at the end she was surrounded by a dense crowd of women. She called me over with welcoming gestures, proudly showed off Dede and Elsa to her Florentine friends, said nice things about me. Some remembered my book, but I avoided it, as if I hadn't written it. The evening was nice, and brought an invitation, from a small, varied group of girls and adult women, to go to the house of one of them, once a week, to talk—they said—about us.

Mariarosa's provocative remarks and the invitation of her friends led me to fish out from under a pile of books those pamphlets Adele had given me long before. I carried them around in my purse, I read them outside, under the gray sky of late winter. First, intrigued by the title, I read an essay entitled *We Spit on Hegel*. I read it while Elsa slept in her carriage and Dede, in coat, scarf, and woolen hat, talked to her doll in a low voice. Every sentence struck me, every word, and above all the bold freedom of thought. I forcefully underlined many of the sentences, I made exclamation points, vertical strokes. Spit on Hegel. Spit on the culture of men, spit on Marx, on Engels, on Lenin. And on historical materialism. And on Freud. And on psychoanalysis and penis envy. And on marriage, on family. And on Nazism, on Stalinism, on terrorism. And on war. And on the class struggle. And on the dictatorship of the proletariat. And on socialism. And on Communism. And on the trap of equality. And on *all* the manifestations of patriarchal culture. And on *all* its institutional forms. Resist the waste of female intelligence. Deculturate. Disacculturate, starting with maternity, don't *give* children to anyone. Get rid of the master-slave dialectic. Rip inferiority from our brains. Restore women to themselves. Don't create antitheses. Move on another plane in the name of one's own difference. The university doesn't free women but completes their repression. Against wisdom. While men devote themselves to undertakings in space, life for women on this planet has yet to begin. Woman is the other face of the earth. Woman is the Unpredictable Subject. Free oneself from subjection here, now, in this present. The author of those pages was called Carla Lonzi. How is it possible, I wondered, that a woman knows how to think like that. I worked so hard on books, but I endured them, I never actually used them, I never turned them against themselves. This is thinking. This is thinking against. I—after so much exertion—don't know how to think. Nor does Mariarosa: she's read pages and pages, and she rearranges them with flair, putting on a show. That's it. Lila, on the other hand, knows. It's her nature. If she had studied, she would know how to think like this.

That idea became insistent. Everything I read in that period ultimately drew Lila in, one way or another. I had come upon a female model of thinking that, given the obvious differences, provoked in me the same admiration, the same sense of inferiority that I felt toward her. Not only that: I read thinking of her, of fragments of her life, of the sentences she would agree with, of those she would have rejected. Afterward, impelled by that reading, I often joined the group of Mariarosa's friends, but it wasn't easy: Dede asked me continuously when we were leaving, Elsa would suddenly let out cries of joy. But it wasn't just my daughters who were the problem. It was that there I found only women who, resembling me, couldn't help me. I was bored when the discussion became a sort of inelegant summary of what I already knew. And it seemed to me I knew well enough what it meant to be born female, I wasn't interested in the work of consciousness-raising. And I had no intention of speaking in public about my relationship with Pietro, or with men in general, to provide testimony about what men are, of every class and of every age. And no one knew better than I did what it meant to make your own head masculine so that it would be accepted by the culture of men; I had done it, I was doing it. Furthermore I remained completely outside the tensions, the explosions of jealousy, the authoritarian tones, weak, submissive voices, intellectual hierarchies, struggles for primacy in the group that ended in desperate tears. But there was one new fact, which naturally led me to Lila. I was fascinated by the way people talked, confronted each other—explicit to the point of being disagreeable. I didn't like the amenability that yielded to gossip: I had known enough of that since childhood. What seduced me instead was an urge for authenticity that I had never felt and that perhaps was not in my nature. I never said a single word, in that circle, that was equal to that urgency. But I felt that I should do something like that with Lila, examine our connection with the same inflexibility, that we should tell each other fully what we had been silent about, starting perhaps from the unaccustomed lament for my mistaken book.

That need was so strong that I imagined going to Naples with the children for a while, or asking her to come to me with Gennaro, or to write to each other. I talked about it with her once on the phone but it was a fiasco. I told her about the books by women I was reading, about the group I went to. She listened but then she laughed at titles like *The Clitoral Woman and the Vaginal Woman,* and did her best to be vulgar: What the fuck are you talking about, Lenù, pleasure, pussy, we've got plenty of problems here already, you're crazy. She wanted to prove that she didn't have the tools to put into words the things that interested me. And in the end she was scornful, she said: Work, do the nice things you have to do, don't waste time. She got angry. Evidently it's not the right moment, I thought, I'll try again later on. But I never found the time or the courage to try again. I concluded that first of all I had to understand better what I was. Investigate my nature as a woman. I had been excessive, I had striven to give myself male capacities. I thought I had to know everything, be concerned with everything. What did I care about politics, about struggles. I wanted to make a good impression on men, be at their level. At the level of what, of their reason, most unreasonable. Such persistence in memorizing fashionable jargon, wasted effort. I had been conditioned by my education, which had shaped my mind, my voice. To what secret pacts with myself had I consented, just to excel. And now, after the hard work of learning, what must I unlearn. Also, I had been forced by the powerful presence of Lila to imagine myself as I was not. I was added to her, and I felt mutilated as soon as I removed myself. Not an idea, without Lila. Not a thought I trusted, without the support of her thoughts. Not an image. I had to accept myself outside of her. The gist was that. Accept that I was an average person. What should I do. Try again to write. Maybe I didn't have the passion, I merely limited myself to carrying out a task. So don't write anymore. Find some job. Or act the lady, as my mother said. Shut myself up in the family. Or turn everything upside down. House. Children. Husband.

78.

I consolidated my relations with Mariarosa. I called her frequently, but when Pietro noticed he began to speak more and more contemptuously of his sister. She was frivolous, she was empty, she was dangerous to herself and others, she had been the cruel tormenter of his childhood and adolescence, she was the great worry of her parents. One evening he came out of his study disheveled, his face tired, while I was talking to my sister-in-law on the phone. He walked around the kitchen, ate something, joked with Dede, eavesdropping on our conversation. Then all of a sudden he shouted: Doesn't that idiot know it's time for dinner? I apologized to Mariarosa and hung up. It's all ready, I said, we can eat right away, there's no need to shout. He complained that spending money on phone calls to listen to his sister's nonsense seemed stupid to him. I didn't answer, I set the table. He realized I was angry, and said, in a tone of apprehension: I'm mad at Mariarosa, not you. But after that night he began to look through the books I was reading, to make sarcastic comments on the sentences I had underlined. He said, Don't be taken in, it's nonsense. And he tried to demonstrate the weak logic of feminist manifestos and pamphlets.

On this very subject we ended up arguing one evening and

maybe I overdid it, going so far as to say to him: You think you're so great but everything you are you owe to your father and mother, just like Mariarosa. His reaction was completely unexpected: he slapped me, and in Dede's presence.

I took it well, better than he did: I had had many blows in the course of my life, Pietro had never given any and almost certainly had never received any. I saw in his face the revulsion for what he had done; he stared at his daughter for an instant, and left the house. My anger cooled. I didn't go to bed, I waited for him, and when he didn't return I became anxious, I didn't know what to do. Did he have some nervous illness, from too little sleep? Or was that his true nature, buried under thousands of books and a proper upbringing? I realized yet again that I knew little about him, that I wasn't able to predict his moves: he might have jumped into the Arno, be lying drunk somewhere, even left for Genoa to find comfort and complain in his mother's arms. Oh enough, I was frightened. I realized that I was leaving what I was reading, and what I knew, on the edges of my personal life. I had two daughters, I didn't want to draw conclusions too hastily.

Pietro came home at around five in the morning and the relief of seeing him safe and sound was so great that I hugged him, I kissed him. He mumbled: You don't love me, you've never loved me. And he added: Anyway, I don't deserve you.

79.

The fact was that Pietro couldn't accept the disorder that was by now spreading into every aspect of existence. He would have liked a life ruled by unquestioned habits: studying, teaching, playing with the children, making love, contributing every day, in his small way, to resolving by democratic means the vast confusion of Italian affairs. Instead he was exhausted by the conflicts at the university, his colleagues disparaged his work, and although he was gaining a reputation abroad, he felt constantly vilified and threatened, he had the impression that because of my restlessness (but what restlessness, I was an opaque woman) our very family was exposed to constant risks. One afternoon Elsa was playing on her own, I was making Dede practice reading, he was shut in his study, the house was still. Pietro, I thought anxiously, is looking for a fortress where he works on his book, I take care of the household, and the children grow up serenely. Then the doorbell rang, I went to open the door, and to my surprise Pasquale and Nadia entered.

They carried large military knapsacks; he wore a cap over a thick mass of curly hair that fell into an equally thick and curly beard, while she looked thin and tired, her eyes enormous, like a frightened child who is pretending not to be afraid. They had asked for the address from Carmen, who in turn had asked my mother. They were both affectionate, and I was, too, as if there had never been tensions or disagreements between us. They took over the house, leaving their things everywhere. Pasquale talked a lot, in a loud voice, almost always in dialect. At first they seemed a pleasant break in my flat daily existence. But I soon realized that Pietro didn't like them. It bothered him that they hadn't telephoned to announce themselves, that they brazenly made themselves at home. Nadia took off her shoes and stretched out on the sofa. Pasquale kept his cap on, handled objects, leafed through books, took a beer from the refrigerator for himself and one for Nadia without asking permission, drank from the bottle and burped in a way that made Dede laugh. They said they had decided to take a trip, they said just that, a *trip*, without specifying. When had they left Naples? They were evasive. When would they return? They were equally evasive. Work? I asked Pasquale. He laughed: Enough, I've worked too much, now I'm resting. And he showed Pietro his hands, he demanded that he show him his, he rubbed their palms together saying: You feel the difference? Then he grabbed *Lotta Continua* and brushed his right hand over the first page, proud of the sound of the paper scraping over his rough skin, as pleased as if he had invented a new game. Then he added, in an almost threatening tone: Without these rasping hands, professor, not a chair would exist, or a building, a car, nothing, not even you; if we workers stopped working everything would stop, the sky would fall to earth and the earth would shoot up to the sky, the plants would take over the cities, the Arno would flood your fine houses, and only those who have always worked would know how to survive, and as for you two, you with all your books, the dogs would tear you to pieces.

It was a speech in Pasquale's style, fervent and sincere, and Pietro listened without responding. As did Nadia, who, while her companion was speaking, lay on the sofa with a serious expression, staring at the ceiling. She almost never interrupted the two men's talk, nor did she say anything to me. But when I went to make coffee she followed me into the kitchen. She noticed that Elsa was always attached to me, and she said gravely:

"She really loves you."

"She's little."

"You're saying that when she grows up she won't love you?"

"No, I hope she'll love me when she's grown up, too."

"My mother used to talk about you all the time. You were only her student, but it seemed as if you were her daughter more than me."

"Really?"

"I hated you for that and because you had taken Nino."

"It wasn't for me that he left you."

"Who cares, I don't even remember what he looked like now."

"As a girl I would have liked to be like you."

"Why? You think it's nice to be born with everything all ready-made for you?"

"Well, you don't have to work so hard."

"You're wrong—the truth is that it seems like everything's been done already and you've got no good reason to do anything. All you feel is the guilt of what you are and that you don't deserve it."

"Better that than to feel the guilt of failure."

"Is that what your friend Lina tells you?"

"No."

"I prefer her to you. You're two pieces of shit and nothing can change you, two examples of underclass filth. But you act all friendly and Lina doesn't."

She left me in the kitchen, speechless. I heard her shout to Pasquale: I'm taking a shower, and you could use one, too. They shut themselves in the bathroom. We heard them laughing, she letting out little cries that—I saw—worried Dede. When they came out their hair was wet, they were half-naked, and gay. They went on joking and laughing with each other as if we weren't there. Pietro tried to intervene with questions like: How long have you been together? Nadia answered coldly: We're not together, maybe *you two* are together. In the finicky tone he displayed in situations where people appeared to him extremely superficial: What does that mean? You can't understand, Nadia responded. My husband objected: When someone can't understand, you try to explain. And at that point Pasquale broke in laughing: There's nothing to explain, prof: you better believe you're dead and you don't know it—everything is dead, the way you live is dead, the way you speak, your conviction that you're very intelligent, and democratic, and on the left. How can you explain a thing to someone who's dead?

There were other tense moments. I said nothing, I couldn't get Nadia's insults out of my mind, the way she spoke, as if it were nothing, in my house. Finally they left, almost without warning, as they had arrived. They picked up their things and disappeared. Pasquale said only, in the doorway, in a voice that was unexpectedly sorrowful:

"Goodbye, Signora Airota."

Signora Airota. Even my friend from the neighborhood was judging me in a negative way? Did it mean that for him I was no longer Lenù, Elena, Elena Greco? For him and for how many others? Even for me? Did I myself not almost always use my husband's surname, now that mine had lost that small luster it had acquired? I tidied the house, especially the bathroom, which they had left a mess. Pietro said: I never want those two in my house; someone who talks like that about intellectual work is a Fascist, even if he doesn't know it; as for her, she's a type I'm very familiar with, there's not a thought in her head.

80.

As if to prove Pietro right, the disorder began to take concrete form, touching people who had been close to me. I learned from Mariarosa that Franco had been attacked in Milan by the fascists, he was in bad shape, and had lost an eye. I left immediately, with Dede and little Elsa. I took the train, playing with the girls and feeding them, but saddened by another me—the poor, uneducated girlfriend of the wealthy and hyperpoliticized student Franco Mari: how many me's were there by now?—who had been lost somewhere and was now re-emerging.

At the station I met my sister-in-law, who was pale and worried. She took us to her house, which this time was deserted, yet even more untidy than when I had stayed there after the meeting at the university. While Dede played and Elsa slept, she told me more than she had on the telephone. The episode had happened five days earlier. Franco had spoken at a demonstration of Avanguardia Operaia, in a packed theater. Afterward he had gone off with Silvia, who now lived with an editor at *Giorno* in a beautiful apartment near the theater: he was to sleep there and leave the next day for Piacenza. They were almost at the door, Silvia had just taken the keys out of her purse, when a white van pulled up and the fascists had jumped out. He had been severely beaten, Silvia had been beaten and raped.

We drank a lot of wine, Mariarosa took out the drug: that's what she called it, in other situations she used the plural. This time I decided to try it, but only because, in spite of the wine, I felt I hadn't a single solid thing to hold on to. My sister-in-law became furious, then stopped talking and burst into tears. I couldn't find a single word of comfort. *I felt* her tears, it seemed to me that they made a sound sliding from her eyes down her cheeks. Suddenly I couldn't see her, I couldn't even see the room, everything turned black. I fainted.

When I came to, I apologized, hugely embarrassed, I said it was tiredness. I didn't sleep much that night: my body weighed heavily because of an excess of discipline, and the lexicon of books and journals dripped anguish as if suddenly the signs of the alphabet could no longer be combined. I held the two little girls close as if they were the ones who had to comfort and protect me.

The next day I left Dede and Elsa with my sister-in-law and went to the hospital. I found Franco in a sickly-green ward that had an intense odor of breath, urine, and medicine. He was as if shortened and distended, I can still see him in my mind's eye, because of the white bandages, the violet color of part of his face and neck. He didn't seem glad to see me, he seemed ashamed of his condition. I talked, I told him about my children. After a few minutes he said: Go away, I don't want you here. When I insisted on staying, he was irritated, and whispered: I'm not myself, go away. He was very ill; I learned from a small group of his companions that he might have to have another operation. When I came back from the hospital Mariarosa saw that I was upset. She helped with the children, and as soon as Dede fell asleep she sent me to bed, too. The next day, however, she wanted me to come with her to see Silvia. I tried to avoid it, I had found it unbearable to see Franco and feel not only that I couldn't help him but that I made him feel more fragile. I said I preferred to remember her as I had seen her during the meeting at the university. No, Mariarosa insisted, she wants us to see her as she is now, it's important to her. We went.

A very well-groomed woman, with blond hair that fell in waves over her shoulders, opened the door. It was Silvia's mother, and she had Mirko with her; he, too, was blond, a child of five or six by now, whom Dede, in her sulky yet bossy way, immediately insisted play a game with Tes, the old doll she carried everywhere. Silvia was sleeping but had left word that she wanted to be awakened when we got there. We waited awhile before she appeared. She was heavily made up, and had put on a pretty long green dress. I wasn't struck so much by the bruises, the cuts, the hesitant walk—Lila had seemed in even worse shape when she returned from her honeymoon—as by her expressionless gaze. Her eyes were blank, and completely at odds with the frenetic talking, broken by little laughs, with which she began to recount *to me*, only to me, who still didn't know, what the fascists had done to her. She spoke as if she were reciting a horrendous nursery rhyme that was for now the way in which she deposited the horror, repeating it to anyone who came to see her. Her mother kept trying to make her stop, but each time she pushed her away with a gesture of irritation, raising her voice, uttering obscenities and predicting a time soon, very soon, of violent revenge. When I burst into tears she stopped abruptly. But other people arrived, mostly family friends and comrades. Then Silvia began again, and I quickly retreated to a corner, hugging Elsa, kissing her lightly. I remembered details of what Stefano had done to Lila, details that I imagined while Silvia was narrating, and it seemed to me that the words of both stories were animal cries of terror.

At a certain point I went to look for Dede. I found her in the hall with Mirko and her doll. They were pretending to be a mother and father with their baby, but it wasn't peaceful: they were pretending to have a fight. I stopped. Dede instructed Mirko: *You have to hit me, understand?* The new living flesh was replicating the old in a game, we were a chain of shadows who had always been on the stage with the same burden of love, hatred, desire, and violence. I observed Dede carefully; she seemed to resemble Pietro. Mirko, on the other hand, was just like Nino.

81.

Not long afterward, the underground war that occasionally erupted into the newspapers and on television—plans for coups, police repression, armed bands, firefights, woundings, killings, bombs and slaughters I was struck again by in the cities large and small. Carmen telephoned, she was extremely worried, she hadn't heard from Pasquale in weeks.

"Did he by any chance visit you?"

"Yes, but at least two months ago."

"Ah. He asked for your phone number and address: he wanted to get your advice, did he?"

"Advice about what?"

"I don't know."

"He didn't ask me for advice."

"What did he say?"

292 · ELENA FERRANTE

"Nothing, he was fine, he was happy."

Carmen had asked everywhere, even Lila, even Enzo, even the people in the collective on Via dei Tribunali. Finally she had called Nadia's house, but the mother had been rude and Armando had told her only that Nadia had moved without leaving any address.

"They must have gone to live together."

"Pasquale and that girl? Without leaving an address or phone number?"

We talked about it for a long time. I said maybe Nadia had broken with her family because of Pasquale, who knows, maybe they had gone to live in Germany, in England, in France. But Carmen wasn't persuaded. Pasquale is a loving brother, she said, he would never disappear like that. She had instead a terrible presentiment: there were now daily clashes in the neighborhood, anyone who was a comrade had to watch his back, the fascists had even threatened her and her husband. And they had accused Pasquale of setting fire to the fascist headquarters and to the Solaras' supermarket. I hadn't known either of those things, I was astonished: This had happened in the neighborhood, and the fascists blamed Pasquale? Yes, he was at the top of the list, he was considered someone to get out of the way. Maybe, Carmen said, Gino had him killed.

"You went to the police?"

"Yes."

"What did they say?"

"They nearly arrested me, they're more fascist than the fascists."

I called Professor Galiani. She said to me sarcastically: What happened, I don't see you in the bookshops anymore or even in the newspapers, have you already retired? I said that I had two children, that for now I was taking care of them, and then I asked her about Nadia. She became unfriendly. Nadia is a grownup, she's gone to live on her own. Where, I asked. Her business, she answered, and, without saying goodbye, just as I was asking if she would give me her son's telephone number, she hung up.

I spent a long time finding a number for Armando, and had an even harder time finding him at home. When he finally answered, he seemed happy to hear from me, and even too eager for confidences. He worked a lot in the hospital, his marriage was over, his wife had left, taking the child, he was alone and eccentric. He stumbled when he talked about his sister. He said quietly: I don't have any contact with her. Political differences, differences about everything. Ever since she's been with Pasquale you can't talk to her. I asked: Did they go to live together? He broke off: Let's say that. And as if the subject seemed too frivolous, he avoided it, moved on, making harsh comments on the political situation, talking about the slaughter in Brescia, the bosses who bankrolled the parties and, as soon as things looked bad, the fascists.

I called Carmen again to reassure her. I told her that Nadia had broken with her family to be with Pasquale and that Pasquale followed her like a puppy.

"You think?" Carmen asked.

"I'm sure, love is like that."

She was skeptical. I insisted, I told her in greater detail about the afternoon they had spent at my house and I exaggerated a little about how much they loved each other. We said goodbye. But in mid-June Carmen called again, desperate. Gino had been murdered in broad daylight in front of the pharmacy, shot in the face. I thought first that she was giving me that news because the son of the pharmacist was part of our early adolescence and, fascist or not, certainly that event would upset me. But the reason was not to share with me the horror of that violent death. The carabinieri had come and searched the apartment from top to bottom, even the gas pump. They were looking for any information that might lead them to

Pasquale, and she had felt much worse than when they had come to arrest her father for the murder of Don Achille.

82.

Carmen was overwhelmed by anxiety, she wept because of what seemed to her the revival of persecution. I, on the other hand, couldn't get out of my mind the small barren square the pharmacy faced, and the shop's interior, which I had always liked for its odor of candies and syrups, the dark-wood shelves with their rows of colored jars, and, above all, Gino's parents, who were so kind, leaning out from behind the counter as if from a balcony: surely they had been there, had been startled by the sound of the shots, from there, perhaps, had watched, eyes wide, as their son fell in the doorway, had seen the blood. I wanted to talk to Lila. But she appeared completely indifferent, she dismissed the episode as one of many, she said only: Of course the carabinieri would go after Pasquale. Her voice knew how to grip me immediately, to persuade me; she emphasized that even if Pasquale had murdered Gino—which she ruled out—she would be on his side, because the carabinieri should have gone after the dead man for all the terrible things he had done, rather than our friend, a construction worker and Communist. After which, in the tone of someone who is going on to more important things, she asked if she could leave Gennaro with me until school began. Gennaro? How would I manage? I already had Dede and Elsa, who wore me out. I said:

"Why?"

"I have to work."

"I'm about to go to the beach with the girls."

"Take him, too."

"I'm going to Viareggio and staying till the end of August.

He barely knows me, he'll want you. If you come, too, that's fine, but alone I don't know."

"You swore you'd take care of him."

"Yes, but if you were ill."

"And how do you know I'm not ill?"

"Are you ill?"

"No."

"So why can't you leave him with your mother or Stefano?"

She was silent for a few seconds, she became rude.

"Will you do me this favor or not?"

I gave in immediately.

"All right, bring him here."

"Enzo will bring him."

Enzo arrived on a Saturday night in a bright white Fiat 500 that he had just bought. Merely seeing him from the window, hearing the dialect in which he said something to the boy who was still in the car—it was him, identical, the same composed gestures, the same physical compactness—gave solidity back to Naples, to the neighborhood. I opened the door with Dede hanging on my dress, and a single glance at Gennaro was enough to know that Melina, five years earlier, had seen correctly: the child, now that he was ten, showed plainly that he had in him not only nothing of Nino but nothing of Lila; he was, rather, a perfect replica of Stefano.

The observation provoked an ambiguous sentiment, a mixture of disappointment and satisfaction. I had thought that, since the boy would be with me for so long, it would be nice to have in the house, along with my daughters, a child of Nino; and yet I noted with pleasure that Nino had left Lila nothing.

83.

Enzo wanted to start off again right away, but Pietro wel-

comed him courteously and obliged him to stay for the night.
I tried to get Gennaro to play with Dede, even if there was
almost six years' difference between them, but while she was
clearly eager he refused, shaking his head decisively. I was
struck by the way Enzo cared for the son who wasn't his, indicating that he knew his habits, his tastes, his needs. Although
Gennaro protested because he was sleepy, Enzo gently insisted
that he pee and brush his teeth before going to bed, and, when
the child collapsed, he delicately undressed him and put his
pajamas on.

While I washed the dishes and cleaned up, Pietro enter-
tained the guest. They were sitting at the kitchen table; they
had nothing in common. They tried politics, but when my husband made a positive reference to the progressive rapprochement of the Communists and the Christian Democrats, and
Enzo said that if that strategy prevailed Berlinguer would be
giving a hand to the worst enemies of the working class, they
ended the discussion in order to avoid a quarrel. Pietro then
politely asked him about his job, and Enzo must have found
his interest sincere, because he was less laconic than usual and
started on a dry, perhaps slightly too technical account. IBM
had just decided to send Lila and him to a bigger company, a
factory near Nola that had three hundred technical workers
and forty clerical employees. The financial offer had left them
stunned: three hundred and fifty thousand lire a month for
him, who was the department head, and a hundred thousand
for her, as his assistant. They had accepted, naturally, but now
they had to earn all that money, and the work to be done was
really tremendous. We are responsible, he explained—and
from then on he used "we"—for a System 3 Model 10, and we
have at our disposal two operators and five punch-card operators, who are also checkers. We have to collect and put into the
System 3 a huge quantity of information, which is necessary so
that the machine can do things like—I don't know—the

accounting, wages, invoicing, the warehousing, management of
the salespeople, orders to suppliers, production, and shipping.
For this purpose we use little cards—that is, the punch cards.
The holes are everything, the effort is concentrated there. I'll
give you an example of the work it takes to program a simple
operation like issuing invoices. You begin with the paper
invoices, on which the warehouseman has marked both the
products and the client they've been delivered to. The client
has a code, his personal information has a code, and so do the
products. The punch-card operators sit at the machines, press
a key to release the cards, then by typing on the keys reduce
the bill number, the client code, the personal-data code, the
product-quantity code, to holes in the cards. To help you
understand, a thousand bills for ten products make ten thousand punch cards with holes like the ones a needle would
make: is it clear, do you follow?

So the evening passed. Pietro every so often nodded to
show that he was following and even tried to ask some questions (*The holes count but do the unperforated parts also count?*).
I confined myself to a half smile while I washed and polished.
Enzo appeared pleased to be able to explain to a university
professor, who listened to him like a disciplined student, and
an old friend who had her degree and had written a book, and
now was tidying up the kitchen, things that they knew nothing
about. But in truth I was quickly distracted. An operator took
ten thousand cards and inserted them in a machine that was
called a sorter. The machine put them in order according to the
product code. Then there were two readers, not in the sense of
people but in the sense of machines programmed to read the
holes and the non-holes in the cards. And then? There I got
lost. I got lost amid codes and the enormous packets of cards
and the holes that compared holes, that sorted holes, that read
holes, that did the four operations, that printed names,
addresses, totals. I got lost following a word I'd never heard

before, *file*, which Enzo kept using, pronouncing it *fi-le,* this *file*, that *file*, continually. I got lost following Lila, who knew everything about those words, those machines, that work, and was doing that work now in a big company in Nola, even if with the salary her companion was earning she could be more of a lady than me. I got lost following Enzo, who could say proudly: *Without her I wouldn't be able to do it.* Thus he conveyed to us his love and devotion, and it was clear that he liked to remind himself and others of the extraordinary quality of his woman, whereas my husband never praised me but, rather, reduced me to the mother of his children; even though I had had an education he did not want me to be capable of independent thought, he demeaned me by demeaning what I read, what interested me, what I said, and he appeared willing to love me only provided that I continually demonstrate my nothingness.

Finally I, too, sat down at the table, depressed because neither of the two had made a move to say: Can we help you set the table, clear, wash the dishes, sweep the floor. An invoice, Enzo was saying, is a simple document, what does it take to do by hand? Nothing, if I have to create ten a day. But if I have to do a thousand? The readers read two hundred cards a minute, so two thousand in ten minutes, and ten thousand in fifty. The speed of the machine is an enormous advantage, especially if it's enabled to do complex operations, which require a lot of time. And that's what Lila's and my work is: to prepare the System 3 to do complex operations. The development phases of the programs are really wonderful. The operational phases a little less. The cards often jam and break in the sorters. Very often a container in which the cards have just been sorted falls and the cards scatter on the floor. But it's great, it's great even then.

Just to feel that I was present, I interrupted, saying:

"Can he make a mistake?"

"He who?"

"The computer."

"There's no he, Lenù, he is me. If he makes a mistake, if he gets in trouble, I've made a mistake, I've gotten in trouble."

"Oh," I said, and then, "I'm tired."

Pietro nodded in agreement and seemed ready to end the evening. He turned to Enzo:

"It's certainly exciting, but if it's as you say, these machines will take the place of men, and skills will disappear; at Fiat robots already do the welding. A lot of jobs will be lost."

Enzo at first agreed, then he seemed to have second thoughts, and finally he resorted to the only person whose authority he credited:

"Lina says it's all a good thing: humiliating and stultifying jobs should disappear."

Lina, Lina, Lina. I asked teasingly: if Lina is so good, why do they give you three hundred and fifty thousand lire and her a hundred thousand, why are you the boss and she's the assistant? Enzo hesitated again, he seemed on the point of saying something pressing, which he then decided to abandon. He mumbled: What do you want from me, private ownership of the means of production should be abolished. In the kitchen the hum of the refrigerator could be heard for a few seconds. Pietro stood up and said: Let's go to bed.

84.

Enzo wanted to leave by six, but already at four in the morning I heard him moving in his room and I got up to make him some coffee. In private, in the silent house, the language of computers disappeared, along with the Italian suited to Pietro's position, and we moved to dialect. I asked about his relationship with Lila. He said it was good, even though she never sat still. Now she was chasing after work problems, now she was squabbling with her mother, her father, her brother, now she was helping Gennaro with his homework and, one way or another, she ended up helping Rino's children, too, and all the children who happened to be around. Lila didn't look after herself, and so she was overworked, she always seemed close to collapse, as she once had; she was tired. I quickly understood that their harmony as a couple, working side by side, blessed by good salaries, should be set within a more complicated sequence. I ventured:

"Maybe the two of you have to impose some order: Lina shouldn't get overtired."

"I tell her that constantly."

"And then there's the separation, divorce: it makes no sense for her to stay married to Stefano."

"She doesn't give a damn about that."

"But Stefano?"

"He doesn't even know that you can divorce now."

"And Ada?"

"Ada has survival problems. The wheel turns, those who were on top end up on the bottom. The Carraccis don't have even a lira left, only debts with the Solaras, and Ada is taking care to get what she can before it's too late."

"And you? You don't want to get married?"

It was clear that he would happily get married, but Lila was against it. Not only did she not want to waste time with divorce—who cares if I'm still married to him, I'm with you, I sleep with you, that's the essential—but the mere idea of another wedding made her laugh. She said: You and I? You and I get married? Why, we're fine like this, and as soon as we get fed up with each other we go our own way. The prospect of another marriage didn't interest Lila, she had other things to think about.

"What?"

"Forget it."

"Tell me."

"She never talked to you about it?"

"What?"

"Michele Solara."

He told me in brief, tense phrases that in all these years Michele had never stopped asking Lila to work for him. He had proposed that she manage a new shop on the Vomero. Or the accounting and the taxes. Or be a secretary for a friend of his, an important Christian Democratic politician. He had even gone so far as to offer her a salary of two hundred thousand lire a month just to invent things, crazy notions, anything that came into her head. Even though he lived on Posillipo, he still kept the headquarters of all his businesses in the neighborhood, at his mother and father's house. So Lila found him around her constantly, on the street, in the market, in the shops. He stopped her, always very friendly, he joked with Gennaro, gave him little gifts. Then he became very serious, and even when she refused the jobs he offered, he wasn't impatient, he said goodbye, joking as usual: I'm not giving up, I'll wait for you for eternity, call me when you want and I'll come running. Until he found out she was working for IBM. That had angered him, and he had gone so far as to get people he knew to remove Enzo from the market for consultants, and hence Lila, too. He hadn't had any success, IBM urgently needed technicians and there weren't many good technicians like Enzo and Lila. But the climate had changed. Enzo had found Gino's fascists outside the house and he escaped because he managed to reach the front door in time and lock it behind him. But shortly afterward an alarming thing had happened to Gennaro. Lila's mother had gone to pick him up at school as usual. All the students had come out and the child was nowhere to be seen. The teacher: He was here a minute ago. His classmates: He was here and then he disappeared.

Nunzia, terribly frightened, had called her daughter at work; Lila returned right away and went to look for Gennaro. She found him on a bench in the gardens. The child was sitting quietly, with his smock, his ribbon, his schoolbag, and he laughed at the questions—where did you go, what did you do—with expressionless eyes. She wanted to go and kill Michele right away, both for the attempted beating of Enzo and the kidnapping of her son, but Enzo restrained her. The fascists now went after anyone on the left and there was no proof that it was Michele who ordered the kidnapping. As for Gennaro, he himself had admitted that his brief absence was only an act of disobedience. In any case, once Lila calmed down, Enzo had decided on his own to go and talk to Michele. He had showed up at the Bar Solara and Michele had listened without batting an eye. Then he had said, more or less: I don't know what the fuck you're talking about, Enzù: I'm fond of Gennaro, anyone who touches him is dead, but among all the foolish things you've said the only true thing is that Lina is smart and it's a pity that she's wasting her intelligence, I've been asking her to work with me for years. Then he continued: That irritates you? Who gives a damn. But you're wrong, if you love her you should encourage her to use her capabilities. Come here, sit down, have a coffee and a pastry, tell me what those computers of yours do. And it hadn't ended there. They had met two or three times, by chance, and Michele had demonstrated increasing interest in the System 3. One day he even said, amused, that he had asked someone at IBM who was smarter, him or Lila, and that person had said that Enzo was certainly smart, but the best in the business was Lila. After that, he had stopped her on the street again and made her a significant offer. He intended to rent the System 3 and use it in all his commercial activities. Result: he wanted her as the chief technician, at four hundred thousand lire a month.

"She didn't even tell you that?" Enzo asked me warily.

"No."

"You see she didn't want to bother you, you have your life. but you understand that for her personally it would be a significant step up, and for the two of us it would be a fortune: we'd have seven hundred and fifty thousand lire a month altogether, I don't know if that's clear."

"But Lina?"

"She has to answer by September."

"And what will she do?"

"I don't know. Have you ever been able to figure out what's in her mind ahead of time?"

"No. But what do you think she should do?"

"I think what she thinks."

"Even if you don't agree?"

"Even then."

I went out to the car with him. On the stairs it occurred to me that maybe I should tell him what he surely didn't know, that Michele harbored for Lila a love like a spiderweb, a dangerous love that had nothing to do with physical possession or even with a loyal subservience. And I was about to do it, I was fond of him, I didn't want him to believe that he was merely dealing with a quasi-camorrist who had been planning for a long time to buy the intelligence of this woman. When he was already behind the wheel I asked him:

"And if Michele wants to sleep with her?"

He was impassive.

"I'll kill him. But anyway he doesn't want her, he already has a lover and everybody knows it."

"Who's that?"

"Marisa, he's got her pregnant again."

For a moment it seemed to me that I hadn't understood.

"Marisa Sarratore?"

"Marisa, the wife of Alfonso."

I recalled my conversation with my schoolmate. He had

tried to tell me how complicated his life was and I had
retreated, struck more by the surface of his revelation than by
the substance. And to me his uneasiness seemed confused—to
get things straight I would have had to talk to him again, and
maybe not even then would I have understood—and yet it
pierced me unpleasantly, painfully. I asked:

"And Alfonso?"

"He doesn't give a damn, they say he's a fag."

"Who says?"

"Everyone."

"Everyone is very general, Enzo. What else does everyone
say?"

He looked at me with a flash of conspiratorial irony:

"A lot of things, the neighborhood is always gossiping."

"Like?"

"Old stories have come back to the surface. They say it was
the mother of the Solaras who murdered Don Achille."

He left, and I hoped he would take away his words, too. But
what I had learned stayed with me, worried me, made me
angry. In an attempt to get rid of it I went to the telephone and
talked to Lila, mixing anxieties and reproaches: Why didn't you
say anything about Michele's job offers, especially the last one;
why did you tell Alfonso's secret; why did you start that story
about the mother of the Solaras, it was a game of ours; why did
you send me Gennaro, are you worried about him, tell me
plainly, I have the right to know; why, once and for all, don't
you tell me what's really in your mind? It was an outburst, but,
sentence by sentence, deep inside myself, I hoped that we
wouldn't stop there, that the old desire to confront our entire
relationship and re-examine it, to elucidate and have full consciousness of it, would be realized. I hoped to provoke her and
draw her in to other, increasingly personal questions. But Lila
was annoyed, she treated me coldly, she wasn't in a good
mood. She answered that I had been gone for years, that I now

had a life in which the Solaras, Stefano, Marisa, Alfonso meant nothing, counted for less than zero. Go on vacation, she said, abruptly, write, act the intellectual, here we've remained too crude for you, stay away; and please, make Gennaro get some sun, otherwise he'll come home stunted like his father.

The sarcasm in her voice, the belittling, almost rude tone, removed any weight from Enzo's story and eliminated any possibility of drawing her into the books I was reading, the vocabulary I had learned from Mariarosa and the Florentine women, the questions that I was trying to ask myself and that, once I had provided her with the basic concepts, she would surely know how to take on better than all of us. But yes, I thought, I'll mind my own business and you mind yours: if you like, don't grow up, go on playing in the courtyard even now that you're about to turn thirty; I've had enough, I'm going to the beach. And so I did.

85.

Pietro took the three children and me in the car to an ugly house in Viareggio that we had rented, then he returned to Florence to try to finish his book. Look, I said to myself, now I'm a vacationer, a well-off lady with three children and a pile of toys, a beach umbrella in the front row, soft towels, plenty to eat, five bikinis in different colors, menthol cigarettes, the sun that darkens my skin and makes me even blonder. I called Pietro and Lila every night. Pietro reported on people who had called for me, remnants of a distant time, and, more rarely, talked about some hypothesis having to do with his work that had just come to mind. I handed Lila to Gennaro, who reluctantly recounted what he considered important events of his day and said good night. I said almost nothing to either one or the other. Lila especially seemed reduced to voice alone.

But I realized after a while that it wasn't exactly so: part of her existed in flesh and blood in Gennaro. The boy was certainly very like Stefano and didn't resemble Lila at all. Yet his gestures, the way he talked, some words, certain interjections, a kind of aggressiveness were those of Lila as a child. So sometimes if I was distracted I jumped at hearing his voice, or was spellbound as I observed him gesticulating, explaining a game to Dede.

Unlike his mother, however, Gennaro was devious. Lila's meanness when she was a child had always been explicit, no punishment ever drove her to hide it. Gennaro, on the other hand, played the role of the well-brought-up, even timid child, but as soon as I turned my back he teased Dede, he hid her doll, he hit her. When I threatened him, saying that as a punishment we wouldn't call his mamma to say good night he assumed a contrite expression. In reality, that possible punishment didn't worry him at all; the ritual of the evening phone call had been established by me, and he could easily do without it. What worried him, rather, was the threat that I wouldn't buy him ice cream. Then he began to cry; between his sobs he said he wanted to go back to Naples, and I immediately gave in. But that didn't soothe him. He took revenge on me by secretly being mean to Dede.

I was sure that she feared him, hated him. But no. As time passed, she responded less and less to Gennaro's harassments: she fell in love with him. She called him Rino or Rinuccio, because he had told her that was what his friends called him, and she followed him, paying no attention to my commands, in fact it was she who urged him to wander away from our umbrella. My day was made up of shouting: Dede where are you going, Gennaro come here, Elsa what are you doing, don't put sand in your mouth, Gennaro stop it, Dede if you don't stop it I'm coming over and we'll see. A pointless struggle: Elsa ate sand no matter what and, no matter what, Dede and Gennaro disappeared.

Their refuge was a nearby expanse of reeds. Once I went with Elsa to see what they were up to and discovered that they had taken off their bathing suits and Dede was touching, with fascination, the erect penis that Gennaro was showing her. I stopped a short distance away, I didn't know what to do. Dede—I knew, I had seen her—often masturbated lying on her stomach. But I had read a lot about infant sexuality—I had even bought for my daughter a little book of colored illustrations that explained in very short sentences what happened between man and woman, words I had read her but which aroused no interest—and, although I felt uneasy, I had not only forced myself not to stop her, not to reproach her, but, assuming that her father would, I had been careful to keep him from surprising her.

Now, though? Should I let them play together? Should I retreat, slip away? Or approach without giving the thing any importance, talk nonchalantly about something else? And if that violent boy, much bigger than Dede, forced on her who knows what, hurt her? Wasn't the difference in age a danger? Two things precipitated the situation: Elsa saw her sister, shouted with joy, calling her name; and at the same time I heard the dialect words that Gennaro was saying to Dede, coarse words, the same horribly vulgar words I had learned as a child in the courtyard. I couldn't control myself, everything I had read about pleasures, latencies, neurosis, polymorphous perversions of children and women vanished, and I scolded the two severely, especially Gennaro, whom I seized by the arm and dragged away. He burst into tears, and Dede said to me coldly, fearless: You're very mean.

I bought them both ice cream, but a period began in which a certain alarm at how Dede's language was absorbing obscene words of Neapolitan dialect was added to a wary supervision, intended to keep the episode from being repeated. At night, while the children slept, I got into the habit of making an effort to remember: had I played games like that with my friends in the courtyard? And had Lila had experiences of that type? We had never talked about it. At the time we had uttered repulsive words, certainly, but they were insults that served, among other things, to ward off the hands of obscene adults, bad words that we shouted as we fled. For the rest? With difficulty I reached the point of asking myself: had she and I ever touched each other? Had I ever wished to, as a child, as a girl, as an adult? And her? I hovered on the edge of those questions for a long time. I answered slowly: I don't know, I don't want to know. And then I admitted that there had been a kind of admiration for her body, maybe that, yes, but I ruled out anything ever happening between us. Too much fear, if we had been seen we would have been beaten to death.

In any case, on the days when I faced that problem, I avoided taking Gennaro to the public phone. I was afraid he would tell Lila that he didn't like being with me anymore, that he would even tell her what had happened. That fear annoyed me: why should I be concerned? I let it all fade. Even my vigilance toward the two children slowly diminished, I couldn't oversee them continuously. I devoted myself to Elsa, I forgot about them. I shouted nervously from the shore, towels ready, only if, despite purple lips and wrinkled fingertips, they wouldn't get out of the water.

The days of August slipped away. House, shopping, preparing the overflowing beach bags, beach, home again, dinner, ice cream, phone call. I chatted with other mothers, all older than me, and I was pleased if they praised *my* children, and my patience. They talked about husbands, about the husbands' jobs. I talked about mine, I said: He's a Latin professor at the university. On the weekend Pietro arrived, just as, years earlier, on Ischia, Stefano and Rino had. My acquaintances shot him respectful looks and seemed to appreciate, thanks to his professorship, even his bushy hair. He went swimming with the girls and Gennaro, he drew them into make-believe dangerous adventures that they all hugely enjoyed, then he sat studying under the umbrella, complaining from time to time about his lack of sleep—he often forgot the sleeping pills. In the kitchen, when the children were sleeping, we had sex standing up to avoid the creaking of the bed. Marriage by now seemed to me an institution that, contrary to what one might think, stripped coitus of all humanity.

86.

It was Pietro who, one Saturday, picked out, in the crowd of headlines that for days had been devoted to the 'fascists' bombing of the Italicus express train, a brief news item in the *Corriere della Sera* that concerned a small factory on the outskirts of Naples.

"Wasn't Soccavo the name of the company where your friend worked?" he asked me.

"What happened?"

He handed me the paper. A commando group made up of two men and a woman had burst into a sausage factory on the outskirts of Naples. The three had first shot the legs of the guard, Filippo Cara, who was in very serious condition; then they had gone up to the office of the owner, Bruno Soccavo, a young Neapolitan entrepreneur, and had killed him with four shots, three to the chest and one to the head. I saw, as I read, Bruno's face ruined, shattered, along with his gleaming white teeth. Oh God, God, I was stunned. I left the children with Pietro, I rushed to telephone Lila, the phone rang for a long time with no answer. I tried again in the evening, nothing. I got her the next day, she asked me in alarm: What's the matter, is Gennaro ill? I reassured her, then told her about Bruno. She knew nothing about it, she let me speak, finally she said tonelessly: This is really bad news you're giving me. And nothing else. I goaded her: Telephone someone, find out, ask where I can send a telegram of condolence. She said she no longer had any contact with anyone at the factory. What telegram, she muttered, forget it.

I forgot it. But the next day I found in *Il Manifesto* an article signed by Giovanni Sarratore, that is, Nino, which had a lot of information about the small Campanian business, underlining the political tensions present in those backward places, and referring affectionately to Bruno and his tragic end. I followed the development of the news for days, but to no purpose: it soon disappeared from the papers. Besides, Lila refused to talk about it. At night I called her with the children and she cut me off, saying, Give me Gennaro. She became especially irritated when I quoted Nino to her. Typical of him, she grumbled. He always has to interfere: What does politics have to do with it, there must be other matters, here people are murdered for a thousand reasons, adultery, criminal activity, even just one too many looks. So the days passed and of Bruno there remained an image and that was all. It wasn't the image of the factory owner I had threated on the phone using the authority of the Airotas but that of the boy who had tried to kiss me and whom I had rudely rejected.

87.

I began to have some ugly thoughts on the beach. Lila, I said to myself, deliberately pushes away emotions, feelings. The more I sought tools to try to explain myself to myself, the more she, on the contrary, hid. The more I tried to draw her into the open and involve her in my desire to clarify, the more she took refuge in the shadows. She was like the full moon when it crouches behind the forest and the branches scribble on its face.

In early September I returned to Florence, but the ugly thoughts rather than dissolving grew stronger. Useless to try to talk to Pietro. He was unhappy about the children's and my return, he was late with his book and the idea that the academic year would soon begin made him short-tempered. One night when, at the table, Dede and Gennaro were quarreling about something or other he jumped up suddenly and left the kitchen, slamming the door so violently that the frosted glass shattered. I called Lila, I told her straight off that she had to take her child back, he'd been living with me for a month and a half.

"You can't keep him till the end of the month?"

"No."

"It's bad here."

"Here, too."

Enzo left in the middle of the night and arrived in the morning, when Pietro was at work. I had already packed Gennaro's bag. I explained to him that the tensions between the children had become unbearable, I was sorry but three was too many, I couldn't handle it anymore. He said he understood, he thanked me for all I had done. He said only, by way of apology: You know what Lina is like. I didn't answer, because Dede was yelling, desperate at Gennaro's departure, and because, if I had, I might have said—beginning precisely with what Lila was like—things I would later regret.

I had in my head thoughts I didn't want to formulate even to myself; I was afraid that the facts would magically fit the words. But I couldn't cancel out the sentences; in my mind I heard their syntax all ready, and I was frightened by it, fascinated, horrified, seduced. I had trained myself to find an order by establishing connections between distant elements, but here it had got out of hand. I had added Gino's violent death to Bruno Soccavo's (Filippo, the factory guard, had survived). And I had arrived at the idea that each of these events led to Pasquale, maybe also to Nadia. This hypothesis was extremely distressing. I had thought of telephoning Carmen, to ask if she had news of her brother; then I changed my mind, frightened by the possibility that her telephone was bugged. When Enzo came to get Gennaro I said to myself: Now I'll talk to him about it, let's see how he responds. But then, too, I had said nothing, out of fear of saying too much, out of fear of uttering the name of the figure who was behind Pasquale and Nadia: Lila, that is. Lila, as usual: Lila who doesn't say things, she does them; Lila who is steeped in the culture of the neighborhood and takes no account of police, the law, the state, but believes there are problems that can be resolved only with the shoemaker's knife; Lila who knows the horror of inequality; Lila who, at the time of the collective of Via dei Tribunali, found in revolutionary theory and action a way of applying her hyperactive mind; Lila who has transformed into political objectives her rages old and new; Lila who moves people like characters in a story; Lila who has connected, is connecting, our personal knowledge of poverty and abuse to the armed struggle against the fascists, against the owners, against capital. I admit it here, openly, for the first time: in those September days I suspected that not only Pasquale—Pasquale driven by his history toward the necessity of taking up arms— not only Nadia, but Lila herself had spilled that blood. For a long time, while I cooked, while I took care of my daughters, I saw her, with the other two, shoot Gino, shoot Filippo, shoot Bruno Soccavo. And if I had trouble imagining Pasquale and Nadia in every detail—I considered him a good boy, something of a braggart, capable of fierce fighting but of murder no; she seemed to me a respectable girl who could wound at most with verbal treachery—about Lila I had never had doubts: she would know how to devise the most effective plan, she would reduce the risks to a minimum, she would keep fear under control, she would be able to give murderous intentions an abstract purity, she knew how to remove human substance from bodies and blood, she would have no scruples and no remorse, she would kill and feel that she was in the right.

So there she was, clear and bright, along with the shadow of Pasquale, of Nadia, of who knows what others. They drove through the piazza in a car and, slowing down in front of the pharmacy, fired at Gino, at his thug's body in the white smock. Or they drove along the dusty road to the Soccavo factory, garbage of every type piled up on either side. Pasquale went through the gate, shot Filippo's legs, the blood spread through the guard booth, screams, terrified eyes. Lila, who knew the way well, crossed the courtyard, entered the factory, climbed the stairs, burst into Bruno's office, and, just as he said cheerfully: Hi, what in the world are you doing around here, fired three shots at his chest and one at his face.

Ah yes, militant anti-fascism, new resistance, proletarian justice, and other formulas to which she, who instinctively knew how to avoid rehashing clichés, was surely able to give depth. I imagined that those actions were necessary in order to join, I don't know, the Red Brigades, Prima Linea, Nuclei Armati Proletari. Lila would disappear from the neighborhood as Pasquale had. Maybe that's why she had tried to leave Gennaro with me, apparently for a month, in reality intending to give him to me forever. We would never see each other again. Or she would be arrested, like the leaders of the Red Brigades, Curcio and Franceschini. Or she would evade every policeman and prison, imaginative and bold as she was. And when the *big thing* was accomplished, she would reappear triumphant, admired for her achievements, in the guise of a revolutionary leader, to tell me: You wanted to write novels, I created a novel with real people, with real blood, in reality.

At night every imagining seemed a thing that had happened or was still happening, and I was afraid for her, I saw her captured, wounded, like so many women and men in the chaos of the world, and I felt pity for her, but I also envied her. The childish conviction that she had always been destined for extraordinary things was magnified. And I regretted that I had left Naples, detached myself from her, the need to be near her returned. But I was also angry that she had set out on that road without consulting me, as if she hadn't considered me up to it. And yet I knew a lot about capital, exploitation, class struggle, the inevitability of the proletarian revolution. I could have been useful, participated. And I was unhappy. I lay in bed, discontent with my situation as a mother, a married woman, the whole future debased by the repetition of domestic rituals in the kitchen, in the marriage bed.

By day I felt more lucid, and the horror prevailed. I imagined a capricious Lila who provoked hatred deliberately and in the end found herself more deeply involved in violent acts. Certainly she had had the courage to push ahead, to take the lead with the crystalline determination, the generous cruelty of one who is spurred by just reasons. But with what purpose? To start a civil war? Transform the neighborhood, Naples, Italy into a battlefield, a Vietnam in the Mediterranean? Hurl us all into a pitiless, interminable conflict, squeezed between the Eastern bloc and the Western? Encourage its fiery spread throughout Europe, throughout the entire planet? Until victory, always? What victory? Cities destroyed, fire, the dead in the streets, the shame of violent clashes not only with the class enemy but also within the front itself, among the revolutionary groups of various regions and with various motivations, all in the name of the proletariat and its dictatorship. Maybe even nuclear war.

I closed my eyes in terror. The children, the future. And I hung on to formulas: the unpredictable subject, the destructive logic of patriarchy, the feminine value of survival, compassion. I have to talk to Lila, I said to myself. She has to tell me every-

thing she's doing, what she plans, so that I can decide whether
to be her accomplice or not.

But I never called nor did she call me. I was convinced that
the long voice thread that had been our only contact for years
hadn't helped us. We had maintained the bond between our
two stories, but by subtraction. We had become for each other
abstract entities, so that now I could invent her for myself both
as an expert in computers and as a determined and implacable
urban guerrilla, while she, in all likelihood, could see me both
as the stereotype of the successful intellectual and as a cultured
and well-off woman, all children, books, and highbrow conversation with an academic husband. We both needed new
depth, body, and yet we were distant and couldn't give it to
each other.

88.

Thus September passed, then October. I didn't talk to anyone, not even Adele, who had a lot of work, or even
Mariarosa, who had brought Franco to her house—an invalid
Franco, in need of help, changed by depression—and who
greeted me warmly, promised to say hello to him for me, but
then broke off because she had too many things to do. Not to
mention Pietro's muteness. The world outside books burdened him increasingly, he went reluctantly into the regulated
chaos of the university, and often said he was ill. He said he
did it in order to work, but he couldn't get to the end of his
book, he rarely went into his study, and, as if to forgive himself and be forgiven, he took care of Elsa, cooked, swept,
washed, ironed. I had to treat him rudely to get him to go
back to teaching, but I immediately regretted it. Ever since the
violence had struck people I knew, I was afraid for him. He
had never given in, even though he got into dangerous situa-

316 · ELENA FERRANTE

tions, opposing publicly what, in a term that he preferred, he called the load of nonsense of his students and many of his colleagues. Although I was worried about him, in fact maybe just because I was worried, I never admitted he was right. I hoped that if I criticized him he would understand, would stop his reactionary reformism (I used that phrase), become more flexible. But, in his eyes, that drove me yet again to the side of the students who were attacking him, the professors who were plotting against him.

It wasn't like that, the situation was more complicated. On the one hand I vaguely wanted to protect him, on the other I wanted to be on Lila's side, defend the choices I secretly attributed to her. To the point where every so often I thought of telephoning her and, starting with Pietro, with our conflicts, get her to tell me what she thought about it and, step by step, bring her out into the open. I didn't to it, naturally, it was absurd to expect sincerity on these subjects on the phone. But one night she called me, sounding really happy.

"I have some good news."

"What's happening?"

"I'm the head of technology."

"In what sense?"

"Head of the IBM data-processing center that Michele rented."

It seemed incredible to me. I asked her to repeat it, to explain carefully. She had accepted Solara's proposal? After so much resistance she had gone back to working for him, as in the days of Piazza dei Martiri? She said yes, enthusiastically, and became more and more excited, more explicit: Michele had entrusted to her the System 3 that he had rented and placed in a shoe warehouse in Acerra; she would employ operators and punch-card workers; the salary was four hundred and twenty-five thousand lire a month.

I was disappointed. Not only had the image of the guerrilla

vanished in an instant but everything I thought I knew of Lila wavered. I said:

"It's the last thing I would have expected of you."

"What was I supposed to do?"

"Refuse."

"Why?"

"We know what the Solaras are."

"And so what? It's already happened, and I'm better off working for Michele than for that shit Soccavo."

"Do as you like."

I heard her breathing. She said:

"I don't like that tone, Lenù. I'm paid more than Enzo, who is a man: What's wrong with that?"

"Nothing."

"The revolution, the workers, the new world, and that other bullshit?"

"Stop it. If you've unexpectedly decided to make a truthful speech I'm listening, otherwise let's forget it."

"May I point out something? You always use *true* and *truthfully*, when you speak and when you write. Or you say: *unexpectedly*. But when do people ever speak *truthfully* and when do things ever happen *unexpectedly*? You know better than I that it's all a fraud and that one thing follows another and then another. I don't do anything *truthfully* anymore, Lenù. And I've learned to pay attention to things. Only idiots believe that they happen *unexpectedly*."

"Bravo. What do you want me to believe, that you have everything under control, that it's you who are using Michele and not Michele you? Let's forget it, come on. Bye."

"No, speak, say what you have to say."

"I have nothing to say."

"Speak, otherwise I will."

"Then speak, let me listen."

"You criticize me but you say nothing to your sister?"

318 · ELENA FERRANTE

I was astonished.

"What does my sister have to do with anything?"

"You don't know anything about Elisa?"

"What should I know?"

She laughed maliciously.

"Ask your mother, your father, and your brothers."

89.

She wouldn't say anything else, she hung up, furious. I anxiously called my parents' house, my mother answered.

"Every so often you remember we exist," she said.

"Ma, what's happening to Elisa?"

"What happens to girls today."

"What?"

"She's with someone."

"She's engaged?"

"Let's put it like that."

"Who is she with?"

The answer went right through my heart.

"Marcello Solara."

That's what Lila wanted me to know. Marcello, the handsome Marcello of our early adolescence, her stubborn, desperate admirer, the young man she had humiliated by marrying Stefano Carracci, had taken my sister Elisa, the youngest of the family, my good little sister, the woman whom I still thought of as a magical child. And Elisa had let herself be taken. And my parents and my brothers had not lifted a finger to stop him. And my whole family, and in some way I myself, would end up related to the Solaras.

"Since when?" I asked.

"How do I know, a year."

"And you two gave your consent?"

"Did you ask our consent? You did as you liked. And she did the same thing."

"Pietro isn't Marcello Solara."

"You're right: Marcello would never let himself be treated by Elisa the way Pietro is treated by you."

Silence.

"You could have told me, you could have consulted me."

"Why? You left. 'I'll take care of you, don't worry.' Hardly. You've only thought of your own affairs, you didn't give a damn about us."

I decided to leave immediately for Naples with the children. I wanted to go by train, but Pietro volunteered to drive us, passing off as kindness the fact that he didn't want to work. As soon as we came down from the Doganella and were in the chaotic traffic of Naples, I felt gripped by the city, ruled by its unwritten laws. I hadn't set foot there since the day I left to get married. The noise seemed unbearable, I was irritated by the constant honking, by the insults the drivers shouted at Pietro when, not knowing the way, he hesitated, slowed down. A little before Piazza Carlo III I made him pull over. I got into the driver's seat, and drove aggressively to Via Firenze, to the same hotel he had stayed in years before. We left our bags. I carefully dressed the two girls and myself. Then we went to the neighborhood, to my parents' house. What did I think I could do, impose on Elisa my authority as the older sister, a university graduate, well married? Persuade her to break her engagement? Tell her: I've known Marcello since he grabbed my wrist and tried to pull me into the Fiat 1100, breaking Mamma's silver bracelet, so trust me, he's a vulgar, violent man? Yes. I felt determined, my job was to pull Elisa out of that trap.

My mother greeted Pietro affectionately and, in turn—*This is for Dede from Grandma, this is for Elsa*—she gave the two girls many small gifts that, in different ways, excited them. My father's voice was hoarse with emotion, he seemed thinner, even more subservient. I waited for my brothers to appear, but I discovered that they weren't home.

"They're always at work," my father said without enthusiasm.

"What do they do?"

"They work," my mother broke in.

"Where?"

"Marcello arranged jobs for them."

I remembered how the Solaras had *arranged a job* for Antonio, what they had made him into.

"Doing what?" I asked.

My mother answered in irritation:

"They bring money home and that's enough. Elisa isn't like you, Lenù, Elisa thinks of all of us."

I pretended not to hear: "Did you tell her I was coming today? Where is she?"

My father lowered his gaze, my mother said curtly: "At her house."

I became angry: "She doesn't live here anymore?"

"No."

"Since when?"

"Almost two months. She and Marcello have a nice apartment in the new neighborhood," my mother said coldly.

90.

He was more than just a boyfriend, then. I wanted to go to Elisa's house right away, even though my mother kept saying: What are you doing, your sister is preparing a surprise for you, stay here, we'll all go together later. I paid no attention. I telephoned Elisa, she answered happily and yet embarrassed. I said: Wait for me, I'm coming. I left Pietro and the girls with my parents and set off on foot.

The neighborhood seemed to me more run-down: the buildings dilapidated, the streets and sidewalks full of holes, littered with garbage. From black-edged posters that carpeted the walls—I had never seen so many—I learned that the old man Ugo Solara, Marcello and Michele's grandfather, had died. As the date attested, the event wasn't recent—it went back at least two months—and the high-flown phrases, the faces of grieving Madonnas, the very name of the dead man were faded, smudged. Yet the death notices persisted on the streets as if the other dead, out of respect, had decided to disappear from the world without letting anyone know. I saw several even at the entrance to Stefano's grocery. The shop was open, but it seemed to me a hole in the wall, dark, deserted, and Carracci appeared in the back, in his white smock, and disappeared like a ghost.

I climbed up toward the railroad, passing what we used to call the new grocery. The lowered shutter, partly off its tracks, was rusty and defaced by obscene words and drawings. That whole part of the neighborhood appeared abandoned, the shiny white of long ago had turned gray, the plaster had flaked off in places, revealing the bricks. I walked by the building where Lila had lived. Few of the stunted trees had survived. Packing tape held together the crack in the glass of the front door. Elisa lived farther on, in a better maintained area, more pretentious. The porter, a small bald man with a thin mustache, appeared, and stopped me, asking with hostility who I was looking for. I didn't know what to say. I muttered, Solara. He became deferential and let me go.

Only in the elevator did I realize that my entire self had in a sense slid backward. What would have seemed to me acceptable in Milan or Florence—a woman's freedom to dispose of her own body and her own desires, living with someone outside of marriage—there in the neighborhood seemed inconceivable: at stake was my sister's future, I couldn't control myself. Elisa had set up house with a dangerous person like Marcello? And my mother was pleased? She who had been enraged because I was married in a civil and not a religious ceremony; she who considered Lila a whore because she lived with Enzo, and Ada a prostitute because she had become Stefano's lover: *she* allowed her young daughter to sleep with Marcello Solara—a bad person—outside of marriage? I had thoughts of that sort as I went up to Elisa's, and a rage that I felt was justified. But my mind—my disciplined mind—was confused, I didn't know what arguments I would resort to. Those my mother would have asserted until a few years before, if I had made such a choice? Would I therefore regress to a level that she had left behind? Or should I say: Go and live with whoever you like but not with Marcello Solara? Should I say that? But what girl, today, in Florence, in Milan, would I ever force to leave a man, whoever he was, if she was in love with him?

When Elisa opened the door, I hugged her so hard that she said, laughing: You're hurting me. I felt her alarm as she invited me to sit down in the living room—a showy room full of flowered sofas and chairs with gilded backs—and began to speak quickly, but of other things: how well I looked, what pretty earrings I was wearing, what a nice necklace, how chic I was, she was so eager to meet Dede and Elsa. I described her nieces in detail, I took off my earrings, made her try them at the mirror, gave them to her. I saw her brighten; she laughed and said:

"I was afraid you'd come to scold me, to say you were opposed to my relationship with Marcello."

I stared at her for a long moment, I said:

"Elisa, I *am* opposed to it. And I made this trip purposely to tell you, Mamma, Papa, and our brothers."

Her expression changed; her eyes filled with tears.

"Now you're upsetting me: why are you against it?"

"The Solaras are terrible people."

"Not Marcello."

She began to tell me about him. She said it had started when I was pregnant with Elsa. Our mother had left to stay with me and she had found all the weight of the family on her. Once when she had gone to do the shopping at the Solaras' super-market, Rino, Lila's brother, had said that if she left the list of what she needed he would have it delivered. And while Rino was talking, she noticed that Marcello gave her a nod of greeting as if to let her know that that order had been given by him. From then on he had begun to hang around, doing kind things for her. Elisa had said to herself: He's old, I don't like him. But he had become increasingly present in her life, always courteous, there hadn't been a word or a gesture that recalled the hateful side of the Solaras. Marcello was really a respectable person, with him she felt safe, he had a strength, an authority, that made him seem ten meters tall. Not only that. From the moment it became clear that he was interested in her, Elisa's life had changed. Everyone, in the neighborhood and outside it, had begun to treat her like a queen, everyone had begun to consider her important. It was a wonderful feeling, she wasn't yet used to it. Before, she said, you're nobody, and right afterward even the mice in the sewer grates know you: of course, you've written a book, you're famous, you're used to it, but I'm not, I was astonished. It had been thrilling to discover that she didn't have to worry about anything. Marcello took care of it all, every desire of hers was a command for him. So as time passed she fell in love. In the end she had said yes. And now if a day went by and she didn't see or hear from him, she was awake all night crying.

Elisa was convinced that she had had an unimaginable stroke of luck and I knew that I wouldn't have the strength to spoil all that happiness. Especially since she didn't offer me any opportunity: Marcello was capable, Marcello was respon-sible, Marcello was handsome, Marcello was perfect. With every word she uttered she was careful either to keep him sep-arate from the Solara family or to speak with cautious liking for his mother, or his father, who had a stomach disease, and almost never left the house, or of the deceased grandfather, sometimes even of Michele, who, if you spent time with him, also seemed different from the way people judged him; he was very affectionate. So believe me, she said, I've never been so happy since I was born, and even Mamma, and you know what she's like, is on my side, even Papa, and Gianni and Peppe, who until a short time ago spent their days doing nothing, now Marcello employs them, paying them really well.

"If that's really the way things are, get married," I said.

"We will. But now isn't a good time, Marcello says he has to settle some complicated business affairs. And then there's the mourning for his grandfather, poor man, he lost his mind, he couldn't remember how to walk, or even how to speak, by taking him God set him free. But as soon as things calm down we'll get married, don't worry. And then, before you get married, it's better to see if you get along, isn't it?"

She began to speak in words that weren't hers, the words of a modern girl picked up from the comic books she read. I compared them with the ones I would have uttered on those same subjects and I realized that they weren't very different, Elisa's words only seemed a little coarser. How to respond? I didn't know at the start of that visit, and I don't know now. I could have said: There's not much to say, Elisa, it's all clear: Marcello will consume you, he'll get used to your body, he'll leave you. But they were words that sounded old, not even my mother had dared to say them. So I resigned myself. I had gone away, Elisa had stayed. What would I have been if I, too, had stayed, what choices would I have made? Hadn't I, too, liked the Solara boys when I was a girl? And besides, what had I gained by leaving? Not even the capacity to find words of wisdom to persuade my sister not to ruin herself. Elisa had a pretty face with delicate features, an unremarkable body, a caressing voice. Marcello I remembered as tall, handsome, muscular, he had a square face with a healthy complexion, and was capable of intense feelings of love: he had demonstrated that when he was in love with Lila, it didn't seem that he'd had other loves since. What to say, then? In the end she went to get a box and showed me all the jewelry Marcello had given her, objects compared to which the earrings I had given her were what they were, small things.

"Be careful," I said. "Don't lose yourself. And if you need to, call me."

I was about to get up, but she stopped me, laughing.

"Where are you going, didn't Mamma tell you? They're all coming here for dinner. I've made a huge amount of food."

I showed my annoyance:

"All who?"

"Everyone: it's a surprise."

91.

The first to arrive were my father and mother, with the two little girls and Pietro. Dede and Elsa received more presents from Elisa, who fussed over them (*Dede, sweetie, give me a big kiss here; Elsa, how nice and plump you are, come to your aunt, you know we have the same name?*). My mother disappeared immediately into the kitchen, head down, without looking at me. Pietro tried to pull me aside to tell me I don't know what serious thing but with the air of one who wants to declare his innocence. Instead, my father dragged him over to sit on a couch in front of the television and turned it on at high volume.

Soon afterward Gigliola appeared with her children, two fierce boys who immediately ganged up with Dede, while Elsa, bewildered, took refuge with me. Gigliola was fresh from the hairdresser, her extremely high heels clacked on the floor, she sparkled with gold, in her ears, around her neck, on her arms. A bright green dress, with a very low décolletage, barely contained her, and she wore heavy makeup that was already cracking. She turned to me and said without preamble, sarcastically:

"Here we are, we've come to honor you professors. Everything good, Lenù? Is that the genius of the university? My goodness, what nice hair your husband has."

Pietro freed himself from my father, who had an arm around his shoulders, jumped up with a timid smile, and couldn't restrain himself, his gaze instinctively rested on the large wave of Gigliola's breasts. She noted it with satisfaction.

"Easy, easy," she said to him, "or I'll be embarrassed. Here no one ever gets up to greet a lady."

My father pulled my husband back, worried that someone would take him away, and started talking to him again about something or other, in spite of the booming television. I asked Gigliola how she was, trying to convey to her with my gaze, my tone of voice, that I hadn't forgotten her confidences and was close to her. The idea must not have pleased her, she said:

"Listen, sweetheart, I'm fine, you're fine, we're all fine. But if my husband hadn't ordered me to come here and bore my ass off, I'd be much better off at my house. Just to be clear."

I couldn't answer, someone was ringing the doorbell. My sister moved lightly, she seemed to glide on a breath of wind, she hurried to open the door. I heard her exclaim: How happy I am, come, Mamma, come in. And she reappeared, holding by the hand her future mother-in-law, Manuela Solara, who was dressed for a party, a fake flower in her dyed reddish hair, sorrowful eyes set in deep sockets, even thinner than the last time I'd seen her—almost skin and bone. Behind her was Michele, well dressed, carefully shaved, with a brusque power in his gaze and in his calm movements. And a moment afterward appeared a big man I had trouble recognizing, everything about him was enormous: he was tall, with big feet, long large powerful legs, his stomach and chest and shoulders inflated by some heavy, compact material; he had a large head with a broad forehead, his long brown hair was combed back, his beard was coal-black. It was Marcello: Elisa confirmed it by offering her lips as if to a god to whom one owes respect and gratitude. He bent over, brushing hers with his, while my father rose, pulling up Pietro, too, with an embarrassed air, and my mother hurried limping from the kitchen. I realized that the presence of Signora Solara was considered exceptional, a thing to be proud of. Elisa whispered to me with emotion: Today my mother-in-law is sixty. Ah, I said, and meanwhile I was surprised to see Marcello, as soon as he came in, turn directly to my husband as if they already knew each other. He gave him a bright smile, shouting: Everything's taken care of, Prof. *What everything was taken care of?* Pietro responded with an uncertain smile, then he looked at me, shaking his head in distress, as if to say: I did everything I could. I would have liked him to explain, but already Marcello was introducing Manuela: Come, Mamma, this is the professor husband of Lenuccia, sit down here next to him. Pietro made a half bow, and I, too, felt compelled to greet Signora Solara, who said: How pretty you are Lenù, you're pretty like your sister, and then she asked me with some anxiety: It's warm in here, don't you feel it? I didn't answer, Dede was whining, calling me, Gigliola—the only one who appeared to give no importance to the presence of Manuela—shouted something vulgar in dialect to her children who had hit mine. I realized that Michele was studying me silently, without even saying hello. I greeted him, in a loud voice, then tried to soothe Dede and Elsa, who, seeing her sister distressed, was about to start crying in turn. Marcello said to me: I'm so happy to have you as a guest in my house, it's a great honor for me, believe me. He turned to Elisa as if to speak directly to me were beyond his powers: You tell her how pleased I am, your sister intimidates me. I said something to put him at ease, but at that moment the doorbell rang again.

Michele went to the door, and he returned shortly afterward with a look of amusement. He was followed by an old man who was carrying suitcases, *my suitcases*, the suitcases we had left in the hotel. Michele gestured toward me, the man placed them in front of me as if he had performed a magic trick for my entertainment. No, I exclaimed, oh no, you're making me angry. But Elisa embraced me, kissed me, said: We have room, you can't stay in a hotel, we have so much space here, and two bathrooms. Anyway, Marcello said emphatically, I asked your husband for permission, I wouldn't have dared take the initiative: Prof, please talk to your wife, defend me. I gasped, furious but smiling: Good Lord, what a mess, thank you Marcè, you're very kind, but we really can't accept. And I tried to send the suitcases back to the hotel. But I also had to attend to Dede, I said to her: Let me see what the boys did, it's nothing, a little kiss will make it go away, go play, take Elsa. And I called Pietro, already caught in the coils of Manuela Solara: Pietro, come here, please, what did you say to Marcello, we can't sleep here. And I realized that my voice was taking on the tones of the dialect, out of nervousness, that words were coming to me in the Neapolitan of the neighborhood, that the neighborhood—from the courtyard to the *stradone* and the tunnel—was imposing its language on me, its mode of acting and reacting, its figures, those which in Florence seemed faded images and here were flesh and blood.

There was another ring at the door, Elisa went to open it. Who else was still to arrive? A few seconds passed and Gennaro rushed into the room. He saw Dede, Dede saw him, incredulous. She immediately stopped whining, and they stared at each other, overwhelmed by that unexpected reunion. Right afterward Enzo appeared, the only blond among so many dark-haired people and bright colors, and yet he was grim. Finally Lila entered.

92.

A long period of words without body, of voice alone that ran in waves over an electric sea, suddenly shattered. Lila wore a knee-length blue dress. She was thin, all sinews, which made her seem taller than usual in spite of her low heels. She had deep wrinkles at the sides of her mouth and her eyes, otherwise the pale skin of her face was stretched over the forehead, the cheekbones. Her hair, combed into a ponytail, showed threads of white over her ears, which were almost without lobes. As soon as she saw me she smiled, she narrowed her eyes. I didn't smile and was so surprised I said nothing, not even hello. Although we were both thirty years old, she seemed older, more worn than I imagined I was. Gigliola shouted: Finally the other little queen is here, the children are hungry, I can't control them anymore.

We ate. I felt as if I were being squeezed in an uncomfortable device; I couldn't swallow. I thought angrily of the suitcases, which I had unpacked in the hotel and which had been arbitrarily repacked by one or more strangers, people who had touched my things, Pietro's, the children's, making a mess. I couldn't accept the evidence—that I would sleep in the house of Marcello Solara to please my sister, who shared his bed. I watched, with a hostility that grieved me, Elisa and my mother, the first, overwhelmed by an anxious happiness, talking on and on as she played the part of mistress of the house, the second appearing content, so content that she even filled Lila's plate politely. I observed Enzo, who ate with his head down, annoyed by Gigliola, who pressed her enormous bosom against his arm and talked in loud, flirtatious tones. I looked with irritation at Pietro, who, although assailed by my father, by Marcello, by Signora Solara, paid attention only to Lila, who sat opposite him and was indifferent to everyone, even to me—maybe especially to me—but not to him. And the children got on my nerves, the five new lives who had arranged themselves into two groups: Gennaro and Dede, well-behaved and devious, against Gigliola's children, who, drinking wine from their distracted mother's glass, were becoming intolerable, and now appealing to Elsa, who had joined them, even if they took no notice of her.

Who had put on this show? Who had mixed together different reasons to celebrate? Elisa obviously, but pushed by whom? Maybe by Marcello. But Marcello had surely been directed by Michele, who was sitting next to me, and who, at his ease, ate, drank, pretended to ignore the behavior of his wife and children, but stared ironically at my husband, who seemed fascinated by Lila. What did he want to prove? That this was the territory of the Solaras? That even if I had escaped I belonged to that place and therefore to them? That they could force on me anything by mobilizing affections, vocabulary, rituals, but also by destroying them, by making at their convenience the ugly beautiful and the beautiful ugly? He spoke to me for the first time since he had arrived. Did you see Mamma, he said, imagine, she's sixty, but who would ever say so, look how pretty she is, she carries it well, no? He raised his voice on purpose, so that everyone could hear not so much his question as the answer that I was now obliged to give. I had to speak in praise of Mamma. Here she was, sitting next to Pietro, an old woman who was a little vague, polite, apparently innocuous, with a long bony face, a massive nose, that crazy flower in her thinning hair. And yet she was the loan shark who had founded the family fortunes; the caretaker and guardian of the red book in which were the names of so many in the neighborhood, the city, and the province; the woman of the crime without punishment, a ruthless and dangerous woman, according to the telephonic fantasy I had indulged in, along with Lila, and according to the pages of my aborted novel: Mamma who had killed Don Achille, to replace him and gain a monopoly on loan-sharking, and who had brought up her two sons to seize everything, trampling on everyone. And now I had the obligation to say to Michele: Yes, it's true, how pretty your mother looks, how well she carries her years, congratulations. And I saw out of the corner of my eye that Lila had stopped talking to Pietro and expected nothing else, already she was turning to look at me, her full lips parted, her eyes cracks, her brow furrowed. I read the sarcasm in her face, it occurred to me that maybe she had suggested to Michele that he put me in that cage: *Mamma's just turned sixty, Lenù, the mamma of your brother-in-law, your sister's mother-in-law, let's see what you say now, let's see if you continue to play the schoolmistress.* I responded, turning to Manuela, *Happy Birthday*, nothing else. And immediately Marcello broke in, as if to help me, he exclaimed, with emotion: Thank you, thank you, Lenù. Then he turned to his mother; her face was pained, sweaty, and red blotches had appeared on her skinny neck: Lenuccia has congratulated you, Mamma. And immediately Pietro said to the woman who was sitting next to him: Happy Birthday also from me, Signora. And so everyone—everyone except Gigliola and Lila—paid respects to Signora Solara, even the children, in chorus: Many happy returns, Manuela, many happy returns, Grandma. And she shied away, saying, I'm old, and, taking out of her purse a blue fan with the image of the gulf and a smoking Vesuvio, she began to fan herself, slowly at first, then more energetically.

Michele, although he had turned to me, seemed to give my husband's good wishes more importance. He spoke to him politely: too kind, Prof, you aren't from here and you can't know the good qualities of our mother. He assumed a confidential tone: We're good folk, my late grandfather, rest his soul, started out with the bar here at the corner, started from nothing, and my father expanded it, he made a pastry shop that's famous in all Naples, thanks also to the skill of Spagnuolo, my wife's father, an extraordinary artisan—right, Gigliò? But, he added, it's to my mother, to *our* mother, that we owe everything. In recent times envious people, people who wish us harm, have spread odious rumors about her. But we are tolerant people, life has taught us to stay in business and to be patient. So the truth always prevails. And the truth is that this woman is extremely intelligent, she has a strong character; there has never been a moment when it would even cross your mind that she has the desire to do nothing. She has always worked, always, and she has done it only for the family, she never enjoyed anything for herself. What we have today is what she built for us children, what we do today is only the continuation of what she did.

Manuela fanned herself with a more deliberate gesture, she said aloud to Pietro: Michele is a wonderful son. When he was a child, at Christmas, he would climb up on the table and recite poetry beautifully; but his flaw is that he likes to talk and when he talks he has to exaggerate. Marcello interrupted: No, Mamma, what exaggeration, it's all true. And Michele continued to sing Manuela's praises, how beautiful she was, how generous, he wouldn't stop. Until suddenly he turned to me. He said seriously, in fact solemnly: There's only one other woman who is *almost* like our mother. *Another woman? A woman almost comparable to Manuela Solara?* I looked at him in bewilderment. The phrase, in spite of that *almost*, was out of place, and for a few instants the noisy dinner became soundless. Gigliola stared at her husband with nervous eyes, the pupils dilated by wine and unhappiness. My mother, too, assumed an expression that was unsuitable, watchful: Maybe she hoped that that woman was Elisa, that Michele was about to assign to

her daughter a sort of right of succession to the most elevated
seat among the Solaras. And Manuela stopped fanning herself
for a moment, she dried with her index finger the sweat on her
lips, she waited for her son to upend those words in a mocking
remark.

But, with the audacity that had always distinguished him,
not giving a damn about his wife or Enzo or even his mother,
he stared at Lila while his face turned a greenish color and his
gestures became more agitated and his words served as a rope,
dragging her attention away from Pietro. Tonight, he said,
we're all here, at my brother's house, first to welcome as they
deserve these two esteemed professors and their beautiful children; second to celebrate my mother, the most blessed woman,
third to wish Elisa great happiness and, soon, a fine marriage;
fourth, if you will allow me, to toast an agreement that I was
afraid would never be made. Lina, please, come here.

Lina. Lila.

I sought her gaze and she looked back for a fraction of a
second, a look that said: Now do you understand the game,
you remember how it works? Then, to my great surprise, while
Enzo stared at an indeterminate point on the tablecloth, she
rose meekly and came over to Michele.

He didn't touch her. He didn't touch a hand, an arm, nothing, as if between them hung a blade that could wound him.
Instead he placed his fingers for several seconds on my shoulder and turned to me again: You mustn't be offended, Lenù,
you're smart, you've gone so far, you've been in the newspapers, you're the pride of us all who have known you since you
were a child. But—and I'm sure you agree, and you'll be
pleased if I say it now, because you love her—Lina has something alive in her mind that no one else has, something strong,
that jumps here and there and nothing can stop it, a thing that
not even the doctors can see and that I think not even she
knows, even though it's been there since she was born—she

doesn't know it and doesn't want to recognize it, look what a mean face she's making right now—a thing that, if it doesn't like you can cause you a lot of problems but, if it does, leaves everyone astonished. Well, for a long time I've wanted to buy this distinctive aspect of her. Yes, buy, there's nothing wrong, buy the way you buy pearls, diamonds. But until now, unfortunately, it was impossible. We've made just a small step forward, and it's this small step that I wish to celebrate tonight: I've hired Signora Cerullo to work in the data-processing center that I've set up in Acerra, a very modern thing that if it interests you, Lenù, if it interests the professor, I'll take you to visit tomorrow, or anyway before you leave. What do you say, Lina?

Lila made an expression of disgust. She shook her head unhappily and said, staring at Signora Solara: Michele doesn't understand anything about computers and I don't know what he thinks that I do, but it's nonsense, it just takes a correspondence course, I learned it even though I only went up to fifth grade in school. And she said nothing else. She didn't mock Michele, as I expected she would, because of that tremendous image he had invented, the living thing that flowed in her mind. She didn't mock him for the pearls, the diamonds. Above all, she didn't evade the compliments. In fact she allowed us to toast her hiring as if she really had been assumed into Heaven, she allowed Michele to continue to praise her, justifying with his praise the salary he was paying her. And all while Pietro, with that capacity of his for feeling at ease with people he considered inferior, was already saying, without consulting me, that he would very much like to visit the center in Acerra and he wanted to hear about it from Lila, who had sat down again. I thought for a moment that if I gave her time she would take away my husband as she had taken Nino from me. But I didn't feel jealous: if it happened it would happen only out of a desire to dig a deeper furrow between us, I took it for granted that she couldn't like Pietro and that Pietro would never be capable of betraying me out of desire for someone else.

Another feeling, however, came over me, a more tangled one. I was in the place where I was born, I had always been considered the girl who had been most successful, I was convinced that it was, at least in that place, an indisputable fact. Instead Michele, as if he had deliberately organized my demotion in the neighborhood and in particular in the midst of the family I came from, had contrived to make Lila overshadow me, he had even wanted me to comply with my overshadowing by publicly recognizing the incomparable power of my friend. And she had willingly agreed to it. In fact, maybe she had even had a hand in the result, planning and organizing it. If a few years earlier, when I had had my little success as a writer, the thing wouldn't have wounded me, in fact would have pleased me, now that that was over I realized that I was suffering. I exchanged a look with my mother. She was frowning, she had the expression she assumed when she was struggling not to hit me. She wanted me not to pretend my usual meekness, she wanted me to react, to show how much I knew, all the high-quality stuff, not that nonsense of Acerra. She was saying it to me with her eyes, like a mute command. But I said nothing. Suddenly Manuela Solara, darting glances of impatience, exclaimed: I feel hot, don't you all, too?

93.

Elisa, like my mother, could not tolerate my loss of prestige. But while my mother remained silent, she turned to me, radiant, affectionate, to let me know that I remained her extraordinary older sister, whom she would always be proud of. I have something to give you, she said, and added, jumping lightheartedly, as was her way, from one subject to another: Have you ever been in an airplane? I said no. Possible? Possible. It turned out that of those present only Pietro had flown, several times, but he spoke of it as if it were nothing much. Instead for Elisa it had been a wonderful experience, and also for Marcello. They had gone to Germany, a long flight, for reasons of work and pleasure. Elisa had been afraid at first, because of the jolting and shaking, and a jet of cold air struck her right in the head as if it were going to drill a hole. Then through the window she had seen white clouds below and blue sky above. So she had discovered that above the clouds there was always fine weather, and from high up the earth was all green and blue and violet and shining with snow when they flew over the mountains. She asked me:

"Guess who we met in Düsseldorf."

I said, unhappy with everything:

"I don't know, Elisa, tell me."

"Antonio."

"Ah."

"He was very eager for me to send his greetings."

"Is he well?"

"Very well. He gave me a gift for you."

So that was the thing she had for me, a gift from Antonio. She got up and went to get it. Marcello looked at me with a smile, Pietro asked:

"Who is Antonio?"

"An employee of ours," said Marcello.

"A boyfriend of your wife," said Michele, laughing. "Times have changed, Professò, today women have a lot of boyfriends and they boast about it much more than men. How many girlfriends have you had?"

Pietro said seriously:

"None, I've loved only my wife."

"Liar," Michele exclaimed, in great amusement. "Can I whisper to you how many girlfriends I've had?"

He got up and, followed by Gigliola's look of disgust, stood behind my husband, whispered to him.

"Incredible," Pietro exclaimed, cautiously ironic. They laughed together.

Meanwhile Elisa returned, she handed me a package wrapped in packing paper.

"Open it."

"Do you know what's in it?" I asked, puzzled.

"We both know," said Marcello, "but we hope you don't."

I unwrapped the package. I realized, as I did, that they were all watching me. Lila looked at me sideways, intent, as if she expected a snake to dart out. When they saw that Antonio, the son of crazy Melina, the illiterate and violent servant of the Solaras, my boyfriend in adolescence, had sent me as a gift nothing wonderful, nothing moving, nothing that alluded to times past, but only a book, they seemed disappointed. Then they noticed that I had changed color, that I was looking at the cover with a joy I couldn't control. It wasn't just any book. It was *my* book. It was the German translation of my novel, six years after its publication in Italy. For the first time I was present at the spectacle—yes, a spectacle—of my words dancing before my eyes in a foreign language.

"You didn't know about it?" Elisa asked, happy.

"No."

"And you're pleased?"

"Very pleased."

My sister announced to everyone proudly:

"It's the novel Lenuccia wrote, but with German words."

And my mother, reddening in return, said:

"You see how famous she is?"

Gigliola took the book, paged through it, said admiringly: the only thing I can understand is *Elena Greco*. Lila then reached out her hand in an imperative way, indicating that she wanted it. I saw in her eyes curiosity, the desire to touch and look at and read the unknown language that contained me and had transported me far away. I saw in her the urgency for that object, an urgency that I recognized, she had had it as a child, and it softened me. But Gigliola started angrily, she pulled the book away so that Lila couldn't take it, and said:

"Wait, I have it now. What is it, you know German?" And Lila withdrew her hand, shook her head no, and Gigliola exclaimed: "Then don't be a pain in the ass, let me look: I want to see what Lenuccia was able to do." In the general silence, she turned the book over and over in her hands with satisfaction. She leafed through the pages one after another, slowly, as if she were reading a few lines here, a few there. Finally, her voice thickened by the wine, she said, handing it to me: "Bravo, Lenù, compliments for everything, the book, the husband, the children. You might think that we're the only ones who know you and instead even the Germans do. What you have, you deserve, you got it with hard work, without hurting anyone, without bullshitting with other people's husbands. Thank you, now I really have to go, good night."

She struggled to get up, sighing, she had become even heavier, because of the wine. She yelled at the children: Hurry up, and they protested, the older said something vulgar in dialect, she slapped him and dragged him toward the door. Michele shook his head with a smile on his face, he muttered: I've had a rough time with that bitch, she always has to ruin my day. Then he said calmly: Wait, Gigliò, what's your hurry, first we have to eat your father's dessert, then we'll go. And the children, in a flash, fortified by their father's words, slipped away and returned to the table. Gigliola, instead, continued with her heavy tread toward the door, saying in irritation: I'll go by myself, I don't feel well. But at that point Michele shouted at her in a loud voice, charged with violence: Sit down right now, and she stopped as if the words had paralyzed her legs. Elisa jumped up and said softly, Come, help me get the cake. She took her by the arm, pulled her toward the kitchen. I reassured Dede with a look, she was frightened by Michele's shouting. Then I held out the book to Lila, saying: Do you want to see? She shook her head with an expression of indifference.

94.

"Where have we ended up?" Pietro asked, half outraged and half amused, when, once the children had been put to bed, we closed the door of the room that Elisa had given us. He wanted to joke about the more incredible moments of the evening, but I attacked him, we quarreled in low voices. I was angry with him, with everyone, with myself. From the chaotic feeling I had inside, the desire that Lila would get sick and die was re-emerging. Not out of hatred, I loved her more and more, I wouldn't have been capable of hating her. But I couldn't bear the emptiness of her evasion. How could you possibly, I asked Pietro, agree to let them take our bags, bring them here, give them the authority to move us to this house? And he: I didn't know what sort of people they were. No, I hissed, it's that you've never listened to me, I've always told you where I come from.

We talked for a long time, he tried to soothe me, I berated him. I said he had been too timid, that he had been put upon, that he knew how to insist only with the well-brought-up people of his world, that I no longer trusted him, that I didn't even trust his mother, how could it be that my book had come out in Germany two years ago and the publisher had said nothing about it, what other countries had it been published in without my knowing, I wanted to get to the bottom of it, et cetera et cetera. To make me feel better, he agreed, and urged me to telephone his mother and the publisher the next morning. Then he declared a great liking for what he called the working-class environment I had been born and brought up in. He whispered that my mother was a generous and very intelligent person, he had kind words for my father, for Elisa, for Gigliola, for Enzo. But his tone changed abruptly when he came to the Solaras: he called them crooks, vicious scoundrels, smooth-talking criminals. And finally he came to Lila. He said softly: It's she who disturbed me most. I noticed, I snapped, you talked to her the whole evening. Pietro shook his head ener-getically, he explained, surprisingly, that Lila had seemed to him the worst person. He said that she wasn't at all my friend, that she hated me, that she was extraordinarily intelligent, that she was very fascinating, but her intelligence had been put to bad use—it was the evil intelligence that sows discord and hates life—and her fascination was the more intolerable, the fascination that enslaves and drives a person to ruin. Just like that.

At first I pretended to disagree, but in fact I was pleased. I had been wrong then, Lila hadn't affected him, Pietro was a man practiced in perceiving the subtext of every text and had easily picked up her unpleasant aspects. But soon it seemed to me that he was overdoing it. He said: I don't understand how your relationship could have lasted so long, obviously you've carefully hidden from each other anything that could rupture it. And he added: either I haven't understood anything about her—and it's likely, I don't know her—or I haven't understood anything about you, and that is more upsetting. Finally he said the ugliest words: She and that Michele are made for each other, if they aren't already lovers they will be. Then I revolted. I hissed that I couldn't bear his pedantic overeducated bour-geois tone, that he must never again speak of my friend in that way, that he hadn't understood anything. And as I was speak-ing I seemed to perceive something that at that moment not even he knew: Lila had affected him, seriously; Pietro had grasped her exceptionality so well that he was frightened by it and now felt the need to vilify her. He was afraid not for himself, I think, but for me and for our relationship. He was afraid that, even at a distance, she would tear me away from him, destroy us. And to protect me he overdid it, he slandered her, in a confused way he wanted me to be disgusted by her and expel her from my life. I whispered good night, and turned the other way.

95.

The next day I got up very early and packed the suitcases, I wanted to return to Florence right away. But I couldn't. Marcello said he had promised his brother to take us to Acerra and since Pietro, although I let him know in every possible way that I wanted to leave, was willing, we left the children with Elisa and agreed to let that big man drive us to a long, low yellow building, a large shoe warehouse. The whole way I was silent, while Pietro asked questions about the Solaras' business in Germany and Marcello equivocated, with disjointed phrases like: Italy, Germany, the world, Professò, I'm more Communist than the Communists, more revolutionary than the revolutionaries, for me if you could flatten everything and build it all again from the beginning I'd be in the first row. Anyway, he added, looking at me in the rear-view mirror in search of agreement, love for me comes before everything.

When we got there, he led us into a low-ceilinged room, illuminated by neon lights. There was a strong odor of ink, of dust, of overheated insulators, mixed with that of uppers and shoe polish. Look, Marcello said, here's the contraption Michele rented. I looked around, there was no one at the machine. The System 3 was completely unremarkable, an uninteresting piece of furniture backed up to a wall: metal panels, control knobs, a red switch, a wooden shelf, keyboards. I don't understand anything about it, said Marcello, this is stuff that Lina knows, but she doesn't have a schedule, she's always in and out. Pietro carefully examined the panels, the control knobs, everything, but it was clear that modernity was disappointing him, all the more since Marcello answered every question with: This is my brother's business, I have other problems on my mind.

Lila showed up when we were about to leave. She was with two young women who were carrying metal containers. She seemed irritated, and ordered them around. As soon as she noticed us she changed her tone, she became polite but in a forced way, as if a part of her brain had broken free and were reaching toward urgent things to do with the job. She ignored Marcello, and addressed Pietro but as if she were also speaking to me. What do you care about this stuff, she said, teasing, if you're really interested in it let's make a deal: You work here and I'll take up your things, novels, paintings, antiquities. Again I had the impression that she had aged before me, not only in her appearance but in her movements, her voice, her choice of a dull, vaguely bored manner in which to explain to us not only how the System 3 and the various machines worked but also the magnetic cards, the tapes, the five-inch disks, and other innovations that were on the way, like desktop computers that one could have at home for one's personal use. She was no longer the Lila who on the telephone talked about the new job in childish tones, and she seemed far removed from Enzo's enthusiasm. She acted like a super-competent employee on whom the boss has dumped one of the many headaches, the tourist visit. She wasn't friendly toward me, she never joked with Pietro. Finally she ordered the girls to show my husband how the punch-card machine worked, then she pushed me into the hall, and said:

"So? Did you congratulate Elisa? Does one sleep well in Marcello's house? Are you glad the old witch is sixty?"

I replied nervously: "If my sister wants it, what can I do, beat her over the head?"

"You see? In the fairy tales one does as one wants, and in reality one does what one can."

"That's not true. Who forced you to be used by Michele?"

"I'm using him, not him me."

"You're deceiving yourself."

"Wait and you'll see."

"What do you want me to see, Lila, forget it."

"I repeat, I don't like it when you act like that. You don't know anything about us anymore, so it's better if you say nothing."

"You mean I can criticize you only if I live in Naples?"

"Naples, Florence: you aren't doing anything anywhere, Lenù."

"Who says so?"

"The facts."

"I know my facts, not you."

I was tense, she realized it. She gave me a conciliatory look.

"You make me mad and I say things I don't think. You did well to leave Naples, you did very well. But you know who's back?"

"Who?"

"Nino."

The news burned my chest.

"How do you know?"

"Marisa told me. He got a professorship at the university."

"He didn't like Milan?"

Lila narrowed her eyes.

"He married someone from Via Tasso who is related to half the Banco di Napoli. They have a child a year old."

I don't know if I suffered, certainly I had trouble believing it.

344 · ELENA FERRANTE

"He's really married?"

"Yes."

I looked at her to see what she had in mind.

"Do you intend to see him?"

"No. But if I happen to run into him, I want to tell him that Gennaro isn't his."

96.

She said to me this and some other fragmented things: *Congratulations, you have an intelligent and handsome husband, he speaks as if he were religious even if he's not a believer, he knows ancient and modern facts, in particular he knows a lot of things about Naples, I'm ashamed, I'm Neapolitan but I don't know anything. Gennaro is growing up, my mother takes care of him more than I do, he's smart in school. With Enzo things are good, we work a lot, we rarely see each other. Stefano has ruined himself with his own hands: the carabinieri found stolen goods in the back of the shop, I don't know what, he was arrested; now he's out but he has to be careful, he has nothing anymore, I give him money, not the other way around. You see how things change: if I had remained Signora Carracci I would be ruined, I would have ended up with my ass on the ground like all the Carraccis; instead I am Raffaella Cerullo and I'm the technical director for Michele Solara at four hundred and twenty thousand lire a month. The result is that my mother treats me like a queen, my father has forgiven me for everything, my brother sucks money out of me, Pinuccia says she loves me so much, their children call me Auntie. But it's a boring job, completely the opposite of what it seemed at first: still too slow, you waste a lot of time, let's hope that the new machines get here soon—they're a lot faster. Or no. Speed consumes everything, as when photographs come out blurry. Alfonso used that expression, he used it in fun, he said that he came out blurry, without clear outlines. Lately he's been talking to me constantly about friendship. He wants to be my friend, he would like to copy me on copying paper, he swears that he would like to be a girl like me. What sort of girl, I said to him, you're a male, Alfò, you don't know anything about what I'm like, and even if we're friends and you study me and spy on me and copy me, you'll never know anything. So—he was having a good time—what do I do, I suffer being the way I am. And he confessed to me that he has always loved Michele—yes, Michele Solara—and he wishes Michele would like him the way he thinks Michele likes me. You understand, Lenù, what happens to people: we have too much stuff inside and it swells us, breaks us. All right, I said, we're friends, but get out of your mind that you can be a woman like me, all you'd succeed in being is what a woman is according to you men. You can copy me, make a portrait as precise as an artist, but my shit will always remain mine, and yours will be yours. Ah, Lenù, what happens to us all, we're like pipes when the water freezes, what a terrible thing a dissatisfied mind is. You remember what we did with my wedding picture? I want to continue on that path. The day will come when I reduce myself to diagrams, I'll become a perforated tape and you won't find me anymore.*

Nonsense, that's all. That talk in the hall confirmed to me that our relationship no longer had any intimacy. It had been reduced to succinct information, scant details, mean remarks, hot air, no revelation of facts and thoughts for me alone. Lila's life was now hers and that was all, it seemed that she didn't want to share it with anyone. Pointless to persist with questions like: What do you know about Pasquale, where did you end up, what do you have to do with Soccavo's death, the kneecapping of Filippo, what led you to accept Michele's offer, what do you make of his dependence on you. Lila had retreated into the unconfessable, any questions of mine could not become conversation, she would say: What are you thinking, you're crazy,

Michele, dependence, Soccavo, what are you talking about? Even now, as I write, I realize that I don't have enough information to move on to *Lila went, Lila did, Lila met, Lila planned.* And yet, as I was returning in the car to Florence, I had the impression that there in the neighborhood, between backwardness and modernity, she had more history than I did. How much I had lost by leaving, believing I was destined for who knows what life. Lila, who had remained, had a very new job, she earned a lot of money, she acted in absolute freedom and according to schemes that were indecipherable. She was very attached to her son, she had been extremely devoted to him in the first years of his life, and she still kept an eye on him; but she seemed capable of being free of him as and when she wanted, he didn't cause her the anxieties my daughters caused me. She had broken with her family, and yet she took on their burden and the responsibility for them whenever she could. She took care of Stefano who was in trouble, but without getting close to him. She hated the Solaras and yet she submitted to them. She was ironic about Alfonso and was his friend. She said she didn't want to see Nino again, but I knew it wasn't so, that she would see him. Hers was a life in motion, mine was stopped. While Pietro drove in silence and the children quarreled, I thought a lot about her and Nino, about what might happen. Lila will take him back, I fantasized, she'll manage to see him again, she'll influence him the way she knows how, she'll get him away from his wife and son, she'll use him in her war I no longer know against whom, she'll induce him to get divorced, and meanwhile she'll escape from Michele after taking a lot of money from him, and she'll leave Enzo, and finally she'll make up her mind to divorce Stefano, and maybe she'll marry Nino, maybe not, but certainly they'll put their intelligences together and who can say what they will become.

Become. It was a verb that had always obsessed me, but I realized it for the first time only in that situation. *I wanted to become*, even though I had never known what. And I had *become*, that was certain, but without an object, without a real passion, without a determined ambition. I had wanted to become something—here was the point—only because I was afraid that Lila would become someone and I would stay behind. *My becoming was a becoming in her wake.* I had to start again to *become*, but for myself, as an adult, outside of her.

97.

I telephoned Adele as soon as I got home, to find out about the German translation that Antonio had sent me. It had come out of the blue, she didn't know anything about it, either. She called the publisher. She called me back after a while to tell me that the book had been published not only in Germany but in France and Spain. So, I asked, what should I do? Adele answered in bewilderment: Nothing, be satisfied. Of course, I said, I'm *very* pleased, but from the practical point of view, I don't know, should I go promote it abroad? She said affectionately: You don't have to do anything, Elena, the book unfortunately didn't sell anywhere.

My mood got worse. I nagged the publisher, I asked for precise information about the translations, I was angry because no one cared to keep me informed, I ended up saying to an indifferent secretary: I found out about the German edition not from you but from a semiliterate friend: can you do your job or not? Then I apologized, I felt stupid. One after the other the French copy and the Spanish arrived, a copy in German without the crumpled look of the one sent by Antonio. They were ugly books: on the cover were women in black dresses, men with drooping mustaches and a cloth cap on their head, laundry hung out to dry. I leafed through them, I showed them to Pietro, I placed them on a bookshelf among other novels. Mute paper, useless paper.

A time of weary discontent began. I called Elisa every day to find out if Marcello was still kind, if they had decided to get married. She responded to my apprehensions with carefree laughter and stories of a happy life, of trips by car or plane, of prosperity for our brothers, of well-being for our father and mother. Now, at times, I envied her. I was tired, irritable. Elsa was constantly getting sick, Dede required attention, Pietro lingered over his book without finishing it. I lost my temper for no reason. I scolded the children, I quarreled with my husband. The result was that all three were afraid of me. The girls, if I merely passed by their room, stopped playing and looked at me in alarm, and Pietro increasingly preferred the university library to our house. He went out early in the morning and came home at night. When he returned he seemed to have on him signs of the conflicts that I, now left out of all public activity, read about only in the newspapers: the fascists who knifed and killed, the comrades who did no less, the police who had by law a broad mandate to shoot and did so even here in Florence. Until what I had long been expecting happened: Pietro found himself at the center of a nasty episode that got a lot of attention in the papers. He failed a youth with an important surname, who was very active in the struggles. The young man insulted him in front of everyone and aimed a gun at him. Pietro, according to the story that an acquaintance told me, not him—nor was it a first-hand version, she wasn't present— calmly recorded the failure, handed the exam book to the boy, and said more or less: Either be serious and shoot or you'd best get rid of that weapon immediately, because in a moment I'm going to go and report you. The boy aimed the gun at his face for long minutes, then he put it in his pocket, took the exam book, and fled. Pietro went to the carabinieri and the student was arrested. But it didn't end there. The young man's family went not to Pietro but to his father to persuade him to withdraw the charges. Professor Guido Airota tried to convince his son, and there were long phone calls, in the course of which, with some amazement, I heard the old man lose his temper, raise his voice. But Pietro wouldn't give in. In great agitation, I confronted him, I asked:

"Do you realize how you're behaving?"

"What should I do?"

"Reduce the tension."

"I don't understand you."

"You don't *want* to understand me. You're just like our professors in Pisa, the most intolerable."

"I don't think so."

"But you are. Have you forgotten how we struggled in vain to keep up with stupid courses and pass exams that were even more stupid?"

"My course isn't stupid."

"You might ask your students."

"One asks for an opinion from those who are competent to give it."

"Would you ask me, if I were your student?"

"I have very good relations with the ones who study."

"So you like the ones who suck up to you?"

"You like the ones who brag, like your friend in Naples?"

"Yes."

"And is that why you were always the most dutiful?"

I was confused.

"Because I was poor and it seemed a miracle to have gone so far."

"Well, that boy has nothing in common with you."

"You don't have anything in common with me, either."

"What do you mean?"

I didn't answer, I avoided it out of prudence. But then my rage increased again, I went back to criticizing his intransigence, I said to him: You'd already failed him, what was the point of pressing charges? He said: He committed a crime. I: He was playing at frightening you, he's a boy. He answered coldly: That gun is a weapon, not a toy, and it was stolen with other weapons seven years ago, from a carabinieri barracks in Rovezzano. I said: The boy didn't shoot. He muttered: The weapon was loaded, what if he had? He didn't, I cried. He, too, raised his voice: I should have waited for him to shoot me and then reported him? I yelled: Don't shout, your nerves are shattered. He answered: Think of your own nerves. And it was pointless to explain to him, anxiously, that even if my words and tone were argumentative, the situation actually seemed very dangerous and I was worried. I'm afraid for you, I said, for the children, for me. But he didn't console me. He went to his study and tried to work on his book. Only weeks later he told me that two plainclothes policemen had come to see him and asked for information about certain students, had showed him some photographs. The first time he had greeted them politely and politely sent them away without giving them any information. The second time he had asked:

"Have these youths committed crimes?"

"No, for now no."

"Then what do you want from me?"

He had seen them to the door with all the contemptuous courtesy he was capable of.

98.

For months Lila never called; she must have been very busy. Nor did I seek her out, although I felt the need. To diminish the feeling of emptiness I tried to strengthen my connection with Mariarosa, but there were many obstacles. Franco now lived permanently at my sister-in-law's house, and Pietro didn't

like me getting too close to his sister or seeing my former
boyfriend. If I stayed in Milan for more than a day his mood
darkened, imaginary illnesses multiplied, tension increased.
Also, Franco himself, who in general never went out except for
the medical treatments he constantly needed, didn't welcome
my presence; he was impatient with the children's voices,
which he found too loud, and at times he disappeared, alarming both Mariarosa and me. My sister-in-law, besides, had endless engagements and was permanently surrounded by women.
Her apartment was a sort of gathering place, she welcomed
everyone, intellectuals, middleclass women, working-class
women fleeing abusive companions, runaway girls, so that she
had little time for me, and anyway she was too much a friend
to all for me to feel sure of our bond. And yet in her house the
desire to study was rekindled, and even to write. Or, rather, it
seemed to me that I would be capable of it.

We discussed ourselves a lot. But although we were all
women—Franco, if he hadn't fled, stayed shut in his room—
we struggled to understand what a woman was. Our every
move or thought or conversation or dream, once analyzed in
depth, seemed not to belong to us. And this excavation seemed
to exasperate those who were weaker, who couldn't tolerate
such an excess of self-reflection and believed that to embark
on the road of freedom it was enough simply to cut off men.
These were unstable times, arcing in waves. Many of us feared
a return to the flat calm and stayed on the crest, holding on to
extreme formulations and looking down with fear and rage.
When we learned that the security force of Lotta Continua had
attacked a separatist women's demonstration, we grew bitter to
the point where, if one of the more rigid participants discovered that Mariarosa had a man in the house—which she didn't
declare but didn't hide, either—the discussion became fierce,
the ruptures dramatic.

I hated those moments. I was looking for inspiration, not

conflict, subjects for research, not dogmas. Or at least so I said to myself, and sometimes also to Mariarosa, who listened to me in silence. On one of those occasions I told her about my relationship with Franco in the days of the Normale, and what he had meant to me. I'm grateful to him, I said, I learned so much from him, and I'm sorry that he now treats me and the children coldly. I thought about it for a moment, and continued: Maybe there's something mistaken in this desire men have to instruct us; I was young at the time, and I didn't realize that in his wish to transform me was the proof that he didn't like me as I was, he wanted me to be different, or, rather, he didn't want just a woman, he wanted the woman he imagined he himself would be if he were a woman. For Franco, I said, I was an opportunity for him to expand into the feminine, to take possession of it: I constituted the proof of his omnipotence, the demonstration that he knew how to be not only a man in the right way but also a woman. And today when he no longer senses me as part of himself, he feels betrayed.

I expressed myself exactly like that. And Mariarosa listened with genuine interest, not the slightly feigned curiosity she displayed with the women in general. Write something on that subject, she urged me. She was moved, she said that she had been too late to know the Franco I was talking about. Then she added: Maybe it was a good thing, I would never have been in love with him, I hate men who are too intelligent and tell me how I should be; I prefer this suffering and reflective man I've taken in and am caring for. Then she insisted: Put it in writing, what you've said.

I nodded somewhat nervously, pleased with the praise but also embarrassed, I said something about my relationship with Pietro, about how he tried to impose his views on me. This time Mariarosa burst out laughing, and the almost solemn tone of our conversation changed. Franco associated with Pietro? You're joking, she said, Pietro has trouble keeping together his own virility, imagine if he has the energy to impose on you his feeling for what a woman is. You want to know something? I would have sworn that you wouldn't marry him. I would have sworn that, if you had, you would leave him in a year. I would have sworn that you would be careful not to have children. The fact that you're still together seems to me a miracle. You're really a good girl, poor you.

99.

We were therefore at this point: my husband's sister considered my marriage a mistake and said it to me frankly. I didn't know whether to laugh or cry, it seemed to me the ultimate and unbiased confirmation of my conjugal unease. Besides, what could I do about it? I said to myself that maturity consisted in accepting the turn that existence had taken without getting too upset, following a path between daily practices and theoretical achievements, learning to see oneself, know oneself, in expectation of great changes. Day by day I grew calmer. My daughter Dede went to first grade early, already knowing how to read and write; my daughter Elsa was happy to stay alone with me all morning in the still house; my husband, although he was the dullest of academics, seemed finally close to finishing a second book that promised to be even more important than the first; and I was Signora Airota, Elena Airota, a woman depressed by submissiveness who nevertheless, urged by her sister-in-law but also in order to fight discouragement, had begun to study almost in secret the invention of woman by men, mixing the ancient and modern worlds. I didn't have an objective; only to be able to say to Mariarosa, to my mother-in-law, to this or that acquaintance: I'm working.

And so I pushed on, in my speculations, from the first and

second Biblical creations to Defoe-Flanders, Flaubert-Bovary, Tolstoy-Karenina, *La dernière mode*, Rose Sélavy, and beyond, and still further, in a frenzy of revelation. Slowly I began to feel some satisfaction. I discovered everywhere female automatons created by men. There was nothing of ourselves, and the little there was that rose up in protest immediately became material for their manufacturing. When Pietro was at work and Dede was at school and Elsa was playing next to my desk and I, at last, felt alive, digging into words and among words, I sometimes imagined what my life and Lila's would have been if we had both taken the test for admission to middle school and then high school, if together we had studied to get our degree, elbow to elbow, allied, a perfect couple, the sum of intellectual energies, of the pleasures of understanding and the imagination. We would have written together, we would have been authors together, we would have drawn power from each other, we would have fought shoulder to shoulder because what was ours was inimitably ours. The solitude of women's minds is regrettable, I said to myself, it's a waste to be separated from each other, without procedures, without tradition. Then I felt as if my thoughts were cut off in the middle, absorbing and yet defective, with an urgent need for verification, for development, yet without conviction, without faith in themselves. Then the wish to telephone her returned, to tell her: Listen to what I'm thinking about, please let's talk about it together, you remember what you said about Alfonso? But the opportunity was gone, lost decades ago. I had to learn to be satisfied with myself.

Then one day, just as I was preoccupied with that need, I heard the key turn in the lock. It was Pietro, coming home for lunch after picking up Dede at school. I closed books and notebooks as the child burst into the room, greeted enthusiastically by Elsa. She was starving, I knew she would cry: Mamma, what is there to eat? Instead, even before throwing down her book bag, she exclaimed: a friend of Papa's is coming to lunch with us. I remember the date precisely: March 9, 1976. I pulled myself out of my bad mood, Dede grabbed me by the hand and drew me into the hallway. Meanwhile Elsa, because of the announced presence of a stranger, was keeping prudent hold of my skirt. Pietro said gaily: Look who I brought you.

100.

Nino no longer had the thick beard I had seen years earlier in the bookstore, but his hair was long and disheveled. Otherwise he had remained the boy of years ago, tall, skinny, his eyes bright, his appearance unkempt. He embraced me, he knelt to greet the two girls, he stood up, apologizing for the intrusion. I murmured some cool words: Come in, sit down, what on earth are you doing in Florence? I felt as if I had hot wine in my brain, I couldn't give concreteness to what was happening: Nino, Nino himself, in my house. And it seemed to me that something was no longer functioning in the organization of internal and external. What was I imagining and what was happening, who was the shadow and who the living body? Meanwhile Pietro explained: We met at the university, I invited him to lunch. And I smiled, I said Yes, it's all ready, where there's enough for four there's enough for five, keep me company while I set the table. I seemed tranquil but I was extremely agitated, my face hurt with the effort of smiling. How is it that Nino is here, and what is *here*, what is *is*? I surprised you, Pietro said, with some apprehension, as when he was afraid of having been wrong about something. And Nino, laughing: I told him a hundred times to call you, I swear, but he didn't want to. Then he explained that it was my father-in-law who had told him to introduce himself. He had met Professor Airota in Rome, at the Socialist Party congress, and there, one thing leading to another, he had said that he had work to do in Florence and the professor had mentioned Pietro, the new book his son was writing, a volume that he had just obtained for him and that he needed urgently. Nino had offered to take it in person and now here we were at lunch, the girls fighting for his attention, he who was charming to both of them, obliging to Pietro, and had a few serious words for me.

"Think," he said to me, "I've come so often to this city for work, but I didn't know you were living here, that you had two lovely young ladies. Luckily there was this opportunity."

"Are you still teaching in Milan?" I asked, knowing perfectly well that he no longer lived in Milan.

"No, I'm teaching now in Naples."

"What subject?"

He made a grimace of displeasure.

"Geography."

"Meaning?"

"Urban geography."

"How in the world did you decide to go back?"

"My mother's not well."

"I'm sorry, what's wrong?"

"Her heart."

"And your brothers and sisters?"

"Fine."

"Your father?"

"The usual. But time passes, one grows up, and recently we've reconciled. Like everyone, he has his flaws and his virtues." He turned to Pietro: "How much trouble we've made for fathers and for the family. Now that it's our turn, how are we doing?"

"I'm doing well," my husband said, with a touch of irony.

"I have no doubt. You married an extraordinary woman and these two little princesses are perfect, very well brought up, very stylish. What a pretty dress, Dede, it looks very nice on you. And Elsa, who gave you the barrette with the stars?"

"Mamma," said Elsa.

Slowly I calmed down. The seconds regained their orderly rhythm, I took note of what was happening to me. Nino was sitting at the table next to me, he ate the pasta I had prepared, carefully cut Elsa's meat into small pieces, ate his with a good appetite, mentioned with disgust the bribes that Lockheed had paid to Tanassi and to Gui, praised my cooking, discussed with Pietro the socialist option, peeled an apple in a single coil that sent Dede into ecstasies. Meanwhile a fluid benevolence spread through the apartment that I hadn't felt for a long time. How nice it was that the two men agreed with one another, liked one another. I began to clear the table in silence. Nino jumped up and offered to do the dishes, provided the girls helped him. Sit down, he said, and I sat, while he got Dede and Elsa busy, eager, every so often he asked where he should put something or other, and continued to chat with Pietro.

It was really him, after so long, and he was there. I looked without wanting to at the ring he wore on his ring finger. He never mentioned his marriage, I thought, he spoke of his mother, his father, but not of his wife and child. Maybe it wasn't a marriage of love, maybe he had married for convenience, maybe he was *forced* to get married. Then the flutter of hypotheses ceased. Nino out of the blue began to tell the girls about his son, Albertino, and he did it as if the child were a character in a fable, in tones that were comical and tender by turns. Finally he dried his hands, took out of his wallet a picture, showed it to Elsa, then Dede, then Pietro, who handed it to me. Albertino was very cute. He was two and sat in his mother's arms with a sulky expression. I looked at the child for a few seconds, and immediately went on to examine her. She seemed magnificent, with big eyes and long black hair, she could hardly be more than twenty. She was smiling, her teeth were sparkling, even, her gaze seemed to me that of someone in love. I gave him back the photograph, I said: I'll make coffee. I stayed alone in the kitchen, the four of them went into the living room.

Nino had an appointment for work, and with profuse apologies left immediately after coffee and a cigarette. I'm leaving tomorrow, he said, but I'll be back soon, next week. Pietro urged him repeatedly to let him know, he promised he would. He said goodbye to the girls affectionately, shook hands with Pietro, nodded to me, and disappeared. As soon as the door closed behind him I was overwhelmed by the dreariness of the apartment. I waited for Pietro, although he had been so at ease with Nino, to find something hateful about his guest, he almost always did. Instead he said contentedly: Finally a person it's worthwhile spending time with. That remark, I don't know why, hurt me. I turned on the television, and watched it with the girls for the rest of the afternoon.

101.

I hoped that Nino would call right away, the next day. I started every time the phone rang. Instead, an entire week slipped by without news from him. I felt as if I had a terrible cold. I became idle, I stopped my reading and my notes, I got angry at myself for that senseless expectation. Then one afternoon Pietro returned home in an especially good mood. He said that Nino had come by the department, that they had spent some time together, that there was no way to persuade him to come to dinner. He invited us to go out tomorrow evening, he said, the children, too: he doesn't want you to go to the trouble of cooking.

The blood began to flow more quickly, I felt an anxious tenderness for Pietro. As soon as the girls went to their room I embraced him, I kissed him, I whispered words of love. I hardly slept that night, or rather I slept with the impression of being awake. The next day, as soon as Dede came home from school, I put her in the bathtub with Elsa and washed them thoroughly. Then I moved on to myself. I took a long pleasant bath, I shaved my legs, I washed my hair and dried it carefully. I tried on every dress I owned, but I was getting more and more nervous, nothing looked right, and I didn't like the way my hair had turned out. Dede and Elsa were right there, pretending to be me. They posed in front of the mirror, they expressed dissatisfaction with clothes and hairdos, they shuffled around in my shoes. I resigned myself to being what I was. After I scolded Elsa too harshly for getting her dress dirty at the last minute, we got in the car and drove to pick up Pietro and Nino, who were at the university. I drove apprehensively, constantly reprimanding the girls, who were singing nursery rhymes of their own invention based on shit and pee. The closer I got to the place where we were to meet, the more I hoped that some last-minute engagement would keep Nino from coming. Instead I saw the two men right away, talking. Nino had enveloping gestures, as if he were inviting his interlocutor to enter into a space designed just for him. Pietro seemed as usual clumsy, the skin of his face flushed, he alone was laughing and in a deferential way. Neither of the two showed particular interest in my arrival.

My husband sat in the back seat with the two girls, Nino sat beside me to direct me to a place where the food was good and—he said, turning to Dede and Elsa—they made delicious *frittelle*. He described them in detail, getting the girls excited. A long time ago, I thought, observing him out of the corner of my eye, we held hands as we walked, and twice he kissed me. What nice fingers. To me he said only *Here go right, then right again, then left at the intersection*. Not an admiring look, not a compliment.

At the trattoria we were greeted in a friendly but respectful way. Nino knew the owner, the waiters. I ended up at the head of the table between the girls, the two men sat opposite each other, and my husband began talking about the difficulties of life in the university. I said almost nothing, attending to Dede and Elsa, who usually at the table were very well behaved but that night kept causing trouble, laughing, to attract Nino's attention. I thought uneasily: Pietro talks too much, he's boring him, he doesn't leave him space. I thought: We've lived in this city for seven years and we have no place of our own where we could take him in return, a restaurant where the food is good, as it is here, where we're recognized as soon as we enter. I liked the owner's courtesy, he came to our table often, and éven went so far as to say to Nino: Tonight I won't give you that, it's not fit for you and your guests, and he advised something else. When the famous *frittelle* arrived, the girls were elated, and so was Pietro, they fought over them. Only then Nino turned to me.

"Why haven't you had anything else published?" he asked, without the frivolity of dinner conversation, and an interest that seemed genuine.

I blushed, I said indicating the children:

"I did something else."

"That book was really good."

"Thank you."

"It's not a compliment, you've always known how to write. You remember the article about the religion teacher?"

"Your friends didn't publish it."

"There was a misunderstanding."

"I lost faith."

"I'm sorry. Are you writing now?"

"In my spare time."

"A novel?"

"I don't know what it is."

"But the subject?"

"Men who fabricate women."

"Nice."

"We'll see."

"Get busy, I'd like to read you soon."

And, to my surprise, he turned out to be very familiar with the works by women I was concerned with: I had been sure that men didn't read them. Not only that: he cited a book by Starobinski that he had read recently, and said there was something that might be useful to me. He knew so much; he had been like that since he was a boy, curious about everything. Now he was quoting Rousseau and Bernard Shaw, I broke in, he listened attentively. And when the children, nerve-rackingly, began tugging at me to order more *frittelle*, he signaled to the owner to make us some more. Then, turning to Pietro, he said:

"You should leave your wife more time."

"She has all day available."

"I'm not kidding. If you don't, you're guilty not only on a human level but also on a political one."

"What's the crime?"

"The waste of intelligence. A community that finds it natural to suffocate with the care of home and children so many women's intellectual energies is its own enemy and doesn't realize it."

I waited in silence for Pietro to respond. My husband reacted with sarcasm.

"Elena can cultivate her intelligence when and how she likes, the essential thing is that she not take time from me."

"If she doesn't take it from you, then who can she take it from?"

Pietro frowned.

"When the task we give ourselves has the urgency of passion, there's nothing that can keep us from completing it."

I felt wounded, I whispered with a false smile:

"My husband is saying that I have no true interest."

Silence. Nino asked:

"And is that true?"

I answered in a rush that I didn't know, I didn't know anything. But while I was speaking, with embarrassment, with rage, I realized that my eyes were filled with tears. I lowered my gaze. That's enough *fritelle*, I said to the children in a scarcely controlled voice, and Nino came to my aid, he exclaimed: I'll eat just one more, Mamma also, Papa, too, and you can have two, but then that's it. He called over the owner and said solemnly: I'll be back here with these two young ladies in exactly thirty days and you'll make us a mountain of these exquisite *fritelle*, all right?

Elsa asked: "When is a month, when is thirty days?"

And I, having managed to repress my tears, stared at Nino and said:

"Yes, when is a month, when is thirty days?"

We laughed—Dede more than us adults—at Elsa's vague idea of time. Then Pietro tried to pay, but he discovered that Nino had already done it. He protested. He drove, I sat in the back between the two girls, who were half asleep. We took Nino to the hotel and all the way I listened to their slightly tipsy conversation. Once we were there Pietro, euphoric, said:

"It doesn't make sense to throw away money: we have a guest room, next time you can come and stay with us, don't stand on ceremony."

Nino smiled:

"Less than an hour ago we said that Elena needs time, and now you want to burden her with my presence?"

I interrupted wearily: "It would be a pleasure for me, and also for Dede and Elsa."

But as soon as we were alone I said to my husband:

"Before making certain invitations you might at least consult me."

He started the car, looked at me in the rearview mirror, stammered:

"I thought it would please you."

102.

Oh of course it pleased me, it pleased me *greatly*. But I also felt as if my body had the consistency of eggshell, and a slight pressure on my arm, on my forehead, on my stomach would be enough to break it and dig out all my secrets, in particular those which were secrets even to me. I avoided counting the days. I concentrated on the texts I was studying, but I did it as if Nino had commissioned that work and on his return would expect first-rate results. I wanted to tell him: I followed your advice, I kept going, here's a draft, tell me what you think.

It was a good expedient. The thirty days of waiting went by too quickly. I forgot about Elisa, I never thought of Lila, I didn't telephone Mariarosa. And I didn't read the newspapers or watch television. I neglected the children and the house. Of arrests and clashes and assassinations and wars, in the permanent agon of Italy and the planet, only an echo reached me; I was scarcely aware of the heavy tensions of the electoral campaign. All I did was write, with great absorption. I racked my brains over a pile of old questions, until I had the impression that I had found, at least in writing, a definitive order. At times I was tempted to turn to Pietro. He was much smarter than me, he would surely save me from writing hasty or crude or stupid things. But I didn't do it, I hated the moments when he intimidated me with his encyclopedic knowledge. I worked hard, I remember, especially on the first and second Biblical creations. I put them in order, taking the first as a sort of synthesis of the divine creative act, the second as a sort of more expansive account. I made up a lively story, without ever feeling imprudent. God—I wrote, more or less—creates man, *Ish*, in his image. He creates a masculine and a feminine version. How? First, with the dust of the earth, he forms Ish, and blows into his nostrils the breath of life. Then he makes *Isha'h*, the woman, from the already formed male material, material no longer raw but living, which he takes from Ish's side, and immediately closes up the flesh. The result is that Ish can say: This thing is not, like the army of all that has been created, *other* than me, but is flesh of *my* flesh, bone of *my* bones. God produced it from me. He made me fertile with the breath of life and extracted it from *my* body. I am Ish and she is Isha'h. In the word above all, in the word that names her, she derives from me. I am in the image of the divine spirit. I carry within me his Word. She is therefore a pure suffix applied to my verbal root, she can express herself *only* within *my* word.

And I went on like that and lived for days and days in a state of pleasurable intellectual overexcitement. My only pressure was to have a readable text in time. Every so often I was surprised at myself: I had the impression that striving for Nino's approval made the writing easier, freed me.

But the month passed and he didn't appear. At first it helped me: I had more time and managed to complete my work. Then I was alarmed, I asked Pietro. I discovered that they often talked in the office, but that he hadn't heard from him for several days.

"You often talk?" I said annoyed.

"Yes."

"Why didn't you tell me?"

"What?"

"That you often talked."

"They were calls about work."

"Well, since you've become so friendly, call and see if he'll deign to tell us when he's coming."

"Is that necessary?"

"Not for you, but the effort is mine: I'm the one who has to take care of everything and I'd like to be warned in time."

He didn't call him. I responded by saying to myself: All right, let's wait, Nino promised the girls he'd be back, I don't think he'll disappoint them. And it was true. He called a week late, in the evening. I answered, he seemed embarrassed. He uttered a few generalities, then he asked: Is Pietro not there? I was embarrassed in turn, I gave the phone to Pietro. They talked for a long time, I felt with increasing uneasiness that my husband was using unfamiliar tones: exclamations, laughter, his voice too loud. I understood only then that the relationship with Nino reassured him, made him feel less isolated, he forgot his troubles and worked more eagerly. I went into my study, where Dede was reading and Elsa playing, both waiting for dinner. But even there his voice reached me, he seemed drunk. Then he was silent, I heard his steps in the house. He peeked in, and said gaily to his daughters:

"Girls, tomorrow night we're going to eat *frittelle* with uncle Nino."

Dede and Elsa shouted with excitement, I asked:

"What's he doing, is he coming to stay here?"

"No," he answered, "he's with his wife and son, they're at the hotel."

103.

It took me a long time to absorb the meaning of those words. I burst out:

"He could have warned us."

"They decided at the last minute."

"He's a boor."

"Elena, what is the problem?"

So Nino had come with his wife; I was terrified by the comparison. I knew what I was like, I knew the crude physicality of my body, but for a good part of my life I had given it little importance. I had grown up with one pair of shoes at a time, ugly dresses sewed by my mother, makeup only on rare occasions. In recent years I had begun to be interested in fashion, to educate my taste under Adele's guidance, and now I enjoyed dressing up. But sometimes—especially when I had dressed not only to make a good impression in general but for a man—preparing myself (this was the word) seemed to me to have something ridiculous about it. All that struggle, all that time spent camouflaging myself when I could be doing something else. The colors that suited me, the ones that didn't, the styles that made me look thinner, those that made me fatter, the cut that flattered me, the one that didn't. A lengthy, costly preparation. Reducing myself to a table set for the sexual appetite of the male, to a well-cooked dish to make his mouth water. And then the anguish of not succeeding, of not *seeming* pretty, of not managing to conceal with skill the vulgarity of the flesh with its moods and odors and imperfections. But I had done it. I had done it also for Nino, recently. I had wanted to show him that I was different, that I had achieved a refinement of my own, that I was no longer the girl at Lila's wedding, the student at the party of Professor Galiani's children, and not even the inexperienced author of a single book, as I must have appeared in Milan. But now, enough. He had brought his wife and I was angry, it seemed to me a mean thing. I hated competing in looks with another woman, especially under the gaze of a man, and I suffered at the thought of finding myself in the same place with the beautiful girl I had seen in the photograph, it made me sick to my stomach. She would size me up, study every detail with the pride of a woman of Via Tasso taught since birth to attend to her body; then, at the end of the evening, alone with her husband, she would criticize me with cruel lucidity.

I hesitated for hours and finally decided that I would invent an excuse, my husband would go alone with the children. But the next day I couldn't resist. I dressed, I undressed, I combed my hair, I uncombed it, I nagged Pietro. I went to his room constantly, now with one dress, now another, now with one hairdo, now another, and I asked him, tensely: How do I look? He gave me a distracted glance, he said: You look nice. I answered: And if I put on the blue dress? He agreed. But I put on the blue dress and I didn't like it, it was tight across the hips. I went back to him, I said, It's too tight. Pietro replied patiently Yes, the green one with the flowers looks better. But I didn't want the green one with the flowers to simply look better, I wanted it to look great, and my earrings to look great, and my hair to look great, and my shoes to look great. In other words I couldn't rely on Pietro, he looked at me without seeing me. And I felt more and more ungainly, too much bosom, too much ass, wide hips, and that dirty-blond hair, that big nose. I had the body of my mother, a graceless body, all I needed was for the sciatica to return and start limping. Nino's wife, instead, was very young, beautiful, rich, and surely knew how to be in the world, as I would never manage to learn. So I returned a thousand times to my first decision: I won't go, I'll send Pietro with the children, I'll have him say I don't feel well. I did go. I put on a white shirt over a cheerful flowered skirt, the only jewel I wore was my mother's old bracelet, in my purse I put the text I had written. I said who gives a damn about her, him, all of them.

104.

Because of all my hesitations we arrived late at the restaurant. The Sarratore family was already at the table. Nino introduced his wife, Eleonora, and my mood changed. Oh yes, she had a pretty face and beautiful black hair, just as in the photograph. But she was shorter than I, and I wasn't very tall. She had no bosom, though she was plump. And she wore a bright-red dress that didn't suit her at all. And she was wearing too much jewelry. And from the first words she spoke she revealed a shrill voice with the accent of a Neapolitan brought up by canasta players in a house with a picture window on the gulf. But mainly, in the course of the evening, she proved to be une-ducated, even though she was studying law, and inclined to speak ill of everything and everyone with the air of one who feels she is swimming against the tide and is proud of it. Wealthy, in other words, capricious, vulgar. Even her pleasing features were constantly spoiled by an expression of irritation followed by a nervous laugh, *ih ih ih*, which broke up her con-versation, even the individual sentences. She was irritated by Florence—*What does it have that Naples doesn't*—by the restaurant—*terrible*—by the owner—*rude*—by whatever Pietro said—*What nonsense*—by the girls—*My goodness, you talk so much, let's have a little quiet, please*—and naturally me—*You studied in Pisa, but why, literature in Naples is much better, I've never heard of that novel of yours, when did it come out, eight years ago I was fourteen*. She was sweet only with her son and with Nino. Albertino was sweet, round, with a happy expres-sion, and Eleonora did nothing but praise him. The same hap-pened with her husband: no one was better than he, she agreed with everything he said, and she touched him, hugged him, kissed him. What did that girl have in common with Lila, even with Silvia? Nothing. Why then had Nino married her?

I observed her all evening. He was nice to her, he let him-self be hugged and kissed, he smiled at her affectionately when she said rude and foolish things, he played distractedly with the child. But he didn't change his attitude toward my daugh-ters, giving them a lot of attention; he continued to talk pleas-antly to Pietro, and even spoke a few words to me. His wife—I wished to think—did not absorb him. Eleonora was one of the many pieces of his busy life, but had no influence on him,

Nino went forward on his own path without attaching any importance to her. And so I felt increasingly at ease, especially when he held my wrist for a few seconds, and almost caressed it, showing that he recognized my bracelet; especially when he kidded my husband, asking him if he had left me a little more time for myself; especially when, right afterward, he asked if I had made progress with my work.

"I finished a first draft," I said.

Nino turned to Pietro seriously: "Have you read it?"

"Elena never lets me read anything."

"It's you who don't want to," I replied, but without bitterness, as if it were a game between us.

Eleonora at that point interrupted, she didn't want to be left out.

"What sort of thing is it?" she asked. But just as I was about to answer, her flighty mind carried her away and she asked me blithely: "Tomorrow will you take me to see the shops, while Nino works?"

I smiled with false cordiality and she began with a detailed list of things that she meant to buy. Only when we left the restaurant I managed to approach Nino and whisper:

"Do you feel like looking at what I've written?"

He looked at me with genuine amazement: "Would you really let me read it?"

"If it wouldn't bore you, yes."

I handed him my pages furtively, my heart pounding, as if I didn't want Pietro, Eleonora, or the children to notice.

105.

I didn't close my eyes. In the morning I resigned myself to the date with Eleonora; we were to meet at ten at the hotel. Don't do the stupid thing—I ordered myself—of asking her if her husband began to read it: Nino is busy, it will take time; you mustn't think about it, at least a week will go by.

But at precisely nine, when I was about to leave, the phone rang and it was him.

"I'm sorry," he said, "but I'm on my way to the library and I can't telephone until tonight. Sure I'm not bothering you?"

"Absolutely not."

"I read it."

"Already?"

"Yes, and it's really excellent. You have a great capacity for research, an admirable rigor, and astonishing imagination. But what I envy most is your ability as a narrator. You've written something hard to define, I don't know if it's an essay or a story. But it's extraordinary."

"Is that a flaw?"

"What?"

"That it's not classifiable."

"Of course not, that's one of its merits."

"You think I should publish it as it is?"

"Absolutely yes."

"Thank you."

"Thank you, now I have to go. Be patient with Eleonora, she seems aggressive but it's only timidity. Tomorrow morning we return to Naples, but I'll be back after the elections and if you want we can talk."

"It would be a pleasure. Will you come and stay with us?"

"You're sure I won't bother you?"

"Not at all."

"All right."

He didn't hang up, I heard him breathing.

"Elena."

"Yes."

"Lina, when we were children, dazzled us both."

I felt an intense uneasiness.

"In what sense?"

"You ended up attributing to her capacities that are only yours."

"And you?"

"I did worse. What I had seen in you, I then stupidly seemed to find in her."

I was silent for several seconds. Why had he felt the need to bring up Lila, like that, on the telephone? And what was he saying to me? Was it merely compliments? Or was he trying to communicate to me that as a boy he would have loved me but that on Ischia he had attributed to one what belonged to the other?

"Come back soon," I said.

106.

I went out with Eleonora and the three children in a state of such well-being that even if she had stuck a knife in me I would not have felt bad. Nino's wife, besides, in the face of my euphoria and the many kindnesses I showed her, stopped being hostile, praised Dede and Elsa's good behavior, confessed that she admired me. Her husband had told her everything about me, my studies, my success as a writer. But I'm a little jealous, she admitted, and not because you're clever but because you've known him forever and I haven't. She, too, would like to have met him as a girl, and know what he was like at ten, at fourteen, his voice before it changed, his laughter as a boy. Luckily I have Albertino, she said, he's just like his father.

I observed the child, but it didn't seem to me that I saw signs of Nino, maybe they would appear later. I look like Papa, Dede exclaimed suddenly, proudly, and Elsa added: I'm more like my mamma. I thought of Silvia's son, Mirko, who had seemed identical to Nino. What pleasure I had felt holding him in my arms, soothing his cries in Mariarosa's house. What had I been looking for at that time, in that child, when I was still far from the experience of motherhood? What had I sought in Gennaro, before I knew that his father was Stefano. What was I looking for in Albertino, now that I was the mother of Dede and Elsa, and why did I examine him so closely? I dismissed the idea that Nino remembered Mirko from time to time. Nor did I think he had ever demonstrated any interest in Gennaro. Men, dazed by pleasure, absent-mindedly sow their seed. Overcome by their orgasm, they fertilize us. They show up inside us and withdraw, leaving, concealed in our flesh, their ghost, like a lost object. Was Albertino the child of will, of attention? Or did he, too, exist in the arms of this woman-mother without Nino's feeling that he had had anything to do with it? I roused myself, I said to Eleonora that her son was the image of his father and was content with that lie. Then I told her in detail, with affection, with tenderness, about Nino at the time of elementary school, at the time of the contests organized by Maestra Oliviero and the principal to see who was smartest, Nino at the time of high school, about Professor Galiani and the vacation we had had on Ischia, with other friends. I stopped there, even though she kept childishly asking: And then?

The more we talked, the more she liked me; she became attached to me. If we went into a shop and I liked something, tried it on but then decided against it, I discovered on leaving that Eleonora had bought it, as a present for me. She also wanted to buy clothes for Dede and Elsa. At the restaurant she paid. And she paid for the taxi in which she took me home with the children, and then had herself driven to the hotel, loaded with packages. We said goodbye, the children and I waved until the car turned the corner. She's another piece of my city, I thought. Outside my field of experience. She used money as if it had no value. I ruled out that it was Nino's money. Her father was a lawyer, also her grandfather, her mother was from a banking family. I wondered what difference there was between their bourgeois wealth and that of the Solaras. I thought of how many hidden turns money takes before becoming high salaries and lavish fees. I remembered the boys from the neighborhood who were paid by the day unloading smuggled goods, cutting trees in the parks, working at the construction sites. I thought of Antonio, Pasquale, Enzo. Ever since they were boys they had been scrambling for a few lire here, a few there to survive. Engineers, architects, lawyers, banks were another thing, but their money came, if through a thousand filters, from the same shady business, the same destruction, a few crumbs had even mutated into tips for my father and had contributed to allowing me an education. What therefore was the threshold beyond which bad money became good and vice versa? How clean was the money that Eleonora had heedlessly spent in the heat of a Florentine day; and the checks with which the gifts that I was taking home had been bought, how different were they from those with which Michele paid Lila for her work? All afternoon, the girls and I paraded in front of the mirror in the clothes we had been given as presents. They were nice things, pretty and cheerful. There was a pale red, forties-style dress that looked especially good on me, I would have liked Nino to see me in it.

But the Sarratore family returned to Naples without our having a chance to see them again. Unpredictably, time didn't collapse; rather, it began to flow lightly. Nino would return, that was certain. And he would talk about my writing. To avoid unnecessary friction I put a copy of my work on Pietro's desk. Then I called Mariarosa with the pleasant certainty that I had worked well and told her I had managed to put in order that tangle I had talked to her about. She wanted me to send it immediately. A few days later she called me excitedly, asked if she could translate it herself into French and send it to a friend of hers in Nanterre who had a small publishing house. I agreed enthusiastically, but it didn't end there. A few hours later my mother-in-law called pretending to be offended.

"How is it that now you give what you write to Mariarosa and not to me?"

"I'm afraid it wouldn't interest you. It's just seventy pages, it's not a novel, I don't even know what it is."

"When you don't know what you've written it means you've worked well. And anyway let me decide if it interests me or not."

I sent her a copy. I did it almost casually. The same morning Nino, around midday, called me by surprise from the station, he had just arrived in Florence.

"I'll be at your house in half an hour, I'll leave my bag and go to the library."

"You won't eat something?" I asked with naturalness. It seemed to me normal that he—arriving after a long journey—should come to sleep at my house, that I should prepare something for him to eat while he took a shower in my bathroom, that we should have lunch together, he and I and the children, while Pietro was giving exams at the university.

107.

Nino stayed for ten days. Nothing of what happened in that time had anything to do with the yearning for seduction I had experienced years earlier. I didn't joke with him; I didn't act flirtatious; I didn't assail him with all sorts of favors; I didn't play the part of the liberated woman, modeling myself on my sister-in-law; I didn't tenderly seek his gaze; I didn't contrive to sit next to him at the table or on the couch, in front of the television; I didn't go around the house half-dressed; I didn't try to be alone with him; I didn't graze his elbow with mine, his arm with my arm or breast, his leg with my leg. I was timid, restrained, spoke concisely, making sure only that he ate well, that the girls didn't bother him, that he felt comfortable. And it wasn't a choice, I couldn't have behaved differently. He joked a lot with Pietro, with Dede, with Elsa, but as soon as he spoke to me he became serious, he seemed to measure his words as if there were not an old friendship between us. And it seemed right to me to do the same. I was very happy to have him in the house, and yet I felt no need for confidential tones and gestures; in fact, I liked staying on the edge and avoiding contact between us. I felt like a drop of rain in a spiderweb, and I was careful not to slide down.

We had a single long exchange, focused entirely on my writing. He spoke about it immediately, upon arriving, with precision and acuteness. He had been struck by the story of Ish and Isha'h, he questioned me, he asked: for you, the woman, in the Biblical story, is no different from the man, is the man himself? Yes, I said. Eve can't, doesn't know how, doesn't have the material to be Eve outside of Adam. *Her* evil and *her* good are evil and good according to Adam. Eve is Adam as a woman. And the divine work was so successful that she herself, in herself, doesn't know what she is, she has pliable features, she doesn't possess her own language, she doesn't have a spirit or a logic of her own, she loses her shape easily. A terrible condition, Nino commented, and I nervously looked at him out of the corner of my eye to see if he was making fun of me. No, he wasn't. Rather, he praised me without the slightest sarcasm, he cited some books I didn't know on relevant subjects, he repeated that he considered the work ready to be published. I listened without showing any satisfaction, I said only, at the end: Mariarosa also liked it. Then he asked about my sister-in-law, he spoke well of her both as a scholar and for her devotion to Franco, and went off to the library.

Otherwise he left every morning with Pietro and returned at

night after him. On very rare occasions we all went out together. Once, for example, he wanted to take us to the movies to see a comedy chosen just for the girls. Nino sat next to Pietro, I between my daughters. When I realized that I was laughing hard as soon as he laughed, I stopped laughing completely. I scolded him mildly because during the intermission he wanted to buy ice cream for Dede, Elsa, and naturally for the adults, too. For me no, I said, thank you. He joked a little, said that the ice cream was good and I didn't know what I was missing, he offered me a taste, I tasted. Small things, in other words. One afternoon we took a long walk, Dede, Elsa, he and I. We didn't say much, Nino let the children talk. But the walk made a deep impression, I could point out every street, the places where we stopped, every corner. It was hot, the city was crowded. He constantly greeted people, some called to him by his last name, I was introduced to this person and that, with exaggerated praise. I was struck by his notoriety. One man, a well-known historian, complimented him on the children, as if they were our children. Nothing else happened, apart from a sudden, inexplicable change in the relations between him and Pietro.

108.

It all began one evening at dinner. Pietro spoke to him with admiration of a professor from Naples, at the time quite respected, and Nino said: I would have bet that you liked that asshole. My husband was disoriented, he gave an uncertain smile, but Nino piled it on, making fun of him for how easily he had let himself be deceived by appearances. The next morning after breakfast there was another incident. I don't remember in relation to what, Nino referred to my old clash with the religion professor about the Holy Spirit. Pietro, who didn't know about that episode, wanted to know, and Nino, addressing not him but the girls, immediately began to tell the story as if it were some grandiose undertaking of their mother as a child.

My husband praised me, he said: You were very courageous. But then he explained to Dede, in the tone he took when stupid things were being said on television and he felt it his duty to explain to his daughter how matters really stood, what had happened to the twelve apostles on the morning of Pentecost: a noise as of wind, flames like fire, the gift of being understood by anyone, in any language. Then he turned to me and Nino speaking with passion of the *virtus* that had pervaded the disciples, and he quoted the prophet Joel, *I will spread my spirit over every flesh*, adding that the Holy Spirit was an indispensable symbol for reflecting on how the multitudes find a way of confronting each other and organizing into a community. Nino let him speak, but with an increasingly ironic expression. At the end he exclaimed: I bet there's a priest hiding in you. And to me, in amusement: Are you a wife or a priest's housekeeper? Pietro turned red, he was confused. He had always loved those subjects, I felt that he was upset. He stammered: I'm sorry, I'm wasting your time, let's go to work.

Such moments increased and for no obvious reason. While relations between Nino and me remained the same, attentive to form, courteous and distant, between him and Pietro the dikes broke. At both breakfast and dinner, the guest began to speak to the host in a crescendo of mocking remarks, just bordering on the offensive, humiliating but expressed in a friendly way, offered with a smile, so that you couldn't object without seeming petulant. I recognized that tone; in the neighborhood the swifter party often used it to dominate the slower one and push him wordlessly into the middle of the joke. Mainly, Pietro appeared disoriented: he liked Nino, he appreciated him, and so he didn't react, he shook his head, pretending to be amused, while at times he seemed to wonder where he had gone wrong and waited for him to return to the old, affectionate tone. But Nino continued, implacable. He turned to me, to the children, he exaggerated in order to receive our approval. And the girls approved, laughing, and I, too, a little. Yet I thought: Why is he acting like this, if Pietro gets mad their relations will be ruined. But Pietro didn't get mad, he simply didn't understand, and as the days passed his old nervousness returned. His face was tired, the strain of those years reappeared in his worried eyes and his lined forehead. I have to do something, I thought, and as soon as possible. But I did nothing; rather, I struggled to expel not the admiration, but the excitement—maybe yes, it was excitement—that gripped me in seeing, in hearing, how an Airota, an extremely well-educated Airota, lost ground, was confused, responded feebly to the swift, brilliant, even cruel aggressions of Nino Sarratore, my schoolmate, my friend, born in the neighborhood, like me.

109.

A few days before he returned to Naples, there were two especially unpleasant episodes. One afternoon Adele telephoned; she, too, was very pleased with my work. She told me to send the manuscript right away to the publisher—they could make a small volume to publish simultaneously with the publication in France or, if it couldn't be done in time, right afterward. I spoke of it at dinner in a tone of detachment and Nino was full of compliments, he said to the girls:

"You have an exceptional mamma." Then he turned to Pietro: "Have you read it?"

"I haven't had time."

"Better for you not to read it."

"Why?"

"It's not stuff for you."

"That is?"

"It's too intelligent."

"What do you mean?"

"That you're less intelligent than Elena."

And he laughed. Pietro said nothing, Nino pressed him:

"Are you offended?"

He wanted him to react, in order to humiliate him again. But Pietro got up from the table, he said:

"Excuse me, I have work to do."

I murmured:

"Finish eating."

He didn't answer. We were eating in the living room, it was a big room. For a few seconds it seemed that he wished to cross it and go to his study. Instead he made a half turn, sat down on the couch, and turned on the television, raising the volume. The atmosphere was intolerable. In the space of a few days it had all become complicated. I felt very unhappy.

"Lower it a bit?" I asked him.

He answered simply:

"No."

Nino gave a little laugh, finished eating, helped me clear. In the kitchen I said to him:

"Excuse him, Pietro works a lot and doesn't sleep much."

He answered with a burst of rage:

"How can you stand him?"

I looked at the door in alarm, luckily the volume of the television was still loud.

"I love him," I answered. And since he insisted on helping me wash the dishes I added: "Go, please, otherwise you're in the way."

The other episode was even uglier, but decisive. I no longer knew what I truly wanted: now I hoped that this period would be over quickly, I wished to return to familiar habits, watch over my little book. Yet I liked going into Nino's room in the morning, tidying up the mess he left, making the bed, thinking as I cooked that he would have dinner with us that evening. And it distressed me that it was all about to end. At certain hours of the afternoon I felt mad. I had the impression that the house was empty in spite of the girls, I myself was emptied, I felt no interest in what I had written, I perceived its superficiality, I lost faith in the enthusiasm of Mariarosa, of Adele, of the French publisher, the Italian. I thought: As soon as he goes, nothing will make sense.

I was in that state—life was slipping away with an unbearable sensation of loss—when Pietro returned from the university with a grim look. We were waiting for him for dinner, Nino had been back for half an hour but had immediately been kidnapped by the children. I asked him kindly:

"Did something happen?"

He muttered:

"Don't ever again bring to this house people from your home."

I froze, I thought he was referring to Nino. And Nino, too, who had come in trailed by Dede and Elsa, must have thought the same thing, because he looked at him with a provocative smile, as if he expected a scene. But Pietro had something else in mind. He said in his contemptuous tone, the tone he used well when he was convinced that basic principles were at stake and he was called to defend them:

"Today the police returned and they named some names, they showed me some photographs."

I breathed a sigh of relief. I knew that, after he refused to withdraw the charges against the student who had pointed a gun at him, the visits of the police—even more than the scorn of many militant youths and not a few professors—weighed on him, as they treated him as an informer. I was sure that was why he was angry and I interrupted him, bitterly:

"Your fault. You shouldn't have acted like that, I told you. Now you'll never get rid of them."

Nino intervened, he asked Pietro, mockingly:

"Who did you report?"

Pietro didn't even turn to look at him. He was angry with me, it was with me he wanted to quarrel. He said:

"I did what was necessary then and I should have done what was necessary today. But I was silent because you were in the middle of it."

At that point I realized that the problem was not the police but what he had learned from them. I said:

"What do I have to do with it?"

His voice changed:

"Aren't Pasquale and Nadia your friends?"

I repeated obtusely:

"Pasquale and Nadia?"

"The police showed me photographs of terrorists and they were among them."

I didn't react, words failed. What I had imagined was true, then; Pietro in fact was confirming it. For a few seconds the images returned, of Pasquale firing the gun at Gino, kneecapping Filippo, while Nadia—Nadia, not Lila—went up the stairs, knocked on Bruno's door, went in and shot him in the face. Terrible. And yet at that moment Pietro's tone seemed out of place, as if he were using the information to make trouble for me in Nino's eyes, to start a discussion that I had no wish to have. In fact Nino immediately interrupted again, continuing to make fun of him:

"So are you an informer for the police? What are you doing? Informing on comrades? Does your father know? Your mother? Your sister?"

I said weakly: Let's go and eat. But right afterward I said to Nino, politely making light of it, and to get him to stop goading Pietro by bringing up his family: Stop it, what do you mean, informer. Then I alluded vaguely to the fact that some time ago Pasquale Peluso, maybe he remembered him, from the neighborhood, a good kid who had ended up getting together with Nadia, he remembered her, naturally, Professor Galiani's daughter. And there I stopped because Nino was already laughing. He exclaimed: Nadia, oh good Lord, Nadia, and he turned again to Pietro, even more mockingly: only you and a couple of idiot police could think that Nadia Galiani is part of the armed struggle, it's madness. Nadia, the best and nicest person I've ever known, what have we come to in Italy, let's go and eat, come on, the defense of the established order can do without you for now. And he went to the table, calling Dede and Elsa, as I began to serve, sure that Pietro was about to join us.

But he didn't. I thought he had gone to wash his hands, that he was delaying in order to calm down, and I sat in my place. I was agitated, I would have liked a nice calm evening, a quiet ending to that shared life. But he didn't come, the children were already eating. Now even Nino seemed bewildered.

"Start," I said, "it's getting cold."

"Only if you eat, too."

I hesitated. Maybe I should go and see how my husband was, what he was doing, if he had calmed down. But I didn't want to, I was annoyed by his behavior. Why hadn't he kept to himself that visit from the police, usually he did with everything of his, he never told me anything. Why had he spoken like that in Nino's presence: *Don't ever again bring to this house people from your home.* What urgency was there to make that subject public, he could wait, he could have an outburst later, once we were in the bedroom. He was angry with me, that was the point. He wanted to ruin the evening for me, he didn't care what I did or what I wanted.

I began to eat. The four of us ate, first course, second, and even the dessert I had made. Pietro didn't appear. At that point

I became furious. Pietro didn't want to eat? All right, he didn't have to eat, evidently he wasn't hungry. He wanted to mind his own business? Very well, the house was big, without him there would be no tension. Anyway, now it was clear that the problem was not simply that two people who had once showed up at our house were suspected of being part of an armed gang. The problem was that he didn't have a sufficiently quick intelligence, that he didn't know how to sustain the skirmishes of men, that he suffered from it and was angry with me. But what do I care about you and your pettiness. I'll clean up later, I said aloud, as if I were issuing an order to myself, to my confusion. Then I turned on the television and sat on the sofa with Nino and the girls.

A long time passed, filled with tension. I felt that Nino was uneasy and yet amused. I'm going to call Papa, said Dede, who, with her stomach full, was now worried about Pietro. Go, I said. She came back almost on tiptoe, she whispered in my ear: He went to bed, he's sleeping. Nino heard her anyway, he said:

"I'm leaving tomorrow."

"Did you finish your work?"

"No."

"Stay a little longer."

"I can't."

"Pietro is a good person."

"You defend him?"

Defend him from what, from whom? I didn't understand, I was on the point of getting mad at him, too.

110.

The children fell asleep in front of the television, I put them to bed. When I came back Nino wasn't there, he had gone to his room. Depressed, I cleaned up, washed the dishes. How foolish to ask him to stay longer, it would be better if he left. On the other hand, how to endure the dreariness of life without him. I would have liked him at least to leave with the promise that sooner or later he would return. I wished that he would sleep again in my house, have breakfast with me in the morning and eat at the same table in the evening, that he would talk about this and that in his playful tone, that he would listen to me when I wanted to give shape to an idea, that he would be respectful of my every sentence, that with me he would never resort to irony, to sarcasm. Yet I had to admit that if the situation had so quickly deteriorated, making our living together impossible, it was his fault. Pietro was attached to him. It gave him pleasure to see him around, the friendship that had arisen was important to him. Why had Nino felt the need to hurt him, to humiliate him, to take away his authority? I took off my makeup, I washed, I put on my nightgown. I locked the house door, I turned off the gas, I lowered all the blinds. I checked on the children. I hoped that Pietro wasn't pretending to sleep, that he wasn't waiting for me in order to quarrel. I looked at his night table, he had taken a sleeping pill, he had collapsed. It made me feel tender toward him, I kissed him on the cheek. What an unpredictable person: extremely intelligent and stupid, sensitive and dull, courageous and cowardly, highly educated and ignorant, well brought up and rude. A failed Airota, he had stumbled on the path. Could Nino, so sure of himself, so determined, have gotten him going again, helped him improve? Again I asked myself why that nascent friendship had changed to hostility in one direction. And this time it seemed to me that I understood. Nino wanted to help me see my husband for what he really was. He was convinced that I had an idealized image that I had submitted to on both the emotional and the intellectual level. He had wanted to reveal to me the lack of substance behind this very young professor, the author of a thesis that had become a highly regarded book, the scholar who had been working for a long time on a new publication that was to secure his reputation. It was as if in these last days he had done nothing but scold me: You live with a dull man, you've had two children with a nobody. His project was to liberate me by disparaging him, restore me to myself by demolishing him. But in doing so did he realize that he had proposed himself, like it or not, as an alternative model of virility?

That question made me angry. Nino had been reckless. He had thrown confusion into a situation that for me constituted the only possible equilibrium. Why sow disorder without even consulting me? Who had asked him to open my eyes, to save me? From what had he deduced that I needed it? Did he think he could do what he wanted with my life as a couple, with my responsibility as a mother? To what end? What did he think he was driving at? It's he—I said to myself—who ought to clarify his ideas. Doesn't our friendship interest him? The holidays are close. I'll go to Viareggio, he said he's going to Capri to his in-laws' house. Must we wait until the end of the vacations to see each other again? And why? Now, during the summer, it would be possible to consolidate the relation between our families. I could telephone Eleonora, invite her, her husband, the child to spend a few days with us in Viareggio. And I would like to be invited, in turn, to Capri, where I've never been, with Dede, Elsa, and Pietro. But if that doesn't happen, why not write each other, exchange ideas, titles of books, talk about our work?

I couldn't quiet myself. Nino was wrong. If he really was attached to me, he had to take everything back to the starting point. He had to regain the liking and friendship of Pietro, my husband asked nothing else. Did he really think he was doing me good by causing those tensions? No, no, I had to talk to him, tell him it was foolish to treat Pietro that way. I got out of bed cautiously, I left the room. I went down the hall barefoot, knocked on Nino's door. I waited a moment, I went in. The room was dark.

"You've decided," I heard him say.

I was startled, I didn't ask *decided what*. I knew only that he was right, I had decided. I quickly took off my nightgown, I lay down beside him in spite of the heat.

111.

I returned to my bed around four in the morning. My husband started, he murmured in his sleep: What's happening? I said in a peremptory way: Sleep, and he became quiet. I was stunned. I was happy about what had happened, but no matter how great an effort I made I couldn't comprehend it *inside* of my situation, *inside* of what I was in that house, in Florence. It seemed to me that everything between Nino and me had been sealed in the neighborhood, when his parents were moving and Melina was throwing things out the window and yelling, racked by suffering; or on Ischia, when we went for a walk and held hands; or the night in Milan, after the meeting in the bookstore, when he had defended me against the fierce critic. That for a while gave me a sense of irresponsibility, maybe even of innocence, as if the friend of Lila, the wife of Pietro, the mother of Dede and Elsa had nothing to do with the child-girl-woman who loved Nino and finally had made love with him. I felt the trace of his hands and his kisses in every part of my body. The craving for pleasure wouldn't be soothed, the thoughts were: the day is far off, what am I doing here, I'll go back to him, again.

Then I fell asleep. I opened my eyes suddenly, the room was light. What had I done? Here, in my own house, how foolish. Now Pietro would wake up. Now the children would wake up. I had to make breakfast. Nino would say goodbye, he would return to Naples to his wife and child. I would become myself again.

I got up, took a long shower, dried my hair, carefully put on my makeup, chose a nice dress, as if I were going out. Oh, of course, Nino and I had sworn in the middle of the night that we would never lose each other, that we would find a way to continue to love each other. But how, and when? Why should he have to look for me again? Everything that could happen between us had happened, the rest was only complications. Enough, I set the table carefully for breakfast. I wanted to leave him with a beautiful image of that permanence, the house, the customary objects, me.

Pietro appeared disheveled, in his pajamas.

"Where are you going?"

"Nowhere."

He looked at me in bewilderment—I never dressed that carefully as soon as I got up.

"You look nice."

"No thanks to you."

He went to the window, looked out, then muttered:

"I was very tired, last night."

"Also very rude."

"I'll apologize to him."

"You should apologize to me."

"I'm sorry."

"He's leaving today."

Dede appeared, barefoot. I went to get her slippers and woke Elsa, who, as usual, her eyes still closed, covered me with kisses. What a good smell she had, how soft she was. Yes, I said to myself, it happened. Fortunately, it could never happen. But now I had to discipline myself. Telephone Mariarosa to find out about France, talk to Adele, go in person to the publishers to find out what they intend to do with my book, if they are thinking about it seriously or just want to please my mother-in-law. Then I heard noises in the hall. It was Nino, I was over-whelmed by the signs of his presence, he was here, for a short time still. I disentangled myself from the child's hug, I said: sorry, Elsa, Mamma will be right back, and I hurried out.

Nino was coming sleepily out of his room, I pushed him into the bathroom, I closed the door. We kissed each other, again I lost awareness of place and time. I was amazed at how much I wanted him: I was good at hiding things from myself. We embraced with a fury that I had never known, as if our bodies were crashing against each other with the intention of breaking. So pleasure was this: breaking, mixing, no longer knowing what was mine and what was his. Even if Pietro had appeared, if the children had looked in, they would have been unable to recognize us. I whispered in his mouth:

"Stay longer."

"I can't."

"Then come back, swear you'll come back."

"Yes."

"And call me."

"Yes."

"Tell me you won't forget me, tell me you won't leave me, tell me you love me."

"I love you."

"Say it again."

"I love you."

"Swear that it's not a lie."

"I swear."

112.

He left an hour later, even though Pietro sullenly insisted that he stay, even though Dede burst into tears. My husband went to wash, and reappeared soon afterward ready to go out.

Looking down he said: I didn't tell the police that Pasquale and Nadia were in our house; and I did it not to protect you but because I think dissent now is being confused with crime. I didn't understand right away what he was talking about. Pasquale and Nadia had completely vanished from my mind, and they had a hard time re-entering. Pietro waited for a few seconds in silence. Maybe he wanted me to show that I agreed with his observation, and wished to face this day of heat and exams knowing that we were close again, that for once, at least, we thought in the same way. But I merely gave him a distracted nod. What did I care anymore about his political opinions, about Pasquale and Nadia, about the death of Ulrike Meinhof, the birth of the Socialist Republic of Vietnam, the electoral advances of the Communist Party? The world had retreated. I felt sunk inside myself, inside my flesh, which seemed to me not only the sole dwelling possible but also the only material for which it was worthwhile to struggle. It was a relief when he, the witness to order and disorder, closed the door behind him. I couldn't bear to be under his gaze, I feared that lips raw from kissing, the night's weariness, the body hypersensitive, as if burned, all would suddenly become visible.

As soon as I was alone, the certainty returned that I would never again see or hear from Nino. And along with it was another certainty: I could no longer live with Pietro, it seemed intolerable that we should continue to sleep in the same bed. What to do? I'll leave him, I thought. I'll go away with the children. But what procedure should I follow, do I simply leave? I knew nothing about separations and divorces, what was the practical part, how much time did it take to be free again. And I knew no couple who had taken that path. What happened to the children? How did one agree about their maintenance? Could I take the children to another city, for example Naples? And then why Naples, why not Milan? If I leave Pietro, I said to myself, I'll sooner or later need a job. Times are hard, the economy is bad, and Milan is the right place, there's the publisher. But Dede and Elsa? Their relations with their father? Must I stay in Florence, then? Never, ever. Better Milan, Pietro could come and see his daughters whenever he could and wanted to. Yes. And yet my head led me to Naples. Not to the neighborhood, I would not return there. I imagined going to live in the dazzling Naples where I had never lived, near Nino's house, on Via Tasso. See him from the window when he was going to and from the university, meet him on the street, speak to him every day. Without disturbing him. Without causing trouble to his family, rather, intensifying my friendship with Eleonora. That nearness would be enough. In Naples, then, not Milan. Besides, Milan, if I were separated from Pietro, would no longer be so hospitable. My relations with Mariarosa would cool, and also with Adele. Not cut off, no, they were civilized people, but, still, they were Pietro's mother and sister, even if they didn't have much respect for him. Not to mention Guido, the father. No, certainly I would no longer be able to count on the Airotas in the same way, maybe not even on the publishing house. Help could come only from Nino. He had strong friendships everywhere, certainly he would find a way to support me. Unless my being close made his wife nervous, made him nervous. For him I was a married woman who lived in Florence with her family. Far from Naples, therefore, and not free. To break up my marriage in a rush, run after him, go and live right near him—really. He would think me mad; I would look like a silly woman, out of her mind, the type of woman, dependent on a man, who horrified Mariarosa's friends. And, above all, not suitable for him. He had loved many women, he went from one bed to the next, he sowed children carelessly, he considered marriage a necessary convention but one that couldn't keep desires in a cage. I would make myself ridiculous. I had done without so many things in my life, I could do without Nino as well. I would go my own way with my daughters.

But the telephone rang and I hurried to answer. It was him, in the background I could hear a loudspeaker, noise, confusion, it was hard to hear the voice. He had just arrived in Naples, he was calling from the station. Only a hello, he said, I wanted to know how you are. Fine, I said. What are you doing? I'm about to eat with the children. Is Pietro there? No. Did you like making love with me? Yes. A lot? Really a lot. I don't have any more phone tokens. Go, goodbye, thanks for calling. We'll talk again. Whenever you like. I was pleased with myself, with my self-control. I kept him at a proper distance, I said to myself, to a polite phone call I responded politely. But three hours later he called again, again from a public telephone. He was nervous. Why are you so cold? I'm not cold. This morning you insisted that I say I loved you and I said it, even if on principle I don't say it to anyone, not even to my wife. I'm glad. And do you love me? Yes. Tonight you'll sleep with him? Who should I sleep with? I can't bear it. Don't you sleep with your wife? It's not the same thing. Why? I don't care about Eleonora. Then come back here. How can I? Leave her. And then? He began to call obsessively. I loved those phone calls, especially when we said goodbye and I had no idea when we would talk again, but then he called back half an hour later, sometimes even ten minutes later, and began to rave, he asked if I had made love with Pietro since we had been together, I said no, he made me swear, I swore, I asked if he had made love to his wife, he shouted no, I insisted that he swear, and oath followed oath, and so many promises, above all the solemn promise to stay home, to be findable. He wanted me to wait for his phone calls, so that if by chance I went out—I had to, to do the shopping—he let the telephone ring and ring in the emptiness, he let it ring until I returned and dropped the children, dropped the bags, didn't even close the door to the stairs, ran to answer. I found him desperate at the other end: I thought you would never answer me again. Then he added, relieved: but I would have telephoned forever, in your absence I would have loved the sound of the telephone, that sound in the void, it seemed the only thing that remained to me. And he recalled our night in detail—do you remember this, do you remember that—he recalled it constantly. He listed everything he wanted to do with me, not only sex: a walk, a journey, go to the movies, a restaurant, talk to me about the work he was doing, listen to how it was going with my book. Then I lost control. I whispered yes yes yes, everything, everything you want, and I cried to him: I'm about to go on vacation, in a week I'll be at the sea with the children and Pietro, as if it were a deportation. And he: Eleonora is going to Capri in three days, as soon as she leaves I'll come to Florence, even just for an hour. Meanwhile Elsa looked at me, she asked: Mamma, who are you talking to all the time, come and play. One day Dede said: Leave her alone, she's talking to her boyfriend.

113.

Nino traveled at night, he reached Florence around nine in the morning. He called, Pietro answered, he hung up. He called again, I went to answer. He had parked downstairs. Come down. I can't. Come down immediately, or I'll come up. We were leaving in a few days for Viareggio, Pietro by now was on vacation. I left the children with him, I said I had some urgent shopping to do for the beach. I rushed to Nino.

Seeing each other was a terrible idea. We discovered that, instead of waning, desire had flared up and made a thousand demands with brazen urgency. If at a distance, on the telephone, words allowed us to fantasize, constructing glorious prospects but also imposing on us an order, containing us, frightening us, finding ourselves together, in the tiny space of the car, careless of the terrible heat, gave concreteness to our delirium, gave it the cloak of inevitability, made it a tile in the great subversive season under way, made it consistent with the forms of realism of that era, those which asked for the impossible.

"Don't go home."

"And the children, Pietro?"

"And us?"

Before he left again for Naples he said he didn't know if he could tolerate not seeing me for all of August. We were desperate as we said goodbye. I didn't have a telephone in the house we had rented in Viareggio, he gave me the number of the house in Capri. He made me promise to call every day.

"If your wife answers?"

"Hang up."

"If you're at the beach?"

"I have to work, I'll almost never go to the beach."

In our fantasy, telephoning was to serve also to set a date, sometime in August, and find a way of seeing each other at least once. He urged me to invent an excuse and return to Florence. He would do the same with Eleonora and would join me. We would see each other at my house, we would have dinner together, we would sleep together. More madness. I kissed him, I caressed him, I bit him, and I tore myself away from him in a state of unhappy happiness. I went to buy, at random, towels, a couple of bathing suits for Pietro, a shovel and pail for Elsa, a blue bathing suit for Dede. At the time blue was her favorite color.

114.

We went on vacation. I paid little attention to the children, I left them with their father most of the time. I was constantly running around to find a telephone, if only to tell Nino that I loved him. Eleonora answered a couple of times, and I hung up. But her voice was enough to irritate me, I found it unjust that she should be beside him day and night, what did she have to do with him, with us. That annoyance helped me overcome my fear, the plan of seeing each other in Florence seemed increasingly feasible. I said to Pietro, and it was true, that while the Italian publisher, with all the will in the world, couldn't bring out my book before January, it would come out in France at the end of October. I therefore had to clarify some urgent questions, a couple of books would be helpful, I needed to go home.

"I'll go get them for you," he offered.

"Stay with the girls, you're never with them."

"I like to drive, you don't."

"Leave me alone. Can't I have a day off? Maids get one, why not me?"

I left early in the morning in the car; the sky was streaked with white, and through the window came a cool breeze that carried the odors of summer. I went into the empty house with my heart pounding. I undressed, I washed, I looked at myself in the mirror, dismayed by the white stain of stomach and breast, I got dressed, I undressed, I dressed again until I felt pretty.

Nino arrived around three in the afternoon; I don't know what nonsense he had told his wife. We made love until evening. For the first time he had the luxury of dedicating himself to my body with a devotion, an idolatry that I wasn't prepared for. I tried to be his equal, I wanted at all costs to seem good to him. But when I saw him exhausted and happy, something suddenly went bad in my mind. *For me that was a unique experience, for him a repetition.* He loved women, he adored their bodies as if they were fetishes. I didn't think so much of the other women of his I knew about, Nadia, Silvia, Mariarosa, or his wife, Eleonora. I thought instead of what I knew well, the crazy things he had done for Lila, the frenzy that had brought him close to destroying himself. I recalled how she had believed in that passion and had clung to him, to the complicated books he read, his thoughts, his ambitions, to affirm herself and give herself the chance for change. I remembered how she had collapsed when Nino abandoned her. Did he know how to love and induce one to love only in that excessive way, did he not know others? Was this mad love of ours the repeat of other mad loves? Was he exploiting a prototype: wanting me in this way, without caring about anything, was it the same way he had wanted Lila? Didn't even his coming to my and Pietro's house resemble Lila's taking him to the house where she and Stefano lived? Were we not doing but redoing?

I pulled back, he asked: what's wrong? Nothing, I didn't know what to say, they weren't thoughts that could be spoken. I pressed against him, I kissed him and I tried to get out of my heart the feeling of his love for Lila. But Nino insisted and finally I couldn't escape, I seized a relatively recent echo— *Here, maybe this I can say to you*—and asked him in a tone of feigned amusement:

"Do I have something wrong when it comes to sex, like Lina?"

His expression changed. In his eyes, in his face, a different person appeared, a stranger who frightened me. Even before he answered I quickly whispered:

"I was joking, if you don't want to answer forget it."

"I don't understand what you said."

"I was only quoting your words."

"I've never said anything like that."

"Liar, you did in Milan, when we were going to the restaurant."

"It's not true, and anyway I don't want to talk about Lina."

"Why?"

He didn't answer. I felt bitter, I turned away. When he touched my back with his fingers I whispered coldly: Leave me alone. We were motionless for a while, without speaking. Then he began to caress me again, he kissed me lightly on the shoulder, I gave in. Yes, I admitted to myself, he's right, I should never ask him about Lila.

In the evening the telephone rang; it must be Pietro, with the girls. I nodded to Nino not to breathe, I left the bed and went to answer. I prepared in my throat an affectionate, reassuring tone, but without realizing it I kept my voice too low, an unnatural murmur, I didn't want Nino to hear and later make fun of me or even get angry.

"Why are you whispering like that?" Pietro asked. "Everything all right?"

I raised my voice immediately, and now it was excessively loud. I sought loving words, I made much of Elsa, I urged Dede not to make her father's life difficult and to brush her teeth before going to bed. Nino said, when I came back to bed:

"What a good wife, what a good mamma."

I answered: "You are no less."

I waited for the tension to diminish, for the echo of the voices of my husband and children to fade. We took a shower together. It was a new, enjoyable experience, a pleasure to wash him and be washed. Afterward I got ready to go out. Again I was trying to look nice for him, but this time I was doing it in front of him and suddenly without anxiety. He watched, fascinated, as I tried on dresses in search of the right one, as I put on my makeup, and from time to time—even though I said, joking, don't you dare, you're tickling me, you'll ruin the makeup and I'll have to start over, careful of the dress, it will tear, leave me alone—he came up behind me, kissed me on the neck, put his hands down the front and under the dress.

I made him go out alone, I told him to wait for me in the car. Although people were on vacation and the building was half deserted, I was afraid that someone would see us together.

We went to dinner, we ate a lot, talked a lot, drank a lot. When we got back we went to bed but didn't sleep. He said:

"In October I'll be in Montpellier for five days, I have a conference."

"Have fun. You'll go with your wife?"

"I want to go with you."

"Impossible."

"Why?"

"Dede is six, Elsa three. I have to think of them."

We began to discuss our situation, for the first time we uttered words like *married, children*. We went from despair to sex, from sex to despair. Finally I whispered:

"We shouldn't see each other anymore."

"If for you it's possible, fine. For me it's not."

"Nonsense. You've known me for decades and yet you've had a full life without me. You'll forget about me before you know it."

"Promise that you'll keep calling me every day."

"No, I won't call you anymore."

"If you don't I'll go mad."

"I'll go mad if I go on thinking of you."

We explored with a sort of masochistic pleasure the dead end we felt ourselves in, and, exasperated by the obstacles we ourselves were piling up, we ended by quarreling. He left, anxiously, at six in the morning. I cleaned up the house, had a cry, drove all the way to Viareggio hoping never to arrive. Halfway there I realized that I hadn't taken a single book capable of justifying that trip. I thought: better this way.

115.

When I returned I was warmly welcomed by Elsa, who said sulkily: Papa isn't good at playing. Dede defended Pietro, she exclaimed that her sister was small and stupid, and ruined every game. Pietro examined me, in a bad mood.

"You didn't sleep."

"I slept badly."

"Did you find the books?"

"Yes."

"Where are they?"

"Where do you think they are? At home. I checked what I had to check and that was it."

"Why are you angry?"

"Because you make me angry."

"We called you again last night. Elsa wanted to say good night but you weren't there."

"It was hot, I took a walk."

"Alone?"

"With whom?"

"Dede says you have a boyfriend."

"Dede has a strong bond with you and she's dying to replace me."

"Or she sees and hears things that I don't see or hear."

"What do you mean?"

"What I said."

"Pietro, let's try to be clear: to your many maladies do you want to add jealousy, too?"

"I'm not jealous."

"Let's hope not. Because if it weren't so I'm telling you right away: jealousy is too much, I can't bear it."

In the following days clashes like that became more frequent. I kept him at bay, I reproached him, and at the same time I despised myself. But I was also enraged: what did he want from me, what should I do? I loved Nino, I had always loved him: how could I tear him out of my breast, my head, my belly, now that he wanted me, too? Ever since I was a child I had constructed for myself a perfect self-repressive mechanism. Not one of my true desires had ever prevailed, I had always found a way of channeling every yearning. Now enough, I said to myself, let it all explode, me first of all.

But I wavered. For several days I didn't call Nino, as I had sagely declared in Florence. Then suddenly I started calling three or four times a day, heedless. I didn't even care about Dede, standing a few steps from the phone booth. I talked to him in the unbearable heat of that sun-struck cage, and occasionally, soaked with sweat, exasperated by my daughter's spying look, I opened the glass door and shouted: What are you doing standing there like that, I told you to look after your sister. At the center of my thoughts now was the conference in Montpellier. Nino harassed me; he made it into a sort of definitive proof of the genuineness of my feelings, so that we went from violent quarrels to declarations of how indispensable we were to each other, from long, costly complaints to the urgent spilling of our desire into a river of incandescent words. One afternoon, exhausted, as Dede and Elsa, outside the phone booth, were chanting, Mamma, hurry up, we're getting bored, I said to him:

"There's only one way I could go with you to Montpellier."

"What."

"Tell Pietro everything."

There was a long silence.

"You're really ready to do that?"

"Yes, but on one condition: you tell Eleonora everything."

Another long silence. Nino murmured:

"You want me to hurt Eleonora and the child?"

"Yes. Won't I be hurting Pietro and my daughters? To decide means to do harm."

"Albertino is very small."

"So is Elsa. And for Dede it will be intolerable."

"Let's do it after Montpellier."

"Nino, don't play with me."

"I'm not playing."

"Then if you're not playing behave accordingly: you speak to your wife and I'll speak to my husband. Now. Tonight."

"Give me some time, it's not easy."

"For me it is?"

He hesitated, tried to explain. He said that Eleonora was a very fragile woman. He said she had organized her life around him and the child. He said that as a girl she had twice tried to kill herself. But he didn't stop there, I felt that he was forcing himself to the most absolute honesty. Step by step, with the lucidity that was customary with him, he reached the point of admitting that breaking up his marriage meant not only hurting his wife and child but also saying goodbye to many comforts—*only living comfortably makes life in Naples acceptable*—and to a network of relationships that guaranteed he could do what he wanted at the university. Then, overwhelmed by his own decision to be silent about nothing, he concluded: Remember that your father-in-law has great respect for me and that to make our relationship public would cause both for me and for you an irremediable breach with the Airotas. It was this last point of his, I don't know why, that hurt me.

"All right," I said, "let's end it here."

"Wait."

"I've already waited too long, I should have made up my mind earlier."

"What do you want to do?"

"Understand that my marriage no longer makes sense and go my way."

"You're sure?"

"Yes."

"And you'll come to Montpellier?"

"I said my way, not yours. Between you and me it's over."

116.

I hung up in tears and left the phone booth. Elsa asked: Did you hurt yourself, Mamma? I answered: I'm fine, it's Grandma who doesn't feel well. I went on sobbing under the worried gaze of Dede and Elsa.

During the final part of the vacation I did nothing but weep. I said I was tired, it was too hot, I had a headache, and I sent Pietro and the children to the beach. I stayed in bed, soaking the pillow with tears. I hated that excessive fragility, I hadn't been like that even as a child. Both Lila and I had trained ourselves never to cry, and if we did it was in exceptional moments, and for a short time: the shame was tremendous, we stifled our sobs. Now, instead, as in Ariosto's Orlando, in my head a fountain had opened and it flowed from my eyes without ever drying up; it seemed to me that even when Pietro, Dede, Elsa were about to return and with an effort I repressed the tears and hurried to wash my face under the tap, the fountain continued to drip, waiting for the right moment to return to the egress of my eyes. Nino didn't really want me, Nino pretended a lot and loved little. He had wanted to fuck me—yes, fuck me, as he had done with who knows how many others—but to have me, have me forever by breaking the ties with his wife, well, that was not in his plans. Probably he was still in love with Lila. Probably in the course of his life he would love only her, like so many who had known her. And as a result he would remain with Eleonora forever. Love for Lila was the guarantee that no woman—no matter how much he wanted her, in his passionate way—would ever put that fragile marriage in trouble, I least of all. That was how things stood. Sometimes I got up in the middle of lunch or dinner and went to cry in the bathroom.

Pietro treated me cautiously, sensing that I might explode at any moment. At first, a few hours after the break with Nino, I had thought of telling him everything, as if he were not only a husband to whom I had to explain myself but also a confessor. I felt the need of it; and especially when he approached me in bed and I put him off, whispering: No, the children will wake up, I was on the point of pouring out to him every detail. But I always managed to stop myself in time, it wasn't necessary to tell him about Nino. Now that I no longer called the person I loved, now that I felt truly lost, it seemed to me useless to be cruel to Pietro. It was better to close the subject with a few clear words: I can't live with you anymore. And yet I was unable to do even that. Just when, in the shadowy light of the bedroom, I felt ready to take that step, I pitied him, I feared for the future of the children, I caressed his shoulder, his cheek, I whispered: Sleep.

On the last day of the vacation, things changed. It was almost midnight, Dede and Elsa were sleeping. For at least ten days I hadn't called Nino. I had packed the bags, I was worn out by sadness, by effort, by the heat, and I was sitting with Pietro on the balcony, each in our own lounge chair, in silence. There humidity was debilitating, soaking our hair and clothes, and our smell of the sea and of resin. Pietro suddenly said:

"How's your mother?"

"My mother?"

"Fine."

"Dede told me she's ill."

"She recovered."

"I called her this afternoon. Your mother has always been in good health."

I said nothing.

How inopportune that man was. Here, already, the tears were returning. Oh good God, I was fed up, fed up. I heard him say calmly:

"You think I'm blind and deaf. You think I didn't realize it when you flirted with those imbeciles who came to the house before Elsa was born."

"I don't know what you're talking about."

"You know perfectly well."

"No, I don't know. Who are you talking about? People who came to dinner a few times years ago? And I flirted with them? Are you crazy?"

Pietro shook his head, smiling to himself. He waited a few seconds, then he asked me, staring at the railing: "You didn't even flirt with the one who played the drums?"

I was alarmed. He wasn't retreating, he wasn't giving in. I snorted.

"Mario?"

"See, you remember?"

"Of course I remember, why shouldn't I? He's one of the few interesting people you brought home in seven years of marriage."

"Did you find him interesting?"

"Yes, and so what? What's got into you tonight?"

"I want to know. Can't I know?"

"What do you want to know? All that I know, you do, too. It must be at least four years since we saw that man, and you come out now with this foolishness?"

He stopped staring at the railing, he turned to look at me, serious.

"Then let's talk about more recent events. What is there between you and Nino?"

117.

It was a blow as violent as it was unexpected. *He wanted to know what there was between Nino and me.* That question, that name were enough to make the fountain flow again in my head. I was blinded by tears, I shouted at him, beside myself, forgetting we were outside, that people tired out by a day of sun and sea were sleeping: Why did you ask that question, you should have kept it to yourself, now you've spoiled everything and there's nothing to do, it would have been enough for you to keep silent, instead you couldn't, and now I have to go, now I have *no choice* but to go.

I don't know what happened to him. Maybe he was convinced he had made a mistake that now, for obscure reasons, risked ruining our relationship forever. Or he saw me suddenly as a crude organism that cracked the fragile surface of discourse and appeared in a pre-logical way, a woman in her most alarming manifestation. Certainly I must have seemed to him an intolerable spectacle: he jumped up, and went inside. But I ran after him and continued shouting all manner of things: my love for Nino since I was a child, the new possibilities of life that he revealed to me, the unused energy I felt inside me, and the dreariness in which he, Pietro, had plunged me for years, his responsibility for having kept me from living fully.

When I had exhausted my strength and collapsed in a corner, I found him in front of me with hollow cheeks, his eyes sunk into violet stains, his tan a crust of mud. I understood only then that I had shocked him. The questions he had asked didn't admit even hypothetical affirmative answers like: Yes, I flirted with the drummer and even more; Yes, Nino and I have been lovers. Pietro had formulated them only to be denied, to silence the doubts that had come to him, to go to bed more serene. Instead I had imprisoned him in a nightmare from which, now, he no longer knew how to escape. He asked, almost whispering, in search of safety:

"Have you made love?"

Again I felt pity for him. If I had answered affirmatively I would have started shouting again, I would have said: Yes, once while you were sleeping, a second time in his car, a third in our bed in Florence. And I would have uttered those sentences with the pleasure that that list provoked in me. Instead I shook my head no.

118.

We returned to Florence. We reduced the communication between us to what was indispensable and to friendly tones in the presence of the children. Pietro went to sleep in his study as he had in the time when Dede never closed her eyes, I in the bedroom. I thought and thought about what to do. The way Lila and Stefano's marriage had ended didn't constitute a model, it was something from other times, managed without the law. I counted on a civil procedure, according to the law, suited to the times and to our situation. But in fact I continued not to know what to do and so I did nothing. Especially since I had just returned and already Mariarosa was telephoning me to tell me that the French volume was progressing, she would send me the proofs, while the serious, punctilious editor at the Italian publishing house was raising various questions about the text. For a while I was pleased I tried to become interested again in my work. But I couldn't, it seemed to me that I had problems much more serious than a passage interpreted incorrectly, or some awkward sentences.

Then, one morning, the telephone rang, Pietro answered. He said hello, he repeated hello, he hung up. My heart began to beat madly, I got ready to rush to the phone ahead of my husband. It didn't ring again. Hours passed, I tried to distract myself by rereading my book. It was a terrible idea: it seemed to me utter nonsense, and made me so weary that I fell asleep with my head on the desk. But then the phone rang again, my husband answered again. He shouted, frightening Dede: Hello, and slammed down the receiver as if he wanted to break it.

It was Nino, I knew it, Pietro knew it. The date of the conference was approaching, surely he wanted to insist again that I come with him. He would aim at pulling me inside the materiality of desires. He would show me that our only chance was a secret relationship lived to exhaustion, amid evil actions and pleasures. The way was to betray, invent lies, leave together. I would fly in a plane for the first time, I would be next to him as it took off, as in films. And why not, after Montpellier we would go to Nanterre, we would see Mariarosa's friend, I would talk to her about my book, I would agree on initiatives, I would introduce them to Nino. Ah yes, to be accompanied by a man I loved, who had a power, a force that no one failed to notice. The hostile feeling softened. I was tempted.

The next day Pietro went to the university, I waited for Nino to telephone. He didn't, and so, in an unreasonable outburst, I called him. I waited many seconds, I was very agitated, in my mind there was nothing but the urgent need to hear his voice. Afterward, I didn't know. Maybe I would attack him, I would start crying again. Or I would shout: All right, I'll come with you, I will be your lover, I will be until you're tired of me. At that moment, however, I only needed him to answer.

Eleonora answered. I snatched back my voice in time before it addressed the ghost of Nino, running breathlessly down the telephone line with who knows what compromising words. I subdued it to a cheerful tone: Hello, it's Elena Greco, are you well, how was the vacation, and Albertino? She let me speak in silence, then she screamed: You're Elena Greco, eh, the whore, the hypocritical whore, leave my husband alone and don't dare telephone ever again, because I know where you live and as God is my witness I'll come there and smash your face. After which she hung up.

119.

I don't know how long I stayed beside the phone. I was filled with hatred, my head was spinning with phrases like: Yes, come, come right now, bitch, it's just what I'd expect, where the fuck are you from, Via Tasso, Via Filangieri, Via Crispi, the Santarella, and you're angry with me, you piece of garbage, you stinking nonentity, you don't know who you're dealing with, you are nothing. Another me wanted to rise up from the depths, where she had been buried under a crust of meekness; she struggled in my breast, mixing Italian and words from childhood, I was a turmoil. If Eleonora dared to show up at my door I would spit in her face, throw her down the stairs, drag her out to the street by the hair, shatter that head full of shit on the sidewalk. I had evil in my heart, my temples were pounding. Some work was being done outside our building, and from the window came the heat and the jangle of drilling and the dust and the irritating noise of some machine or other. Dede was quarreling with Elsa in the other room: You mustn't do everything I do, you're a monkey, only monkeys act like that. Slowly I understood. Nino had decided to speak to his wife and that was why she had attacked me. I went from rage to an uncontainable joy. *Nino wanted me* so much that he had told his wife about us. He had ruined his marriage, he had given it up in full awareness of the advantages that came from it, he had upset his whole life, choosing to make Eleonora and Albertino suffer rather than me. So it was true, he loved me. I sighed with contentment. The telephone rang again, I answered right away.

Now it was Nino, his voice. He seemed calm. He said that his marriage was over, he was free. He asked me:

"Did you talk to Pietro?"

"I started to."

"You haven't told him yet?"

"Yes and no."

"You want to back out?"

"No."

"Then hurry up, we have to go."

He had already assumed that I would go with him. We would meet in Rome, it was all arranged, hotel, tickets.

"I have the problem of the children," I said, but softly, without conviction.

"Send them to your mother."

"Don't even say that."

"Then take them with you."

"Are you serious?"

"Yes."

"You would take me with you anyway, even with my daughters?"

"Of course."

"You really love me," I whispered.

"Yes."

120.

I discovered that I was suddenly invulnerable and invincible, as in a past stage of my life, when it had seemed to me that I could do anything. I had been born lucky. Even when fate seemed adverse, it was working for me. Of course, I had some good qualities. I was orderly, I had a good memory, I worked stubbornly, I had learned to use the tools perfected by men, I knew how to give logical consistency to any jumble of fragments, I knew how to please. But luck counted more than anything, and I was proud of feeling it next to me like a trusted friend. To have it again on my side reassured me. I had married a respectable man, not a person like Stefano Carracci or, worse, Michele Solara. I would fight with him, he would suffer, but in the end we would come to an agreement. Certainly breaking up the marriage, the family, would be traumatic. And since for different reasons we had no wish to tell our relatives, and would in fact keep it hidden as long as possible, we couldn't even count, at first, on Pietro's family, which in every situation knew what to do and whom to turn to in handling complex situations. But I felt at peace, finally. We were two reasonable adults, we would confront each other, we would discuss, we would explain ourselves. In the chaos of those hours one single thing, now, appeared irrevocable: I would go to Montpellier.

I talked to my husband that evening, I confessed to him that Nino was my lover. He did everything possible not to believe it. When I convinced him that it was the truth, he wept, he entreated, he got angry, he lifted up the glass top of the coffee table and hurled it against the wall under the terrified gaze of the children, who had been awakened by the shouts and stood in disbelief in the living room doorway. I put Dede and Elsa back to bed, I soothed them, I waited for them to go to sleep. Then I returned to confront my husband: every minute became a wound. Meanwhile, Eleonora began to batter us with phone calls, day and night, insulting me, insulting Pietro because he didn't know how to act like a man, telling me that her relatives would find a way of leaving us and our daughters with nothing, not even eyes to cry with.

But I didn't get discouraged. I was in a state of such exaltation that I couldn't feel that I was wrong. In fact, it seemed to me that even the pain I caused, the humiliation and attacks I endured, were working in my favor. That unbearable experience not only would help me to *become* something I would be satisfied with but in the end, by inscrutable means, would also be useful to those who now were suffering. Eleonora would understand that with love there is nothing to be done, that it's senseless to say to a person who wants to go away: No, you must stay. And Pietro, who surely in theory already knew that precept, would only need time to assimilate it and change it to wisdom, to the practice of tolerance.

Only with the children did I feel that everything was difficult. My husband insisted that we tell them the reason we were quarreling. I was against it: They're small, I said, what can they understand. But at a certain point he reproached me: If you have decided to go, you have to give your daughters an explanation, and if you don't have the courage then stay, it means you yourself don't believe in what you want to do. I said: Let's talk to a lawyer. He answered: There's time for lawyers. And treacherously he summoned Dede and Elsa, who as soon as they heard us shouting would shut themselves in their room, in a close alliance.

"Your mother has something to tell you," Pietro began, "sit down and listen."

The two girls sat quietly on the sofa and waited. I started:

"Your father and I love each other, but we no longer get along and we have decided to separate."

"That's not true," Pietro interrupted calmly, "it's your mother who has decided to leave. And it's not true, either, that we love each other: she doesn't love me anymore."

I became agitated:

"Girls, it's not so simple. People can continue to love one another even though they no longer live together."

He interrupted again.

"That's also not true: either we love each other, and then we live together and are a family; or we don't love each other, and so we leave each other and are no longer a family. If you tell lies, what can they understand? Please, explain truthfully, clearly why we are leaving each other."

I said:

"I am not leaving you, you are the most important thing I have, I couldn't live without you. I only have problems with your father."

"What?" he pressed me. "Explain what those problems are."

I sighed, I said softly:

"I love someone else and I wish to live with him."

Elsa glanced at Dede to understand how she should react to that news, and since Dede remained impassive, she, too, remained impassive. But my husband lost his composure, he shouted:

"The name, say what this other person is called. You don't want to? Are you ashamed? I'll say it: you know that other person, it's Nino, you remember him? Your mother wants to go and live with him."

Then he began to cry desperately, while Elsa, alarmed, whispered: Will you take me with you, Mamma? But she didn't wait for my response. When her sister got up and almost ran out of the room, she immediately followed her.

That night Dede cried out in her sleep, I woke with a jolt, hurried to her. She was sleeping, but she had wet her bed. I had to wake her, change her, change the sheets. When I put her back to bed, she whispered that she wanted to come to mine. I agreed, I held her next to me. Every so often she started in her sleep, and made certain I was there.

121.

Now the date of the departure was approaching, but things with Pietro didn't improve, any agreement, even just for that trip to Montpellier, seemed impossible. If you go, he said, I'll never let you see the children again. Or: If you take the children I'll kill myself. Or: I'll report you for abandonment of the conjugal home. Or: let's the four of us go on a trip, let's go to Vienna. Or: Children, your mother prefers Signor Nino Sarratore to you.

I began to weaken. I recalled the resistance that Antonio had put up when I left him. But Antonio was a boy, he had inherited Melina's unstable mind, and he had not had an upbringing like Pietro's: he hadn't been trained since childhood to distinguish rules in chaos. Maybe, I thought, I've given too much weight to the cultivated use of reason, to good reading, to well controlled language, to political affiliation; maybe, in the face of abandonment, we are all the same; maybe not even a very orderly mind can endure the discovery of not being loved. My husband—there was nothing to be done—was convinced that he had to protect me at all costs from the poisonous bite of my desires, and so, to remain my husband, he was ready to resort to any means, even the most abject. He who had wanted a civil marriage, he who had always been in favor of divorce, demanded because of an uncontrolled internal movement that our bond should endure eternally, as if we had been married before God. And since I insisted on wanting to put an end to our relationship, first he tried all the paths of persuasion, then he broke things, he slapped himself, suddenly he began to sing.

When he overdid it like that he made me angry. I insulted him. And he, as usual, changed suddenly, like a frightened beast, sat beside me, apologized, said he wasn't upset with me, it was his mind that wasn't functioning. Adele—he revealed one night amid tears—had always betrayed his father, it was a discovery he had made as a child. At six he had seen her kiss an enormous man, dressed in blue, in the big living room in Genoa that looked out on the sea. He remembered all the details: the man had a large mustache that was like a dark blade; his pants showed a bright stain that seemed like a hundred-lire coin; his mother, against that man, seemed a bow so tensed that it was in danger of breaking. I listened in silence, I tried to console him: Be calm, those are false memories, you know it, I don't have to tell you. But he insisted: Adele wore a pink sundress, one strap had slid off her tan shoulder; her long nails seemed like glass; she had a black braid that hung down her back like a snake. He said, finally, moving from suffering to anger: Do you understand what you've done to me, do you understand the horror you've plunged me into? And I thought: Dede, too, will remember, Dede, too, will cry out something similar, as an adult. But then I pulled away, I convinced myself that Pietro was telling me about his mother only now, after so many years, deliberately to lead me to that thought and wound me and hold me back.

I kept going, exhausted, day and night; I no longer slept. If my husband tormented me, Nino in his way did no less. When he heard me worn out by tension and worries, instead of consoling me he became irritable, he said: You think it's easier for me, but it's an inferno here, just as much as for you, I'm afraid for Eleonora, I'm afraid for what she could do, so don't think that I'm not in as much trouble as you, maybe even worse. And he exclaimed: But you and I together are stronger than anyone else, our union is an inevitable necessity, is that clear, tell me, I want to hear it, is it clear. It was clear to me. But those words weren't much help. I drew all my strength, rather, from imagining the moment when I would finally see him again and we would fly to France. I had to hold out until then, I said to myself, afterward we'll see. For now I aspired only to a suspension of the torture, I couldn't stand it anymore. I said to Pietro, at the end of a violent quarrel in front of Dede and Elsa:

"That's enough. I'm leaving for five days, just five days, then I'll return and we'll see what to do. All right?"

He turned to the children:

"Your mother says she will be absent for five days, but do you believe it?"

Dede shook her head no, and so did Elsa.

"They don't believe you, either," Pietro said then. "We all know that you will leave us and never return."

And meanwhile, as if by an agreed-on signal, both Dede and Elsa hurled themselves at me, throwing their arms around my legs, begging me not to leave, to stay with them. I couldn't bear it. I knelt down, I held them around the waist, I said: All right, I won't go, you are my children, I'll stay with you. Those words calmed them, slowly Pietro, too, calmed down. I went to my room.

Oh God, how out of order everything was: they, I, the world around us: a truce was possible only by telling lies. It was only a couple of days until the departure. I wrote first a long letter to Pietro, then a short one to Dede with instructions to read it to Elsa. I packed a suitcase, I put it in the guest room, under the bed. I bought all sorts of things, I loaded the refrigerator. I prepared for lunch and dinner the dishes that Pietro loved, and he ate gratefully. The children, relieved, began again to fight about everything.

122.

Nino, meanwhile, now that the day of departure was approaching, had stopped calling. I tried to call him, hoping that Eleonora wouldn't answer. The maid answered and at the moment I felt relieved, I asked for Professor Sarratore. The answer was sharp and hostile: I'll give you the signora. I hung up, I waited. I hoped that the telephone call would become an occasion for a fight between husband and wife and Nino would find out that I was looking for him. Minutes later the phone rang. I rushed to answer, I was sure it was him. Instead it was Lila.

We hadn't talked for a long time and I didn't feel like talking to her. Her voice annoyed me. In that phase even just her name, as soon as it passed through my mind, serpentlike, confused me, sapped my strength. And then it wasn't a good moment to talk: if Nino had telephoned he would find the line busy and communication was already very difficult.

"Can I call you back?" I asked.

"Are you busy?"

"A little."

She ignored my request. As usual it seemed to her that she could enter and leave my life without any worries, as if we were still a single thing and there was no need to ask how are you, how are things, am I disturbing you. She said in a weary tone that she had just heard some terrible news: the mother of the Solaras had been murdered. She spoke slowly, attentive to every word, and I listened without interrupting. And the words drew behind them, as if in a procession, the loan shark all dressed up, sitting at the newlyweds' table at Lila and Stefano's wedding, the haunted woman who had opened the door when I was looking for Michele, the shadow woman of our childhood who had stabbed Don Achille, the old woman who had a fake flower in her hair and fanned herself with a blue fan as she said, bewildered: I'm hot, aren't you, too? But I felt no emotion, even when Lila mentioned the rumors that had reached her and she listed them in her efficient way. They had killed Manuela by slitting her throat with a knife; or she had been shot five times with a pistol, four in the chest and once in the neck; or they had beaten and kicked her, dragging her through the apartment; or the killers—she called them that—hadn't even entered the house, they had shot her as soon as she opened the door, Manuela had fallen face down on the landing and her husband, who was watching television, hadn't even realized it. What is certain—Lila said—is that the Solaras have gone crazy, they are competing with the police to find the killer, they've called people from Naples and outside, all their activities have stopped, I myself today am not working, and it's frightening here, you can't even breathe.

How intensely she was able to give importance and depth to what was happening to her and around her: the murdered loan shark, the children undone, their henchmen ready to spill more blood, and her watchful person amid the surging tide of events. Finally she came to the real reason for her phone call:

"Tomorrow I'm sending you Gennaro. I know I'm taking advantage, you have your daughters, your things, but here, now, I can't and don't want to keep him. He'll miss a little school, too bad. He's attached to you, he's fine with you, you're the only person I trust."

I thought for a few seconds about that last phrase: *You're the only person I trust*. I felt like smiling, she still didn't know that I had become untrustworthy. So that, faced with her request, which took for granted the immobility of my existence amid the most serene reasonableness, which seemed to assign to me the life of a red berry on the leafy branch of butcher's broom, I had no hesitation, I said to her:

"I'm about to go, I'm leaving my husband."

"I don't understand."

"My marriage is over, Lila. I saw Nino again and we discovered that we have always loved each other, ever since we were young, without realizing it. So I'm leaving, I'm starting a new life."

There was a long silence, then she asked me:

"Are you kidding?"

"No."

It must have seemed impossible to her that I was inserting disorder into my house, my well-organized mind, and now she was pressing me by mechanically grasping at my husband. Pietro, she said, is an extraordinary man, good, extremely intelligent, you're crazy to leave him, think of the harm you're doing to your children. She talked, making no mention of Nino, as if that name had stopped in her eardrum without reaching her brain. It must have been I who uttered it again, saying: No, Lila, I can't live with Pietro anymore because I can't do without Nino, whatever happens I'll go with him; and other phrases like that, displayed as if they were badges of honor. Then she began to shout:

"You're throwing away everything you are for Nino? You're ruining your family for him? You know what will happen to you? He'll use you, he'll suck your blood, he'll take away your will to live and abandon you. Why did you study so much? What fucking use has it been for me to imagine that you would enjoy a wonderful life for me, too? I was wrong, you're a fool."

123.

I put down the receiver as if it were burning hot. She's jealous, I said to myself, she's envious, she hates me. Yes, that was the truth. A long procession of seconds passed; the mother of the Solaras didn't return to my mind, her body marked by death vanished. Instead I wondered anxiously: Why doesn't Nino call, is it possible that now that I've told everything to Lila, he'll retreat and make me ridiculous? For an instant I saw myself exposed to her in all my possible pettiness as a person who had ruined herself for nothing. Then the telephone rang again. When I grabbed the receiver, I had words on my tongue ready for Lila: Don't ever concern yourself with me again, you have no right to Nino, let me make my own mistakes. But it wasn't her. It was Nino and I overwhelmed him with broken phrases, happy to hear him. I told him how things had been arranged with Pietro and the children, I told him that it was impossible to reach an agreement with calm and reason, I told him that I had packed my suitcase and couldn't wait to hold him. He told me of furious quarrels with his wife, the last hours had been intolerable. He whispered: Even though I'm very frightened, I can't think of my life without you.

The next day, while Pietro was at the university, I asked the neighbor if she would keep Dede and Elsa for a few hours. I put on the kitchen table the letters I had written and I left. I thought: Something great is happening that will dissolve the old way of living entirely and I'm part of that dissolution. I joined Nino in Rome, we met in a hotel near the station. Holding him tight, I said to myself: I'll never get used to that nervous body, it's a constant surprise, long bones, skin with an exciting smell, a mass, a force, a mobility completely different from what Pietro is, the habits we had.

The next morning, for the first time in my life, I boarded an airplane. I didn't know how to fasten my seat belt, Nino helped me. How thrilling it was to squeeze his hand while the sound of the engines grew louder, louder, and louder, and the plane began its takeoff. How exciting it was to lift off from the ground with a jerk and see the houses that became parallelopipeds and the streets that changed into strips and the countryside that was reduced to a green patch, and the sea that inclined like a compact paving stone, and the clouds that fell below in a landslide of soft rocks, and the anguish, the pain, the very happiness that became part of a unique, luminous motion. It seemed to me that flying subjected everything to a process of simplification, and I sighed, I tried to lose myself. Every so often I asked Nino: Are you happy? And he nodded yes, kissed me. At times I had the impression that the floor under my feet—the only surface I could count on—was trembling.

Elena Ferrante was born in Naples. She is the author of *The Days of Abandonment*, *Troubling Love*, and *The Lost Daughter*. Her Neapolitan novels include *My Brilliant Friend*, *The Story of a New Name*, *Those Who Leave and Those Who Stay*, and the fourth and final book in the series, *The Story of the Lost Child*.

THE NEAPOLITAN NOVELS
By Elena Ferrante

BOOK 1

"Ferrante's novels are intensely, violently personal, and because of this they seem to dangle bristling key chains of confession before the unsuspecting reader."
—James Wood, *The New Yorker*

978-1-60945-078-6 • September 2012

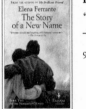

BOOK 2

"Stunning . . . cinematic in the density of its detail."
—The *Times Literary Supplement*

978-1-60945-134-9 • September 2013

BOOK 3

"Everyone should read anything with Ferrante's name on it."—Eugenia Williamson, *The Boston Globe*

978-1-60945-233-9 • September 2014

BOOK 4

"One of modern fiction's richest portraits of a friendship."—John Powers, *NPR's Fresh Air*

978-1-60945-286-5 • September 2015

"Imagine if Jane Austen got angry and you'll have
some idea how explosive these works are."
—John Freeman, critic and author of *How to Read a Novelist*